After a working life as an academic, civil servant and international management consultant, retirement allowed Robert Ferguson to return to the imaginative writing which he had so much enjoyed as a boy. Finding himself in the West Midlands of England, he became immersed in the region's little known but vibrantly energetic literary life, writing, publishing and occasionally winning prizes for his short stories, poetry, reviews and novel.

For all those who have to manage their depression on their own.

Robert Gordon Ferguson

A Magic Flight

AUSTIN MACAULEY PUBLISHERS™

LONDON ∗ CAMBRIDGE ∗ NEW YORK ∗ SHARJAH

A CIP catalogue record for this title is available from the British Library.

ISBN 9781398437333 (Paperback)
ISBN 9781398437340 (ePub e-book)

www.austinmacauley.com

First Published 2022
Austin Macauley Publishers Ltd®
1 Canada Square
Canary Wharf
London
E14 5AA

Immense thanks are due to:

The members of the Solihull Writers' Workshop, the Happy Heart Fiction Night Group and Cannon Poets, for the warmth of their welcome and their encouragement and advice, when I joined them and began to write again.

Sarah Head, Dawn Bolton and Helen Combe, who so willingly undertook to read and offer such constructive criticism on the first draft of this book.

Dr N P Lawson and His Honour Judge Stephen Eyre QC for their technical advice on psychotherapeutic, police and courtroom practices, and the production team at Austin Macauley for bringing this book to the marketplace in its final form.

I must also give fulsome appreciation to Dr Peter Marshall, author of *A Handbook of Hypnotherapy: A Practitioner's Guide*, and to John Bradshaw, author of *Healing the Shame that Binds You*, on whose books in particular I drew in an attempt to present my heroine's story credibly.

Despite these mountains of practical help, lacunae will remain, for which I must and do take full and sole responsibility.

R. G. Ferguson
Autumn 2021

Chapter One

"Oh, you stupid, irresponsibly careless, bloody tart!" he shouted. He raised himself onto his knees and slapped me hard, open-handedly, across the face, first on one side and then the other, before rolling sideways away from me.

"Don't you have the first bit of self-interested common sense?" I had always known he had a temper, but it nowhere near offset his bank balance. I had been hit by men before, so I could take this, though it made my jaw ache like hell.

"However did you manage it, you stupid woman?" He could call me stupid as long as he liked. He hadn't been attracted to my brain, after all. That wasn't why I was here, and we both knew it.

"I must have forgotten to take my pill one morning," I muttered, trying to draw a tear from the corners of my eyes.

"Well, you'll have to get rid of it, Irene, won't you. And I suppose the bill for that will come to me, too, won't it?"

"The doctor says it's too late for that," I said as clearly as I could through the stiffening muscles of my face.

He pushed himself off the bed and towered over me.

"I see." His face was stony. "OK, that's the end then, isn't it. It's been good while it lasted. I want you out of here by noon tomorrow. You understand? One of my staff will be around tomorrow noon to make sure you've gone."

I tried the "But where will I go, I shall be homeless" line on his retreating back, as he walked off into his dressing room, but I knew it would do no good. He was a hard man, and employed hard people on his staff. That was how he had grown his business, and it was a strong contributing factor to his physical attraction, too. But he would not stand for inefficiency, and he no doubt thought of my pregnancy as such a failure.

Well, I'd been in such a position before. It wasn't the end of the world. But I would be hard pressed financially to support myself for the months before the birth, and those after it, until I could regain my figure and another 'sponsor', as I liked to think of them.

I managed. I found a poky room above a shop in Holloway. It wasn't the first, or the worst, I'd lived in since I came to London as a teenager. I lived on benefits, if you could call it living, and eventually gave birth on the National Health Service.

"She's a lovely little girl," the vast Nigerian midwife said, beaming, as she put the bundle into my lap on top of the thin blanket that had been put over me. "What are you going to call her?"

"I have no idea," I replied. I glanced up at the nametag on the midwife's generous bosom. "Hannah's as good as anything, I suppose."

The beam widened.

"It never done me no harm," she said. "Father Adrian will be happy to baptise her for you, before you leave," she offered.

"Whatever," I said. If they wanted all that folderol, they could have it, as long as I wasn't expected to contribute in any way. All I wanted was a good night's sleep before I had to face the world and any more decisions.

Of course, the hospital's social worker had to add her four pennyworth.

"So this is little Hannah Lethbridge," she said, glancing into the transparent plastic cot beside my bed. "Now, your forms suggest you're on your own, Irene. Is that right?"

I nodded.

"Have you planned how you'll look after little Hannah?" she went on. "I have to ask…you'll be keeping her with you?"

I hadn't kept the previous one. She'd been adopted, by goodness knew who. I had no idea where she was, or who she was, these days, and had thought I didn't care. But I had cared, did care. Every now and then, I wondered what had happened to her, still felt responsible for her, still missed her, cried a bit occasionally in private places. I had planned all through my latest pregnancy to have this one adopted too. It was only sensible, given my inescapable lifestyle. But now I wasn't sure I could handle worrying about two of them, even just now and then.

I don't know why I said it, but I did.

"No, I'll keep her. We'll manage somehow, I suppose."

***

10

Some of the girls looked lovely in their uniforms on Hannah's first day at her grammar school. The blazers were cherry-red, with a cream shirt-blouse and a red tie with dark blue diagonal stripes. They could wear a black kilt-skirt with a red pinstripe check, and black tights, or knee-socks with a red stripe around the turnover at the top, and black shoes. Or black trousers. They were lovely colours when they were fresh, of course. But Hannah's uniform was second-hand, and she was deeply ashamed of it. When the uniform list had come from the school, with the name of the school outfitter and the price list, her mother had thrown a fit.

"My goodness, girl, where do you expect me to get the money for all this? I can't afford those prices! My goodness, the nerve of them, to *demand* such things! It'll just be the posh Mums from the top of the hill, who bring their children to school in their *cars*, who'll spend this much. Ah, this is more like it, on the back. They do a second-hand sale of uniforms in the school hall, the day before the beginning of term. That'll be perfectly adequate for you, my girl. After all, you're growing, up and out. What we buy now won't fit you in another year. Even so, it's going to cost a total *fortune*! Oh, the *cheek* of the bloody people!"

"But I can't start a new school looking down-and-out! I can't!" Hannah protested. "They'll all laugh at me, and tease me—"

"Oh, just don't grizzle, like you usually do at the least little thing. I've told you before. If you cry, you just encourage them. Give them some back. Fight, my girl. I've always had to. It's a hard world out there. Maybe it's time you learned to deal with it. And don't look like that. *I'm* not impressed, not a bit. For goodness' sake, straighten your back. Hold your head up. At least, *look* as if you don't have all the troubles of the world on your shoulders. Nobody's going to help a *loser*, I can tell you that."

"But you don't have a regular job, or a regular income," Hannah said, "and yet you smoke a packet of cigarettes a day, and not the cheaper little thin ones that some of our neighbours in the other flats smoke. And there are always bottles of drink on the shelf, and your cut-glass drinks glasses are your most prized possessions, after your clothes. Oh, why can't you get a job of *some* sort?"

"Get a job? Get a job? When do I have time to have a job, let alone to demean myself going around looking for one? Sitting there in front of an impertinent, trumped up little nobody, being interviewed for some nothing 'yes, madam, no madam' job, and having to stand up all day being polite with my best smile plastered across my face? Is that all you think I'm worth? Honestly, sometimes you sound just like my mother, Hannah, and I don't know where that comes from, I'm sure!"

"But, even if it wasn't an important job, it would give you some regular money, like everybody else," Hannah pointed out. "There'd be regular food, and regular clothes, and bus fares instead of walking in the rain and ending up bedraggled. Even if it were only in a shop, or something, it would help, wouldn't it?"

"In a shop?" her mother shrieked, horrified. "I was born for better things than shop-work, my girl, and one day you'll know it. If my father had let me go to university, I'd have had a decent start. But, oh, no, 'what do you need all that book-learning for, girl,' he said. 'You're pretty enough to make your way without book-learning. You can do something in the business. The business will look after you.' But of course, it didn't.

"The old fool spent all the profits on impressing his friends in the pub, and at the dogs, while my own mother worked her fingers to the bone at home and hadn't a clue what he was doing. And then the creditors took the business, and we were left with nothing. Well, I'm not going there again, my girl. I've lived on my wits since then, and managed, most of the time.

"Mr Right will turn up sooner or later, you'll see. But catching Mr Right needs as much cleverness as business. It *is* business, and doesn't leave time for me to work for somebody else. That's just a limitation on getting to where you want to be, where *I* want to be, and deserve to be, after all I've suffered already."

"But, Mother—"

"Don't you 'but, Mother' me, my girl, I won't have it. I know what I'm doing."

"But you don't!" Hannah almost shouted. "You never know where you are, and nor do I. I never know who's going to be in the house when I get home, or when I wake up, or anything! It's confusing and frightening, and…oh, I wish you'd get a proper job. I wish we could be *ordinary*, just like everybody else!"

***

As doctors' surgery receptionists, we're quite used to people turning up in front of us looking less than healthy. They wouldn't have come here otherwise, would they? But the young woman in front of me that morning looked ready to collapse.

12

"My name is Hannah Lethbridge," she said, in no more than a whisper.

We get to know most of the patients by sight, especially the 'regulars', what young Dr Jones calls the 'worried well'. But this one I couldn't remember at all. She had quite a pretty, heart-shaped face behind her big, circular-rimmed spectacles, and a lot of well-washed brown, wavy hair. You wouldn't describe her as smartly dressed. Her overcoat was obviously an old friend, and more appropriate to winter than to this summer day, but the slim—skinny—young woman inside it was still shivering as she stood in front of me.

I checked the basic screen of patients registered with the practice, and there she was.

"Oh, you're a student," I said.

"No, not anymore," she muttered.

"Well, your address will have changed from the one we have here, I expect, so I'll need you to fill out our form with your new details."

I turned and drew a blank copy from the pigeon-hole behind me. Turning back, I asked, "Do you have a pen?"

"Um, I expect so," she said, "but I really do think I need to see a doctor fairly urgently."

Her hands were gripping the edge of the reception desk so hard that her knuckles were white with strain.

"Well, that might be a problem this morning," I said firmly. "You can see how many people are waiting already." Sad though it is, doctors only have twenty-four hours in a day, the same as the rest of us. "Why don't you fill out the form this morning, and then telephone us from home later to make an appointment in a couple of days?"

She didn't say anything. Just picked up the registration form and turned away looking tragic. Well, students with their yuppie flu were best off at home drinking lots of water until they recovered and didn't need to bother a busy doctor. Hannah staggered dramatically to a chair in the waiting area. I watched her sit down, and was turning towards the next patient in front of me when, suddenly, there was a slithering sound as Hannah slipped forward off her chair and sat, totally rigid, on the floor.

Her eyes behind the spectacles were staring. Her legs were stretched out in front of her, slightly apart, as stiff as fallen branches. She was holding her back and shoulders motionless, as if she didn't dare to move any part of her body a fraction of an inch. She was clearly in intense pain. A couple of helpful patients sprang up to help her as I hit the emergency bell-push on my desk, and I called across to them, "No, leave it to the nurses, please! It's easy to do more harm than good in these situations."

They subsided back into their seats, looking horror-stricken at the girl now propped up against her chair and beginning to relax her body, though not the muscles of her face. Two of the practice nurses rushed in.

"What's her name?" one of them said to me.

"Er…Hannah Lethbridge," I replied.

"Hello, Hannah. I'm Patsy and this is Shona. Can you stand up, if we help you?"

Hannah said nothing, just looked at Patsy and tried unsuccessfully to raise her arms. With no apparent effort, the nurses more or less picked Hannah up bodily, got her into a vacant examination room, and closed the door. I told the open mouths in the waiting area, "All over, folks. The nurses will take care of her now. Everything's back to normal. Now, Mrs Hogarth, what can we do for you today?"

***

At the factory, Mrs White spoke testily, "Janice, you'll have to come and help me in my office this morning. Hannah hasn't appeared, again, and I've got a mountain of letters to get through by the end of the afternoon."

Mrs White in a good mood was all right, Janice thought, but, for her, the work was everything. Anything which delayed it had to be bulldozed efficiently out of the way, regardless of who else's work had to be disturbed. Oh, well, it would make a change. She wiped her pen, put it down beside her drawing board, and obediently followed Mrs White into her glass box at the end of the Drawing Office.

"So where's Little Hannah this morning, then?" Daryll asked of nobody in particular. "Ah, well, everybody knows Hannah's a write-off."

"Oh, shut up Daryll!" one of the other girls said. "What do you mean, 'everybody'?"

"Well, everybody. Well, all the fellows in the Drawing Office, anyway. She never comes out drinking, does she, lunch-times or after work? She's never up for a laugh. We dared Chris to ask her out. He'll have a go at anybody, won't you, Chris?"

Chris looked up and leered proudly.

"Anyway," Daryll continued, "he asked her, Hannah, but she just turned bright red, spun around and dived back into Mrs White's office like a bunny down a burrow, didn't she? Everyone wet themselves!"

No one did on this occasion, but Daryll was not to be stopped.

"Even Cherry invited her to one of her girlie evenings," he went on, "but she wouldn't go. And when Jack the foreman in the Print Shop patted her bum, you could hear her shriek in the bus station. But Jack didn't mean any harm. He pats all the girls' bums, doesn't he? It's a matter of routine for him, isn't it? Anyway, Hannah was too chicken to report him, even, so we all had another good laugh, and wrote her off, didn't we? Let her get on with it, and left her be."

"Get on yourself, Daryll, and concentrate," said Len. "None of us wants to be re-doing what you've made a mess of. Anyway, Hannah's all right. Just quiet, which makes a change in here. And she's not bad-looking."

"Yeah, she's quite pretty, I suppose." There was no quietening Daryll when he got onto his favourite subject. "Good legs, nice hair, long and dark. The glasses aren't a help, like she hides behind them. And keeps her skirts on her knees. No thigh, know what I mean? But, yeah, she'd have been all right if she'd been human, like."

There was a murmured chorus from the rest of the drafting crew.

"Shut up Daryll, or you'll have Mrs White back in here."

"Anyway," Wyn whispered to Cherry, whose board was just beside hers, "you thought she was a nice girl when she first arrived, didn't you?"

"Well, yes," Cherry whispered back, "but mainly I was sorry for her when Jack had a go at her. She obviously isn't used to that kind of thing. And I'm not scared of Jack. I'm not scared of anybody, man or woman." She thought for a moment. "Hannah's all right, now those morons have given up teasing her. They got bored once they found out they'd get no reaction except that she nearly died of fright every time they tried anything. I told Jack, told him straight, if he tried it on with Hannah again, I'd report him to HR, with all the details! So he gave up as well."

"I'll bet you would, and all!" Wyn murmured admiringly.

Cherry contemplated her sparse memories of Hannah.

"Yeah, I asked her out with the girls, but she wasn't interested. No, not a drinker. Not a dancer, I guess. Doesn't smoke. Doesn't swear. Doesn't speak, hardly. Doesn't anything we know about. Just a kid, as if she was about twelve, but OK, you know?"

***

When Hannah's open-ended sick-note did come in, Mrs White went down to see her friend Amanda in Human Resources. They had both been with the firm for quite a while.

"Yes, she came to us straight from the university," Amanda confirmed, once she had extracted Hannah's file from her cabinet, and opened it on the desk in front of her.

"This was her first real job, apparently," she said, glancing through Hannah's original application form, "apart from shop-work on Saturdays while she was at school, and in her gap-year. She had done secretarial college after school, and kept up her skills at Uni. Adequate references from a couple of female tutors. Run-of-the-mill. "Nothing known against", effectively. But that's OK."

"It sounds as though you got the same sort of impression that I did," Mrs White observed. "Not much personality, but we can do without too much of that in the junior roles. I was very happy with her."

"I'm glad to hear it," her colleague smiled. "Once she'd done the induction morning. I sent her to you, dear, and I haven't heard anything more of her since then. I know you give your people a good grounding and knock them into shape. Now I've got to find you a temp, I suppose. I'll get onto that this afternoon, and see what the agencies have to offer."

"I'd be obliged if you could push it along for me, Amanda," Mrs White said. "I really miss Hannah, I can tell you."

***

"Up we go, Hannah," Patsy said kindly, as she and Shona lifted me onto the couch in the examination room. Shona gave me a sip of water while Patsy put a thermometer under my tongue and shone her tiny torch into each of my eyes in turn.

"Are you warm enough, Hannah?" Patsy asked. "Too warm?"

"I am a bit warm," I managed to say. "May I take off my coat?"

I tried to sit up, but couldn't. I hadn't the strength of a new-born kitten. I was close to crying with frustration.

"Not to worry," Shona said. "We'll do that. You just get over whatever has happened to you."

She flipped undone my tie-belt and unbuttoned and opened my coat. Putting their arms around my back from either side, the nurses lifted me, slipped my arms from my sleeves and hauled the coat from beneath me.

"I am so sorry," I tried to murmur, but my eyes were closing. All I wanted was to go to sleep.

"Dr Walmsley will be in to see you soon, Hannah," Patsy said. I was just aware of something hard and plastic being pushed under my hand, and of her saying, "If you need one of us, just press that bell," and then I passed out.

I was told later that Dr Walmsley had come in to see me between appointments, just for a first look, but had left me there until the end of morning surgery. I slept and woke up and slept again repeatedly, but hadn't the strength to move. When I did wake up, the form lying on the cabinet beside my head showed that either Patsy or Shona had checked me every half an hour.

About 12.30, the doctor came back, and woke me gently. I wasn't much help as he tried to build a picture of my medical background. My answers to his questions wouldn't come together, and, when I had formed an answer, the words wouldn't come to express it. Anyway, almost all my answers were negative. Some of his questions, though necessary, were just plain embarrassing. No, I wasn't pregnant (that made me blush). No, I didn't have a boyfriend. Yes, I was a virgin (deeper blush).

Usual childhood illnesses, no surgery apart from tonsillectomy aged seven. PA to Mrs White at the factory, and could I please have a sick-note to send in? Live alone, only child, mother in London, or away somewhere, but please don't phone her, there was nothing she could do, or ever had. Father abroad, but I didn't know where. No close friends, no one from university with whom I'd kept in touch.

I tried to tell the doctor that I just needed a week or so's rest. I'd be perfectly all right then... And so on. Anyway, he decided he couldn't risk sending me home with no one there to look after me, and asked the receptionist to call an ambulance to take me to hospital, "for a night, at least, Hannah, just till your system settles down a little." I didn't want to go, of course. I'd be fine at home, I tried to say, but it only came out in a whisper, and he was clearly so right!

"It is just an ordinary hospital, isn't it, Doctor?" I managed to say. "You're not sending me to a mental hospital? I'm not mad, am I, Doctor?" I was on the verge of panic, though such a diagnosis would not have come as a total surprise.

"No, no, it will probably be Addenbrooke's, if they have the space," he reassured me. "You won't receive any medication, and you won't be there more than two nights, I expect. Then, when you're stronger, you can come and see me again, and we'll talk about where this might have come from and what we're going to do about it together."

Chapter Two

The stay in hospital was bliss. I just slept, nibbled at whatever food was put in front of me, and sipped the tepid water from the glass on the trolley-table across my bed, which was mysteriously refilled whenever I emptied it. Nothing more was required of me. I was allowed to go home on the third day, after assuring the doctor and nurses that I had food in the house, and that it was going to be warm. I explained to them that, being a bungalow, my 'home' had no stairs, and demonstrated that I could walk again sufficiently to get around it. Once satisfied, they sent me off in a taxi, and I crept into the house, curled up on the sofa and went back to sleep.

A couple of days later, I was feeling—at least physically—a little better, made the required appointment, and caught the bus into town to see Dr Walmsley again. We talked about my job, and the bungalow and my neighbours, whom I hardly knew, and—superficially—about living in London before university. Then he sent me to Shona, who took several ampules of blood from my arm for analysis, and told me to make another appointment with Dr Walmsley in a week's time to review the results. I was almost worn out by then, and couldn't face having to wait for a bus, so I got the receptionist to call me a taxi to take me home. I was beginning to realise that, although medical treatment in this country is "free at the point of delivery", being ill could be quite an expensive business!

Frustratingly, for me anyway, the blood tests showed no signs of disease. When we next met, however, Dr Walmsley declared that to be good news, signed off another medical certificate for me to post to the factory on my way home (I had brought with me a stamped envelope for the purpose), and then turned towards me with a reassuring smile.

"Hannah," he said very kindly, "I believe I've done as much as I can to help you at this stage. However, I'd like you to see a colleague of mine who specialises in addressing problems beyond those we can usefully treat with pills."

I could feel the panic rising again.

"You mean a psychologist, doctor! So you *do* think I'm going mad!"

"No, no, far from it, Hannah. But what many people don't grasp is that the mind and the body are linked together inextricably. Mostly, both mind and body absorb the normal slings and arrows of life. However, if too many hurts build up over time, the mind can become overwhelmed and simply say to the body, 'Enough! Close down while I get reorganised.' I suspect that this is what has happened to you, and I believe that the colleague I am thinking about will be just the person to help you. She is here in Cambridge, so getting to her will be no more difficult for you than getting here to me."

I wasn't going to tell him how difficult it had been to come to see him, how determined I had had to be in insisting to my unwilling body that I must get out of bed and shower and dress and stagger to the bus shelter. Fortunately, the shelter has those horrible, hard iron seats for which I was really grateful that morning. But what could I say? He was doing everything he could for me, with a gentle kindness that I wasn't used to receiving.

"Thank you, doctor," I managed to tell him. "Perhaps that does sound like the best thing."

"I'll write to my colleague at once, then," Dr Walmsley said, "and you'll no doubt hear directly from her receptionist in a few days' time to set up an appointment for you."

He smiled at me, satisfied, and I thanked him again, I hope a little more graciously, before getting the bus back to my empty home.

***

My first appointment with Mrs Margaret Turner, psychotherapist, was made for 3 weeks later. The address was on my usual bus route into town, so the journey there was a little more convenient than going to Dr Walmsley's surgery. I was perhaps slightly stronger in my legs by then, but every chance to minimise the making of an effort was much appreciated!

Mrs Turner's consulting room was in a very calm-looking, old-fashioned red-brick house with big windows, set back from the pavement behind an old-fashioned fence of black-painted iron stakes and a slightly overgrown lawn. The canopies of two big trees shaded the path to the front door. It looked suitably like a haven, I thought, as I pressed the bell. Inside, I was shown to an elegant, bright sitting room with a high ceiling. The morning sun flooded the room from the window, and made it very cheerful. After a short wait, a woman came in. She was in her forties, I supposed, with comfortable, fluffy, shoulder-length brown hair and a warm smile.

"Ms Lethbridge?" she said. We shook hands. Wearing her neat, neutral-coloured skirt and jacket, and attractive pastel blouse, she looked very like a college tutor, which I found comforting. Still smiling, she said, "Come into my room, and be comfortable." She turned towards a door further down the waiting room, opened it and ushered me through.

"Is that chair all right for you," she inquired. "Can I take your coat?" It was comfortably warm in her house, even now that we weren't on the sunny side. Here, the window behind the desk looked out over another lawn, with fruit-trees growing at intervals around the surrounding wall. All very calm again.

Mrs Turner took my old coat and hung it on a peg behind the door through which we'd come, waved me into the big padded chair she had previously indicated, and went around to sit behind her desk.

"May I call you Hannah? You have had a horrid time," she said very gently, once we had settled in our respective chairs. "So how are you feeling now?"

"Better, thank you, though I'm still sleeping a lot, and feel very tired continuously."

"Apart from seeing Dr Walmsley, have you been out of the house since you left the hospital?" she asked me next.

"Only to the corner shop, once. I was running out of food."

"And how did that go?"

"Well, I got there, and back. Mr Ahmed, the shopkeeper, sent his son to carry my shopping home for me. It isn't far, but I was very grateful. They're very kind people."

"And when you'd got home?"

"Oh, I went back to bed for the rest of the day. And the day after."

Even that short exchange used up a lot of my depleted store of energy, to say nothing of the determination I had needed to get here in the first place. I was grateful to be allowed to sit silently for a moment.

"I don't know what's wrong with me," I finally murmured. "I'm not sure why Dr Walmsley suggested that I should come and see you. All I need is a few days' rest, and I'll be fine."

"Do you feel fine now?" Mrs Turner asked.

"Well, no, but after a few days—"

"I think Dr Walmsley is afraid that this will take more than a few days," she said, still gently. "It looks as though you've suffered a fairly serious depressive incident, Hannah, and neither he nor I, nor, I suspect, you, know where all this came from. We have to find that out first, so that we'll know how to deal with it."

She gave me another long moment to grasp this, before going on.

"I understand that one of the practice nurses has taken samples of your blood. Did you mind that happening?"

"I'm not sure I noticed, really. She was very quick and efficient, and very kind. They both were."

"Well, Dr Walmsley tells me that the laboratory found nothing amiss, so we don't need to worry about medication at this stage."

I was sincerely thankful for that. I remembered having seen a girl on my staircase in college who had been prescribed 'medication' after a breakdown. She had gone around like a zombie and I certainly didn't want that.

There was another pause. Having given me a chance to rest, Mrs Turner said, "Now, I'd like you to take me through what happened to you a month ago. The day you didn't go in to work."

Suddenly, I could think of nothing to say. My mind had gone blank. It was as though a thick bank of fog had suddenly materialised in my head, and cut me off from the world. The only words that would come through the increasing panic were, 'I don't know. I don't know what happened,' and I burst into floods of tears. The tears went on and on running, and my face felt as stiff as if it had been turned into stone. It took me a couple of minutes to notice that Mrs Turner had pushed a box of tissues across the table towards me, but I couldn't reach out to take one. I just sat and wept, sobbing. My face was as wet as if I'd been swimming and had just that second raised my face from the water. Except that the tears and the moans didn't stop, and my face didn't dry, as she let me cry out of myself the pain of all the past twenty-two years.

Eventually, I ran out of sobs, drew in a breath to the bottom of my lungs, tried to sit up a little straighter, and muttered, "I'm s-s-so sorr-y-y."

"You needed that, Hannah. Don't be sorry, not for a second!" Mrs Turner said; and then, conversationally, as if it had been the most normal scene in the world, asked me, "When did you last cry?"

That almost set me off again, but I must have been completely cried out. I was able to tell her, "I never cry. I haven't cried for years and years. I can't remember crying since infant school."

I took a tissue from Mrs Turner's box, and then another. They were big, family-size tissues, and I needed them both. I must have looked a complete fool, sitting there and mopping myself up. At least it was only tears I had to mop. I didn't use make-up in those days.

"Do you remember what made you cry then?"

"It was when my father didn't collect me one lunchtime, and I knew he would never be there to collect me ever again," and that did break me. The tears burst out as if from a broken dam, and I was off once more, back into that remembered despair. Between the renewed sobs, I gulped, "And that was my fault, too."

When finally I had recovered myself, and taken some more deep breaths, Mrs Turner smiled at me and said, "Going back to the start of all this that Thursday, can you describe, however briefly, Hannah, the sequence of events that morning?"

"Well, I simply woke up," I began, "and couldn't face getting out of bed. I stayed there four days. By the Monday, I realised I needed a sick-note for work, and got myself down to Dr Walmsley's surgery, and collapsed."

"We all fancy a naughty day in bed, from time to time," Mrs Turner said, "and I don't suppose it does too much harm, if it doesn't cause anyone else any difficulty. It really doesn't sound like one of those, though?"

The question mark at the end of her sentence was only just audible, but it was definitely there.

"No, I've never been able to take a day off, casually, like that," I assured her. "It honestly wasn't like that at all."

Over the next couple of meetings, a week apart, we didn't get much further. I dug deeply into her store of tissue-boxes, but it seemed that it could take it. By the third meeting, I was eating more and sleeping less, though I was still exhausted by lunchtime every day. Gradually, I had begun to be able to tell Margaret something of my background, beginning—at her suggestion—at the reverse end, perhaps because she recognised that this was where I would feel safer.

"So where did you go to university?" she had asked.

"Here, in Cambridge" I replied. I was still at the almost monosyllabic stage, not yet fully trusting her with my life, my identity. It was all I had left, and I was clutching it protectively.

"Did you enjoy it?"

"Um. Mostly."

"Good tutors? Good friends?"

"Mostly, yes, thank you"

"Have you kept in touch with some of them?"

"No, not really."

She changed direction.

"What subject did you read?"

"English."

"Were you brought up here in Cambridge?"

"No. In London."

"But you decided to stay here, after you'd graduated," she observed.

"It was easiest. For interviews and job opportunities, and so on," I explained.

I knew I was giving her a hard time, but I hadn't the strength for much more. It must have seemed to her like trying to dig into frosty soil with a blunt spade, but she was very patient with me.

"Was job hunting a nightmare?"

"No. I bought a local paper, and phoned, and the Human Resources Manager at the factory said come in and have a chat. I filled in an application form for her, and she wrote to me a few days later to offer the job."

"I should think, with your qualifications and skills, they'd almost bite your hand off," Margaret said. "Did you enjoy the work?"

"Once I'd learned what it was all about, it was fine, thank you."

"And the people?"

"Fine, thank you."

"And the men?" she asked, in what she seemed to hope was a girls-together, we-know-what-men-are-like tone.

"They leave me alone now, and that's fine."

"That 'now' doesn't sound too promising?" she said. I wasn't ready yet to tell her about Daryll and Jack the foreman, so I said nothing and she left the issue for the present.

"Knowing the town after being here for three years, it wasn't difficult to find somewhere to live, I suppose?" she next inquired. "What is it? A flat, or a house?"

"I rent a small bungalow, on the edge of…" I named the almost rural suburb to the South of the town-centre.

"That's a long way out. What's it like for transport? Or do you drive?"

"No. I can't drive. It's right at the end of the bus route into the centre, and the 'bus goes past the factory, so that's easy, too. And it's quiet, around there."

Quiet? It was wonderful! Even the fieldmice seemed to go about on tiptoe. I liked my bungalow, and felt very comfortable there.

"It's a bit different from what you were used to in London, I guess?"

"Um."

"So tell me about London." That was blunter, and gave me a start. Her voice was harder, for the first time rather demanding, or perhaps it was just that we both knew she was approaching a sensitive area. I resorted to silence again for a while, but then felt she deserved an answer of some sort.

"We lived in flats mostly, or rooms. Sometimes in houses."

"Who's we?"

"My mother and I."

"It sounds like quite a sequence of places. Nice places?"

"As long as they were near a library, I didn't mind. The rooms were mostly foul. Some of the flats were all right."

"What about the houses?" She was feeling her way carefully. This time, I was quiet for quite a long time. Eventually, I told her, "They were always very well furnished. And spacious. Easy to get lost in."

"At least they sound a nice contrast to the flats."

Another long silence. Then, I burst out, "They were never ours."

We both left the silence to grow, this time, until, after a while, I murmured, "They belonged to friends of my mother."

Apparently, that was enough for one day. It certainly was for me, even if the appointment-time hadn't been up. Margaret escorted me back into the waiting room.

"Just sit here for a few minutes, and gather yourself, and then go when you feel ready," she said, and I sat there, gathering my strength.

Margaret and her receptionist took no notice of me, just getting on with their normal morning business in quiet voices, until I felt strong enough for the trek to the bus stop. It was only a hundred yards or so, but I was feeling very wobbly. Eventually, I felt able to begin my little journey, and stood up. The receptionist gave me a lovely smile, and said, "See you next week, Ms Lethbridge. Take care, and call us if you need us."

It was said sincerely, though I was determined to fight my way through this by myself if I possibly could.

***

When I came back the next week, Margaret had rearranged the chairs in her consulting room. We were to sit opposite one another in front of her desk, which felt much more relaxed and friendly. I was pleased. Once we had settled, she began.

"You were saying, last time, Hannah, that, when you were in London, it was just you and your mother. So, tell me about your father."

For minutes together, I couldn't. At last, fighting for control, I said, "He left when I was six, but I don't think he was my biological father," and broke down again.

After a while, and still through streaming tears, all I could say was, "Why am I here? What's wrong with me? Why can't I stop crying? What am I supposed to do?" followed by more tears, floods of them, accompanied by a loud, uncontrolled wailing. Even at school, even at the worst times with my mother, I had never made such a frustrated, shameful noise.

When my distress had declined to just an occasional sob, Margaret got up and went around her desk to pull yet another box of tissues from the bottom drawer. She efficiently ripped open the top of the box, passed me a generous handful, and waited while I wiped my face and blew my nose.

"I can't go on like this," I said. "I've had a breakdown, haven't I? I've failed again, haven't I?" With a huge effort, I managed to maintain control this time. Just sat there, feeling infinitely sad, but unsurprised.

With her lovely, gentle smile, Margaret said, quite firmly, "Hannah, you have just taken the biggest, most important step anyone can take onto the road to recovery. Yes, you've had a breakdown, but you've faced it! Twenty years of life have finally overwhelmed all the strength and courage with which you have dealt with their demands, and, inside you, something has finally said, 'I've been holding you together, your mind and your body, for so very long, and quite an effort it has been at times, I can tell you! Quite an effort, to help you avoid shouting back at your oppressors, or curling up on the floor in a heap. We did it, again and again, consistently, together, you and I,' it is finally saying, Hannah, 'but everything has a breaking point, whether it's cake or tungsten steel, and I've reached mine. So now we need to put ourselves together again, and start over.' That's what it's saying, Hannah, and being a very intelligent young woman, you know it's right."

She paused, for me to let all that sink in. I had stopped sniffing by now, though I was still curled down into the chair by my despair. But at last I was able to look up into Margaret's warm, calm eyes and concentrate on what she was saying. She was the only source of hope I had, the first in a very long time, and I wanted so badly to reach out towards it. As I held her eyes, she went on.

"So now we can begin to leave that awful past behind, and that is why you're here. I'm your guide back out of the forest, down the mountain, out of the swamp, because I've been here with other people in a similar state. In fact I've been there, where you are sitting, myself. There is a way back! You *will* begin again, and you've a lot of life still to live, never mind having a lot to catch up."

***

At our previous meeting, Margaret had sounded like a kindly headmistress encouraging a sixth-former with examination nerves. Perhaps that really was what I needed, just then. Now, however, it was time for us to get down to work in earnest, it seemed. She began by explaining more about the working of the human mind, and I started to set into context the significance of her previous questions, and my reactions to them.

"The first thing to understand," she said, "is that the mind adjusts to accepting whatever its environment permits. When hurtful things happen, as they do to everyone, and that person has enough confidence, they fight for their rights and win. However, if they don't feel confident about winning, or it becomes obvious that they are not going to win, they just tuck the hurtfulness into a bag at the bottom of their mind and pretend it didn't happen and didn't hurt. But the bag has a finite capacity. Furthermore, the hurts in the bag fester and swell, as if they were rotting garbage. One day, if the hurts are left long enough, and there are enough of them, the bag just bursts. The hurts spill out all over the person's consciousness and take it over, and the person suffers a collapse."

She stopped, and looked me full in the face, as if to make sure how I was taking this, if I was taking it in. Her eyes were fixed on my face, and mine on hers. Then I realised that my hands were twisting uncontrollably in the lap of my old, navy blue, pleated skirt.

Margaret had noticed the twisting, too, for she glanced down and then up to my face again, very quickly, smiled as if to say, "Never mind", and continued, "I believe that's what happened to you, Hannah. The day came when the bag burst, and laid you out like a defeated boxer in the ring. You didn't recognise that it was the accumulated hurts that had laid you low, because you'd got so used to not thinking about them. You had just pushed them deeper and deeper into the bag and unconsciously hoped that they were in the past, dealt with. But they weren't, and never will be until they are brought out into the open and accepted for what they were when they happened. What they remain today.

"That's not going to be comfortable," she went on, as if to prepare me for the hard work in front of us, "but it will all happen here, in the security of this room, with just you and I present, or on your own in the privacy of your bungalow. And, as you sort out each of those hurts, and see them as having been imposed on you, as not being your fault in any way, their power over you will weaken, and your strength will grow back towards what it was before you collapsed."

And so, finally, I began to describe to Margaret the details of the non-life of my childhood and youth, experiences and emotions which had committed me to a non-life at university and to a job far beneath the ability of which I used to think I was capable. The process was very slow. At first, from the habits of a lifetime, I felt I could trust nobody, not even Margaret.

There was so much about which I felt so ashamed. I was horribly afraid of losing Margaret's respect, however little I deserved it, however limited it might be. I felt I had no experience of love. I wasn't even sure that love, as I longed for it to be, did actually exist in the world I occupied. I had no confidence that any attraction, any affection, I might feel for someone else would be reciprocated. So, I suppose I had got used to offering as little of myself as I politely could, in order to minimise the hurt that I feared would inevitably result from a human relationship.

***

It was almost twelve months later that I thought Hannah might be ready to move into a more demanding phase of her analysis. One particularly bright, sunny morning, she seemed a little more relaxed than usual, perhaps in response to the weather. That does happen to people, even when they don't appear to notice it. Her hair, which had been growing down below her shoulder-blades, had been trimmed to just less than shoulder-length, and she was wearing a blouse which I hadn't seen before in uncharacteristically bright colours.

After a brief recapitulation of the matters we had touched on at our previous meeting, I said carefully, "Hannah, I'm getting a broad picture of some of the events we've discussed, but I'm aware of a lack of detail. I think it's time we dug into some of these events, so that I can come to recognise how and why they arose, and the effects they might have had on you. Is that all right with you?"

"Ye-es?" tentatively. Pause. "What do you have in mind?"

She clearly wasn't totally comfortable with the prospect of a move beyond what had become, for her, a comfort zone.

"I'm particularly interested in your mother," I said. "Mothers are desperately influential on their children, especially on girls growing up through all the social and physical changes that happen to us. But I feel that perhaps you didn't talk to your mother very much, or she to you. Not talk as mothers and daughters need to do. So I wonder if it isn't time you talked to her as you'd have liked to do all those years ago."

As I had been speaking, Hannah had been curling further into her chair, as if to protect herself; uncharacteristically, she interrupted me, with something like panic in her voice.

"No! Where is she? She isn't here, is she? You said this would be private, just you and I and never anybody else! No, I can't..."

She was sitting bolt upright in her chair, pale as a sheet, and very near to tears.

"No," I reassured her. "She's nowhere near, and certainly not here. She never will be, physically, unless or until you want her to be. Nobody ever will, I promise. That's not what I have in mind at all. But I believe that there's a lot you didn't say to her, over the years, and that those unsaid words are still causing you hurt. They are forming a blockage, a barricade, over which, at the moment, you can't climb. Until you can climb past that blockage, dismantle it, remove it, it will go on preventing you from moving forward, and that is what you want to do, isn't it? That is what you need, isn't it?"

She nodded stiffly, like a jointed doll, but didn't sit up any straighter. She still wasn't sure where this was going, and was terribly fearful that it was going to be painful again.

"But you can talk to her now as you wanted to do all those years ago," I continued. "She isn't here, but you can remember what she said, or imagine what she might have said if you'd said some of the things you didn't dare say to her then." I tried to think of an analogy which would strike a chord of realism with this particular girl. "It's rather as if you were writing a play, hearing in your mind the words you want to write, seeing in your imagination the stage, and the lights, and your characters in their costumes, with their postures and gestures, performing before you. But you'll be speaking both parts, those of both you and your mother."

Hannah had curled back hard into her chair. I needed to encourage her to relax, if I could, her body first. Then her mind would follow.

"You can stand up, if you want to," I suggested, "to make the scene feel more realistic, but you don't have to. Just do it from where you are in that lovely, comfortable chair, if you'd rather. Shall we try? Shall we start, for example, in your school-days? Was there something that you would have liked to tell your mother about, receive her comfort and support, but didn't feel able to do?"

There was a silence of some length. Hannah hadn't stood up but she had uncurled slightly. She said, "I'm not sure I can do this."

"Close your eyes," I said. "You're quite safe. There's only you and I here."

Hesitantly, she closed her eyes. After another minute, haltingly, she began.

"Other girls had school-friends, but I didn't."

She dropped straight into a deeper, stronger, more dominating voice, the voice of her mother.

"No! Certainly not! Of course you can't bring anyone here for tea! We don't eat 'tea'. Good gracious, girl, you know that. Anyway, just look around you at this room. Whatever would they go back and tell their snobby mothers? I'd be *mortified*! Whatever are you thinking of?"

Hannah, in her own voice:

"Well, can I go to hers after school one afternoon?"

"What, and leave me *obligated*? I can just hear *that* going round the coffee shops! 'I fed that drab little girl because Heidi, or Petra, or whatever her name might be, insisted. And there's *no* sign of her mother responding, and it's been *weeks…*'."

"But…"

Hannah sprang to her feet, and turned on the chair as if she were still sitting there.

"Once and for all, Hannah, no! Let that be enough. You must see how impossible it would be to entertain here."

"But your friends come here…"

"Only when I've known them for some time, and know them quite well, and know that there is some likely benefit to be had from letting them in. Benefit for both of us. They see how difficult it is for us to live here, and invite us to move in with them. We've lived in some nice houses in that way. You've had lovely rooms when I've succeeded like that, haven't you? But your little friends aren't going to invite us to live with them, are they? Or their mothers? They'd just gossip." Hannah's voice rose to a mimic-squeak. "'Mummy, they've got great cracks all over their kitchen wall, and their bathroom has no bidet!' And that would be around the district in no time."

"Oh, it's not fair, it's not fair."

And suddenly, Hannah's words stopped short. She clapped her hand to her cheek, as if, here, today, she'd been slapped again.

"That's enough of that grizzling," her mother's voice said sharply. "I said no, and that's that."

Hannah sat down again in the client chair. The intensity of those memories had hit her hard.

"Were you often slapped?" I asked gently.

There was a pause before Hannah could bring herself to answer.

"No, not often. Only when I made her particularly cross. And then, usually on the backs of my legs. Not often across my face."

I thought 'cross' was an understatement. Mother seemed to have something of an anger management issue. But she wasn't my client. It was Hannah that I could help today, hopefully, eventually.

Chapter Three

At my next appointment, Margaret asked me, "So how has your week been, Hannah?"

"The best word I can find for it, I think, is 'stony'," I replied. "I seem to have been a little calmer, but I've kept tripping over my feelings when I wasn't thinking about them. It was distracting. Is that normal?" I asked.

"Perfectly usual," she assured me, "and quite healthy and helpful. Would you like to tell me about some of these feelings?"

"The strongest one is…" I hunted for the word, "…humiliation, I suppose. I remember feeling worth so much less than the other girls at school. Not in classwork. I did all right at most things there. I had to struggle with the sciences, but, apart from maths, we could give them up after the third year, and I did, very happily! No, it was the feeling of being different, an outsider, and everything that arose from that."

To my relief, Margaret took a new line.

"And how are you sleeping?" she asked.

"Sleeping is what I do best," I said, and managed a little smile. "I fall asleep anywhere I sit down in a chair, even an upright one in the kitchen. I do it in buses, and nearly miss my stop. I am constantly tired. I'm in bed never later than nine in an evening, unless I fall asleep earlier in my armchair. Once I'm in bed, though, I only sleep in patches. After two or three hours, I wake up and can't get back to sleep, so I get up and have a drink or a cup of soup, and read something for an hour or so before going back to bed. Then I probably don't wake up before ten or eleven the next day."

"That must make for very disrupted days," she suggested.

"Yes," I replied. "It doesn't help, I suppose, that I have nothing to get up for, except coming to see you, or going to the shop for food, or to the local branch-library, so I seem to have lost the sense of organisation I used to have." I paused, suspicious of what she'd make of what I needed to say next. But I had to say it. "And, when I am asleep, I'm dreaming a lot more than I used to do."

"What sort of dreams are you having, Hannah?" she inquired.

There was another pause. I couldn't help it.

"Sort of, scenes from my childhood, mostly," I muttered.

"Happy dreams?" she prompted, to keep me going, though she must have been pretty sure they hadn't been.

"Not really," I said. "More like nightmares. Sometimes. I wake up frightened and crying." I could feel the tears gathering in my eyes again.

I took a tissue from the box on her desk beside me, removed my glasses, mopped my eyes, and gave Margaret an apologetic smile. Inevitably, she said, "Would you like to tell me about one of these bad dreams?"

I realised that, under the influence of the awful memories Margaret was asking me to face, my body had twisted in my chair, and my legs had become tightly twined around each other like those of a gauche little girl.

"Sit very straight," she suggested. "Put your feet flat on the floor, breathe very deeply, and relax. You're quite safe here, Hannah. Whatever has frightened you in the past can't touch you now. Close your eyes and consciously relax your toes. Think about your toes, and let them relax. Now the rest of your feet. Now your ankles. Now think about your knees and let them relax."

We moved all the way up my body like this, until I had uncurled and most of the tension seemed to have gone.

"Now, let that dream back into your memory, Hannah. You're quite safe here and now," Margaret repeated. "Stay as relaxed as you can, and let it come back bit by bit, under your control, so that it no longer overwhelms you. You know it's only a memory. Now, replay it, like a film, for me. Play the parts. Let it all happen, here where you know you're safe."

So, eventually, I began.

***

A lot of my work as a therapist involves getting my clients to let go of their accumulated stress. Sometimes, this is very hard to watch while it's happening, as it was then with Hannah. Suddenly, she sprang to her feet, her left arm twisting behind her back.

"Ow! Stop it, Lauren Bates! Leave me alone. Stop it! That hurts!"

33

In a different, rougher voice, she said,

"That's nothing, softy! Now let's see what's in this pocket."

Hannah's voice again.

"There's nothing there. You know I never have anything you want."

"On your knees, little Hannah Lethbridge."

Another voice.

"Give us her bag. Let's see what's in there."

"Tip it out. In the puddle."

Hannah was kneeling on the carpet now, bent forwards, her arm still behind her back.

"Ah, there, then. All that lovely neat writing being smudged in the wet. And her textbooks. Nicely soaked!"

"Try the other pocket, Lauren."

"Get off me, get off!"

Hannah was wriggling on the floor now.

"Nar, there's nothing again."

"Nice tear in her pocket, though, Lauren. Bit of sewing practice for you there, Hannah Lethbridge."

"Ah, come on. There's nothing here for us."

Hannah's body folded down onto her knees. She looked like a painting of a martyr on a cell-floor after torture. It took her a minute or two to recover enough to put out a hand to her chair. Slowly, she pushed herself upright, and slumped into her chair, eyes closed, totally spent. I let her sit quiet and recover until she looked up at me again.

"Did that happen often?" I asked.

"There were gangs of bigger girls who used to pick on the smaller ones, and take their sweets, or handkerchiefs, or money, if anyone had any. They'd just dig their hands straight into your pocket and grab. If they didn't find anything there, you'd be pushed up against a wall or forced down onto the ground, and one of them would tip out your bag, so that they could take what they wanted."

"That must have been pretty demeaning," I said. "You couldn't report it to a teacher, I suppose?"

"No," Hannah murmured, head down.

"How long did they go on picking on you?"

"Oh, for about a year or so. But it wasn't just me they bullied, so it wasn't continuous. And they soon learned that I never had any money, which was what they were really after. They just knocked me about a bit, called me weakling and drip, and sometimes worse. Mostly, I avoided them, and avoided parts of the school where there wouldn't be many people. But if they did get me, I could do nothing but put up with it and wait for it to end. It was the inability to do anything to stop it that was worst."

She continued, "The pocket of my blazer was almost torn off that day and I knew Mother had no means of mending it, and nor did I. So, at lunchtime, I went to Mrs Hutchison, who taught Domestic Science, and asked if she could let me have a needle and thread to take home that evening to do the repair." She looked down at her lap, shamefaced at the memory, and then looked up at me again earnestly, as though she still could not believe what had happened next.

"In fact, she told me to come to her at the end of the afternoon, and she put the pocket through one of the sewing machines and mended it in a twink. She didn't ask why my mother couldn't have done it, or why there were no needles and thread at home, or why none could be bought, but she looked at me very straight, and I knew she was thinking, 'What a poor, useless child!' It was horrible. I felt so small. I could never meet her eyes again if I met her in a corridor, never mind in class. But she was always very friendly and helpful, so perhaps she forgot about me fairly quickly. It was quite a big school."

"She didn't ask you how it had come to be ripped so badly?" I asked. There was something more here that needed to be unearthed. Hannah looked sideways out of the window, and didn't answer. Eventually, I said, "And, when you told your mother…?" but I knew she hadn't told her mother anything of all this. "Would you like to tell her now?"

Hannah thought for a moment. She was getting used to the technique now. She stood up, straightened her shoulders, raised her chin and said, in her own voice, "It's horrible when they catch me. I dodge them as much as I can, but…if there are only two or three of them, and I don't wait for them to start, I can sometimes push through them and run away. But they pinch and poke you, and try to make you kneel on the ground. If it's wet, they destroy all your things, and then you have to make up a story to explain to teachers how the books got so filthy, and your tights wet and muddy. Oh, Mother, I hate them! I hate them, and I wish they could be made to stop!"

Her voice dropped in pitch.

"Well, what do you expect me to do about it, girl? You wouldn't want me shepherding you everywhere. They'd just treat you worse, wouldn't they? You'll just have to fight them off when they start. It's a hard world out there, and the sooner you realise that the better."

"But you could give me a hug…"

Hannah took a couple of steps back.

"Not in this frock, my girl. And I've just finished my make-up, so softness like that will have to wait. There's a time for that sort of thing, and it isn't now."

"It's never now! You never hug me. Nobody ever hugs me, no one will ever hug me."

Then she came out of role. This time, there were no tears, but she looked straight at me, and said, "No one ever has, and I don't see how anyone ever will."

***

By the time we met again in my consulting room, I thought Hannah might have had enough gloom for a while. I wondered if there could have been a happy episode of *any* sort in her life. It seemed a thin chance, but I thought I'd try.

"Hannah, you've been through some very difficult situations. But was there one that really made you happy, even for the very shortest time?"

"Oh, yes," she answered, and briefly almost smiled. "But it was horrible to begin with. It almost didn't happen, and would not have done if it were not for one particular person's kindness. I'll never forget her for that."

"Would you like to tell me about it?" I asked.

When she was in the Sixth Form, Hannah told me, it was announced that there was to be a trip to Paris for 10 days' experience of the true Parisienne accent in preparation for the A-level French oral examination. Her mother's negative reaction was to be expected. Hannah stood up and slid easily into role.

"*Darling*, of course not. Where am I going to find *that* sort of money? I ask you! It's quite out of the question."

In her own voice, Hannah said, "It would be such a help, with the A-level examination coming up in the summer. It's an incredible opportunity, and I've never been out of London, let alone abroad. I suppose you couldn't ask Tony to pay for it, could you? Or to lend you the money?"

Hannah immediately twisted away from the chair as though having been hit in the face again. She sat down and was quiet as she absorbed her mother's reaction. After a moment or two, she raised her eyes to meet mine again.

"At the time, we were living with Tony," she explained. "The house was in Chelsea, not far from the river. I used to have lovely walks along the Embankment, and could go into the Tate Gallery when it was cold after school."

"That sounds a lovely house. He must have been quite well off to live there," I said.

"Oh, yes, loaded," Hannah replied a little bitterly. "Mother wouldn't have bothered to pick up a man who hadn't enough money to support her needs. In all fairness, though, he was generous enough to me, when he wanted me out of the way."

"So what happened next?" I asked.

Her face brightened as she explained how it had all been sorted out.

"When I didn't bring the form back, and everybody else in the French Set had done so, wonderful Mrs Paladyne, our teacher, told me to see her after school one day, and said that she had to know final numbers by the end of the week, in order to finalise the booking. I had to tell her that I wouldn't be going because Mother and I couldn't afford it. Oh, that was really humiliating! I went bright red and hot all over, and I couldn't look at her." Even now, years later, Hannah blushed at the memory, but then smiled again and went on with the story.

"Anyway, she just said, 'All right, run along, Hannah,' and I went back to Tony's as usual. That was on the Tuesday. In the morning break on the Thursday, Mrs Paladyne sent a junior to fetch me to her. She wanted to tell me that the school had a limited fund to provide bursaries to pay for 'educationally essential experiences' for selected pupils. 'If the Paris trip isn't such an experience, I don't know what is,' Mrs Paladyne said to me. 'The Head agrees. All we need is for your mother to give her consent and sign a few forms.' Well, Mother berated me again when I told her about the bursary, of course."

The pitch of her voice dropped temporarily, but she stayed in her chair this time. When she spoke, there was a surprisingly sarcastic edge to her emphases, as though her happiness at the outcome had enabled her to see this incident as a tiny victory over her mother.

"Hannah! How *could* you show me up like this! Again! I've never taken charity like *that,* and won't allow *you* to do so, my girl. I won't *dare* go near that school again, *ever.*"

"But I didn't care," Hannah continued in her own voice. "I was determined to go to Paris, even if I had to forge her signature on the forms. I truly was prepared to do that," she said earnestly, her eyes taking on a new hardness behind her spectacles, "and I was sure Mrs Paladyne wouldn't look at them too closely…"

I believed that even good, naïve Hannah had been prepared to turn forger in the interest of such a cause. Her determination showed in every taut line in her body, as she remembered how she had felt. Then she relaxed, and went on with her narrative.

"Anyway, the next morning, Mother gave me all the forms, signed, and I went to Paris the next Easter with everybody else. I think Tony told her to sign them and get rid of the girl for ten days, because he took Mother skiing for a week in Switzerland while I was away. She came back very proud of herself, with loads of new clothes that Tony had bought for her."

"And Paris in the spring was wonderful?" I asked.

"Oh, it was amazing!" Hannah replied, with the brightest smile I had seen from her since I had met her. "By the time we went, I'd saved up a little money, which I changed as we went through the ferry port. Mrs Paladyne took us around the sites during the day, and made us order our own drinks and treats in cafes and so on.

"Best of all, though, she allowed us to go off without her for two hours in an evening, provided we went in groups of never fewer than three and were back where we were staying by ten o'clock. I tagged on to a couple of other girls, not really friends, but their French wasn't great and they let me choose where we went and get their tickets on the Metro and so on, so we got on all right for just that little time. Oh, it was wonderful!"

Hannah actually grinned to herself as remembered it.

"You really enjoyed that experience," I suggested.

"Yes," she agreed. "It made all the difference, after the previous horrors of my years at school. I realised that there was kindness in the world, and that, even if I found it only occasionally, it was like finding a treasure which could support me in the outside world." She took a deep breath. "It was a turning point, in a way. After that, I knew I had to get away. I really started working hard to get to university, any university. That would be my way out. To get away, where I could be alone."

***

The memory, from Hannah's previous appointment, of Paris and her moment of hope, had cheered her so very much that, when we next met, its influence still showed in her face and in the warmth and confidence of her greeting. I was sad that I had to bring her back to the harsh reality of why she was in my consulting room.

"So Tony served your purpose," I smiled. "Has he always been thoughtful to you?"

"Oh, he wasn't around much longer than the rest. By the end of the summer, he and Mother were beginning to row, as usual, and Mother moved back into a really foul place. But I was up here at the university by then, so this time it didn't really affect me."

"Hannah, I must ask you... What is all this about moving into your mother's friends' houses?" I asked. "Would you like to tell me about that?"

"Oh," Hannah said, looking down again and clasping her hands tightly in her lap. "Every so often, we'd go and live in somebody's house for a few weeks or months. A friend of my mother's, a man-friend." Hannah blushed slightly. She clearly understood the superficial implications of that explanation. She moved on quickly, and said, "Sometimes it was just an ordinary house, sometimes something almost palatial, with lots of bedrooms and staircases. I always got my own bedroom in those houses, that's true, and I enjoyed that. I could keep myself out of their way, Mother's and her friend's, and that seemed to suit all of us. All I had to do was be invisible, Mother said."

"Did you have to change schools every time this happened?"

"Oh, no. It just meant getting more buses, different buses. And there were other advantages, sometimes."

I waited for her to tell me about the advantages.

"Well, from time to time, often at weekends, her current friend would slip some money into my hand or my pocket and suggest I took myself off to the cinema or something. That usually meant they were having other people to the house, and especially didn't want me to be seen. It was a great help, though, because I never had regular pocket money from Mother.

"I used to wander about, when I was sent out like that, perhaps go up to the second-hand bookshops in the Charing Cross Road, or go to a library or a museum, where it would be warm for as long as they stayed open. Or I'd ride a bus." She looked at me earnestly, as though to impart a great truth of which I was unlikely to be aware.

"You can spend a long time on a bus for very little money, you know. Then I could save most of the money I'd been given to buy a book, or something I needed, or something I really wanted of my own. I kept my savings in a box, wrapped in a tissue so that the coins wouldn't rattle if someone found the box and moved it. But I had to keep moving the box from place to place because, now and then, money disappeared from it, especially when we'd gone back to another pokey flat."

"Your mother took money from your savings?"

"Oh, yes, if we were behind with the rent, or she needed money for a taxi, or cigarettes, or something. If I bought a blouse, or a brooch or necklace, which wasn't often, and only because they were particularly beautiful, and she found them, they'd sometimes disappear. I'd have to wait for her to go out so that I could get them back from her wardrobe or her dressing table drawer."

"And what did she say when you protested?"

"Oh, I didn't. There wasn't any point. She'd take it anyway. I just moved the box to a new hiding place, if it were money she'd taken. Anything else I simply reclaimed when circumstances permitted. At least that way there wouldn't be another row."

"And how did you get on with your mother's friends?" I inquired eventually.

"I didn't really. I just kept out of their way as much as I could. She seldom left me alone with them. She sent me to my room if that was likely to happen." She blushed. "I know what you're asking, but nothing really dreadful actually happened. I suppose I was very naïve when I was young. Some of them occasionally patted my arm, or my head, in passing.

"But Mother was very insistent that I should never leave my room without getting fully dressed and to always lock the bathroom door when I was in there. I always pulled a chair across my bedroom door, once I realised what she meant about such things. She hated anyone else receiving attention, though. She always had to be the one in the limelight, and that suited me."

"Did she tell you the 'facts of life'?"

"No, never. But we did Sex Education at school. I hated it. So embarrassing! Even in an all-girls school." She blushed again. "But I suppose it was useful, as a warning." All the mechanics, and none of the emotions, I thought. Poor Hannah, to be excluded from yet another joy of adult life.

Time was up for that week, and I was glad. The next area we needed to face up to was her life in the immediate run-up to her collapse, and that would be tough enough for her, but, after more than a year's experience, Hannah was used to the process of analysis, and I was confident she would handle those matters effectively.

Chapter Four

At Hannah's next appointment with me, I approached her more recent past.

"So you came up to the university here in Cambridge," I said, and paused to see in which direction she would take the narrative.

"Yes," she said, but nothing more.

"That was a great success," I ventured, trying to insert a positive note into the exchange. There hadn't been many of those so far. But Hannah showed none of the satisfaction for which I had hoped.

I noticed that, today, she was wearing brown. Jumper, skirt, even her tights and shoes, were brown. It was as if she had chosen the clothes to be drab. She wore no jewellery other than a simple wristwatch with a thin black strap. Nothing relieved the drabness, not even her lovely hair, the waves of which fell to just below her shoulders and were as disciplined as ever. I tried once more to dangle the bait of pride before her, to give her a memory which might cheer her up.

"The entry standards are very high here, of course," I suggested, and she almost smiled before giving a slight shrug, as if to say "It was only luck", which I well knew it never was. There was something here that needed to be explored. If Hannah was trying to keep me out of this bit of her story, I couldn't let her get away with that, for her own good.

Reluctantly, I decided that, if Hannah wouldn't take the easy road of telling me what had happened to her at the university, I would have to push her until she did.

"But it is also very expensive to live and to study here," I pressed. "However did you manage, financially?"

"Oh, I won a scholarship," she said, and did brighten, slightly but visibly. "To Newnham, which was where I had always dreamed of going."

"And did the scholarship provide you with sufficient money?"

"With vacation jobs, I made it do so," Hannah said. "Even in the second year, when we had to live out of college. I couldn't afford to house-share, like most of the other girls. But I only needed a room, so I became a 'paying guest' in the tiny terraced house of an elderly relative of one of the College porters. She needed the extra cash, I was told, and I needed somewhere cheap." She shrugged. "But it worked, for both of us. And, anyway, it was the sort of thing I had been used to, in the times when Mother was between men. Better than some of those times, actually."

"And why Newnham?" I asked.

"Because it's an all-women college," Hannah replied. "I'd had enough of men throughout my teenage years. There had always been men hovering around my mother, making a fuss of her, encouraging her to play at being someone she wasn't, ignoring me as far as they could, and cutting me off from her." She sat up a little straighter as she remembered all this.

However, there was a discomforting edge to her voice as she explained what she had believed to be her motivation. "I thought that, in an all-women College environment at Cambridge University, of all places, I would be free of all that silliness. I thought that everyone would be like me, that everyone would have gone there to be away from men, to concentrate on their studies, to prepare for lives in which they wouldn't just be playthings, or nuisances, but would be the equal of men, with equal chances of successful careers."

"And how was it?" I enquired.

"Well, I didn't mix much. I couldn't afford to. Many of the girls had brilliant minds and were very stimulating in tutorials and seminars. Others spoke in nothing but slogans, or show-off pseudo-philosophical clichés, or they concentrated on chasing men just as my mother had done. Nothing was as important as their latest ball-dress and their latest conquest, and the jealousies between them were vicious.

"Most of them had enough money to do it, while the rest pretended as convincingly and desperately as they could that they had parents as wealthy as anyone else. When they were around, it was as bad as school, if not worse. I got to recognise some of those who spent a lot of their time in the libraries." She looked down at her hands, now twisting again in her lap. "We smiled at each other as we came and went, but I never got to know any of them beyond that, even those in the same College."

"Were all your tutors women?" I enquired. "Surely you must have had some male tutors?"

"One or two," she agreed, "but they were tutors, and mostly frightfully distant and disparaging."

"And there would have been boys in your tutorial pairings?" I pressed.

"Occasionally, when we were sent to study under some particular eminence in another college." Abruptly, she stopped talking and I realised that I needed to know why.

"Hannah," I said, "was there a particular boy?"

She shrank, twisting slightly in her chair but remaining silent.

"Hannah, it's only me. It's only us. Hannah, what happened?"

I could hardly hear her reply.

"It wasn't a boy, it was a tutor. And I think he tried to rape me." She looked up, with the despair in her face which I had seen when she first came to me. I had thought we had dispersed it months before. In a somewhat stronger voice, she went on, "But it was afterwards that was even worse."

***

I let the following silence hang in the room between us until she was ready to continue.

"It was in my third year," she eventually said. "My personal tutor thought it would be good for me to go to him. Almost all my tutorials had been in my own college up until then, and she thought that I ought to be able to demonstrate "some more breadth". Hannah's voice was strengthening as she told the story. There was an expanding element of anger in it, perhaps disgust. "He's an 'Authority', my tutor told me, 'with a capital A, and has great influence in the Department. Catch his eye, and your First may well be confirmed.' I can hear her saying that now. Well, she was right about all that. He had written three books about the Romantic Poets, and lots of papers, most of which I read before going to my first meeting with him. And he *was* decisive in fixing the class of my degree!" She said that with an unusual degree of vehemence, and then stopped.

Again, I waited. She would have to tell this part of her story at her own speed, in her own time, or she would not tell it at all; and she needed to tell it if she was to break free from it. Eventually, she went on.

"One morning, my pair didn't turn up. I never knew why not. She was in another college, and we hadn't become close. Anyway, with two of us, we had sat side by side on his sofa. When I got to his rooms on this particular morning, though, I was almost late, and it was obvious that my pair wasn't coming, so I went to sit on the armchair, but he insisted that I sit on the sofa as I normally did."

"So he bothered you a little, even before that morning?" I suggested.

"Um." She looked uncomfortable. "A bit. Well, more than a bit. He liked to walk around the room while he talked. He liked to stroke the backs of our heads or twirl his fingers in the ends of our hair, from behind the sofa. When this first happened, we didn't know what to do. The second or third time he did it to her, my pair tossed her head to try to suggest that she wanted him to desist, but we were both aware of his influence, and neither of us wanted to upset him. And he was good at his subject, without a doubt."

"But he didn't stop doing it?"

"Oh, no," Hannah said, "he'd obviously done it for years." She paused again, and again I waited. "Well, that morning, he sat behind his desk as usual while I read my essay, and then got up to wander about while he commented on it. And, yes, he did his hair-twirling thing, but by then I just tried to ignore it, and went on making notes on what he was saying.

"We were talking about Shelley, and whether he had loved his sister, or Southey, or whoever. But then he sat down beside me." Another pause. She bowed her head, and, when she went on this time, I could barely hear her voice. "Then he put his hand under my skirt, right...under my skirt. I could feel him groping for the top of my...under things, and I must have screamed. I thought that would stop him, but it didn't. He just pulled all the harder." By now, Hannah was staring at the sky out of the window of my consulting room.

"Whatever did you do?" I prompted her.

"I hit him across the face with my folder. It was hard plastic, and I hit out as hard as I could. He let go of me then. His nose was bleeding hard. The blood was dripping off his chin onto his shirt-front. I didn't see any more. I ran from the room as fast I could, and down the stairs into the quad." She stood up and went to the window. "I must have looked a mess, and I was crying. A couple of girls who were passing stopped.

"One put her arm around me, and the other said, 'Had a go at you, too, has he?' so I knew I wasn't the first. I couldn't stop crying, and I couldn't tell anyone what had happened, so I just took off again through the college gates and into the street, and thought that would be the end of it. I'd stopped crying by the time I got back to my own college. I'd begun to realise that, whatever his intentions, nothing really dreadful had happened, and that it could have been so much worse. I'd forgotten about hitting him, I think. It was only the next day, when my personal tutor called me to her rooms, that the real trouble began."

While she had been telling this part of her story, Hannah had kept her face turned away from me. Now she looked straight at me, earnestly, beseechingly.

"She told me that he was claiming I had assaulted him without any provocation! I couldn't believe it. 'No, no,' I told her, 'it wasn't like that at all!' 'But there was no one else there to witness what happened,' she said, 'and he will be believed against you. I'm afraid you've blown your First,' she said, though she assured me that she'd fight hard for an Upper Second for me if I didn't contest what he was saying. The assault allegation would go no further in the university, she said. He wouldn't want any more fuss, as long as no one openly challenged his reputation, and he got his way, his revenge, over the class of my degree. So I just gave up."

She stood up and walked across to the window at which she had been staring.

"You have a beautiful garden," she said, "so open to the sky. I would love to just fly out into it, out of my whole human life."

***

I was so very sad for poor Hannah, but almost ecstatic about the progress of her treatment. At last, I was convinced we'd uncovered the trigger-point for her collapse.

"Gave up, how?" I asked, when she had come back to her chair and almost flumped down into it in a most un-Hannah-ish manner.

"Well, it was nearly Finals. I just stopped working. It wouldn't make any difference now, anyway. I was appalled at the injustice of it all, of the whole system. I'd believed Cambridge degrees were given on the basis of achievement, and it obviously wasn't so, in my case at least. I couldn't win here in the university, where I'd proved I'd been fitted to be, so I probably wouldn't be able to win anywhere else. I wrote what I could at Finals—I still loved what I was writing and thinking about—was given an Upper Second Class degree, and looked round for a job of some kind which would keep body and soul together. It didn't matter what."

I gave her space for her emotions to settle down, all the anger and despair her mind had generated, even if she had not been fully aware of those feelings at that time.

When she seemed ready, I said, "You didn't consider going back to London, at this point?"

"Not for a minute." She was very definite about that. "I'd escaped from there, actually and mentally. I hadn't heard from my mother for almost three years, but I hadn't given that any kind of thought, except for being sure that I wasn't going to tell her I'd failed again, and hear her crow. 'I knew you'd never get on in the world, Hannah. You were always going to be a loser,' she would have said, and I could do without that."

"You still had an excellent degree, Hannah."

"But it wasn't what I was worth, what I could have had!" she almost spat out at me.

"And so you ended up at the factory?"

"Um." She was looking down at her hands again.

"So how would you characterise your mood at that point, Hannah?" I asked.

"Oh, knowing what I now know," she smiled at me briefly, "I suppose I was depressed. I didn't know that then. I had just given up. Nothing mattered. Nothing would ever matter." Unusual anger again entered her tone. "I'd live, eat, sleep. Fairly quickly, I learnt enough to do that job at the factory automatically. I quite liked it that Mrs White gave me increasing amounts of responsibility, drafting letters for her, and so on. But it was all purely mechanical. I didn't have to think. I didn't have to enjoy it. The factory didn't interest me, nor the people there. It was just a way of getting a regular income, something more secure than anything I had previously known."

The tutor's attack on Hannah had clearly been an attempted rape, and as clearly could not possibly be proved in court. But its impact on Hannah's mental stability, the impact of her total incapacity to oppose the aftermath, had been extreme. I was sure she had become clinically deeply depressed, and might well have eventually become a danger to herself into the bargain. Her collapse was by far the least of the possible outcomes to which she had been exposed at that point.

Obviously, the lack of an exemplar father-figure in her conscious life, and her mother's habitual attitude and behaviour, had had a huge effect on Hannah's inability to form supportive and comforting relationships, or to manage those which she could not avoid forming among the people she inevitably met in her day-to-day life. Finally, it had all overwhelmed her. It was only surprising that such an outcome had taken as long to arrive as it did.

Dealing with all that took several weeks. Eventually, however, it was time to lay the foundation for the next stage of our work together.

"Hannah," I therefore said at the end of one of our sessions, "before our next meeting, I'd like you to think about the patterns in your life." Hannah looked puzzled and slightly fearful. "Don't worry about it," I tried to reassure her. "This is a long-term project, and will probably occupy us for quite a little while, but it is central to finding yourself in the present, separating yourself from what has happened in the past and has left its marks on you."

***

When I left Margaret's consulting room that morning, I had little clear idea of what she was asking me to do. She seemed to have wanted me to look at my part in the events of my past. But I hadn't thought that I had had a part. I hadn't been responsible for all those moves, for my mother never having any money, for her taking my things if she fancied them... All this went round and round in my head on the bus back to where I was living. Mother, Mother, Mother. What she'd done, and not done.

But Margaret wanted me to put Mother aside, and look at myself. That was scary. That meant accepting some responsibility for what had happened, for how those things had developed and how I had—or rather had not—dealt with them. Only gradually did it dawn on me that I had been criticised constantly by my mother, humiliated repeatedly by my peers, to the extent that I expected and feared criticism whenever I was to be judged by someone else. When it happened, I knew that the critic had to be right, that there was no way I could reasonably question the criticism, or the judge's right to criticise me. Finally, I realised that what I feared most of all in the world was to lack the respect of the people among whom I lived.

Gradually, over several months, Margaret and I worked on all this, until one morning she said, "Hannah, we now have some idea why your mind is liable to react as it does to the normal, unthinking cruelties of human life. But you are likely to continue to react like that unless we can find an alternative reaction to use in the face of threatened injustice or inappropriately imposed power.

"So I'd like to suggest something of that sort, and ask you to start it into your mind, repetitively, over the coming week. I want you to spei. time remembering events for which you have always—but inappropriately accepted the blame, and then get into the habit of saying to yourself, 'I am not my mother. I am not responsible for her actions or their consequences.'"

An expression of satisfaction started to spread over Hannah's face as she tried out, silently, the words I had suggested to her. She certainly liked the idea they conveyed. Neither of us would know for several years how valuable their use would actually prove to be.

***

I totally trusted Margaret. Whatever was to come, I knew she would look after me. Nonetheless, that morning, after we had done our usual review, I felt myself becoming wary when she broached a new subject. I was much less liable to panic now at the prospect of new experiences. I hardly ever cried these days, and was beginning to feel increasingly comfortable with myself.

"Hannah," she said, "you have been working hard and successfully at all this for some time, but I believe that there is still a major issue that we need to address, and that is the matter of other people."

Oh dear. I really didn't like the sound of this! "Other people populate the world," she reminded me with a big smile. "We human beings can't avoid each other. In fact, we depend on each other. That is how we are made. You have been hurt by other people, but not everyone you have met has hurt you. Your lovely French teacher, Mrs Paladyne—"

"Yes, she was wonderful to me," I murmured.

"How would you describe what she did for you, Hannah?" Margaret asked.

"She supported me. She gave me a chance to get outside my usual environment, where I could make decisions for myself, and for the others around me. I think that was the greatest gift she gave me. I really appreciated that opportunity. And she didn't have to do that. She did it freely. And so did Mrs White at the factory. Once I'd settled in there, she trusted me, as though that was the normal way of people dealing with each other."

"And those gifts, of generosity and trust, made a huge difference, didn't they?" Margaret suggested, "especially as you hadn't seen much of either previously."

I nodded. I couldn't trust my voice.

"Well, even though you might find it difficult to believe at the moment, there are other people out there who will offer you similar gifts, if you will give them the opportunity," she said.

"Umm," I replied, doubtfully.

"On Monday evenings," Margaret went on, "I facilitate a group of about a dozen people who, for different reasons and in different ways, have been hurt much as you have. Like you, they need to rebuild their trust in other people."

I still wasn't totally comfortable, and I suppose Margaret could see this. She could always see how I was feeling, especially when I couldn't recognise it for and in myself. Nonetheless, she pressed on.

"No one has to say anything at our meetings. It is not uncommon for newcomers to say nothing for months after they join. But nobody minds that. They all joined the group with the same sorts of baggage, the same sorts of difficulties."

"What sort of people?" I asked.

"All sorts. Solicitors, house-wives, shop-assistants, students, people working on the railway and in local government. You wouldn't know what they did outside the group unless they chose to say. They are a fascinating mixture."

"So why are they there, and what do you do?"

"The purpose of the group is to provide a source of trust and support for each other when that is needed," she explained. "That may be in the meetings, or between particular individuals who have come to recognise that another member might be one whom they can trust with whatever is bothering them. And everyone is free, if approached by someone else in the group for support, to say, no, I can't do that, or no, not at the moment, or no, not yet." She hesitated. "I'd love you to join us, Hannah."

I didn't know what to say. I wanted to say yes, but was frightened to do so. I bought time, as usual.

"I'm not sure," I said eventually. "Can I think about it, and then we can talk about it again next week?"

I wasn't at all sure that I was ready for this. The prospect of stepping out into society again was terrifying after so many months of more-or-less seclusion. On the way home on the bus, I did think about it, and my fear began to shrink away. I trusted Margaret. She was the only person I did trust just now. If she thought it was time to at least crawl to the door of my shell and put out an antenna, maybe it had to be done. It would have to be done sooner or later, I supposed.

By the time I got off the bus outside my bungalow, I had decided to tuck the whole thing into the back of my mind and not face it until after the weekend, and then see how I felt about it. That wasn't so much cowardice as wariness, I told myself, as I unlocked the front door and, thankfully, left the world behind again for a while.

Chapter Five

I eventually found the discreet entrance to the little chapel where Margaret's group met, and followed the sign inside the door to a surprisingly large hall at the rear of the building. I had told Margaret that I would like to come and sit in on a group meeting, and she had warned me that I might feel reluctant to come in when I actually got there.

"This will be a big step for you, Hannah," she had repeated, "but you're a courageous girl. I'm sure that, if you can bring yourself to join us, it really does have the potential to be helpful."

Having avoided social company for so long, I could see that she might be right. Nonetheless, as I went into the hall, I was not just feeling wary. I was terrified!

I took a folded cardboard name-plate with my first name written on it from a small table just inside the door, as she had instructed me, and took my first look around the room. At the far end, about a dozen folding chairs had been arranged in a tight circle, and three other people were already sitting there. Margaret herself was standing by another small table, putting out teacups and saucers and spoons around a generously-sized electric kettle, which was just coming to the boil, and a carton of milk, a bag of sugar, and what looked like a biscuit tin.

"Hello, Hannah," Margaret greeted me brightly, smiling as she turned at the sound of my footsteps. "Come and have a cup of coffee, and a biscuit or two."

I took a coffee, and went to find a seat in an unoccupied segment of the circle. Gradually, the seats filled up. One or two people spoke to each other. Most people smiled generally and usually weakly, as they sat down. Promptly at seven-thirty, Margaret slipped the catch on the door-lock—"for privacy" as she had previously explained to me—and joined the circle on the chairs.

"Well, good evening, everyone," she said. There was a low rumble of response. "It's good to see you all again," she continued. "So, just begin whenever anyone is ready, and remember, no interrupting a speaker while they are still talking."

The silence extended, but I gradually realised that it was a comfortable silence. Everyone around the circle looked relaxed. After about ten minutes, a young woman a few seats to my right sat up a bit straighter and said quietly, "I got out to the supermarket this week."

"Well done, Trudy," several voices congratulated her.

"It was only a quick trip, and I didn't stay in the store very long. I just needed some vegetables and a loaf, and they're both stacked quite near the door. But it's a start, isn't it?" She looked appealingly at Margaret, who beamed back at her encouragingly.

"Are you eating any more, Trudy?" a man's voice asked.

"A bit," she said, but without any great conviction.

There was another silence, then another man, on far the side of the circle from me, said, "My wife and I are still together, but we're still not getting below the surface. I do try, but she won't respond to anything much other than what we need to arrange to keep the house in order, and where I'll be when I'm away overnight. She won't talk about anything…personal, and I'm having real trouble with that. It's so bloody lonely."

He was choking slightly as he finished speaking, and seemed likely to burst into tears, but he made a visible effort and kept his tears under control.

"You were going to suggest she might come along here with you," another man said.

"Fat chance! So I tried suggesting she find another group she can go to, but no, 'I'll find help when I need it', she said, 'but I don't like people knowing personal things about me'. And then she said I wasn't to talk about such things here, either. 'But that's what the meetings are for,' I tried to tell her, but she wouldn't have it."

"Man, it's lonely when someone you depend on won't talk to you, or let you talk," a tall West Indian man said sympathetically. "Keep trying, mate. All you can do, there."

Someone else, a woman this time, said gently, "Are you still sure you want to stay in the marriage, Barry? It's obviously hurting you most terribly. I know, believe me, that divorce is horrible, but…"

Barry was still fighting his tears, and said nothing. He had clearly considered that possibility before, and hated it, but it was not yet off the table for him, apparently. Several people glanced at Margaret to check that the question hadn't been too intrusive, but she said nothing. No doubt she would follow up on the progress and the on-going difficulties of individuals in her consulting room sessions with them. Here, apart from making the refreshments and welcoming everybody, I wasn't sure what her role was, unless it was to referee arguments if they ever broke out.

An Asian woman on my right suddenly said, angrily, "My mother-in-law has the opposite problem. Always poking into our personal things, mine and my husband's. Won't shut up. When are we going to have a baby, why haven't we had a baby, how often do we try, how do we try. It's never right, and I so much want to have children, but it just won't happen," and she pulled her hijab over her face and burst into floods of tears and almost wailing sobs.

There was universal sympathy for her in the expressions around the circle. Two people covered their faces with their hands in distress. Nobody moved from their chair or spoke until she had regained control, however. She was allowed to sob out her grief and her distress without interruption. When she had calmed down again, smiled shyly round the circle, and muttered, "Sorry, sorry," a couple of times. Several voices told her 'not to worry, let it out, dear'.

"No apologies needed here, Jahida, you know that," Margaret said, still smiling warmly, and everyone sat back again more comfortably, and the silence was resumed.

At about a quarter to nine, Margaret got to her feet and said briefly, "OK, folks?" No one disagreed. "Right. Time for a cuppa, then, I think," and she walked away to take the catch off the door.

"She always takes her time doing that," said the girl next door to me. "Gives us time to have a word with each other, if we want to. Sort of marks the end of the session."

I noticed that one of the other women was giving Jahida a huge hug, and nearly reducing her to tears again through her brave, grateful smile. My neighbour straightened up after retrieving her handbag from the floor beneath her chair, and began to walk over towards the refreshments table. That was more than I could face that evening, however. I left, and no one seemed to mind.

I had come through the evening unscathed. No one had required me, let alone pressed me, to say a word, not even to say who I was or why I was there. Apart from Margaret, and my neighbour at the end of the session, it seemed quite possible that no one else had really noticed I was there, which suited me fine.

The circle had felt welcoming. I began to think that this could be a pleasant way to spend an evening, if it went on like this. And, if it didn't, I simply wouldn't come.

Also, I had learned several useful things. In the first place, there *were* pleasant, unthreatening, ordinary people in the world just like me, who went about suffering from the weight of appalling, hidden burdens imposed on them by other people. I was not the only one, nor even the one with the heaviest burden. I was not alone, nor even particularly unusual, as I had so often thought I must be.

Secondly, those people *understood* what it felt like to be so burdened, to be so in need of support. Not material support. Just a word and a touch, and perhaps the opportunity to pick up advice from hearing how someone else was handling their own particular difficulties. By the time I left the hall, I still had not said anything beyond the normal politeness, but I had listened and been heartened and strengthened. I found that I was looking forward to the next meeting more than I had looked forward to anything for a very long time.

***

Gradually, I got used to the group, and continued to appreciate its members' uncritical, supportive attitude to each other, and their unspoken acceptance of my presence. I became comfortable with the woman beside whom I had happened to sit on the first evening. Whichever of us arrived first, the other came and sat in the next seat, if it were still free. She was in her thirties, I thought, slightly plump beneath the thick woollen jumper and simple trousers she wore every week.

I began to wonder if the cold from which she seemed to need to protect herself was inside or outside her. She would have looked confident if it wasn't for the slightly haunted expression she habitually wore, except when she smiled. Then, you could see the happy person inside her who had been damaged by whatever had brought her to the group. But she didn't smile often, except when we first saw each other, or were leaving at the end of a meeting.

After a few weeks, as it was approaching Christmas, I began to stay for the refreshments at the end of group meetings. There was no pressure at that stage either, as I had feared. The group broke into little gaggles, standing quietly or talking generalities about the outside world, or in pairs or threes, usually offering advice and support to someone who had spoken in the circle. There was no feeling of exclusion. I supposed it was how close families behave, though I had no experience, first-hand or second-hand, on which to base that supposition. Nothing was private here, but there was great sensitivity in the way people dealt with each other's vulnerabilities. Shared experience and understanding were obvious. I finally grasped the meaning of the word 'community', something I had not understood until then.

I did not contribute for quite a while after I joined the group. By then, some new people had joined, and some had stopped coming, but the character of the group, and the nature of the members' issues, remained much the same. We had all been damaged, in one way or another, by parents, partners, neighbours, teachers or bosses, and we were all struggling to get back on terms with ourselves and with the world in which we had to exist. By the time I did decide to speak, I was feeling much better about myself in many ways, more ready to face life again.

This was indicated, I realised, by the fact that the big, practical issue of an income had begun to poke its head over my horizon like a sailor's first sight of a coastal mountain as, at last, she approached the end of a long, lonely voyage. However, it was an issue that I kept postponing. I did not want to go back to the factory, to its sympathy and its boredom, but I could not see what other sort of job I might be able to get, let alone do, especially after what had happened to me over the last eighteen months.

Gradually, I began to wonder whether this was a matter on which I could obtain useful advice in the group. One evening, therefore, having carefully planned a minimal sentence or two by which I could introduce the subject, I waited for a suitable silence. In one such space, I gathered myself together and said, "I'm Hannah. I collapsed a couple of years ago, but, sooner or later, I'm going to have to go back to work. Does anyone have any useful tips on that subject, please?"

There was a discernible straightening of backs around the circle. This was different from the usual 'cries for help' that members were used to hearing, seemingly more practical, though I didn't doubt that most of them recognised it as the camouflage that it was for the issues which I had attempted to use it to hide.

A middle-aged, professional-looking man on my right said, "Was your collapse work-related, Hannah?"

"No," I replied, "not directly. It seems to have resulted from a build-up of previous things which finally I could no longer withstand. I had an easy job. I was comfortable with my boss, and more or less everyone was kind to me."

"Do you feel ready to go back to work?" somebody else asked.

"No, not yet," I said, "but I will have to do so, very soon."

Several people nodded, no doubt thinking of their own difficulties in managing on benefit-payments. There was a short pause.

"Will you want to go back to the same sort of work?" was the next question.

"Probably not," I said, "though I have no idea what else I might be able or accepted to do."

"What's stopping you going back to work now, Hannah?"

"At the moment, I don't yet feel strong enough to do a day's work. I still get up late, go to bed early and, more often than not, I have to have a sleep in bed in an afternoon. Travelling on a bus tires me, and so does walking further than to my local shops."

"Have you thought of starting on something part-time, when you're feeling stronger?" someone on my left offered.

"Your public library might have something about training-courses," someone else said. "Give you a new skill, and pointers to new job-opportunities."

"Yes," someone else suggested. "You might be able to develop something you could do freelance, from home like, as a start."

"Something based on IT, if you've got your own computer," another voice added.

Again, there was a pause. Eventually, when it seemed that the group had got as far as they wanted to go on this subject, I said, sincerely, "Thank you. Those sound like very good ideas. Thank you all."

They *were* good ideas, and I *was* grateful for them. I suddenly realised that, in those last few minutes, I had said more to anyone other than Margaret than I had done for almost two years. Most of all, though, I was grateful for the feeling of having been fully accepted into the group at last. It had not been their fault that I had continued to feel like an attender rather than a member for so long. That was down to me alone. But tonight, I had spoken up, trusted them, and they had reached out to me generously.

As we walked over to the refreshments table at the end of the meeting, my next-door neighbour said quietly, "I'm starting back to work next week after a year and a half. Do you want to talk about it?"

We gathered our cups and saucers, and my new friend took a couple of biscuits from the tin.

"Can't resist them," she said, with a rueful smile. "My day seems to be one long nibble. Don't know what I'll do when I'm back at work. Expand like a balloon, I expect."

"Was it hard," I asked carefully, "deciding to go back?"

"Um," she said. "I'm only going back part-time to start with, which won't make it any easier to find the rent. But I still get tired by lunchtime. I'm hoping I'll get stronger with practice, like going for a run, and going a little further every week. I used to do that, until …"

Her voice died on her, and she looked down into her cup. I gave her space to regain control. Eventually, she looked up again, and gave me another brief, wan smile.

"Are you going to be doing…what you did before?" I tried.

"Not exactly, but more or less." She paused. "I'm a fully qualified management accountant, actually. I worked very hard for that," she said proudly, "and was doing quite well. Now, I'm going back as a lowly book-keeper." She sighed. "But it's a start." Another pause. "I asked where I used to work, but they wouldn't risk it. 'Sorry, Trish, we've filled your position long since,' the bloody little HR director told me, pompous little… 'It's been a while, hasn't it? Feeling a bit better now, are we?' Fat lot of good he was, either, when…it happened."

Another pause.

"That's awful," I tried to commiserate.

"Anyway, it's water under the bridge now," she said, taking a deep breath and standing straighter. "New start, and all that. Better luck next time."

"I think you're being very brave," I said, and meant it. She obviously wasn't looking forward very much to her new start. "When exactly are you starting?"

"Monday morning, sharp at 8.30," she replied.

"Look, I don't want to be pushy," I suggested, "but would you like us to meet for a coffee on Saturday? A sort of *bon voyage* event, to send you off into the future? Do you live around here? Do say no if you don't fancy it."

"I'd love to," she said. "I'm Trish, by the way. Trish Cox."

"I'm Hannah," I said, and left it at that, for now.

We fixed a time and place to meet, put down our cups, thanked Margaret, called a general goodbye to those who were still left, most of whom would help her with the washing up and putting away—no doubt we'd all do our share eventually—and left to go to our slightly less lonely homes.

Trish and I did meet on that Saturday. It was my first time out with a girlfriend for…I don't know whether it helped Trish, but it cheered me up no end. Afterwards, I did indeed go into the local library for a general look at their careers and training leaflets. I sat down at a table to examine what I had collected, and gazed round at all the neatly shelved books. Another possibility began to emerge in my mind.

Trish didn't appear at the next week's meeting of the group, and I wondered if, for her, it had done its job. She reappeared the week after, however, and we arranged to meet for coffee again the following Saturday afternoon. I arrived first at the little café we had chosen, got a fair-trade coffee, and sat half-expecting she wouldn't come after all. When she did arrive, had got a hot chocolate and had sat down heavily opposite me, she said, with a tired smile, "Sorry to be late. I overslept. Right through the morning, until two o'clock. I keep doing that at weekends, when I don't set the alarm."

She looked down and stirred the cream topping into her chocolate.

"How's it all going?" I asked tentatively.

"I'm still finding it exhausting," Trish said. "I can do the job, and I'm only working mornings, thank goodness. By one o'clock, I'm worn out, and go home and back to bed, get up about seven or eight, eat something, go back about ten and sleep right through till the alarm goes off next morning. I've got to shop this afternoon, later. I'm almost out of food. And I must get something else to wear. I've been living in jumpers and trousers for eighteen months. Everybody else in the office wears skirts, and make me feel dowdy, though nobody's said anything. Yet."

I noticed that, while she still looked haunted, she seemed younger this morning. Then I noticed she was wearing a touch of lipstick, and a pale eyeliner.

"You look very nice this afternoon," I said.

"Decided I had to make an effort for the office," she smiled, "and it's started to become a habit again. Do you ever try a bit of lippy? Your lovely eyes and dark lashes don't need any help, but a little colour lower down might sort of balance your face. Make it a bit broader." She stopped. "Hope I'm not sticking my great nose in, Hannah?"

I was used now to the carefully polite form which suggestions took between members of the group.

"I've never used make-up," I said, "which was quite a help when the finances got a bit thin. One fewer thing to have to buy."

"Oh, yes, that's when I stopped using it. Still, there was nobody else to bother about it, so …"

"Do you want to talk about what happened?" I said, before I'd really thought about it.

"No, not really, if you don't mind. It's all over and left behind. New start, new life, new adventures. Drink up, and you can come and help me find a skirt. If you've time?" she offered.

As Trish had said, new adventures. I had hardly ever shopped for clothes in my life, though I was very good at looking after what I had.

"That would be fun," I decided. "Thank you."

We looked at skirts in all the bigger shops, and dresses in the new autumn colours, and jumpers and shoes…We had a thorough rummage, and a lot of giggles and gossip about what other women were apparently looking for, and their poor husbands lurking at the edges of the women's departments and trying not to show their embarrassment when called upon for an opinion. It wasn't until we got to the 'cheap and cheerful' store that Trish bought anything, and then it was just a plain black pencil skirt, of which we must have seen a dozen versions by then.

"What about this one with a pinstripe?" I had suggested, and Trish was obviously tempted, looked at it and then at me, sideways. But she said, no, she wasn't ready for anything quite so daring yet, and we giggled again and put it back on the rack. I bought nothing, though we saw so many things that I loved, and several that Trish insisted on taking off the rack and holding against me.

"Maybe next year," I had to keep telling her, thinking 'if I can get a job and some income by then'.

Out in the street, the sky was dark, of course, being December, and the buildings and shop windows were bright with Christmas lights and decorations.

"What are you doing for Christmas, Hannah?" Trish asked as we walked down to the cluster of town-centre bus-stops.

This was an old chestnut. I gave her the answer I'd used for years.

"Oh, the usual, I expect."

Trish stopped, and a dozen shoppers diverted past the sudden obstruction she made. She looked at me carefully, before saying, "Does that mean what I think it means?"

I realised that, on this occasion, it was too difficult to kid this kidder.

"Probably," I admitted.

She put her arms around me, and we both let go a couple of tears.

"Together, then?" she said into my ear, still holding me close.

"Yes, please," I murmured back.

We released each other.

"Ooh, there's my bus," she said, looking up the road. "Let's fix details at next week's meeting."

"Have a good week," I called after her as she hurried away. "Take care."

At the end of next week's meeting, having collected our drinks, and Trish a handful of biscuits, we went back to the circle of chairs and sat down.

"How are you doing?" I asked Trish.

"Quite well, I think," she said. She certainly looked less haunted. "I'm finding out where things are, like buses and cheap shops and cafes near the office, and I've laid out a budget for myself which I can manage, mostly. It's tight, but maybe I'll be able to go full-time in the spring, which will bring in a bit more cash. How about you?"

"OK, thanks," I replied. "My life circles around this," I waved at the hall and the other members of the group gathered near Margaret's kettle, "and sessions with Margaret, and, on a good day, I go and find a library, or walk down to the Fitzwilliam for a browse. I'm beginning to feel restless. I need to get out beyond the same four walls now and then."

"Being poor so easily becomes being lonely," Trish philosophised. "Have you thought any more about a job, yet?"

"I'll see how things are after Christmas," I said, continuing to put off serious thinking in that direction. I really didn't feel strong enough yet to face all that, though I recognised the danger of letting an excuse become a habit.

"Speaking of Christmas…" Trish began, and then stopped, and picked up the last biscuit balancing precariously on the edge of her saucer. Was there a tear at the corner of her eye?

I decided to be practical.

"There's no public transport on Christmas Day, and not much on Boxing Day," I said. "Shall we do something on Christmas Eve?"

"That's a good idea!" Trish agreed enthusiastically. "What about meeting for supper?" She named a little restaurant near the chapel. I knew it wasn't too expensive, or at least it hadn't been when I occasionally ate there on a "cheer-me-up" indulgence as a student.

Trish looked up again, and met my eye.

"Hannah," she said, quietly, "no presents, not even little ones."

She was becoming really upset. Obviously, Christmas had once meant a lot more to her than it had ever meant to me. For a second, I wondered what had brought her to Margaret, but there was no way I was going to ask. If she wanted to tell me, when she wanted to, she'd do so. But I felt a huge sympathy for her. She had clearly had a dreadful time.

"Not this year," I agreed, regarding the issue of presents. "See how we get on next year, when we're both a bit more flush."

She smiled, as relief took over her face from its expression of sad embarrassment.

Christmas Eve supper was a strange, heart-shaking success. The restaurant was packed, and it was a good thing Trish had booked a table in advance. The food was good, and I enjoyed eating something somebody else had cooked. Trish seemed determined to be cheerful, if not exactly festive, and our table was tucked away in a corner where, despite the volume of voices from everyone else, we could still talk freely. We put aside the paper hats, and decided to take our crackers home with us, more because we didn't want the fuss and mess of pulling them at our table than with any future celebration in mind.

We were into our main courses (helpings far too large for either of us), when Trish said, "Christmas hurts! And I used to love it so much!" And then she reimposed her happyish face, and said, "I'm so sorry, Hannah."

"Don't worry," I told her. "I've a fair idea where you are. Probably I've a better idea than anybody in the town outside the group."

She sniffed, smiled briefly as she reached for a tissue from the handbag by her feet, and blew her nose firmly but discretely.

"It's all to do with a man, of course," she murmured reluctantly. "I loved him so much." She stopped again. "He was married, but he left his wife and we lived together for eight months. I was the happiest…"

I waited. She would get there in her own time.

"I still love him!" she said, face and voice bleaker than I had seen or heard on her before.

"He died. Hit and run driver. He went out on Christmas Eve afternoon two years ago, and didn't come home. I didn't worry at first. Then, by seven o'clock I did, but didn't know what to do. Shortly after nine, I 'phoned the hospital, and…they told me…he had been brought in hours before, but they hadn't known who he was."

There was nothing to say. It's unlike me, but I had to get up and go around the table to hold her. I gave no thought to what any of the other people in the room thought. She needed to be held, and we hugged each other for minutes. When her arms slackened around my waist, I let her go and went back to my seat.

Eventually, slightly pink, she looked up at me and tried to grin, and I tried to grin back. Neither attempt was particularly successful, but was the best we could do. For a distraction, I said, "Coffee?" and began to signal to our waitress.

"Come back to mine for coffee?" Trish invited, almost begged.

So I did, and slept on her sofa at the end of the evening. Late the next morning, Trish came out of her bedroom, we had yet more coffee, and, once she had satisfied me that she had returned to some sort of stability, I got a taxi home. I had had some peculiar Christmases before, and not a lot of memorable presents. That year, I was given a friend with whom I've stayed in touch ever since, even though we seldom see each other from one year's end to the next.

Chapter Six

From time to time in my consulting room, I realised that I had no clear idea of how Hannah had managed financially through the period of her difficulties. The factory had paid her for the first three months of her illness, which was reasonably generous, but had then notified her by letter that, with great regret, they had had to terminate her employment. They trusted that, on full recovery, she would feel free to approach them if she might care to consider re-joining them. With some prompting, she was able to agree that that was as much, and probably more, than a lot of employers would have done in the circumstances.

Thereafter, I presumed, she had lived on the various available benefits. Dr Walmsley and I had written the appropriate supportive letters to the relevant plethora of central and local government agencies, when Hannah requested them. Not wanting her to be distracted by avoidable money-worries, I asked her briefly from time to time if she was managing, and she always said she was. She was a sensible girl, and well used to living with hardly any available cash, but we had been working together for almost three years now. It can't have been easy, or much fun, struggling on a limited budget for so long a period of time.

I was therefore very pleased, one Wednesday morning in spring, when Hannah sat down in the client-chair and said, "I'm thinking it's time I got a new job."

"Well, well," I replied, assessing silently whether she was strong enough at last to go back out into the world. Certainly, she looked and sounded strong enough. Moreover, she was wearing a blouse and skirt that I hadn't seen before, and was carrying what looked like a new handbag.

"The fact that you're actually thinking that way is a good sign that you may indeed be ready to move on," I said. "What sort of job are you considering?"

"I went to tea with my tutor at the university last week," Hannah said "It's possible that she might be prepared to put me in touch with a friend of hers who runs a small publishing house, and might take me on as a reader. But it's in Edinburgh."

I almost said, "Well, well," again, but managed to stop myself in time.

"That sounds like very good news," I said instead. "It'll be a big effort, finding a new home and moving, and everything. You're really feeling ready for all that now?"

"Oh, yes, I'm confident I can manage it, though I couldn't and wouldn't have felt like this six months ago."

I was so glad to hear her use the word "confident".

"And Dr Walmsley is comfortable with that?" I asked, touching all the bases.

"I spoke to him last Friday," Hannah said earnestly, "and he asked the same questions that you just have. He said how pleased he was that I felt so much better, and saw no reason from his point of view why I shouldn't go ahead."

"I'm very pleased for you too, Hannah," I agreed, and received a proper smile. "If you felt you would like support up there in Edinburgh, just let me know," I added. "I'd be more than happy to find someone to whom I could refer you, if you wished."

"Thank you," she said, "and I'll contact you if I feel the need, of course. But I'm pretty sure I'll be all right now, with all you've done for me."

"No, you've done it, Hannah, and done it well," I congratulated her. It has to be the client's effort, every time, in this business.

And, as far as I was concerned at the time, as her therapist, that was Hannah. A new life, a new identity, in effect. She wrote me a very nice "thank you" letter, a few weeks later. She was enjoying her new job, and was finding it very rewarding. It was much more suited to her abilities than her previous one. No boyfriend mentioned yet, but I knew it would come in time. I could stop worrying about Hannah, I was sure. Which was a good thing, because there are always plenty more poor souls to be picked up in my world, and helped through their darkness.

***

A 'Dear Hannah' note from my former tutor arrived the following week, telling me how I should go about contacting MacWhinney, Preston, the publishing house of which she had spoken to me. In the meantime, I began to haunt Cambridge libraries to research the firm, its products, the publishing industry, Edinburgh itself and places to live there…well, everything I could think of in preparation for, I suppose it had to be called, 'beginning a career'.

My tutor suggested that I should write to the Managing Editor in Edinburgh, mentioning her name, saying something of my 'particular interests' in contemporary English literature (there hadn't been any for the last three years, but I could resurrect the essays I had done in College, I supposed) and asking to be considered for the post of a reader in his 'house'. "It's all just a formality," my tutor had written, "if you maintain the standard of the work you used to do for me." That "if" was the catch, of course. Could I get back to that standard from a standing start? At least all I had to write now was a letter, not a complete thesis.

It took me four days of intense work to prepare the letter to my increasingly fearful satisfaction, and send it off. Some three weeks later, I received a reply from Mr James MacWhinney, saying that he had heard 'great things' of me, was indeed seeking a junior reader, and was looking forward to meeting me. Would I please let him know when I might next conveniently be in Edinburgh, and, in the meantime, would I perhaps care to let him have an outline ("not more than 3,000 words, on this occasion") of the principles which I felt should direct the assessment of the commercial potential of such manuscripts as no doubt I was already aware that his firm attracted and, ultimately, published.

This was horrifying! Mr MacWhinney was clearly prepared to do a favour for an old friend's protégée, but he wasn't prepared to risk his firm's reputation or resources on a totally lame duck. He wanted some measure of the duck's quality before he offered it his favour, or allowed it to unduly delay his recruiting process. This was not the 'mere formality' I had expected. It was not at all the same as when I went to work for Mrs White at the factory. This was job-hunting for professionals, among professionals. And it was going to be expensive, too!

I immediately went to the bus and train stations to check the price of a ticket to Edinburgh, and my horror deepened. If I didn't in fact land this job, it was going to cost an awful lot of money to traipse about the country after others for which I might be remotely qualified, and for which I might suitably apply. My benefits, though generous and appreciated, were not intended to pay for extensive country-wide travel. Nor was I going to have any more income until, presumably, at least a month after I started whatever job I did manage to get.

Well, I had squirrelled away a little money, as it was my habit to do; but only a very little by comparison with the fare to Edinburgh, and the cost of an over-night stay there. It wouldn't go far.

I again called on the goodwill of my former tutor, telling her of the task Mr MacWhinney had set me, and begging a contact in the University Press who might advise me briefly how to go about it. Between them, she and her friend at the Press—she knew *everybody* in the literary life of the university, apparently, but I couldn't keep on running to her whenever I needed a leg up—outlined what MacWhinney was probably hoping that I would give him. Ten days of intense library work did the rest, and I took the resulting paper to my tutor, feeling just like an undergraduate all over again.

"Coffee, sherry or gin?" she enquired, as she always had. She liked her students to be relaxed sufficiently to say what they thought, while still sufficiently sober as to be lucid and respectful. When we were settled with our drinks, I read her what I had prepared, and she listened intently, as she always did.

"My, Hannah," she said when I came to the end, "you have been working hard to produce that in such a short time. Your research has been very thorough. You've covered all the points, I think. I'm glad to see that Penny, at the Press, was useful to you. However…" There was always a 'however' after the initial praise, with this woman, but the 'howevers' were almost always worth their weight in gold. "However," she went on, "MacWhinney is not an academic, he's a businessman. For him, time is money, your time in particular, as someone he will be paying to invest their time on his behalf. What he wants you to show him is whether you have a system."

I began to scribble notes furiously on the margin of my paper.

"When you pick up a manuscript from the pile in his office, what will you look for it to offer, first, then second, then third? What will your priorities be, in judging that this manuscript could be knocked into publishable shape, while that one couldn't be published profitably in a thousand years? What will the market support? What tell-tale signs will you look for in a manuscript to enable you to judge between one and another?"

She had put her finger on what was missing from my paper, as usual. My admiration for her as a practical, professional woman, as well as an appropriately respected academic, increased even further. It took me four more long days to reorder and expand my material into the structure she had suggested, and then I felt ready to send it off to Edinburgh. In my covering letter, I suggested that I might meet Mr MacWhinney in his office in two weeks' time, if that were convenient to him. Then I sat back to hoard my cash against the forthcoming unavoidable expenditure.

***

As my train pulled out of Cambridge station and headed through the modern suburbs to the North of the city, I realised that this would be the first time I had left Cambridge for almost seven years. I had always lived in a city, had seen almost nothing of the countryside. All the way to Peterborough, I was mesmerised by the desolate flatness and vast, wide skies of the Fenlands. I was slightly depressed by the drab yellow-black brickwork of the tiny towns through which the train passed after Ely—Manea, March, Whittlesea.

Each one seemed to be in danger of sinking into the peaty Fen fields, and disappearing for ever. I was overawed by the apparently endless bucket-chains carrying, first over the railway and then the river, the clay which had been extracted to make the Fletton bricks from which those towns had apparently been built.

I had to change trains at Peterborough. Sitting uncomfortably on a cold, garishly-painted metal bench bolted down to the platform there, I ate one of my homemade sandwiches while waiting for the mainline train from Kings Cross which would take me to Edinburgh. Once that train had pulled out of Peterborough station, it became obvious that I was no longer going to be distracted on this part of the journey. The speed of the train blurred the view of the passing country, and made me feel slightly sick when I tried to look beyond the less-than-clean carriage window beside my seat.

I read through the scheme I had sent to Mr MacWhinney, and a couple of my university essays that I had brought with me. With the prospect of the next day's interview, it felt—quite comfortingly, actually—as if I were revising for yet another examination. Despite stretching to a coffee from the refreshment trolley somewhere near Doncaster, and finishing my sandwiches, I fell asleep after we had passed York, under the influence of the warmth in the hermetically-sealed carriage. The journey passed fairly quickly, therefore, and the disembodied voice announced our arrival at Edinburgh soon after three o'clock.

I invested in a street-map of the city, as I passed the newsstand on the station concourse. Once off the station, the people I asked were most helpful in directing me to the bus stop I needed in order to get to my hotel, and less difficult to understand than I had feared. Their accent was usually quite gentle, though the meaning of some of the (presumably) dialect-words I heard, in the conversations around me on the bus, were less easy to interpret. The bus ride was only short. In ten minutes or so, I was on Beaufort Street. I could see no sign for the King's Hotel, but found it—no more than a pretentiously-named guest house—just a little further down the road.

It wasn't grand, but I couldn't afford grand. The receptionist made me welcome, though with a stronger accent than some I had heard so far. Nonetheless, I gathered the gist of most of what she told me, I believed. My room, on the second floor, was small but, again, more adequate than I had feared. The controls for the shower in the tiny *en suite* bathroom puzzled me for several minutes, but I worked them out eventually, and everything was perfectly clean. The small window of my room, also clean, looked out over an extensive cemetery, but that didn't bother me. This would do fine for the one night I would be here, I thought. I'd existed in far worse surroundings in the past.

Edinburgh, in the next morning's early sun, was not yet even pleasantly warm. It was not crowded by visitors as it would be for the festival later in the year. I hardly noticed those who were there. All I could think of was impressing Mr MacWhinney. I had read and reread yet again the paper I had sent him, in my hotel room and in the cheap café where I took a coffee the following morning in lieu of breakfast. I found the city centre conveniently compact. I could walk everywhere I needed to go, it seemed, and the walk to MacWhinney, Preston's offices in St Andrew's Square was welcome and relaxing.

***

The firm (I was soon to learn that the term was to be spoken in two syllables, with a strongly rolled 'r') was located on three upper floors of one of the narrow Georgian properties, disguised behind the imposingly wider stone frontages which surrounded the square. I was welcomed by the raised eyebrows and gleaming grey eyes of a warmly dressed woman in her 50's who was clearly expecting me.

"Are you Hannah?" she enquired, without approaching me. "Aye, you will be."

She raised her chin and her voice.

"Mr James, your visitor's here!" She turned back to the broad unpolished table on which she had been arranging her armful of papers into separate piles. "He'll be out directly," she told me, without looking up.

I stood just inside the double glass entrance doors, and looked around the room. Not so much a room as a space. High ceiling. Bare board floor. Lit by two tall windows at one end which looked out over the square. Well used, clean, and warm in atmosphere if not in temperature. An older man came slowly through one of the doorways opening off the space. His grey hair was thinning and as if blown about by a breeze, of which there was none around him.

Over several warm Fair Isle pullovers and a formal shirt and wool tie, he wore what had once been a good tweed suit, no doubt, some decades previously. Comfort clearly transcended appearance here, I realised gratefully.

"Ach, so you'll be Hannah," he said, looking up at last from the papers he was carrying to give me a very friendly smile. "Come away in here, now, come away. Will you be having a cup of tea, maybe? No? Aye, I'll have one, Elisabeth if you please," this to the paper-sorting woman, "and a biscuit, perhaps."

"Yes, Mr James, I'll mash for us all, it being our break-time."

"Hm," said Mr MacWhinney. The issue of breaks and tea was obviously one of some contention. This bore out my tutor's observation of him as a businessman, canny enough to watch carefully the expenditure of time and money under his management.

His office, like the outer one, was bare floored, but had a huge, old-fashioned radiator all along one wall. I was glad to see it. The big window looked out to the South, over the city to the Castle and the Old Town, but would gain no natural heat until the sun had come around later in the morning. In front of the equally huge, and hugely piled, desk was a big, squashy leather chair, comfortingly reminiscent of the one in Margaret's consulting room, but, of course, several generations older.

"Sit you down, lassie," Mr MacWhinney said, "sit you down. Ah, thank you, Elisabeth," as she came in and put his cup and saucer precariously on one of the piles on his desk.

"If you'd at least leave a corner of the desktop for your cup, Mr James, we'd maybe have fewer accidents," Elisabeth suggested in the tone of a mother remonstrating yet again with a long-standing habit of her grown-up son.

"Aye, aye," Mr MacWhinney responded through something of a sigh. "Now, Hannah, you had a good journey? And you've somewhere to stay in the city?"

"Yes, thank you, Mr MacWhinney," I said, "I was perfectly comfortable last night, and I'd planned to be going back South again later this afternoon."

"Indeed, indeed," he said through another sigh. "That might be a great pity, now, perhaps."

I wasn't sure what this meant. I had assumed that I was only here for a brief interview. Nothing to the contrary had previously been mentioned. Not being sure where the conversation was intended to go, I said nothing.

"Hm, hm," Mr MacWhinney said. I was getting used to his repetitions. They were to provide him with thinking time, I realised, as well as to bolster the gravitas of his dignity.

"Aye, well, lassie, I'd in mind you might be persuaded to stay for the rest of the week, maybe, you see."

I was still too confused to say anything yet.

"Aye, you see," Mr MacWhinney continued, "I was very impressed by the paper you sent me. From someone who doesn't know the publishing business, at least. You don't know the publishing business at first hand, I understand?" His face opened, as if at a totally new thought that had never previously crossed his mind. Was there something he hadn't been told? If so, out with it, now. He was not to be fished like a salmon.

"No, Mr MacWhinney, but I did what research I could, and spoke to a very helpful contact in the business."

"Did you so?" MacWhinney more-or-less murmured. "Did you so? Hm, hm." His voice returned to its normal volume. "Well, to continue, I liked the structure you were proposing in your paper, the orderliness of it. And the economy of the whole thing. Aye, I was very impressed, lassie. Your criteria won't always be applicable just precisely as you've suggested, of course. Books are like people. Everyone an individual. Systems often need to be adapted, in any field of activity. But I liked the bones of what you were saying. I thought, she'll maybe do. Aye, given a few years work on her, she'll maybe do."

I was still not sure what all this added up to, but it sounded as though a thank-you might be polite. So,

"Thank you, Mr MacWhinney," I said.

"Aye, aye," he replied. "Anyway, its Dr MacWhinney, if we're to be so formal, lassie, and we're not, here among ourselves. I'm Mr James in the office, and that goes for everyone. And everyone else is Christian names. Hm?"

The final 'hm' made me wonder how comfortable he really was with all this. Already, I smelled Elisabeth's power, however limited, at work here.

"I'm sorry, I didn't know about the doctorate, Mr James," I said. "I'll try to remember the conventions in future."

"Aye, aye," he repeated. "Now, lassie, what I have in mind is this. If you'd like to stay in Edinburgh until Friday week, and start work here this morning, I'll pay you per diem what I have in mind to offer you if you join us permanently. And maybe I'll add a daily expense line to cover your accommodation and three meals. There's not a lot to you, lassie," he said, looking me over briefly but unthreateningly, in the manner of a fond uncle, "you'll be no good to us without your strength."

He paused and lifted his eyebrows and his cup, to take a sip of tea. I took the opportunity to be practical, in a way I wouldn't have dared to do a year or two ago. I was tougher now.

"That's a very attractive proposal, Mr James," I said. "May I ask exactly what salary you had in mind, and what might happen after Friday week? I have to say that I'm really looking for a permanent job." In fact, I very much *needed* a permanent job, but I had the wit not to say that to a prospective employer at this stage.

"Oh, aye, lassie?" MacWhinney said. His tone seemed to express surprise. I was afraid that he was taking a dim view of a woman asking about money, especially so early in their acquaintance, but it was soon clear that his concern was elsewhere.

"Now, you see, Hannah," he said, "our practice here is to outsource as much of the work as we can to specialist readers, editors, designers, illustrators, printers, proof-readers, salespeople and so on." I looked straight at him, and nodded seriously, as though I fully understood the vocabulary and economics of the publishing industry. "That keeps our direct staff-costs low," he continued, "but we do need at least one of every skill-area on our staff here, in order to stay on top of quality-issues, as well as to administer the distribution and monitor the progress of each project, and the necessary liaison with the authors of accepted texts. I take it you're young enough to understand these damned electronic machines?"

"I am computer literate, Mr James," I said, crossing my fingers mentally. Looking round the room, I could see no computer, although it could have been buried under the mountains of accumulated paper on his desk. "I completed a

72

secretarial and book-keeping course before going up to the university, and worked as a Personal Assistant in industry for some time. I'm sure I could obtain a reference from that employer, if you wished."

"No, there'll be no need for that," MacWhinney said. "You'll show me what you can do in that regard, no doubt. I don't understand the things at all, at all," he smiled, "but Elisabeth does, so we get by." Obviously, Elisabeth was the proverbial treasure in his eyes, which perhaps began to explain the origin of their mutually respectful and dependent working relationship.

MacWhinney reached for his teacup again. After another sip, he put it down precariously on its tilting saucer, and said, "The first step in this business is a wee bit hit-and-miss, maybe. Agents send us manuscripts with flowery, enthusiastic letters of commendation. Sometimes, such extravagance is justified, sometimes it really isn't." He wagged his head from side to side sadly. "We need to judge between the two promptly. Otherwise, an agent might send copies of a good manuscript to several houses, and the quickest to recognise its quality wins the business. On the other hand, authors send their manuscripts to us direct, and most of them are unpublishable. But maybe one in thousands is a jewel of remarkable value, and, if we don't give such material a reasonable degree of attention, we could miss it. That would be too sad." He almost grinned. Clearly, he enjoyed what in his words sounded like a sort of strolling commercial cut-and-thrust.

"Now, we've had no in-house reader for a few weeks," he continued. "Your predecessor—I hope—decided to bet on herself and try being a freelance editor. Ah, well, good luck to her. Why shouldn't she? We'll use her when we need." She had obviously left with his blessing and with no animosity whatsoever. Was there a soft heart beneath his sharp business carapace?

"But, upstairs," he continued, "there's a small room with a big table, on which there's an even bigger pile of manuscripts which are just going on accumulating. I wouldn't know, and I'm not going up there to see. But Elisabeth tells me so." He raised his mobile eyebrows once more, and tucked in his chin like a defensive boxer. "Frequently!"

"That part of the work sounds fun," I said, giving him my best and most confident smile. "And after Friday week?"

"Hm, hm," he began, "well, lassie, if we're all comfortable with how you're getting on by then," I imagined that he meant himself, me and Elisabeth, "I'd thought maybe you'd just...carry on. We'd give you a contract, of course, say two years to start, with mutual review-and-break clauses at the first three and six months. That's the sort of thing we start new people off on. Aye. Hm, hm." It sounded as though Mr James wasn't at his most comfortable in the HR role. I was sure Elisabeth had no such qualms.

"And the salary, Mr James?" I smiled to take the sting out of my persistence.

"Aye, you're a business-like lassie, I can see," he mumbled, and said a figure.

I paused as if to consider the sum offered, and to arrange my face so that it showed neither the shock nor the overwhelming happiness it had made me feel. It was far more than I had been earning at the factory, let alone what I had received on benefit for the past two years, but this was a more professional and responsible position. When I recalled the salary-levels I'd seen in the course of researching the publishing industry, in advertisements for similarly titled jobs, it wasn't a lot, of course. I was new to the work, the firm was prestigious but small.

However, Mr James' offer could be expected to cover the rent on a modest Edinburgh flat, and provide a rather more comfortable existence than I had previously known. I hoped I could get out of the remaining few months on the lease of my bungalow. I didn't want to be paying for it when I wasn't using it. And I hoped I could get a refund on the return half of the train ticket I wouldn't be using that evening. That would help with the immediate issue of the limited cash in my purse.

Perhaps I had paused for rather longer than I had intended, because Mr James again raised his eyebrows, and spoke before I could do so.

"The salary would be reviewed annually, of course, in the light of performance?" The pitch of his voice rose at the end of the sentence. I was being wheedled, I realised. He wanted me to say yes! I was succeeding! I felt a surge of satisfaction which was unlike anything I had ever experienced before.

"I'm sure that would be very satisfactory, Mr James," I said, and—I could not help it—I beamed at him over his piled-high table. "It all sounds most generous, and I will be very happy to accept."

He beamed back at me, and we both relaxed visibly.

"Now, can you stay on up here without inconvenience to yourself for the next ten days?" he asked.

I did a mental check around my abandoned bungalow. Windows, lights, plugs, front and back door locks. I had no appointments that could not be rearranged by telephone. In fact, cancelled!

"Thank you, Mr James," I said, "I shall be happy to do so."

It looked as though I was now an Edinburgh resident, for better or worse, and, all being well, for the foreseeable future. I was overwhelmed with happiness and pride.

Chapter Seven

"Elisabeth," MacWhinney called. "Elisab ... Oh, there you are. Young Hannah here will be with us, at least until Friday week."

Elisabeth gave me a smile.

"I minded she might be," she said.

"Aye," MacWhinney went on, "She'll need keys, and one of those mobile gizmos, I suppose."

"She can have the ones Flora left," Elisabeth said.

"Well, show her around upstairs, if you will, and introduce her to whoever is in this morning." Turning back to me, he said, "I'll see you whenever you need to see me, no doubt, Hannah, but Elisabeth is the fount of all knowledge here, and your first port of call for advice." His descriptions of his right-hand woman were surrounded by invisible inverted commas and loaded with irony, but were spoken fondly and evinced no change in Elisabeth's expression. She'd heard it all before, no doubt, and took no notice of it. She picked up his cup and saucer just as it began to slide off his desk. That too was habitual, I thought. The interview was clearly at an end.

"Thank you, Mr James," I said, but he had finished with me and had returned to whatever it was he had been reading when I arrived. He waved his hand towards the door without looking up, and I followed Elisabeth out into what I soon learned to call 'the lobby', outside his office door.

Elisabeth had a tiny office just off the lobby, with a little scullery at the back where she put Mr James' cup and saucer on the draining board beside a huge Women's Institute teapot. Her office desk was at least as big as Mr James', and as deeply buried in paper. How many trees died in the service of the publishing industry, I wondered, even today? In front of her desk-chair was a very efficient-looking computer, however, with a telephone switchboard beside it, and a printer and processor on a big trolley to one side. Cupboards covered all the walls except where her own huge radiator, and numerous grouped, waist-height power-points, interrupted the space. A big window showed the city to the East. Morning warmth, I thought.

Elisabeth reached over and opened a drawer in the desk.

"Here are your keys and mobile telephone," she said, offering them to me. "The phone is charged. And here's the charger. You'll probably have to charge it where you're living. You've not as many power-points upstairs as I have here—after something of a struggle, I might say! Mr James is not especially minded of modern appliances."

She didn't say 'hm' at the end of her statement, but it hung in the air between us almost visibly.

"I'll show you your office," she announced.

My own office! I thought, and felt the warmth of achievement.

Leading the way, Elisabeth turned sharply into a patch of deep darkness between the doors of her office and that of Mr James. This was the stairwell. Literally! Elisabeth went up three flights of stairs like a steeplechase horse addressing the first fences at Ayr racecourse.

"There's no lift," she said, "just a dumbwaiter to move documents between floors when necessary. You'll get fit here, Hannah, if nothing else."

On the way up the stairs, I looked sideways at the landings and realised that both the upper floors were laid out similarly. At some point, probably long in the past, the interior of the building had been totally gutted and replaced. The narrow staircase gave onto a small landing on each floor, from which a dark corridor opened out on either side. The solid wooden floor-boards were unpolished and uniformly bare, but had been swept clear of accumulated dust. The corridors were no wider than the staircase. Working space had been prioritised over communication space. Whatever happened when people met coming from opposite directions, and both were carrying armfuls of stuff—no doubt papers, in this place—I wondered.

I finally reached the third floor, somewhat behind Elisabeth's brisk progress.

"The corridors are dark if no one remembers to leave their door open," Elisabeth grumbled. It being early in the day, most of the doors were shut. Such greyness as there was on this floor percolated through scarce skylights which were liberally scattered with what I presumed were pigeon-droppings. I could just about see where I was going on this floor, but on the one below, without skylights, the electric light would be on all day. I expect they're on timers, I thought, smiling to myself, for the economy.

"This is your office," Elisabeth said, opening the last door on the left. I was appalled.

The office was tiny, little bigger than my hotel room. It was dominated by a large, old-fashioned table, which was covered with what I presumed to be manuscripts. Each one seemed to be hundreds of pages thick. At random points in the pile, there were big envelopes and even thicker parcels wrapped in brown paper. I felt like the girl in the story of Rumpelstiltskin, faced with a ton of straw to spin into gold. Perhaps one day a prince…I put the thought firmly away from me.

"Where on earth do I start?" I blurted.

"Start at the top of the pile and go on until you get to the table-top," Elisabeth said, with a wicked grin, "or until Mr James says stop. Most of them are worth no more than the bin. Just don't miss the one that isn't." Another grin. "Or at least, don't let Mr James know you have!"

In the farthest corner, but at least near enough to the window to catch some light, was a much smaller table than the one which dominated the centre of the room. Behind it was a stout wooden chair. The back curved round into the arms, and a worn but generously-filled cushion of indeterminate original colour softened the wooden seat. Beside the chair stood a huge plastic rubbish bin.

On the neighbouring wall, there were four columns of oversized pigeon-hole shelves. Three columns were marked with hand-written paper labels, "To Editorial", "Back With Author" and "Possible". All of them were empty. The last column seemed to hold things like staplers, scissors, biros, highlighters, sticky tape and a variety of stationery, in no particular order. On the desk was a laptop, printer and telephone.

"You'll not be using the telephone for personal calls. Dial 9 to get an outside line, 0 for me," Elisabeth said briskly. "There's a hook for your coat behind the door. The lavatory," she gave equal emphasis to each syllable of the word, apparently to express her disapproval of the need for it to exist at all, "the lavatory is on the entrance-floor, beneath the stairs. Not something for visitors to remember, but enough for us, I suppose."

I recalled her remark that Mr James had little interest in 'modern appliances'. Presumably, the lavatory counted as just such another one.

"Switch off the light on leaving the room, if you please," Elisabeth continued. "That goes for every room." There was a firm emphasis on the word *every*. I noted that she had made no attempt to switch on the light when we came into my office, despite the indoor gloom.

I slipped off my coat and obediently hung it behind the door. Reaching over my 'desk', I dropped my handbag onto the seat of the chair behind it. Only the most determined thieves would penetrate this far into the building through the shadows. Even then, they'd be unlikely to see my bag without putting on the light, which would be a complete giveaway. Anyway, they wouldn't get rich on the meagre pickings of my purse. And they'd be sure to ignore the tiny, ancient mobile that Elizabeth had issued to me.

"Does the firm have an archive of what it's published?" I asked. "I've seen a lot of your recent titles, but I'd like to actually read some more of them, if possible, to get a thorough feel for what you favour, and perhaps why."

Elisabeth spun on her flat heel, crossed the corridor in one firm stride and opened the door opposite to my own. Over her shoulder, I saw that the room was of exactly the same dimensions as my office, but differently furnished. Apart from the window-space, every inch of the walls was covered by ancient, floor-to-ceiling, mahogany bookshelves. A further double-sided bookcase of the same sort of design and construction occupied the middle of the room like a spine, and a librarian's stool sat forlornly on one side of that bookcase to provide access to the upper shelves—for someone rather taller than myself!

"There's a copy of every book the firm has published since it was founded in 1863," Elisabeth said, "but only the one copy, so what you borrow, make sure you put it back. Most of the earliest ones are priceless now, being so long out of print. Quite irreplaceable."

The dust on the largest, presumably the oldest, volumes looked as though no risk of loss had been incurred for several decades. However, I would take a few of the books back to the hotel each evening, starting with the most recently issued—and bring them back each morning, religiously!

"This door is kept closed to keep out the dust," Elisabeth said, firmly closing the door to the archive and pursing her lips slightly at the futility of the requirement. "Bring your own beaker for your tea," she continued. "You can use the kettle in my office if you want a cup outside break-hours."

"What are the hours?" I asked. "Mr James didn't say."

"As many as you want, when you want. You can come in at weekends, if you wish. You've the keys to get in, but after five o'clock and at weekends, lock the outer door behind you once you're in the building. We do not want all

Edinburgh's taggle in here after you when you're likely on your own. There's no time-clock. Mr James will judge your productivity by what you get through. How you do that is up to you. And I mash tea twice a day, morning and afternoon, when I get a minute to switch on the kettle."

As a coffee drinker, I resolved to get a cheap electric kettle of my own, and a multi-point extension lead, as soon as possible.

"Will I leave you to settle?" she said. "There seems to be nobody else in at present, but they're friendly enough when they are. You can introduce yourself, no doubt, when you come across them."

"Yes, I'll be fine, Elisabeth, thank you," I said. An opportunity to explore the working of the computer systems would be welcome, I was thinking.

"Aye, well," she said, and set off back along the corridor through the gloom to return downstairs.

***

Fifteen minutes later, I had discovered neither a biro that worked, nor any reference anywhere to the codes which would open the computer or allow me to use the mobile telephone. I picked up the telephone on the desk and dialled 0.

"Aye, Hannah?" Elizabeth answered. She didn't sound as though she particularly welcomed an interruption from the most junior member of staff quite so early in our relationship.

"Elisabeth," I said, trying not to sound pleading or desperate, "do you have a record of the passwords Flora used for her computer and mobile, please?"

"No."

Oh, goodness. Now what?

"Well, do you think you could give me her telephone numbers, so I can ask her? I can't really do much until I know how she organised things, and where she was up to, as it were."

"Hm." There was a pause. I doubted Elisabeth was considering the proprieties of Personal Data Protection. "Aye," she said eventually. "I've found her numbers. I'll call her when I get a minute, and transfer her to you."

"Thank you," I started to say, but the line was dead already. "Hm," I found myself thinking. (How many more of the firm's habits was I going to pick up?) Elisabeth wasn't unfriendly. She just didn't waste words. But clearly the place was still run as Mr James and Elisabeth had taken it over, and when on earth was that?

Having nothing else to do until I had heard from the fabled—mythical?—Flora, I reached for a pair of scissors and a packet from the central table, and took from my bag a biro that I knew worked, together with the criticism scheme I had prepared for Mr James. He hadn't commented on it in any detail, and, with the additions made in view of my tutor's advice, it seemed likely to provide the only sensible basis I had for reviewing submitted manuscripts, at least until somebody told me otherwise. Characters. Plots and subplots. Credibility and anachronisms. Grammar, spelling (how much editing would be needed), flow, current literary fashions, target market, preparation and production costs.

By eleven o'clock, I had reviewed and rejected three manuscripts, on the basis of reading the first and last ten pages or so of each. I decided that if I was sufficiently inspired by those passages, I would open other pages at random to check my initial impressions. So far, no such inspiration had arisen. This was slow work, and not yet hugely rewarding. No doubt it would become quicker with practice. Or perhaps wouldn't. That might explain the size of the heap of unexamined manuscripts on the table, of course.

At twenty past eleven, Elisabeth telephoned.

"The kettle's boiled. Shall I pour your tea?" she asked abruptly. "And I've Flora on the line for you." The order of priorities was…interesting.

"May I speak to Flora first, please, and then I'll pop down for a drink." She must have some coffee granules for visitors, I thought hopefully.

There was a crackle on the line, and then a soft Scottish voice said, "Is that Hannah? This is Flora. Welcome to MacWhinney, Preston. Congratulations!"

"Thank you," I said warmly. Contact at last with someone whom I could ask about what I was supposed to do here, and perhaps how.

"You'll no doubt have loads of questions. Will we meet for lunch at Geordie's in St Andrew's Square at 12.30?"

This was more than I could ever have hoped.

"Um," I said, in surprise rather than indecision. "Oh, that would be wonderful. Thank you so much."

"See you then!" she said, and put down the phone. Before I could take the receiver from my ear, there was a second click on the line. Elisabeth had been monitoring the call. To see what Flora might say about the firm, I wondered? Or did she monitor everybody's phone-calls? Did she report back all her findings to

Mr James? Or did she just find it efficient to keep an eye and an ear on what was going on? Hm, I thought again. (It was becoming a habit!) Here was something else about which to ask Flora at lunch.

***

I found Geordie's easily by simply walking around the Square from MacWhinney, Preston's building. With the upper floors of all the neighbouring buildings apparently being taken up by offices, it was not surprising that the little restaurant was busy. The clientele seemed mostly young, and were taking sandwiches or salads from the counter, or chattering noisily at the small, square tables. As I stood inside the door looking around, a tall, well-built woman stood up and waved vigorously. It must be Flora, I supposed, and waved back, pointing at the counter to indicate that I would get some lunch and come over to her.

Once served, I threaded my way over to where Flora was sitting, and put down my coffee and sandwich on the table.

"I'm Flora," she said, "though you know that, of course."

She was wearing a light-weight blue coat, stylish but not expensive, over a neat black jumper and skirt. Her blonde hair was wiry, cut short and curled at the ends. She looked every inch the publishing professional, with a full, warm smile that softened the smartness of her overall appearance.

"Hannah," I said, and reached out my hand.

Her handshake was confident, firm and welcoming.

"So, how's your first morning been?" she asked.

"A roller-coaster," I replied. "Everything happened hugely quickly at the beginning, and then slowed to snail-pace once Elisabeth had shown me to my office. Your office, I guess."

"Oh, I remember it well. Did I leave it in an awful mess?" Flora said apologetically.

"Not at all. I'm sure the pile of manuscripts has just sat there and grown organically since you left."

"Is it mountainous again?" Flora laughed. "Don't worry. It'll go down, but never disappear. Have you met Andrew yet?"

"I've only met Mr James and Elisabeth so far. There was nobody else about when I was being shown around. Apart from getting a coffee at break-time, I stayed in my room until coming out to meet you."

"Oh, they'll all come in to see you when they've given you a wee while to settle in," Flora said. "They're a good crowd. Andrew's very quiet—that's a euphemism by the way, he says almost nothing—but strong as an ox and very efficient. He'll be bringing you up a mailbag of manuscripts every afternoon, when the post has arrived and Elisabeth has sorted it. And he takes your reject-bin downstairs every evening, via the dumbwaiter, for Elisabeth to go through and send off the 'We regret' letters to the aspiring authors."

Flora took a graceful bite from the sandwich in front of her.

"That's how she and Mr James know how much work you're getting through," she explained, "by the number of rejects you send downstairs each day. They'll know about the 'query-pursues' soon enough. You'll be so pleased to see one of those that you'll want to dash down the stairs to tell Mr James straight away. Just don't dash downstairs in heels," she grinned. "It's not safe."

"Elisabeth seems to be the kingpin in the whole organisation," I suggested.

"Oh, yes," Flora confirmed. "Nothing would get done without Elisabeth Preston."

This stopped me up short.

"Oh, she's *that* Mrs Preston!" I remembered her brief but efficient letter calling me to Mr James' interview. "Is she a partner?" I asked. "I hadn't realised."

"No, you wouldn't," Flora confirmed. "She's Mr James' secret weapon. He hides her in a silo, like a guided missile. She watches, and she waits. When there's a difficulty he'd rather not handle, Elisabeth lifts off from her silo and deals with it."

Flora paused for a sip of coffee.

"But don't worry too much. Such things don't often arise," she continued. "Oh, Elisabeth is a bit daunting until you get to know her, but she'll do anything for Mr James and for the firm. That includes supporting the rest of the staff. For the good of the firm, of course," ironic smile this time, "but it can be a great comfort to know she's always there to back you up—provided you've made the right decision of course! When you haven't, she'll tell you, and still back you up."

Flora grinned again, hearteningly, and then said, "Oh, by the way, Elisabeth listens to phone calls made through her switch-board. That's why, this morning, I made our lunch date so briskly. I hope I didn't put you off." She smiled again, disarmingly. "I was afraid you'd ask about things better not answered in Elisabeth's listening ear, for both our sakes. Anyway," she reached down into her bag for a piece of notepaper, "here are the passwords you'll need, and my phone numbers and email address, so you can call and ask me anything you like. It's a rubbish mobile I've left you," she grimaced. "But at least you can make any calls you like on it, and you don't pay the monthly bill. I don't know whether Elisabeth gets a calls-list with the bill. She probably does, in fact," we both laughed, "but at least she can't tell what you said. I think!" We giggled, and paused to take nibbles of our lunch, and then Flora outlined the filing system she used on the computer.

"All my contacts are on there, too," she said, "so you'll be able to see from the emails what I was up to when I left, and how far I'd got. They'll give you an idea of the processes involved when you do find a speck of gold in the heap of hopelessness. It does happen, honestly, but you'll probably have to wait a while to find one." She smiled fondly. "My husband Ian says it's like fishing. You sit and watch the float for ages, and nothing happens. You get cold and wonder if it's worth doing at all, and then the float bobs, and you think you might have got one. It's a great feeling," she said with enthusiasm. "Not only that, but MacWhinney, Preston's a comfortable place to work. You'll get a good grounding in the essentials. I always felt lucky to be there."

"You obviously enjoyed it," I said. "Do you mind me asking why you left?"

"Oh, I've a bairn," she said with another smile.

I glanced at her hand and saw her wedding ring.

"Ian and I have been waiting years for it to happen. Now it has, I hate being away from her. But, in my bit of the business, I can do most of the work from home."

"It's very good of you to meet me like this," I offered.

"Oh, I break out now and then for myself, and when necessary for clients. Next door has two bairns under three, and we take turn-and-turn. She's a fabric-designer, so our lives are not dissimilar and fit together nicely," she said comfortably. "Also, I left because I was ready to move on up the chain. I had begun to do some editing, when Munro was stretched. Have you met Munro yet? He's on your floor, first door on the right at the head of the stairs. Tall guy, thin, red hair and glasses. Meticulous. Does very complex crossword puzzles and eats semi-colons for breakfast." She laughed. "But absent-minded. I kept waiting for him to tumble down the first flight of stairs through it, but he wouldn't have noticed if he had, probably. Just picked himself up and gone on to wherever he was going." She giggled again. "Anyway, I got a taste for editing, but there

84

wasn't going to be much chance of displacing Munro, even if I'd wanted to. So I decided, all in all, I'd go freelance. I had a few contacts, and I've made a few more since I left MacWhinney, Preston."

"It sounds as though you're doing very well," I congratulated her.

She smiled, again, a happy girl, comfortable in her niche, for a while anyway. She gave me some more invaluable information and advice, and then said, standing up, "Call me whenever you like. Preferably on the mobile. I'll get back to your mobile as soon as I can. I try to remember to put mine on silent mode when Veronica's asleep. The landline tends to wake her up. And she sleeps whenever and wherever she needs to, at the moment, so there's no routine to it. Let's have lunch again. I've enjoyed meeting you. In a month or so?"

"I've only been taken on until Friday week," I said.

"Oh, you'll be here for years," Flora said merrily. "They do that 'just for a few days' thing to everyone, but they only give you a start if they fancy you'll fit their need. Call me. Bye," and she gathered up her bag and rushed off baby-wards.

***

I finished my lunch. The next thing I had to do was to extend my reservation at the hotel. Eventually, if I was to stay in Edinburgh, I'd find a place of my own to rent. For now, however, my new 'salary and allowance' from Mr James would cover what the hotel was charging me. It wasn't an expensive hotel, even by my standards! I telephoned to the hotel on the office mobile, and made the necessary arrangement—the manager seemed very pleased to know I'd be staying—and walked back to MacWhinney, Preston to finally break into Flora's systems on the computer.

The rest of the week passed very quickly. I did indeed meet Andrew and Munro, who were exactly as Flora had described them. Malcolm, the designer/printer, popped up from the second floor to make himself known, and to tell me that the technical branches—design, print/production, sales, accounts and despatch—were all down there below me. There couldn't have been many of them, I thought. There wasn't room.

Phylida, the resident proof reader, also looked in briefly. Of unfathomable age, spectacles, modestly—slightly old-fashioned—dressed, very well spoken with the slight Edinburgh accent of a Miss Jean Brodie, she had an air of someone of great experience and professional precision. I decided on the spot to cultivate her, very gently. I was sure she would have much to teach me, if I could break through her obvious, but not unfriendly, reserve. Her room was opposite Munro's, next door to mine. We were all on the same floor, so that would help in getting to know them.

I dug into the mass of information on Flora's computer. There were so many names. Authors, agents, freelance editors as she herself now was, external readers and proof-readers. I would not be commissioning any of these by myself for quite a while, I knew. However, I made sure I knew where on the system I could find their names and the histories of their former contacts with the firm.

Flora had clearly been very organised. Her systems had separate files with easily-understood labels for the names and functions of her contacts, and the various contexts of their work for MacWhinney, Preston. And it was all cross-referenced. It fitted together like a jigsaw puzzle. By the end of my first Friday afternoon at MacWhinney, Preston, I thought I was beginning to get the hang of it all. Or some of it, at least.

I did a lot of my reading in cafés at lunchtime or wherever I ate a frugal supper. The rest I did in my office, huddled up to the radiator, or at the hotel late into the nights. In addition to manuscripts, I tried to skim at least three of the firm's most recent publications each day, and make notes on the sorts of books the firm seemed to favour. I bought two 'lifetime' bags from a supermarket, and was well on the way to having destroyed them by the end of the week.

Carrying a heap of books and manuscripts back to the hotel in an evening was heavy work. Elisabeth had been right. I would soon become very fit, physically, in this job, and not just from running up and down the stairs. But I made sure there was always something in the plastic reject bin for Andrew to cart down to Elisabeth each evening, as an indication that I was trying my best for the firm, at the very least.

At just before half-past four that first Friday afternoon, Elisabeth rang me on the telephone from downstairs.

"Will you pop down to see Mr James, Hannah, if you please," she said. "He wants to find out what you've been about these past few days."

I was exhausted. I had worked from early in the mornings to late at night for several days together. However, there was nothing to be done but to comply. As usual, Elisabeth had rung off before I could say I was on my way. I imagined her sitting at her desk, timing the promptness of my arrival on the ground floor with a stopwatch. Or perhaps an egg-timer. I knew that was unfair, but…To arm myself, I gathered up the sheaf of papers on which I had made sheet after sheet of notes on each of the manuscripts I had read, and addressed the stairs.

Carrying all these documents, I thought to myself with a slightly rueful smile that I really was fitting into the MacWhinney, Preston culture. When I reached the foot of the stairs and crossed the lobby, I could see that Mr James' door was open. He called me to come straight in, and said, "Sit down, Hannah, sit down. How have you found us this week? Tell me what you've been doing, what you've enjoyed, what's confused you, made you feel uncomfortable, how you've approached the work. How are you feeling about Edinburgh, and about us here at MacWhinney, Preston?"

He smiled amiably at me, with his brows down over his eyes like a concerned uncle with a niece whom he had received into his house, but hadn't yet decided whether that had been a good idea.

"Well, Mr James." I tried to gather myself and plan something of a strategy for responding to his questions. Concentrate on the professional things, I thought. That's what he really wants to know about. "Well, I've been made very welcome by everybody. Flora gave me a very good introduction to how she'd been working, and I'm beginning to come to grips with the procedures she followed. I haven't yet had any contacts from outside the building, of course, but I feel confident that, if and when someone does 'phone me or write in, I'll know where to look for a precedent for dealing with them. Or I'll find out quickly that I don't know enough to help them, and where to ask what I should do. Probably Elisabeth, first of all."

"Aye." Mr James slumped slightly in his chair, as he settled himself more comfortably. "Aye, Elisabeth's your first port of call. She's been keeping the routine calls off your back these last few days. It's what she's been doing since Flora left us, so it's no trouble to her. But she'll be glad of the relief when you can begin to take a few of them for her. Would you feel ready to begin to do that next week, do you think?" One eyebrow rose, and the ends of the lips curled slightly upwards.

"Oh, yes," I said, meeting his eyes, and trying to show a confidence I was not sure I felt. "Gladly."

"Aye, it'll do you good to get your hands on the reality of it all, no doubt. And you've been looking at some of the manuscripts, I understand? Have any of them stood out to you?" Thanks to Flora, I knew that he and Elisabeth knew exactly how many manuscripts I had examined and rejected, and which ones.

"The manuscripts can be sorted into a variety of overlapping groups," I said. "The easiest to deal with, perhaps, are those on subjects or themes that the firm doesn't usually, or even never has, published. Then there are those which achieve a negative score on more than three-quarters of the characteristics I identified on that scheme I sent you before we met, Mr James." I paused slightly to see whether he yet wanted to comment on my scheme.

How on earth could it be beyond criticism? It was based on nothing but theory and other peoples' advice, untouched by any personal experience of the commercial demands of the publishing industry. But Mr James said nothing so I went on, hoping that I would be able to climb out of any pit I might be digging for myself.

"I've been forming those conclusions on the basis of skim-reading the first and last few pages of each manuscript. When I've found one that I haven't rejected on that basis, I've been reading some more passages at random within the bulk of the book, to see whether I could easily pick up the characters and plots and themes that I recognised in the first and last pages, and to get an impression of the quality of the writing. Anything that still scored fewer than a quarter of the scheme's negatives after that would be a possible, I thought. I was proposing to read right through such cases, to see if they might actually be probable successes."

"And have you found any such 'probable successes'?" Mr James asked.

"Um, no, not yet," I said.

"Aye, I'm not surprised, lassie. But go on, go on."

"I did notice, from Flora's records," I said, "that there are a number of authors who have sent us a manuscript before." Flora had meticulously kept a brief record of every manuscript she'd ever looked at in MacWhinney, Preston. Author, title, date received, decision, and main reason or reasons for that decision. "Some people seem to favour us, even though we consistently reject their work."

"Aye, they do, and we're publishers, not a Creative Writing tutorial college," Mr James grunted. "They must find their own ways to improve their writing, or their judgement. Or both. But you're right, Hannah, you never know when a frog will turn into a prince or princess, and we wouldn't want to miss such an opportunity just because they'd been churning out rubbish we couldn't use for years and years." Abruptly, he changed the angle of his attack. "Now, do you recall the best manuscript and the worst of those you've seen this past week? Or should I say, the least worst and the worst?"

I pulled a couple of sheets of notes from my bundle, and mentioned a title and author. He leaned forward and took from the pile on his desk a particular manuscript. Had he got there every single manuscript I had looked at in the last few days?

"Hm," he said. "Go on."

I nominated one which I had found, at first, to be superficially attractive.

"Well, I thought that the characters in this one were pretty well drawn, and the plots and subplots were quite interesting, if a bit well-worked by other authors," I said. "But the writing style seemed to me rather careless. I finally suggested rejecting that one because it would need an awful lot of editing before it was really presentable."

And that was where my education in the ways of MacWhinney, Preston really began. In each of the cases I presented to him, he considered my criticisms, and then began to place his views into the context of the financial parameters of the publishing industry. The average cost of each step in the process was this, the minimum number of copies that might be sold for each type of book was that, the required minimum profit to MacWhinney, Preston per 1000 copies of each type of book was so.

"Everything here must pay for itself, Hannah," he told me rather firmly, "or we'll all go down to perdition. Everything except me, of course," he said, and chuckled to himself. Then he turned to the firm's house-style, "what people expect when they see 'MacWhinney, Preston' at the bottom of a book's spine. We've kept to that, broadly, for more than a century, and it's done us no harm so far, no harm at all. It's not written in stone, you know, but you'll have to make me a case for doing anything, hm, radical." He drew out the first syllable of radical to a great length, as if anything radical was like a foul-tasting medicine. It was to be avoided except when it would do more good than harm.

With that, he lifted another manuscript from his table.

"Now, let's review this one in the light of what I've been saying." He read out the author and title from the front sheet of the manuscript, and I sorted through my bundle to find the notes I'd made when I 'read' it. "Now, you rejected this one. If I were to suggest, Hannah, that I fancied this one might have legs, what would you say to me?" He clearly wanted me to explain and defend the reasons why I had rejected this manuscript, and so our discussion continued. Finally, he said, "Well, you seem to be finding your way, Hannah."

I glanced at my watch. It was five minutes to seven. We had been at it for almost two and a half hours. To me, it felt like no more than thirty minutes. I had been fascinated, involved. I had grown up some more in one of those sudden spurts that happen under the stimulus of someone rather special providing a unique opportunity.

"We'll stop now, I think," Mr James went on, "but we'll maybe do this again. I've quite enjoyed it, and I hope you have too. Hm, hm. Now, you've worked hard this week. Take the weekend for yourself. Walk around the city. Enjoy the sun. And do me another week like this afterwards. Off you go, then, off you go."

Chapter Eight

I hadn't enough money to make the most of Edinburgh that weekend, and I hated and feared spending more than my hard-pressed bank account could stand. When I wasn't reading manuscripts and recent MacWhinney, Preston publications, therefore, I spent most of my time walking around the city in ever widening circles based on St Andrews Square and the Royal Mile. The weather held fair, and I felt renewed by the exercise. By the following Monday morning, I was feeling increasingly comfortable in the Old Town, and had noted where to catch the buses I would need to extend my explorations.

The following week, I followed much the same routine as I had set for myself in the first few days at the firm, but rather less intensively. By the Wednesday morning, however, something rather more pressing was increasingly bothering me. I had not seen anything of Mr James all week, other than glimpses of him sitting behind his desk as I glanced at him through his office doorway when passing through the lobby. I had no idea where I was likely to be working, let alone living or earning, next week. I was feeling somewhat insecure, despite Flora's confidence in my permanent employment at MacWhinney, Preston. By eleven o'clock, I had decided that I simply must ask Elisabeth for an interview with Mr James as soon as possible. I picked up the telephone and dialled the dreaded 0.

"Yes, Hannah."

"Elisabeth, I am so sorry to bother you, but I really feel I need to see Mr James. Is he likely to be free sometime today, please?"

"I'll let you know." The line went dead, and I went back to the manuscript I had been examining.

As I crossed the lobby at about one o'clock, on my way out to buy a sandwich to eat at my desk, Elisabeth called from her office, "Hannah, Mr James will see you at two o'clock. And I've an envelope here for you." Turning, I went into Elisabeth's office.

"It's your pay for the past two weeks," Elisabeth said. "I didn't doubt you'd prefer it in cash, after what you'll have had to spend since you came up here. I'll be needing your bank details and an address, and so on, later, when you've seen Mr James."

Did that mean…? Could I properly ask her…? I decided on prudence. If she'd felt it correct to tell me more, she would have done so. With such good omens, though, I could perhaps afford to go to lunch with a slightly less worried heart.

"Thank you, Elisabeth," I said. "I'm certainly glad of the cash. I'll be back by two o'clock."

"He'll want another talk like last Friday," Elisabeth warned me. "Bring your notes again, he said to tell you."

So was it the good news I wanted it to be? Or just a 'wind up the week, and see what she's been doing' talk? Elisabeth's mention of bank details suggested the former. My self-doubts were less optimistic. My pet tummy-butterflies started to flutter again. I settled for just a bowl of soup for lunch. If Mr James was to give me good news, I could treat myself to a decent supper this evening. I was back at my desk well before two o'clock, but Elisabeth didn't summon me until ten past. Did that mean something about me, or had some other bit of business diverted Mr James? When I got down to his office, however, he was in his usual chair, in his usual comfortably slumped posture, with his nose in a paper as ever.

"Well, Hannah," he said genially. He leaned forward to put down the paper on the heap on his desk. "Have you enjoyed your time with us?"

Whatever did that mean? I was reading implications into every syllable. My nerves were all over the place.

"Very much, thank you, Mr James."

"And will you be prepared to put up with us all for a while longer, maybe?" he enquired. "On the terms we discussed when we first met?"

"Thank you, Mr James," I said. "I would like that very much."

"Aye. Well," he said. "Hm." He seemed satisfied, and there was the briefest of pauses as he changed gear to what really interested him. "Now, I'd like to hear the details of what you thought about a couple of the offerings you considered last week." And we were off into discussion mode again, for which, emotionally, I was totally unprepared. I had officially joined MacWhinney, Preston! I was a professional reader to a prestigious publishing house! I wanted to run around his desk and kiss him! And then run out to Elisabeth and kiss her. And Andrew, though that might well have frightened him even more than I would have been frightened if he had kissed me.

***

Rather than kissing anyone, I sat demurely in Mr James' clients' chair, and spent an hour arguing with him the merits and demerits of a couple of particular authors and their unsolicited manuscripts. And learning from his accumulated wisdom.

"And you've been talking to a few of our callers, I understand?" he eventually said. "And making a fair fist of it, I hear. Hm."

I thanked him.

"But you mustn't waste too much time on them, Hannah. Aye, we'd not want to be brutal to anyone, of course, but time's baubies. We're not a charity. If we were, I believe we might make more from the Revenue than we do from the books." He wagged his head from side to side in mock-sadness which we both recognised for what it was. "You've done well with the callers you've had this week. You're developing a fair set of responses. Just stick to them, deliver them crisply, cut across their waffle, and don't be diverted by the bullies or the broken hearts. We've no time for either sort here."

"Now, go and see Elisabeth," he continued, reaching for the paper he had been reading when I came in almost two hours earlier, "do me another two days hard work, and then have a good weekend thinking through what's gone right this week and what's gone wrong, and how all of it can be improved. Go on, go on" he said, waving me out of his office doorway with the document which was now in his hand.

As I left Mr James' office, I found Elisabeth standing in the middle of the lobby, smiling broadly.

"He'll likely not have said it to you," she spread her arms towards me, "but welcome to the firm!" and literally folded me up in the biggest hug I had ever, ever had. Pressed to her chest, I wept as I hadn't since those early days in Margaret's consulting room. Acceptance overwhelmed me. There were people who cared about me, cared for me. I was no longer just Hannah Lethbridge, I was Hannah Lethbridge of MacWhinney, Preston. I couldn't believe the relief of no longer being alone against the world. Elisabeth didn't seem to mind my tears.

She pushed a tiny, tidy handkerchief into my hand, and I mopped up and apologised for making such a silly fuss. Elisabeth just said, "Whisht!", gave me another squeeze and then let me go.

"Now, go and get your things and go away until tomorrow," she said. "I want you out of here in no more than twenty minutes. Is that clear, young lady?" She was smiling again, and so was I.

"Yes, Elisabeth," I said obediently, for the first of many, many times in the years to come, I was sure.

Upstairs, I pushed a manuscript from each of three piles into one of my lifetime bags, and stepped across the corridor to select a couple of recent publications from the archive. I was just taking my coat from its hook when I realised that the ancient mobile was buzzing insistently in my bag. I plucked it out and accepted the call.

"MacWhinney, Preston," I said. "Hannah Lethbridge speaking."

"You're still in Edinburgh then?" said Flora's voice. "Do I take it you're a fully-fledged member of the firm by now?"

"Yes," I confirmed, and nearly broke down all over again. "Oh, Flora!"

She squealed with pleasure for me, and then stopped suddenly, no doubt careful not to startle her baby.

"Come to supper," Flora said. "It's only domestic, but it'll be wholesome. We're not far out of the city centre." Her directions were efficiently precise. "About seven-thirty? Ian won't be back before then, and I will have put Veronica down, hopefully. For the twentieth time, probably. Bye."

I didn't get a chance to refuse, even if I had wanted to do so. I glanced at my watch and saw that I just had time to get back to the hotel to arrange a further extension of my stay.

The manager was behind the tiny reception desk when I got back to the hotel.

"Well, Ms Lethbridge, bookings are beginning to come in. May I enquire if you might still intend to be in Edinburgh over the weekend and into next week?" she asked.

I had not known that morning what my situation was going to be by the evening, so I had not felt able to book my room beyond Thursday night.

"Oh, Mrs MacCrae, I'll be staying on in Edinburgh for the foreseeable future, apparently," I said. "Can I keep my same room, for at least another month, please?"

"Hm," Mrs MacCrae murmured. It was obviously a characteristic utterance in Edinburgh parlance. She looked down at the ledger which was open before her on the desk. "I'm afraid I've a problem there, Ms Lethbridge," she continued. "I'm fully booked this weekend, you see. You did not tell me you might be staying longer, and the new guest is a regular, who always stays up there in what has been your room."

I was nonplussed. Were all my new arrangements going to be as complicated as this? Probably, I realised, or at least some of them. Oh, well. Get down to it, Hannah. There must be somewhere else to stay around here.

Mrs MacCrae pursed her lips.

"Now, when I'm pressed, my friend Kathleen Gordon, around the corner at the Stag Hotel, is sometimes able to oblige. You could move back here on Monday evening, if you wished, Ms Lethbridge." She was clearly reluctant to lose a solid month's booking, which suited me fine. "Will I be telephoning my friend to see if she could take you just for the weekend?"

"That would be very helpful, Mrs MacCrae," I thanked her.

She picked up the telephone and dialled briskly.

"Kathleen, is that yourself, hen?" Her accent had thickened noticeably. "It's Helen, around the corner at the Royal. Aye. Aye. And yourself? Och, aye. Now, Kathleen, I've a guest in some difficulty here, just for the weekend. Could you oblige, perhaps? Aye. She'll be coming back here to me on Monday. Aye. A Ms Lethbridge. Will I be sending her around to you now, then? Aye. No, not a lot to carry, and she's fit enough for that, I'd say." Mrs MacCrae looked up at me with a friendly smile. "Aye. As soon as we've settled her bill for the last while, then. Aye. Thanks, Kathleen. See you soon."

She rang off, still smiling at me.

"I am most grateful, Mrs MacCrae," I told her.

"Oh, that's nothing, Ms Lethbridge. Now, will you be settling up for what's owing so far, and I'll book you in for the next month from Monday, shall I?"

I paid her in cash from Elisabeth's envelope. I would have to check the balance on my bank account tomorrow. I was aware that I could too easily lose control of my finances in the forthcoming maelstrom of new arrangements. Now that I had a regular earned income, however, I could apply for a credit card, of course. That would help, I thought gratefully.

The appearance and proportions of the room I was given at the Stag Hotel, around the corner, were much the same as those at the Royal, less the view of the neighbouring cemetery. It was a hassle having to go back to the Royal on Monday, but stability beckoned for a while, once I had returned to Mrs MacCrae's kindly custody. I dumped my suitcase and bag of books in my new room, had a quick shower and then set out for Flora and Ian's flat.

***

Flora and Ian's home was on the first floor of a fairly modern-looking building. The stairs were nothing to me after ten days' training at MacWhinney, Preston. I poked the tiny plastic bell-push on the door, and had to wait only briefly before it opened and Flora gave me my second huge hug of the day.

"So many congratulations, Hannah," she said, and then, pushing me to her arms' length to look at me properly, she asked, "Are you really happy?"

"I am so relieved!" I said. "And very, very happy. Elisabeth gave me a hug!"

"Of course she did," Flora beamed. "She knows they've picked up a real asset, and she is actually human underneath her metronomic efficiency. Believe it or not, I'm very fond of her, as well as holding her in great respect. She grows on you, given time." She let me go and turned towards the inside of the flat. "Now, come away in," she said, "and meet Ian. He's only just home."

Several doors led off the small vestibule. One was closed, presumably Veronica's nursery. From the furthest, there was a wonderful smell of cooking food. Flora led me towards its origin.

"We're in the kitchen," Flora said. "We're mostly in the kitchen when we're both home, which is little enough. I hope you don't mind. It's the warmest room, and the most convenient." I followed her closely, and came into a square, compact room with a long window on the further side above the smart steel sink.

The wall opposite the window was furnished with a stove, worktop and cupboards. A modest television set, turned off, was supported above the draining board by a fragile-looking metal frame. To one side, a sofa was spread with the bright, cheerful fabrics of several throws. In the centre of the room was a table rather smaller than any I'd seen in MacWhinney, Preston's offices, around which stood four simple wooden chairs. As I came in, a comfortable-looking man of about Flora's height looked up from setting the table with mats and cutlery.

"Ian," Flora said, almost closing the door behind me, "this is Hannah."

"How are you, Hannah," he greeted me, offering a strong-looking, square hand.

"She's exhilarated," Flora said. "Can't you tell?"

"So the job's settled, is it?" Ian said, with a broadening smile. "I heard James MacWhinney was keeping you in suspense as usual."

"Oh, he doesn't mean to be hard," Flora said. "He just doesn't realise what it's like to live outside his own little world."

"Yes, until this afternoon, it was all a bit uncertain," I concurred. "But everything's wonderful now. I feel like a new person. Which is just as well," I added, "since I'm beginning to realise how many things will need to be done pretty quickly before I can really settle down to enjoy my new situation. But Flora's right, Mr James is a dear. And so professional and experienced! I shall learn so much very quickly in this job, I think."

A baby-monitor on the worktop beside the sink squeaked quietly.

"Oh, that's madam," Flora said fondly. "I'll go and sort her out."

She turned out of the door again, and disappeared.

"Flora's feeding Veronica herself," Ian said placidly, "so it won't take long to settle her down again. She's a very contented baby. So far." He was clearly as besotted with his daughter as was her mother. "Once she's gone off, she'll stay asleep until the middle of the night, and then she'll come in with us for a wee while for another feed. But sit yourself down," he said, pulling out a chair for me at the table. He turned towards a big saucepan on the stove, and gave it a stir with a wooden spoon which had been lying to hand on the draining board.

"I'll just turn up the heat on these potatoes," he continued, lifting the lid on a slightly smaller saucepan on the second ring of the stove. "They'll be done by the time Flora's back, and then we can eat." He was obviously used to taking his share of the domestic duties. What a very nice arrangement they had together, I thought.

"And how are you finding Edinburgh?" he asked. "Have you somewhere comfortable to stay?"

I told him about the Royal Hotel, and the weekend stay at the Stag.

"But I'll need to find a flat as soon as I can," I said.

"Aye," he agreed. "You'll have no difficulty. This is a transient city, for all it's not too big. People are always moving in and out of flats. And they're generally quite helpful. You've only to ask."

"Yes, I've found that already," I agreed.

He gave each of the saucepans another stir as Flora returned from her motherly duties.

"There," she said. "That's Veronica settled for a while. Let's eat!"

Ian took three plates from where they had been warming in the stove, and began to serve the stew and potatoes. It smelt amazingly good! Nothing like the minimal meals I had heated up, rather than cooked, for myself for so long.

"Were you both born in Edinburgh?" I asked. "All the Edinburgh people I've met seem very proud of their city."

"I was born here," said Flora, "but went to Dublin for university. Ian comes from a wee town up near Aberdeen."

"I'm an engineer," Ian explained. "University in Aberdeen, two years on the oil rigs, three years in the Antarctic Survey, and now a quieter job with the City Council. It's less pay than the rigs, but more secure, and a decent pension."

"He misses the adventures he used to have, so he goes climbing in the Cairngorms with his mad friends four or five times a year," Flora mock-complained, "when the boredom has nearly driven him wild."

"Oh, my job's not exactly boring," Ian said. "But a lot of it is routine. There's compensations, though." They smiled at each other.

"How long have you two been together?" I asked. "How did you meet?"

"It seems we've been together for ever," Flora teased, grinning, "but it's about four years now, I suppose. I've loved every minute, especially now we've got Veronica."

She launched into the story of their first meeting, Ian's subsequent tentative approaches and how she'd had to push him along the romantic road.

"I knew he was the one as soon as we met," she said, and sighed.

"So did I," said Ian, "but I was afraid she wouldn't want to know. I'd had little to do with women for so many years."

"Just penguins," Flora smiled.

They told me about their families, their growing up, their friends and their social life in Edinburgh. Under pressure from Flora, Ian brought out stunning photographs of his time in Antarctica and up mountains in Scotland and Switzerland, and, more readily, photographs by the dozen of Veronica at each stage of her five-month life. I was shocked when Flora suddenly said, "I'm not throwing you out, but if you don't go in the next five minutes, you'll miss the last bus for Beaufort Street."

We flurried quietly so as not to wake Veronica. I was given another hug by Flora and another firm handshake by Ian, gathered my coat and bag, and, as I got out onto the pavement, saw the bus approaching. But what a grand evening they had given me! I was totally relaxed in a way I'd never known before, and, in my bed at the Stag Hotel, I slept more solidly and longer than I had done in years.

***

As I approached the top of MacWhinney, Preston's precipitous stairs the next morning, I saw that the light was on in Munro's office.

"Is that yourself, Hannah?" he called as I passed his office doorway.

"Yes, it is," I called back. "Good morning, Munro."

"I thought it was your step," he said from the depths of his room. "Will you be making some tea, perhaps?"

I am no great feminist despite three years at a women-only college. Also, I supposed that, since I was the most junior person in the firm, and he was clearly working hard already this morning, I could do him a favour on this occasion. Pity I had to go downstairs again, and back up, just as soon as I'd got to the top floor. However, he might well prove to be my leg up in the firm, if he put some editing work my way one day.

"Just this once," I called to him. "Milk and sugar?" I was ready for another coffee, anyway, I supposed.

"A wee drop of milk, if you please," Munro ordered from within the room. Downstairs, his tea and my coffee made and dispatched aloft in the dumbwaiter, I climbed the stairs yet again.

At the top, I took the beakers out of the lift and, at Munro's doorway, called, "Tea."

"Come in, Hannah, come in," he replied.

It was the first time I had been into his office. It was the same size as mine next door, with the same big central table and two chairs, and it had the same small corner desk, the surface of which was totally clear. Spread across the central table, however, was a dismembered manuscript. He seemed to have split it into a number of sections and individual pages, across which were scattered a series of hieroglyphs, apparently scratched by the red biro Munro was holding in his left hand.

I put down the beakers on his desk and made no secret of my interest in what he was doing with the manuscript. His markings looked much like those of a school teacher's marking a pupil's essay. *Sp* in the left margin clearly noted a spelling mistake, with the correction written neatly above the offending word.

Para, I presumed, indicated the need to break up an overlong portion of continuous text. But many of the other marks were quite arcane. Munro put down his pen and turned towards me, reaching for his beaker.

"Editing seems to have a whole vocabulary of its own, a different language," I suggested.

"Aye, it's a sort of shorthand. There's a basic, universal system that most editors and proof-readers use, but Phylida and I have extended the basic system with some additions we've found useful."

"Is there a 'teach yourself' textbook?" I asked.

"Of course." He reached behind him towards a bookcase, drew out a much-used volume and offered it to me. "You can borrow that in the office, if you're interested, but leave it in full view somewhere on your desk. We still refer to it now and then, when something unusual turns up."

"Thank you," I said, taking the book from his hand. I looked at the broad spine. 'MacWhinney on Editing' the gold letters spelled out.

"Not our Mr James?" I asked.

"No, no, his great-grandfather, Mr Joseph, who founded the firm in 1863. At that time, every editor used his own system, which made for difficulties when several editors were reviewing the same manuscript sequentially. So Mr Joseph compiled a system from what seemed to be the best practices he and his colleagues and friends used, and it became an industry standard, certainly in Edinburgh. Very useful for training new editors." He looked me in the eye. "Will you be interested in doing a little editing, in due course?" he asked me.

Careful, I thought. If I say yes, will he see that as a challenge to his position in the firm, or a potential help to him? If I say no, will he think I'm no more than an unambitious time-server?

"I'd certainly be interested," I replied, "but I've no idea what Mr James has in mind for me in the long term. Perhaps I'd better get to grips with the initial processes of reading first."

"Aye, he plays his cards very close, Mr James," Munro said. "But I do miss Flora. She used to take a bit of weight off me when I was pressed, from time to time. There are people in this firm who make promises to people outside the firm which the likes of you and I have to fulfil for them, Hannah. Hm."

"Is this one of them?" I enquired, leaning over his current work.

"Indeed. The subject-matter is very interesting, but the quality of the English is appalling. The author is the nephew of a friend of Mr James. Everyone's keen to see his work in print before Christmas. I wanted to ask which Christmas, but…ah, well." Munro took a deep drink from his beaker, leaned around the other way to put the beaker on his desk, and picked up his pen again. Tea-break was clearly over.

"Thanks for the book," I said, and went off to my own room.

The first thing I had to do was to look for a flat in Edinburgh that I could afford to rent. I turned on the computer on my desk, clicked on the browser icon, pulled Andrew's 'dump' chair towards me, and spread my street map across its seat. An hour later, I had assembled a 'long list' of possible flats. Taking the ancient mobile from my bag, I began calling letting agencies to arrange viewings as soon as possible. Having done all I could in that regard, I took up Mr Joseph MacWhinney's textbook on editing, which was of much more interest to me.

Just before three o'clock, Munro put his head around my door.

"I'm off, then, Hannah. I'll lock the front door when I'm out, and you'll do the same, no doubt, when you finish." He saw what I was reading, smiled slightly and raised his eyebrows, but said nothing. I gathered that he approved, and was looking forward to obtaining occasional support when necessary. I realised that I hadn't eaten since Flora and Ian's wonderful stew the previous night. Time for me to go, too. I put down the book on the corner of my desk where it would be easily seen, gathered up my coat and bag, and switched off the ceiling light in the office.

Carefully leaving my office door open so that I could see my way down the corridor to the stairs, I glanced into Munro's office. The manuscript on which he had been working was now in one stack, reconstituted, in the centre of his table. I longed to go through the pages to see what he had done with them, but did not dare. That would have taken interest beyond the bounds of impertinence. I carefully descended the stairs, locking the outer door as I reached the street.

Sunday was colder. The air was full of mist, and the moisture gathered on my too-thin coat. I decided to buy something warmer next week, and perhaps some kind of hat into which I could tuck my hair. I both needed them and could afford to pay for them at the same time, at last.

Mrs Gordon, seeing me leave the hotel, referred to the weather as 'dree', which she explained as meaning dreary. That seemed particularly apt. It wasn't much of a day for walking, so I went back into the office, and read and made notes. It would be useful to put in the extra few hours, since my output was going to be reduced, as was the content of the reject-bin, when I had to spend working-time viewing prospective places to live.

On Monday, I telephoned the Cambridge Job Centre to announce that I was now employed, which precipitated another deluge of form-filling and letter writing. After that, however, and until the viewing appointments started to be lined up, I was able to settle into a reasonably comfortable routine. Phylida and I took our morning break in each other's offices once or twice a week. Elisabeth put through more telephone calls from authors seeking news of their manuscripts. Munro narrowly avoided falling down the stairs regularly while trying to walk, read and write at the same time, and, altogether, I began to feel thoroughly at home.

As summer passed into autumn, the city became less busy with tourists. Flora and Ian fed me at their flat now and then. I met Veronica and fawned, I hoped appropriately, though my inexperience of babies must have shown. Once my finances had begun to strengthen, I took them out to a real restaurant for supper as a payback for all their kindnesses; and Flora and I met for lunch once a month or so.

Through her, I began to meet other members of the Edinburgh publishing fraternity, which was both pleasant and enlightening. I said little on those occasions, as befitted my very junior status, but kept my ears open to learn how other firms, and freelancers, dealt with the day-to-day events of our particular working world.

Six weeks later, I found a suitable furnished flat, at the top of a four-storey building behind Broughton Road, not far from the Royal Botanical Gardens. After so long in my room at Mrs MacCrae's hotel, the flat seemed to offer me acres of space, though it had only a lounge-dining room, one bedroom and a bathroom the size of a large cupboard. The kitchen was little larger, but the views from the windows southwards across the city centre were very pleasant. The nearby bus route to St Andrew's Square was going to be increasingly convenient as the winter set in. The furniture, and the walls, were slightly battered. I suspected the flat had been recently vacated by students.

However, I bought bedding, throws and some cheap, colourful curtains, to hide as far as possible the evidence of what seemed likely to have been a fairly mixed history. And there was a laundrette only a couple of streets away! It would do me very well, for a year, at least. I agreed to move in at the beginning of November, which necessitated returning to Cambridge for a long weekend to pack up the bungalow and arrange for all my things to be brought up to Edinburgh.

Leaving Cambridge after so long, I felt nothing but the excitement of beginning a new adventure. I would keep in touch with the few special people there—my analyst Margaret, Penny at the University Press and my lovely tutor—by telephone and letter.

Mrs MacCrae was pleased for me, I could tell. For some weeks, my stay had represented a welcome continuity of cashflow at her modest establishment, although we were both aware that she could have let my room many times over during the festival season at a much more profitable rate. She seemed to have accepted the trade-off philosophically and kindly, however.

"We'll miss you, Ms Lethbridge," she assured me. By then, I had become something of a fixture at the Royal. "Just take care of yourself out there." She was in grave doubt, apparently, that I could exist safely in the city without her fond oversight.

At MacWhinney, Preston, I found my first tiny speck of gold among the unsolicited manuscripts which continued to stack up on my office table. It was winter now, and cold and wet outside on most early mornings. In my office, I huddled up to the radiator for warmth, and had pulled the reject bin close beside me for convenience.

The special one was the third manuscript I had plucked from my table that morning. The first two had gone into the bin, break-time was approaching (I hoped) and I had picked up this manuscript at random from the table, expecting nothing more than usual. From the first page, it grabbed me by the throat, I could not wait to turn the pages. I was there, with the central character, in his world, in his horrifying situation. Glancing down, I realised that I had reached page 25 without a pause, without a sigh, without a thought other than for the next stage of the plot.

I ignored the ringing of the telephone on my desk, flicked on to page 84, read and found myself bewitched again. The same at around page 200. The last ten pages almost made me cry with relief as the hero emerged triumphant into the rest of his life. I couldn't believe it. This one really looked as though it might have a future. I could hardly wait to go out for something to eat, come back as quickly as possible, and settle down to read the whole story through from beginning to end this afternoon.

Elisabeth called to me as I crossed the lobby.

"You've not been down for your coffee this morning, Hannah," she said. Just that, no recrimination implied, a question barely hinted but needing to be answered. But it was too early to tell her, to tell anyone, of what I thought I had found.

"I got myself buried in a job," I said, prevaricating.

Elisabeth's lips twitched slightly.

"Was it a useful morning, then?"

"Yes, I think so," I replied. "It needed doing."

"Mm. Well, remember, publishing isn't government. The world won't end for a ten-minute break, but the mind gets tired if too much is demanded of it."

"I'm just off now to get something to eat," I said.

"Aye, well, eat it there. Don't bring it back to your desk. Start fresh this afternoon."

"Yes, Elisabeth," I called as I started to go down the stairs to the outside door. There was no fooling Elisabeth. She had been in the business too long not to know that I had something on my mind. Was I as transparent as all that? Apparently so, to Elisabeth at least.

Warmed by a bowl of soup in my favourite nearby café, I returned to the office. The lobby was empty. No sign of Elisabeth or Mr James. I made myself a beaker of coffee and took it upstairs with me. Back in my room, I felt like a mineral prospector whose months of chipping rock have finally brought him some hopeful signs. I settled back into my find, beginning at page one, took a sip of coffee, and lost myself again. This one really was as gripping as I had hoped and suspected. Inevitably, there were points and passages that jarred slightly. I marked them in pencil for future attention and moved on, carried forward by the story's tide.

At about three o'clock, the telephone rang, insistently. I reached behind me blindly to pick up the receiver, my eyes locked onto the text before me.

"Is your beaker upstairs, Hannah?" Elisabeth's voice asked. "I saw it down here this morning."

"Oh, yes, I brought a drink up here with me after lunch," I said.

"Well, I'm mashing and the kettle's boiled."

I thanked Elisabeth, put the manuscript aside carefully and took my beaker downstairs. What would I say if she probed the cause of my distraction again, especially if any of the others were there as well? But she didn't. She just smiled briefly at me as I passed her on my way into the scullery and out of it again, going back towards the stairs.

"You'll not be working too late up there tonight, Hannah," she said. "A long view is usually rewarding with something that seems exciting."

She knew! She actually knew that something was up, or that I thought it might be, and, as always, her advice was excellent. But I needed to read through the manuscript all the way, in one go, before reading it again critically. Only then would I feel ready to tell anyone exactly what we might have on our hands. But the further I read that afternoon, the more convinced and excited I became. At five minutes to six, the telephone rang again.

"Oh, you are still there, Hannah," Elisabeth said. "Well, you're the last. You'll mind to lock up securely when you do leave, no doubt."

"Yes, Elisabeth," I said, as neutrally as possible. "I'll be going soon."

"Hm," said Elisabeth. "There'll likely be another day tomorrow," and she put down the phone.

I was not sure if she was teasing me or caring for me. Either way, I returned to my find, finished it shortly before nine o'clock, and found myself exhausted. Taking no work with me, I went back to the flat, ate something light on rye biscuits, showered and was asleep by ten. I expected to need all my physical and mental strength on the following day.

Late the next afternoon, back in the office, I went downstairs to find Elisabeth.

"Um, Elisabeth…" I began tentatively.

"Is it a man or a manuscript?" she asked, giving way to one of her rare wicked grins.

"Oh, it's a manuscript," I almost stammered.

"I'd a mind it was one or the other," she said, still grinning. "I'm glad to know which. The fuss we had with Flora when Ian was courting her so slowly…" She waggled her head from side to side comically. "Well, write a pitch for Mr James, attach your notes and everything the author's sent us this time, and any history you can find out about him or her, and give it to me when you're ready. I'll give it to Mr James to consider."

The telephone beside her elbow rang. She reached for the receiver, and I turned to go back upstairs. Of course, these were the earliest days for my protege, and, at MacWhinney, Preston, the finding of a possible future publication was their *raison d'etre*. It was routine. Would I go the same way, in due course? Lose the surge of excitement, after finding a few more possibles? That would be sad, I thought as I got back to my room. I am so much enjoying this feeling of fulfilment. I shall look back on it so happily, even if Mr James damns this manuscript. Well, it's up to me to make sure that he doesn't, I decided, settling down to write the most persuasive pitch he'd probably ever see!

It took me the rest of the week to go through the manuscript, making succinct notes on its strengths and more extensive notes on its weaknesses. The reject bin remained empty, but no one, neither Andrew nor Elisabeth, commented on that. On the Saturday, I composed 2,000 words to persuade Mr James to agree with my assessment, and spent Sunday in and around the flat doing chores, while what I had written was left to germinate in the back—and in the forefront, truth to tell—of my mind. On the following Monday morning, I finalised what I wanted to present to Mr James, printed it out and assembled everything and took it down to Elisabeth.

"Thank you, Hannah," Elisabeth said when I gave her my bundle. "We'll be seeing something in your bin this week, then, now you're back with us, perhaps." But she smiled. I knew I was forgiven, but needed to forget my pet manuscript. It was out of my hands. My job now was to apply my attention to all the other authors whose dreams were stacked on the table in my office.

I climbed the stairs, willing Elisabeth to take my pitch straight in to Mr James and tell him to read it IMMEDIATELY. But I didn't really believe that she would. I had to be satisfied with the fact that, by the time I left the office at the end of the day, my distinctive bundle had disappeared from her desk, as far as I could see.

Chapter Nine

It was late-December before I heard more of my speck of gold. In the meantime, I had skim-read and rejected more than a hundred manuscripts, answered dozens of calls from authors impatient for stardom, progressed in my reading of Mr Joseph MacWhinney's handbook on editing and successfully relegated my pet manuscript to the back of my mind—mostly.

I had sent Christmas greetings to new friends in Edinburgh, and to my few contacts in Cambridge. Flora and Ian had invited me for lunch on Christmas Day. I had arranged to meet a couple of other girls in the publishing industry over the forthcoming holiday, and had booked a seat for a theatre production on another evening. I had worked hard since arriving in Edinburgh, and was ready for a few days' break.

Christmas Day was to fall on a Thursday, that year. It was on the preceding Tuesday that Elisabeth called me down to see Mr James. Yet again, I made the mistake of assuming it was to be a routine 'wind-up before Christmas' meeting.

"Well, Hannah," he greeted me as I entered his office. "Well, well, well. We did right to bring you to MacWhinney, Preston, then, did we? You'll be making all our fortunes before we die, no doubt? Which, I must say, we seemed very unlikely to do at this time last year." Was this the deepest irony? It had to be. But what had I done to deserve it? I was used to Mr James' heavily veiled teasing. We all were. He even teased Phylida gently, from time to time. I smiled and said nothing until he showed me firmer ground on which to stand.

"Aye, well, that Englishman's manuscript you spotted, Johnstone, was he?" I knew Mr James knew the author's name as well as he knew mine. "It seems that other people share your view. And so do I, lassie, so do I. So he's had an offer from us of a contract and a wee advance. Perhaps he'll not realise how wee in his excitement, and Christmas, and all. I'm hoping so, anyway." He grinned from beneath his brows, "So you did well to spot him, and his manuscript, Hannah. Well done, indeed."

I could hardly speak with excitement.

"Thank you, Mr James," I managed to say, with as much proper modesty as I could muster.

"Aye, well, now let's find the next one, hm?" he grunted, all business again. "But maybe not in the lot you've been reading recently, hm? Just one thing, though, Hannah. It took you the best part of a week between recognising Johnstone's value and pitching it to me. It was your first such exercise, I know, and the result was fine, but it took you too long, Hannah, hm?"

"The next one will be quicker, I promise, Mr James," I said firmly. "Next time, I won't be learning the technique from scratch. I'll follow the same sort of structure I used for Johnstone, if that one gave you what you needed?"

"Oh, it was fine," Mr James said, "fine."

I had to concentrate hard on what he said after that. My elation kept distracting me. Anyway, it wasn't a long meeting, and finished at a time suitable for an early lunch. When he released me, I dashed upstairs to my room, closed the door, and telephoned Flora on the office mobile. She seemed to take ages to answer. When she did, I could contain myself no longer.

"Flora, Flora, I found one! I found one!"

"I know," she said. "Mr James gave it to Munro and to me for second reading. We were so happy for you. Did he not tell you?"

"Nor did you," I mock-complained. But without any anger. I could hear her pleasure for me in her voice.

"It's a lovely find," she said. "A strong story, well written. An absolute gem. Well done you, Hannah! Was Mr James pleased?"

"I think so," I confirmed. "He told me to go away and find him the next one."

"Yes, he would," said Flora. "Oh, there's Veronica. Congratulations, again and again, Hannah. See you on Christmas Day," and she rang off.

***

Nothing much got done on the Wednesday. Elisabeth, Phylida and I, Jenny from Accounts and Frances from Dispatch, all went out for a girls' lunch, and there was a holiday air throughout MacWhinney, Preston's premises. Christmas lunch the next day, with Flora, Ian and Veronica, was wonderful. I had bought Ian a bottle of malt whiskey, on Flora's advice, and a soup-maker for Flora which she said she had been dying to get for months, and she gave me a very large, very

108

warm, bright pink scarf, "to cheer up your journeys to work on winter mornings," she said.

For Veronica, by now crawling, I took a collection of noisy toys for her to chase about the floor, which seemed to amuse her greatly. Ian and I washed up after lunch, and I walked back to my flat in the gloom of a late afternoon, relaxed and refreshed and unusually full of good food. Those feelings of general satisfaction carried me through the following weekend. By Monday morning, I was ready to get back to work.

The next great event was the firm's New Year's Eve party for loyal and valued authors and agents, and our regular external readers, editors, printers and booksellers, to be hosted by all the office staff. Assisted by Flora, I had invested in a new frock and shoes, smarter than anything I had ever previously possessed. I prepared for the occasion with both excitement and a degree of dread. I knew the limitations of my experience—or rather non-experience—of big social events.

Even at university, I had avoided all such things. That was not going to be possible this time. I spent a lot of time researching the profiles of as many of the guests as I could find, or could get Elisabeth or Phylida to describe to me, so that I might have something with which to start a conversation. No doubt the characteristic self-confidence of successful authors would then take over, and I could simply follow their leads with polite admiration and appreciation until they moved on to someone else.

The party was to be held in the huge banqueting room at one of the city's better hotels. Elisabeth had organised everything perfectly, of course. There was an ample buffet and bar, crowds of people of whom I knew almost none, and a noise-level I had not experienced since break-time at school on a wet, windy day.

Following Elisabeth's 'advice', I prepared to spend the evening spotting the unattached and approaching them with my hand extended, saying, 'I'm Hannah Lethbridge, with MacWhinney, Preston.' There were few people who were not taking advantage of the occasion to expand their own personal networks, however, so my strategy was little used. Elisabeth, Phylida, and Flora, who was also there of course, pulled me into their circles and introduced me frequently, often before slipping away to make contact with someone else.

After a while, I was finding the whole thing much easier than I had feared.

"I'm Hannah—" I began with one very tall, already balding, younger man.

"Aye, so I've heard," he said. "I'm George Herald, from the *Evening News*. A colleague tells me you write an insightful drama review. Pithy, he says."

I could feel my face warming. I had only been writing the reviews for a hobby, to see if I could, and could get them printed. A few had appeared in the *Evening News*, much to my delight, and had indeed been noticed, it seemed.

"Thank you. Are you here in a personal capacity, or for the paper?"

"Oh, no, just for the paper. Tasked with picking up next year's big thing before he or she happens, as usual. But this is always a good party to measure the strength of the city's publishing industry. You haven't been up here long, I understand?" he enquired. "Settled in and enjoying it?"

"Very much, thank you."

"Maybe we could go to the theatre together sometime, and I could observe your technique?" He realised what he had said, and we both blushed. "Your critical technique, I mean. Oh dear, it's getting worse, isn't it?"

We were both giggling by then.

"That would be fun. Thank you," I said.

"I'll call you. Now," he continued, looking around, "have you met Edward Spears, of…" he mentioned a competitor company. "Edward, come and meet Hannah Lethbridge of MacWhinney, Preston. I'll be in touch, Hannah," he said, leaving me to the mercies of Mr Spears, not expecting for a minute that George would make good on his offer.

The party continued. Edward introduced me to Ann, an agent whose name I had heard mentioned in the office. Ann introduced me to Gerald, another agent, who introduced me to Mr Alexander, his boss at one of the very prestigious firms in the city, who introduced me to his well-known new star writer, Corinne Hambleton, professor of biochemistry at the university and latest successor to the leadership of the determinedly atheist faction in Scottish society. Occasionally, the sequences of introductions tailed out, but I soon found another one to begin, and so the evening passed enjoyably and profitably.

As midnight approached, Mr James quieted the room and made a speech thanking everyone for the success of their efforts last year and looking forward confidently to MacWhinney, Preston's achievements in the coming year. The windows were opened the better to hear the city's bells ring in the New Year, and to enable everyone to see the fireworks let off on the Castle walls. Auld Lang Syne was sung vigorously. And then it was over. Our guests gradually drifted away, and we could finally make our own ways home in the early hours of the morning.

***

By Tuesday, the world had returned to normality. In the almost complete absence of postal deliveries over the holiday, the stacks of manuscripts on my table were discernibly smaller. I turned over some of the shorter ones, to give a chance to at least a few of those which had been on my table longest, and settled in again to feed the reject bin. I found no more gems, but still enjoyed seeing in the manuscripts the patterns of thoughts which had been passing through our aspiring authors' experiences or imaginations.

As the weeks passed, I found increasingly trying the long northern nights and short days, and the much colder weather than I had generally experienced further South. By now, I was equipped with thick sheepskin mittens, long, warm, shiny, lined boots (of which I was very proud!), and an anorak "fit for the rigs", as Ian described it. I spent almost every day in trousers and thick woolly jumpers, and my office chair and reject bin were permanently located hard up against my radiator. One morning in mid-February, Munro tapped on the door and came into my office.

"Do you have a minute, Hannah?" he enquired.

"Of course, Munro. Good morning."

"Oh, yes, of course. Good morning." He looked at me and smiled as he realised I was teasing him. "Erm…how are you getting on with Mr Joseph?"

"Almost finished it, for the first time through," I said. "It's dense, isn't it? It's on the desk, by the phone." The handbook of editing practice had been migrating irregularly between Munro's office and my own for months now, according to his (infrequent) need and the occurrence of my spare time.

"No, I don't need it," he said, looking earnest. "Do you feel you might be interested in having a first go at editing a manuscript yourself, though?" Perhaps I hesitated for a fraction of a second. "I've cleared it with Mr James. He's quite happy for you to have a go, if you'd like to do so."

"I'd love to," I said enthusiastically. In secret, I had been unofficially 'editing' passages I had been reading in my manuscripts, just for practice, and hoping that one day I might be asked to do it for real.

111

"It's only a wee book of short stories, which Martin Consort has persuaded Mr James to accept on behalf of the cousin of one of Martin's better clients." I'd met Martin briefly among the agents at the firm's New Year party, a man of Mr James' generation, and of a similar bearing. "It's not a high priority, time-wise," Munro continued, "though Mr James would like it on the market for the summer holiday season. He's hoping it might sell a few copies in train stations and airports to people going away on boring journeys." Munro drew a face. There wasn't going to be any great prestige to be derived from this one, so the donkey-work could reasonably be passed down the line to me. What did I care? It was a start, a toe in the door to the future I wanted.

"Is that it?" I said, waving at the bundle under his arm.

"Um," he agreed, unwilling to let go of a manuscript, even with all the i's dotted and t's crossed. Not a natural team-player, our Munro.

"May I see it?" I asked as mildly as I could.

"Um," he said again, and held it out, reluctantly.

It looked to be about three or four hundred pages long.

"Is this the only copy we have?" I enquired.

"Um."

"Would it be sensible for me to get another copy to work on, then?" I suggested. "That might mean, when I give it back to you, that you don't have to mark up both the author's errors and mine on the same copy, which could make everything very messy and confusing."

"Yes," he said thoughtfully. "Go and see Malcolm downstairs in Design and Production. He has a bigger photocopier than Elisabeth's."

I knew Munro wasn't one for idle chat, but this was like getting blood out of a stone.

"I'll give it two hours a day for a start, and see how I'm getting on by the end of the week. Does that sound about right?"

"Um," he said yet again. Then, "Remember, Hannah," this most seriously, "MacWhinney, Preston doesn't believe in colons or semicolons, or split infinitives. And we don't like too many conjunctions, either. Check each one for validity, if you please. Do a quick line-edit first and get the feel of the thing, before going for structure and characters."

"Can I show you how far I've got next Monday morning, Munro," I asked, "and you can set me right where I'm not quite up to speed?"

"Aye, that would be best." He turned to go back to his own room. "Thank you, Hannah. Much appreciated," he said over his shoulder. It wasn't fulsome thanks, but that was Munro, I already knew. He wasn't rude, just very, very focussed on what he was going to do next.

The next stop was Malcolm, on the floor beneath. His office was the size of mine and Munro's combined, and took up the whole depth of one side of the building on the second floor. As I approached his door, I could hear the clatter of a large-volume photocopier going full tilt.

"Good morning, Malcolm," I said from the doorway.

"Hallo, stranger," he replied. "What can we do for you?"

At the far end of the room, a fleshy young man with long, dark hair and heavy-rimmed glasses was clearing copies from a machine and stacking them on the table beside him.

"I wondered if you could run me just one copy of this manuscript, please?" I said.

"It'll cost you twenty pounds," said the dark-haired boy, "or there's a Speediprint shop around the corner."

"Shut up, Kenny. This is Miss Hannah from upstairs. Show her the respect you give to Mrs Elisabeth, now."

"Och, she doesn't frighten me like Mrs Elisabeth," Kenny said, grinning at me.

"Enough," said Malcolm. To me, "Leave it on the side here, Hannah. Want it yesterday, I suppose? Kenny will bring it up after lunch."

"Thank you very much." I retreated through the door again, and headed for the stairs, glancing into the quieter room on the other side of the corridor.

"Hallo, Hannah," said Jenny's voice from inside. "What are you doing down here?" I stepped into her office. The partitioning on this side of the corridor was as on the floor above. Her room was the same size as mine, but the large table was clearly her desk. A massive, ancient-looking safe stood in one corner, and stationery and files of all sorts filled the shelves on three walls.

"Have you met Tansy, my assistant accountant," Jennie said, waving towards a homely girl seated at another, smaller table behind the door.

"What a power-house," I commented, smiling at Tansy, who blushed and smiled back shyly.

"Oh, yes, this is where the firm's money is really made," Jenny boasted. "All you clever-clogs people above and below are just there to make it look good for the taxman." We gossiped pleasantly for a minute or two, and then I resumed my climb to the third floor.

Kenny brought me my copy, and the original manuscript, about twenty past one. I wrapped the original in bubble-paper preserved from another submitted manuscript, and took the copy with me when I left the office to find a bowl of soup at lunchtime. I was later than usual, and chose a café that was warm and steamy, but not too crowded at this time of year. I had no trouble spreading the opened manuscript beside my bowl.

A couple of hours later, I had read pretty well half of the fourteen stories it comprised. Several were quite attractive. One or two were no more than scraps, and seemed to me to be out of balance with the rest of the collection. MacWhinney, Preston seldom published flash-fiction, I knew. Mr James apparently felt that it was rather beneath the position the firm held in the industry, and that exaggerated brevity demonstrated want of application by the author, rather than any particular, if fashionable, skill. "If it bored the author after only a page or two, it'll likely bore the reader," I'd heard him say, perhaps slightly harshly I thought, but there it was.

Back in my own office, I addressed the demands of the reject bin until about seven o'clock, when Andrew arrived at my door to take away the results of my day's work. He nodded to me silently as he came in, and again as he left with the bin. I took the hint, gathered up my belongings, and went home, with the short stories in my shopping bag to finish the preliminary read-through at home after supper.

The next morning, I began the detailed line-edit. The spelling was quite good, I found, but there were too many long, complex sentences. I scattered full stops extensively, deleted conjunctions wherever possible and broke up large blocks of text into separate new paragraphs at several points. This was rather fun! Like doing a word-search puzzle, I thought irreverently, pressing on.

After Elisabeth's call to take a break, I returned to the manuscripts piled on my table for the rest of the day. I was finding the novelty of editing dangerously attractive. However, the thought of Elisabeth's assessment of the volume of my rejects helped me keep my expanding roles in balance.

***

On Wednesday afternoon, the telephone on my desk rang.

"I've a Mr Herald asking to speak to you," Elisabeth announced. "If this is personal, Hannah, keep it short, please."

"Yes, Elisabeth," I said.

The telephone clicked, and George's voice said, "Hallo, Hannah, I'm told personal calls are frowned upon in office hours." I could hear the amused smile in his voice, and wondered if Elisabeth had heard it too. "Will you call me back this evening?" He gave me a mobile number which I scribbled on the corner of the sheet of scrap on which I was making notes. "I'll be here until seven this evening."

"Oh, thank you, George," I said, taken completely by surprise. "I'll call you between six and seven."

"Aye. Right. Speak to you then," and he rang off.

I imagined Elisabeth saying 'hm' as she put down her receiver.

Curiosity got the better of me by four o'clock. Returning to my office with my afternoon coffee, I extracted my mobile from my handbag and called the number George Herald had given me.

"Hallo, it's Hannah Lethbridge at MacWhinney, Preston," I said.

"Ooh, Hannah, in working hours?" he teased. "This really is thoroughly personal."

I said nothing, wondering how sensible I had been to call him. He had seemed a pleasant man when we met at the New Year's party, but I didn't want him or anybody else to think I was encouraging him socially.

"Well, not quite thoroughly," George continued. "Our regular drama critic is out of town for a day or two, and there's a show he would otherwise have covered. There are complimentary press tickets." That sounded good. "Would you like to cover it with me for the *News*?"

"If I'm free, I'd love to," I said, trying to keep my voice as even as possible. "Tell me where and when."

He gave me the details. It was a student production. In Edinburgh, that didn't necessarily mean an unprofessional shambles. New stars had been known to have been born from such companies. I had been wondering whether to go to this one, anyway. I decided. George still sounded a nice man. Not pressing or threatening, so far.

"That sounds fine," I said. "Shall I meet you in the foyer there?"

"I'll look forward to it," he said, with a slightly old-fashioned politeness, and, I thought, so will I.

By the Friday afternoon, I had line-edited about two-thirds of the stories. The next morning, after doing some essential shopping and the necessary weekend chores in the flat, I decided to stay there rather than go in to the office. The flat was too snug to leave that day. At weekends, I had found by experience, the heating in the office was only enough to keep the plumbing from freezing. I got down to my editing again, and reached the end of it on Sunday evening. Munro was already in his office by the time I got to MacWhinney, Preston on Monday morning.

"Good morning, Munro," I said, tapping on his door. "May I have a word?"

He looked up and waited for me to speak.

"I've line-edited those short stories you gave me right through once, but I'd quite like to go through them again to make sure I haven't missed too much. Can I aim to let you have them by, say, close-of-play on Wednesday?"

He looked dubious.

"I can't do anything with that job this morning," he said, "but I'd quite like to see what you've done this afternoon. There's no point in you going too far before we've had a chance to discuss your first attempts."

That was blunt, but fair enough, I thought.

"Well, could I get Kenny to make a copy of what I've done? Then I could leave it with you, and review the copy until you've time for a talk."

"OK," Munro agreed, as briefly as ever, and turned back with what looked like relief to the manuscript before him. Talk about single-tracked! But usefully decisive, I supposed.

When I had taken off my coat and hung it behind the office door, I went down to see Malcolm and Kenny again.

"Good morning," I said to them. They were both hard at work on their computers, with a stack of floppy disks on the desks beside them.

"Could I have another copy…"

"Put it there," Malcolm said, not looking up. The level of concentration in this place was almost overwhelming. "You'll have your copy by eleven."

I thanked him, put my edited copy of the manuscript down on a corner of his worktop and turned to leave their hive of activity.

Just before twelve, Kenny came up to my office.

"There's your original material, with all its squiggles," he said, "and a copy of it."

I took my original line-edited version of the stories in to Munro and settled down to my stacks of manuscripts again.

***

George and I went to see the students' production on the Wednesday of that week. It was a modern-dress, somewhat adapted, version of *The Merchant of Venice*, set in Frankfurt, without any artificial German accents, thank goodness, and well-enough done overall, with particularly good lighting but without future star-material among the cast so far as I could see. As we were leaving the theatre, George said, "I don't think Duncan missed anything much. Shall we have a drink around the corner, maybe?"

I knew of his colleague Duncan, the regular theatre critic for the *News*. I needed to know if George's assessment of his likely view of the evening was Duncan's or George's, however. There was no point in my writing something that would be completely at odds with Duncan's tastes. Such a review would simply go on the peg faster than it reached his desk.

"A drink would be lovely," I said, in the interest of getting more of my work into his paper.

In the pub, George went to get my mineral water and his pint, while I found two seats at an already occupied table, and sat to look over the notes I had scribbled in the dark of the theatre. Setting down the drinks, George glanced at my notebook.

"Is that some kind of private shorthand?" he smiled. "I can't read a word of it."

"Some of it is my own abbreviations," I returned, "but mostly it's a mixture of my careless handwriting, and the influence of the darkness. I can read it, anyway. Well, most of it, by the morning after."

"So will you pan it, in the review?" he asked. He really hadn't much enjoyed the play, it seemed.

"Not completely," I said. "It was an interesting take on the economic rise of a newly reunified Germany…"

"You're a born journalist," he teased. "You're already composing your opening paragraph!"

We both laughed. I took it that I was somewhere close to the house-style of the drama column of the *News*, and turned to ask about his own field.

"So what sort of subjects do you mostly cover?"

He was very willing to tell me his war-stories, as he called them, and it made an amusing end to a relaxing evening. He was still telling them when he walked me to my bus-stop, and we agreed we'd had a lovely evening, and must do it again.

Munro returned my first attempt at line-editing the following morning. As soon as he put down the manuscript on my desk and I opened it, I could see how many additional amendments he had marked. I was mortified!

"Don't worry," Munro said. "You've been trying too hard, for too long at a time. Go back to the beginning, and start again in small bites. I may have missed something as well. None of us are invulnerable. Bring it back to me on Tuesday next, if you will."

At least I was being allowed to go on editing. Also, Munro had been very kind and constructive. This was a side of him that I had not seen before, one he did not show in his concentrated, day to day, behaviour. I was touched.

Chapter Ten

The months passed. The winter eased, and suddenly I realised that I had been in Edinburgh a whole year. I was being paid the compliment of everyone taking for granted my presence in the firm, and had been given an open contract, and a pay-rise. I had thought I might have found another manuscript that we might bring to publication, but, after prolonged rumination, Mr James had disagreed. The piles on my table maintained their maturity, though there was achievement in my not letting them become overwhelming large.

My editing was becoming more accurate, though not yet to the point of independence from Munro's meticulous oversight. George and I had been to the theatre together a few times. I had bullied my landlord into letting me repaint half the rooms in my flat, and spring was in sight over a near horizon.

And, in fact, the next three years passed in much the same way. I was now a confirmed inhabitant of Edinburgh. I readily understood most of the dialect I heard from time to time on the buses and in the shops near my flat. My drama reviews appeared regularly in the *News*. In the Firm, I was being given more, and more significant, manuscripts to edit without Munro's supervision, talking directly to authors about the results, and generally playing a greater part in the company's work. Unless I was feeling particularly tired, I seldom remembered not having been here, and was very happy not to do so.

One afternoon, Elisabeth called me on the phone from downstairs.

"Mr James would be grateful if you'd step down to see him, Hannah," she said.

"Of course, Elisabeth. Do I need to bring anything specific?"

"No, no. He just wants to discuss something with you."

I couldn't think of anything I hadn't done recently, or of anything other than routine matters that he might want to discuss. He hadn't bothered to give me one of his tutorials for several months.

"Ah, Hannah," he greeted my tap on his office door. His tone almost suggested surprise to see me, as though he hadn't issued his summons to our meeting.

"Good afternoon, Mr James," I replied.

He waved me to his client-chair and put down the paper he had been examining.

"Aye, aye. Now, Hannah, you've been pretty busy recently, hm?"

"Nothing out of the ordinary, Mr James. Better that way than the other."

"Hm. Well. Hm. I've a friend, you see, in Dundee…"

Here we go, I thought, he wants a rush-job to get an otherwise no-hoper to market for the friend of a useful friend.

"He's a very eminent man, I understand," Mr James continued. "A full professor, no less, though I first met him when he was much more humble." He grinned to himself at his memories. Then he raised his bushy eyebrows to their fullest extent, for emphasis, and looked straight at me. "He heads the English Department at the university in Dundee, hm."

I tried to look suitably impressed.

"He's short a junior lecturer, he tells me, at short notice," Mr James went on. "Part time. There's no great amount of money in it, and there's the cost of the travel to Dundee, unless you could negotiate for them to pay that."

I finally realised that Mr James was effectively offering me the job.

"They want someone with a good general background in literature, who could also build up undergraduate potential for eventually producing publications, for the greater glory of the university, his department and no doubt himself. He was aye one to value himself," Mr James smiled again fondly at his memories. "You've got what he's looking for, Hannah, and it would do MacWhinney, Preston no harm to make a small long-term investment in future Scots talent."

"It would mean me spending time away from the office," I murmured, "and what exactly would your friend want me to teach?"

"It isn't so much the what," Mr James said, "but the how. My friend envisages workshops, apparently, 8 half-days a term plus marking-time. Are you aware of workshops?" he asked. He clearly wasn't.

"Oh, yes, Mr James. I'm sure I could manage that." My mental fingers were crossed, but I could find out what I didn't yet know. It sounded like the concept of seminars with exercises and a modernised name. I could check that with my contacts in the university here in Edinburgh. "I suppose it would be a matter of telling the students what publishers look for in submitted manuscripts, and what damns them." It was no more than I'd been learning since I joined MacWhinney, Preston. "I'd like to take up the offer, if I may. Thank you for asking me."

"I'll expect no great drop in your productivity here," Mr James said, looking at me mock-sternly. Then he smiled. "I don't foresee any great problem there, however." He gave me the name and contact details of his friend the Professor, and suggested I telephone him after a few days, by which time Mr James would have paved the way for me.

***

Not surprisingly, Professor MacAlister turned out to be a very similar character to Mr James, though with a personal drive that was a little more obvious. I went to Dundee one morning to meet him, and was soon passed down to a senior lecturer to be told what was to be required of me.

"What we have in mind is quite a revolutionary idea, we think," Morag MacIver explained enthusiastically. She was a short, strongly-built woman with a mass of bright red, curly hair, a huge amount of inner energy, and the wonderful soft burr to her voice which I now knew suggested a Hebridean origin. "The aim of the first-degree course is to turn out people with a sound background in English literature who will be capable of making a living from writing, or if not, from teaching or publishing, after they've completed their studies here." I liked this idea immensely. It was different from, and more than, my own undergraduate experience of the dry academic analysis of texts.

"We envisage you leading very practical workshops," Morag continued, "in which the students will be required, through your guidance, to work and rework what they write into forms that publishers or theatrical producers will accept." Her expression took on an almost anxious intensity. "We'd like them to have published something, somewhere, by the end of their first year, so we look to your knowledge and experience of the industry to help them identify to whom they might most appropriately and successfully pitch their work, how to pitch it, and in what form. We've an idea that they might be encouraged to start a literary magazine of their own, and we'd like you to help them with that, especially the practical aspects."

I quickly saw that such a project could be somewhat demanding of my time. The hour-and-a-half's train journey from Edinburgh to Dundee and the same back, plus marking time (some of that could be done on the train, perhaps), plus the establishment and general editorship of a new literary journal... Still, I wanted to do this. I was already feeling the excitement of a new project, and of other people believing that I could bring it off. Morag wanted practical workshops. Well, an awful lot of the work on the new journal could be included under the heading of 'practical', and done by the students. Anyway, a whole three-hour period with the students every week would need to be broken up. It would have to be task-based rather than traditional, old fashioned, straight teaching. And it would require pretty detailed planning, term by term, though it must still provide space for flexibility. I wouldn't know exactly what would be needed until the students' own capabilities and aims became apparent, as they developed through the year.

"You're already thinking how you'll do this, aren't you?" Morag was smiling, and I realised that I had been so taken up with my own thinking that I had temporarily lost consciousness of her presence beside me.

"Um," I said, "I've a lot of preparation to do. I take it that this will be a new course? The Department hasn't offered anything similar, with a course structure I could look at...?"

"No, this will be totally new to us, Hannah. Is that maybe slightly daunting?"

"Yes and no," I replied. "It gives me a lot of freedom to shape the course, and to integrate all the materials and resources. What a wonderful challenge!"

"Will I tell Prof you'll be here at the beginning of October, then?"

"Subject to my boss giving his final approval," I said, "but I don't think that's going to be a problem. What are the precise dates and times involved, and who do I have to see about pay and administration?"

We talked details and exchanged telephone numbers, and I went back to Edinburgh, planning and making notes all the way.

***

I was so afraid that my first session of the course in Dundee would be a nightmare. A few days after meeting Morag, when my initial excitement had died down, the nerves started up. As my overall plan came together, I kidded myself that I had got my nerves under control, but I hadn't, not really. I had just let them be pushed down temporarily beneath my other crowding thoughts, like a child being pushed under water by an older sibling in a swimming pool. I did most of the planning in the evenings and at weekends. It didn't need much original research.

I had been employed by the university to pass on and inculcate in the students the skills I used every day in the office. It was more a matter of planning the time-use, breaking up each of the eight 3-hour afternoon sessions in the first term into units of time and activity that would be sufficiently intense as to avoid boredom in the participants without driving them so hard as to render the less able unproductive and marginalised. My job was to teach, not to forge steel.

So there I was, on that first afternoon of my course in October, sitting a third of the way around a circle of tables in a big, otherwise bare, sun-filled room. Gradually, eighteen boys and girls—it was all they seemed to me, though I was not yet double their age—pushed open the door to the room and came in according to their characters. Some knew each other already.

They greeted each other in subdued voices, but took not a bit of notice of me. I could have been a mature-student member of the course, I suppose, though the heaps of bags and materials against the wall behind my chair suggested otherwise—to me, at least. At precisely two o'clock, I stood up and began.

"Ladies and gentlemen, good afternoon. My name is Hannah Lethbridge. I'm an initial reader and editor with MacWhinney, Preston, the publishers in Edinburgh."

"Och, it's another English invasion," a voice said.

He was a short, heavy boy slumped in his chair a few seats round the circle from me. Quiet chuckles came from one or two of what were clearly already his acolytes. I paused and looked at him as neutrally as I could, saying nothing for a couple of seconds, then went on.

"Most of your courses in this Department will give you the skills to analyse English literature. My purpose is to turn you into publishable writers." There was a new quality of silence in the room. That had interested them!

"It will necessarily be a practical course, a series of workshops in which we will all contribute to each other's learning. We will be resources for each other, and the course will work only if everyone provides their share of the raw material on which we will feed and grow." I outlined the assessment plan which was to be applied to grade their work, and the time-demands which would be made of them. "I will not be grading work handed in to me after the deadlines indicated. No work, no grade."

I wasn't sure if I could get away with this, but I needed to take control from the beginning. "You will also write in your sessions with me. I won't be talking at you for a solid three hours at a time, though I'll be talking more in the first few weeks, to give you a common basis in a particular set of skills. After that, you will gradually take over the time allocated to us, and I will be here more and more to be available to you as you, or sometimes I, feel the need."

I paused and looked around the group again. Well, at least open rebellion had not broken out yet, and most of them had their eyes on me rather than on their pads or out of the windows.

"So now I need to know who you are." I walked to the flip-chart at the side of the room on which I drew a circle, and chairs were scraped as those on my side of the circle turned around slightly, the better to see what I was about to do. "I'd like each of you tell me, in no more than five crisp sentences, your name, the sort of writing you particularly like to read and to write, and what you've been writing in the past two years. Would you begin, please?" I pointed my marker-pen at the girl who was sitting on the opposite side of the circle from my chair. She made to stand.

"No need to stand up unless you wish to do so, at this stage," I said. She looked grateful, and promptly sat down again to speak her name, which I wrote in its place on the circle on my chart, and to inform us of her literary likes and dislikes.

It was a quarter to three by the time I had identified each of the students on my chart. They would all sit somewhere else next week, just to confuse me, of course, but at least by then I would have linked appearances to names for most of them. It was time for their first task.

"Now, I want each of you, by four o'clock, to write me a piece of prose about your hometown. You can do it here or anywhere else you fancy. I'm hoping for about 800 words, but don't strain or worry if you get a little less," I stressed 'little', "or more. Just make sure you're back here by four. Thank you." The room emptied, needless to say, and I too went down to the cafeteria in a nearby building for a cup of coffee.

When we had all returned at four o'clock, I gave them their next instruction.

"What I want you to do next is to swap what you have written with a colleague, read through what your colleague has written, read it a second time and then offer them constructive criticism on their material." I laid extra stress on the word 'constructive'. "So begin with the strengths you can see in their work, and communicate them first. Only then put forward what you see as weaknesses, always saying why you think it's a weakness and always suggesting how you think what they have written at that point could be improved.

"Do not interrupt your critic while they are delivering their criticism," I emphasised, "however misplaced their criticism might appear to be, however strong the emotions they have raised in you of disappointment or anger or whatever, however they may have completely misunderstood what you were trying to say. Your turn to respond will come when your partner has finished offering the points they want to make, and when you do respond, do it calmly.

"Take as many deep breaths as you need to retain your calmness, but stay calm. That will leave your brain clear to think, rather than simply to react to whatever emotion your partner's criticism has evoked. Finally, remember that your partner is likely to be feeling just what you would feel if somebody criticised your work as you are criticising theirs. Put yourself in their place. Your purpose is to build them up, not tear them down. And finish this exchange no later than 4.45, please, so that we can have a quick review before finishing the session."

I sat down, beginning to feel exhausted, while the group settled into pairs and began reading each other's work quietly. *So far, so good*, I thought.

At 4.45, I stood up again, called a halt to their exchanges, asked for views on constructive criticism as a technique, which were generally positive, set them another small task to bring to next week's meeting and closed the session. I had survived! There hadn't been a riot. I was a teacher in a university! It was the fulfilment of a dream that I had given up thinking might become a reality. However the students reacted to me the next week, I now knew I could do this, and I caught my train back to Edinburgh with a happy heart.

***

That autumn was hectic. I had made fairly detailed plans for the Dundee course during the summer. Nonetheless, I found it demanding to keep up with my everyday work at MacWhinney, Preston as well as thinking through the tweaks to the course required by the particular needs of the student group and my own inexperience of teaching. Everything seemed to take longer than I had allowed. We were all learning intensively together, though I tried to hide as well as I could the surprises that occasionally pounced on me in the course-room. The students were generally a friendly, hard-working lot.

Even my pet Scottish nationalist gradually seemed to come to accept me as a necessary, even a useful, evil. Morag had sat in on a couple of my sessions, once the course was well under way, and seemed happy at the way it was going. I had met other members of the faculty in passing, in the corridors or the cafeteria, and had no doubt that they were discussing my progress among themselves, but no one offered particular comment.

I soon adopted a routine of getting the train from Edinburgh just before noon, setting up my resources in the course-room when I got to Dundee, and popping into the campus cafeteria for a bite to eat before my sessions started. I reversed that sequence after each session, and got back to my flat in Edinburgh about eight-thirty or nine o'clock, ready for an early night, and an early start in the office the next day. It was all very organised and thoroughly enjoyable.

One evening at the end of November, however, everything changed. The cafeteria was more crowded than usual when I went in for a meal after my session with the students. I had been lucky to find a table where I could spread a MacWhinney, Preston manuscript beside my plate. However, I was not surprised when a man of about my own age, carrying his plate and cutlery, stopped beside me and enquired whether he could share my table.

"Of course," I said, closing the manuscript to make space for him, and popping it into the shopping bag beside my feet.

"You'll be teaching here perhaps?" he said, once he'd sat down and picked up his fork.

"Yes, just part-time," I replied, "in the English Department. I do a writing-workshop with first-year students once a week."

He raised his eyebrows.

"Oh, you're a writer, then?" he asked.

"No, I'm an editor with a publisher. MacWhinney, Preston, in Edinburgh."

"Will you be publishing the work of some of our students, then?" he smiled.

"We'll have to see. The course only began this term." Guessing that he wasn't a student, from his age and serious facial expression, I said, "What do you teach?"

"I'm a chemist," he said self-deprecatingly, as though it was the easiest work in the world and of no great matter. "I don't do much teaching these days. I run a laboratory, exploring the useful characteristics of various substances for the food industry." His lips curved slightly, self-mockingly. "How long have you been in Scotland?" he asked, with another smile.

And so we chatted. He seemed a warm, pleasant man, and, in the way of such things, we entertained each other over an otherwise slightly boring meal. I couldn't believe that it was after seven o'clock when I caught sight unintentionally of the watch on his wrist.

"I must go," I said, gathering up my things, "but thank you for lightening the evening."

"Will you perhaps be here next week? Maybe we could lighten each other's evening again then?"

"That might be very pleasant," I said, carefully rather than enthusiastically. "Thank you. Let's see how we go."

But we did meet the next week, and the next, and then it was the end of term, and I wouldn't be back in Dundee until January.

I can't say that I really missed Drummond the chemist over the holiday. There was Christmas, and the firm's New Year party, and catching up on my work in the office. Nonetheless, I was surprised how pleased I was to see him when I started back at Dundee in January for the second term of my workshops with the students. Drummond and I ate together and chatted in the cafeteria. I told him about getting the students to be practical in their writing, not just artistic, and also in the planning of the literary journal the Prof wanted us to produce.

He told me about his enzymes and sugar-substitutes, though not much of what he said made any sense to me. Perhaps it was a relief to him to have someone other than another chemist to talk to occasionally. I could only hope so. At least he showed no sign of boredom while he was with me. Ours was becoming a comfortable, if not a close, relationship, and I felt that that suited me very well.

I had continued to submit theatre reviews to the *News* through the summer's Festival season, and then covered the pantomime season in December and January. However, the increase in work in the autumn, especially that arising from my Dundee commitment, had reduced their number significantly, so it came as a pleasure when, over a cafeteria supper at the end of January, Drummond announced, "Scottish Opera is doing *Eugene Onegin* at the Festival Theatre in Edinburgh in a couple of weeks. Would you like to go?"

I knew nothing about music, and opera was not something to which anyone had ever introduced me. Perhaps this showed, because Drummond said, "It's by Tchaikovsky, very Russian and emotional. Beautiful music and costumes. I'd really be glad if you'd come with me."

Why not? I thought. It will be a new experience, yet another new adventure, and I hadn't had one of those recently.

"Thank you, I'd love to," I decided, and we arranged to meet at the theatre on the following Monday fortnight.

Just before going out for lunch the next day, I telephoned Flora, my fairy godmother in all new experiences.

"How are Ian and Veronica?" I asked, after establishing that she could be interrupted and was not in the middle of something which was actually important.

"Ian's fine, and Veronica's at her playgroup, though I must go and collect her in twenty minutes or so." I heard no more of Ian, but was given a full account of her daughter's development. Eventually, Flora ran out of news about her, and asked, "How's Dundee going?"

"The course is fine, thank you," I assured her, "going very well, in fact. But that's not the problem." I paused and Flora waited for me to go on. "I've been invited to the opera," I finally blurted out. "Flora, I know nothing about opera, and I don't know what to wear."

"But you said yes, anyway. Is it a man?"

"Um, actually, yes."

"Ooh, Hannah," Flora shrieked down the telephone, almost deafening me. "Oooh, Hannah. And about time too, my dear! Come round for supper tonight after work. I need to hear *all* about him! And we'll go shopping on Saturday. Princes Street, no less. Only the best for this occasion."

That evening, Flora contained herself until we had finished eating. Once the washing-up had been done, however, she said commandingly, "Ian's going to watch the football on television in here," Ian looked mildly surprised but didn't demur, "so we'll take our coffee into the other room, Hannah."

I had not been into their lounge previously, so I was interested to see that it was no bigger than my office, and not much more luxuriously furnished. There was a central, oval coffee table and a comfortably firm three-piece suite, including a two-seat sofa, scattered with brightly coloured cushions, all on neutral-coloured wall-to-wall carpeting. There were several of Ian's photographs of startling scenery, enlarged and framed, on the walls, and a mirror opposite the door, presumably for the purpose of making the room seem larger as one came in. Sitting down, Flora turned to me, and said firmly, but grinning like an ape, "Now!"

"Now what?" I said weakly. "There's nothing special to tell. I've just been asked out to the opera for the first time, and I'm—"

"You're completely flummoxed!" Flora said delightedly. "Who is he? What's he look like? What does he do? How do you feel? Oh, Hannah, you're hopeless!"

It was all true. All of it. I was not sure that I wanted to feel what I was beginning to feel about Drummond. I was not sure if my excitement was over being taken to the opera, or being taken to the opera by Drummond.

"Hannah, dear," Flora said, very gently. "Have you never been invited out by a man before?"

I burst into tears. Just like I used to do, so long ago, when I was ill. Why could other people see so easily what I was feeling when I couldn't? Why was I so pathetic, weeping at the least little thing? Flora came and sat beside me on the sofa and put her arms around me. Gradually, I stopped crying. She pulled back from me slightly to look at me.

"What is it, Hannah?" she said. "Is it the man or the situation? If it's the man, he's best seen off straight away!"

I knew she'd 'see off', in no uncertain terms, anyone who frightened me.

"No, no," I tried to reassure her through my dying sobs, "I think he's lovely. He's gentle and impeccably polite, and seems kind and generous. He works long hours, and he's a chemist at the university in Dundee, and he wears these warm-looking jackets and doesn't look after his shoes particularly well, and his hair could do with a trim, but…"

"Has he tried to kiss you yet?" Flora asked.

"Goodness, no!" I protested. "There's never been a word out of place."

"So how did you meet him, and how long have you known him?"

"Oh, it seems he's been there forever!" I could hear myself almost sighing. What *was* all this? "But I suppose it's only been a few months." Pulling myself together, I insisted, "What I really need to know is, whatever am I going to wear, and what will it cost?"

Flora was not so easily deflected. She persisted, very sensitively, until she had extracted from me every detail I knew about Drummond, and then instructed me carefully how to learn more, from him and from seeking out and making mutual friends on the campus who had known him for longer than I had.

Then she became seriously serious.

"Hannah, dear, will you forgive me if I talk to you like a mother? I know you haven't had much to do with your own mother for a while, and I'm guessing she didn't do a lot for you when you were around each other. There are times when a girl needs a mother to tell her things, and the girl's first serious date is one of them. Don't be embarrassed. Just look at your hands, if you like, and listen, but there are some things I really need to be sure you know."

What a friend Flora always had been, and now in particular was! There was so much of 'this sort of thing' that no one had ever told me. I knew there was, from books and films, in the general way that every child knows it. I had so many questions on these subjects, and I'd never had anyone I dared to ask. I looked up at her, waiting for her to go on.

She smiled, and said, "Firstly, take all this excitement very slowly. Not so slowly as to put him off," she grinned this time, "but slowly enough for you to keep control. That shouldn't be difficult, as far as he's concerned. He's a scientist devoted to his work, and won't give you a thought for hours together, a lot of the time. Though, characteristically, they're very loyal and loving, when you're with them. Well, mine is, anyway." She nodded towards the kitchen, from where the sounds of televised football had swelled and died throughout our conversation.

"Secondly," she went on, reaching for a pad on the corner of the dresser near her hand. She turned to a clean page, wrote on it and ripped it off. "This is the name and details of my doctor. She's excellent on the gynaecological bits and pieces. I take it you haven't…"

I must have been bright pillar-box red! I certainly felt it, as I shook my head, feeling silly and sheepish.

"Do you have a doctor of your own yet up here?" Flora enquired.

"Not one I'd want to talk to about these things," I said firmly.

"Well, mine's a brick, and a personal friend. I'll ring her on Monday and ask if she will fit you in sometime next week."

"But, Flora, I'm only going out for an evening with him," I protested, "there's no question of anything…more…yet. If ever."

"Better safe than sorry," Flora said, "especially in these matters. You never know when it might happen. It just does, at the right time. And I want regular progress reports, Hannah. Regular," she emphasised. "And detail! All the details." She gave me another vast hug and we both collapsed giggling on her tiny sofa. "Now, clothes," she said. "The last time my husband and I went to the opera…" She said 'my husband and I' in a mocking, pseudo-smart voice. "It's no good asking me, Hannah. I've never been to the opera either! But I know where to go to find out."

We fixed a time and place to meet on Saturday morning to go shopping, and her advice then was as good as it had always been. Another dress and shoes, and a smarter coat than I had ever previously possessed, were added to my wardrobe, with quite an impact on my credit card but nothing I couldn't manage if I was careful for the rest of the month. She insisted on lending me a particular scarf which she said would just set off the dress, and I was grateful. All mine were woven for warmth rather than style. I was going to look the part at the opera. All I had to do was mind my tongue, to protect my ignorance.

It truly was a wonderful evening. Drummond was the perfect escort. He looked after me so generously, allowing the music and the costumes and the whole experience to just consume me without pressing his greater knowledge on me in any way. By the end of the evening, when he walked me to my bus stop, I was both exhausted and exhilarated and could still hear and see the opera continuing in my mind. I really was not paying attention to Drummond, therefore, when, as the bus drew up at the stop, he bent forward and kissed my cheek.

"Goodnight, dear Hannah," he murmured. "See you soon," and put his hand on my back to gently push me forward onto the bus.

How I remembered where to get off the bus, I am not at all sure. I could think of nothing other than Drummond's kiss. The next morning, dressing in my everyday jumper and skirt for the office, and taking my oil-rig anorak from its hook in my hall, I had recovered slightly. It was only a kiss on the cheek. Everybody kissed that way at the end of an evening. The fact that no one, certainly no man, had ever kissed me that way was neither here nor there. It was no more than a politeness, an expression of his pleasure at an evening's entertainment which we had both thoroughly enjoyed.

Nonetheless, Elisabeth gave me a decidedly funny look as she wished me good morning on my way past her to go up to my office. And indeed, I did feel different. Lighter. Did it show so easily? How frightening! I took a firm grip on myself, and tried to settle down to scan a newly-arrived manuscript. I knew that I could no more have given the necessary concentration to the process of editing than I could swim in a bath of treacle, or even one of asses milk, though the latter possibility was suddenly wonderfully attractive. "Stop it, Hannah," I told myself, without much success, until Elisabeth put through a call to me from an even more needy author than usual, which forced me to focus on something other than myself.

My ancient mobile telephone buzzed at about eleven o'clock.

"Lunch," said Flora's voice, with her usual smiling command barely dressed up as a question. "Usual place, about twelve-thirty?"

"Thank you," I said, "yes, of course."

"Are you all right, Hannah?" Flora asked.

"I'm wonderful, thank you," I replied.

"Ah," Flora said, and rang off.

By the time we met, I had realised that of course she would quiz me over our lunch. How much would I confess? In fact, it all just poured out. I began by trying to tell her about the performance, the lights, the thrill of the auditorium, the grandness of the music...

"Yes, yes, yes," she said impatiently, "and...?"

I paused.

"Oh, come on, Hannah!" she said, exasperated. "Did he take your hand, did he kiss you good night? You're a new girl this morning. Whatever happened?"

"He only kissed my cheek," I told her, "only the once, right as he was putting me on my bus. Oh, Flora, I don't know where I am! I know that a kiss like that needn't mean anything at all, but—"

"But you hope it does," Flora asserted. "So when will you see him again?"

"Next week, in Dundee, I suppose," I replied, realising how long it seemed until then, and that our meetings in the cafeteria always seemed a matter of coincidence, of wonderful good luck. Neither of us had ever suggested a particular time or table. It just seemed to happen. Now I was asking myself how I could handle my students in the three hours before I might meet Drummond— or might not, I realised—in the cafeteria afterwards.

"And does he have your mobile number?" Flora asked, "or you his? Do you know where he lives?" My face gave her the answers. "Oh, Hannah, you know nothing about him, my dear, do you?"

And I realised that, apart from his being a university research chemist of pretty wide aesthetic interests, no, I knew nothing about him at all. But it didn't matter! He was a lovely man, who had kissed my cheek.

Chapter Eleven

A week later, I was still in a dreadful tizzy. I was afraid Drummond would not kiss me again, and even more afraid that he would, and that things would get out of hand, and…a girl at school, in the sixth form, had got pregnant. I knew the biology of how it had happened, and I remembered the gossip after she had not come back to finish her A-level course. "She's had to get a job, to pay for the baby," I heard, and she had been expected to go on to university, but didn't, couldn't.

And yet, how was I supposed to tell a stranger that I wanted, felt I needed, contraception? I havered for days. It was too early, it might never happen, I couldn't go on living if it did, if it did not. Better to act now than to have to ask for a morning-after tablet, or whatever. In the end, I telephoned the surgery, mentioned Flora's name, was told that my call had been expected, and was given an appointment for a few days ahead.

I sat in the doctor's reception area, quaking. The receptionist took as little notice of me, gave me the same brief smile as she gave to the couple of other patients whom I had followed into the building. In due course, she said to me, in the same impersonal tone she had used for my predecessors, "Doctor will see you now, Ms Lethbridge. Along the passage, second door on the right." I tapped on the door, heard a firm "Come in," and found a neat, grey-haired woman, probably in her 50s, wearing a white linen overall-coat, who smiled her welcome.

"Good evening, Ms Lethbridge. May I call you Hannah? Flora tells me that you need contraception. Do sit down while I run through a few essential questions."

I sat, and so did she, on chairs on the same side of her desk, from which she took a prepared clipboard and ballpoint pen.

"Now, you're twenty-eight years old, I believe. And your precise date of birth is…?" I gave it, together with my address and my National Health Service number.

"Have you been having sexual relations regularly?" she asked.

"Um, no, Doctor, in fact…um…I haven't…but I thought…precautions…"

I was almost incoherent, and she took pity on me at once.

"May I guess? This is all very strange to you. It's what I do every day, with a dozen or more girls every week, so please relax and be comfortable. I'm sorry about the questions, but I have to know where we're starting from so that I can offer you the best advice."

She had a lovely, gentle, sensible, comforting voice. The more she spoke, the less tense I felt.

She asked about my general health, my periods, and gave me a physical examination, after which she said, as if asking how I had my coffee,

"Well, all that seems to be fine." She had picked up a bunch of brochures from her desk. "There are so many forms of contraception these days, and…" she looked straight at me for emphasis, though still smiling, "none of them can be considered to be totally, 100% reliable." She went carefully through the options, and the combinations which were practical, and I gradually recovered my wits.

Eventually, she said, "What I'd advise for you is the Pill, and encouragement for your partner to use condoms, but you must let me know if you get any persistent side-effects, as you begin your course." She told me what side-effects to look for, and instructed me to read the whole of the information which would be in the box of tablets.

"And you must take the pill every day, without fail. Take it at a regular time, for example, when you scrub your teeth first thing in the morning."

After more advice, she wrote me a prescription, and I was able to escape. Outside her surgery, I went into the first café I came to, and sat down with as strong a coffee as I could get. I was shattered, but it was almost done. Just a call at a strange pharmacy where I wouldn't be known, to get the prescription made up. Then I needn't dwell on the matter anymore. It hadn't been so bad.

The doctor had been amazingly kind, and the examination which I had so much dreaded had not been the terrible experience I had feared. By the time I had finished my coffee, I was beginning to feel much more capable of returning to the world, and would soon be fully prepared for whatever it might bring.

***

134

Drummond and Hannah continued to meet on the days she was in Dundee. She told him a little of her life at MacWhinney, Preston, and gave him a skeletal outline of the activities of the factory in which she had worked before moving to Edinburgh. He mentioned something of his current work, and of the house which he shared with a couple of other people on the outskirts of Dundee. She knew he had a car, because, on one occasion when they had talked longer over their supper than usual, he had driven her to the station to catch her train back to Edinburgh, and had kissed her cheek again.

That had been the evening on which Drummond had drawn back the curtain, if only a little way, on the history of his family. Drummond MacKeagh's great-grandfather had landed at Stranraer from a small Irish coasting ship a few years after the First World War. He had walked the twenty-odd miles to Wigtown, obtained labouring jobs in the small docks there, and lived frugally.

Somehow, he attracted the attention of Deidre MacKinnon, the much more practical and good-looking daughter of a fish-dealer who lived above the town quay. He and Deirdre produced three strapping sons. Two left Wigtown as early as they could to make their fortunes, or at least a decent living, in England. The third and youngest, however, became an apprentice to the local cobbler, eventually replacing his master and building himself a respected if limited place in the local community.

This enabled him to educate his son and daughter at the ancient grammar school in the town, and eventually at the Universities, respectively, of Glasgow and St Andrews, from the former of which his grandson Drummond also graduated, and made a modest beginning to his academic career.

At his school in Glasgow, Drummond had been known as an able but somewhat narrow student. He applied his undoubted intelligence and intense curiosity to the subjects for which he felt an innate interest and ability, but did no more than enough elsewhere in the life of the school to satisfy his mentors and peers. He kept fit, but made no effort to gain a place in the school's sports teams. He passed every examination for which he was entered, but only excelled in the sciences. He was not without friendships, but they were not deep. As soon as he could, he took a holiday job as a technician in the laboratories of a large food-processing factory, to which he returned regularly and worked reliably. Here, he built up a precocious understanding of the practical details of food-chemistry, a subject in which he eventually gained a higher degree and an appointment at the University of Dundee to further his researches.

By the time he was thirty, Drummond had a respectable reputation as a useful scientist, and as a man of quiet, pleasant charm, but with little in the way of a social life.

"Who's that pretty girl you've been seen eating with in the cafeteria so regularly, Drummond?" someone had asked him one day.

Drummond had simply smiled pleasantly and said nothing, and there was not enough interest in him among his colleagues to press the point, or to try to find out more. Little additional detail was added to Hannah's knowledge by the man and woman who had sat at their table in the unusually crowded cafeteria one evening, for want of anywhere else being available. Introductions had been inevitable.

"This is Isobel, who works in the labs with me, and Sandy," Drummond said.

"Are you both chemists?" Hannah enquired.

"No, Sandy's an engineer," Isobel replied. "We're engaged," she explained, unconsciously turning a solitaire diamond up into Hannah's view, "though goodness knows when we'll be able to afford to get married. What do you do, Hannah?"

"I'm a publisher's editor," Hannah responded, "in Edinburgh, but I teach a course in the English Department here, on a temporary basis."

"Hannah is growing Scottish literary talent for the future," Drummond said, and the talk turned to personalities in the university's senior administration, and the reasons why they were rather less popular than usual at the time. Perhaps conscious that Hannah had been slightly left out of their conversation, Isobel insisted on swapping mobile numbers with Hannah before she and Sandy left, together with an open invitation for them to meet for lunch or coffee sometime when Hannah was in Dundee.

"Or when you're in Edinburgh?" Hannah suggested hospitably. Isobel agreed that she did sometimes go down to Edinburgh for shopping, and that meeting there would be nice.

In fact, Isobel was in the cafeteria with another girl when Hannah popped in for a quick coffee in the middle of her afternoon session the next week.

"This is Sylvia," Isobel said, as Hannah joined them. "She's a colleague in Drummond's lab. Sylvia, this is Hannah, Drummond MacKeagh's friend."

"Ooh, the mystery lady from Edinburgh," Sylvia said archly. "Hi, Hannah. We've all been fascinated by Drummond's new social interest. So unusual for him. He generally keeps himself very much to himself. You must have something *very* special."

They all giggled, and Hannah demurred politely.

"He seems to be very keen on his work," Hannah said.

"He's well-respected in his field," Isobel said. "His papers have been attracting increasing attention, but none of us know what he does when he's not in the lab. So what do you do together, Hannah?"

"Oh, we've been to theatres, and once to the opera," Hannah says. "He knows a lot about opera, apparently, a lot more than I do, though I did thoroughly enjoy the one we saw."

"He lives in…" Sylvia named accurately the suburb in which Drummond lived, obviously poking to see if Hannah had been to his house, but Hannah simply nodded silently.

"He grew up in Glasgow, and went to the university there, I believe," said Isobel, but again Hannah side-stepped the implied question about how well Hannah knew his family.

"I presume that's a good Department?" Hannah suggested, hoping to deflect the conversation into less personal matters. Isobel and Sylvia took the hint, and the talk turned to the various merits of other universities before all of them decided that break-time was over and they must return to their afternoon's work.

"I'll be in Edinburgh on Saturday week," Isobel said as they were leaving the cafeteria. "Shall we meet for coffee?" Hannah thanked her, and agreed she would phone to set up a meeting.

***

Through the summer term, Hannah's students kept her increasingly busy, as the first edition of their literary magazine neared publication. There was also a burst of energetic activity at MacWhinney, Preston, as the negotiations over the final preparations of several books all came to fruition together. Hannah was grateful for such free evenings as she could squeeze in between long days in the office or in Dundee, and, as often as they could, she and Drummond began to walk above the river, or go to the cinema, as a way of relaxing. Mostly, Drummond came down to Edinburgh for these evenings, and Hannah assumed that he drove back to Dundee afterwards.

Neither of them was particularly bothered what sort of films they went to see. For Hannah, it was enough that Drummond wanted to make the effort to see her, and Drummond seemed to be content simply to have an evening doing something other than working now and then. His kisses on her cheek were by now his routine way of saying goodnight to her, though he made no move to kiss her when they were in the cafeteria at Dundee. On one evening, however, they ended up in a cinema watching a rather *noire* film. At one intensely violent point in the film, Hannah buried her face impulsively in Drummond's shoulder, and he put his arm around her comfortingly and left it there. That was the evening that, bending to kiss her goodnight, he turned her face towards him and kissed her fully and unavoidably on the lips, and Hannah melted into him, returning his kiss.

On their next two visits to the cinema, one in Edinburgh and the second in Dundee, Drummond put his arm around Hannah's shoulders soon after the beginning of the film, and she took his spare hand from his knee, firmly and possessively. Their kisses in the dark became longer and longer, breaking up only reluctantly as the crescendo of music announced the climax and end of the film. As they left the cinema at the end of the first of these evenings, Hannah could not look into Drummond's face. On the second occasion, she could look nowhere else. Her body rang like a soprano bell. She could not let go of his hand, so he had to grin at her to remind her that he needed both hands to put on his light raincoat.

A week later, rather than going to a cinema, Drummond suggested, after they had eaten at the university, that they walk to Dudhope Park and enjoy the evening sun. Hannah left her bags in Drummond's car for safe-keeping, and they walked to the park with their arms around each other. There were several couples in the park, sitting and lying to enjoy the feelings which Hannah and Drummond were sharing, but they found an unoccupied dell and sat, pressed hard against each other. Drummond laid back on the grass, and pulled Hannah down onto his chest.

When the passion of Drummond's exploration of her mouth and body became too passionate, Hannah sat up, and said, "No, Drummond, not here. Take me home."

"It'll have to be Edinburgh," Drummond said. "Everybody's at home at mine this evening."

Together, hand in hand, they returned briskly to the university car park, saying little or nothing as their mutual passion cooled to a controllable level. On the drive to Edinburgh, Hannah sat, almost quivering, beside him, leaning over to kiss his cheek at traffic lights as they entered the city. At Hannah's building, they almost skipped up the stairs, calling a terse goodnight to a neighbour whom they met on the stairs, and giggling while cursing inwardly at the delay required by courtesy.

In Hannah's flat, Drummond hardly gave her time to put down her bags before gathering her into his arms.

"Oh, Drummond," she said, "what are we doing?"

"You know fine," he said in a deeper voice than usual, and kissed her deeply again. She led him to her bedroom, and snatched the curtains closed. They were fumbling with each other's clothes. Naked, they fell together onto Hannah's single bed as if superglued together.

Totally beyond any control, his hands were like feathers on her body, and then like fetters. He held her down beneath him as he entered her, and she felt the fierce initial pain, and quickly the joy, of being utterly, completely loved for the first time in her life.

Afterwards, she struggled out from beneath him, sat up and turned to look down into his eyes. They were smiling up at her, as were his lovely lips, so she kissed each expression of his love in turn, but could summon no words.

"Wow, Little Hannah," Drummond said.

"Oh, Drummond, whatever are we going to do? The term ends in four weeks, and the year, and I've no idea whether they'll want me for next year, or what I'm going to do through the summer if they do."

"We'll do a lot of travelling, I guess," Drummond said, smiling complacently. "And a lot of this, perhaps?"

"Yes, please, yes please," Hannah squealed, and they became too occupied to say more for a while.

At some point, Hannah freed herself and switched on the lamp on her bedside table.

"I'd offer you a proper drink if I had any," she said, "but I've only coffee."

"No teabags?" Drummond enquired.

"No, I'm sorry, I don't use them."

"Nor invite visitors here often, I presume."

"Almost never, except my friend Flora."

"I've a mind to send you for a carryout, you dreadful girl. Like that, just as you are. The Lady Godiva of Edinburgh."

"Can you drink coffee?" Hannah asked.

"Oh, yes, but we'll need some supplies if we're going to do this often."

More prolonged kisses, before Hannah swung her legs over the side of the bed and stepped quickly to her wardrobe for a robe.

"You are so very beautiful," Drummond said, admiring her from the bed.

Hannah blushed, and wrapped her robe around her. She found her spectacles where Drummond had carefully left them on her dressing table, and put them back on her nose.

"Coffee," she said, and hurried out to her tiny kitchen before she was deflected from her intention again back into the bed.

***

The rest of the summer was filled with the most intense activity I had ever known. It began with Morag waiting for me as I came into the room for my teaching-session the next week.

"Hannah, I hear wonderful things about the magazine!" Morag said, beaming.

"It's all down to the students," I replied with enthusiasm. "It really is. They've done the writing, the editing, the cover design, the printing, everything, and the galleys look amazing."

"Well, you're a very popular young lady with them, from what their tutors can gather," Morag insisted. "They all seem to have enjoyed their year with you, apart, clearly, from profiting by it hugely. They're all convinced they're on the cusp of brilliant writing careers! Reality will strike soon enough, I guess. Anyway, Prof wants you to come back and do it again next year. Might that be possible, do you think?"

"I'd love to do it again, Morag. Thank you. But I'll have to clear it with my boss in Edinburgh, of course."

"Oh, yes, of course. Will I have Prof phone him, then?"

"Yes, please," I said, "and then I can act surprised and gratified. I hope. But I'm pretty sure he'll agree."

"Now, here's the next thing," Morag went on. "Prof wants a launch-party for the magazine, in the last week of the term. He wants to make a big splash of it, show off the whole project, not only in Dundee, but with the other Scottish

Universities and the publishers in Edinburgh and Glasgow. Can you manage that, do you think, Hannah?"

"Well, I'm sure the students will do all the donkey-work," I said, quickly thinking through the bones of the job. "I'll just set parameters, give them sources, and generally oversee progress. And deflect them from the inevitable wilder ideas, as usual."

We both laughed. Morag had no difficulty in grasping the importance of that skill of control without constraint in relation to young, energetic imaginations; or the effort it so often required.

"May I tell them this afternoon that it's in the wind, and get them started? There isn't much time to make all the preparations," I suggested.

"Yes, I think so," Morag said, "though Prof will want to approve the date and guest-list, no doubt."

"I'll keep you both posted as the planning develops," I reassured her. "But, Morag, are you not placing a lot of confidence in the youngsters? After all, we haven't got a final proof of the first edition of the magazine yet. I was hoping to pass a first few copies to you and Prof and everybody in the Department in about ten days' time, but—"

"Oh, don't you worry," Morag grinned. "Your students have been so full of what they've been doing with you that the whole Department's seen more or less every line of the content, and of the design at its various stages of development, in more drafts than probably you've seen yourself. And so have a lot of the Art Department. It's a wonder the youngsters haven't tapped into the skills of the Physics Department for advice on moving their drafts from one place to another! Of course, with you only dashing up here for an afternoon a week, you won't have picked up the full measure of their excitement. Oh dear, Hannah, everyone's recognised success when they've seen this. Now we just need the exposure for the product, as widely-spread as possible."

The launch-party was a great success. The students took over the planning, as I had expected. All I provided, with Elisabeth Preston's help, was a list of people from the publishing industry and, with Morag's help, those from other Scots universities who needed to be invited. I took a firm hand over the appearance of the invitations to the VIPs, and that of the decorations in the senior common room in which the party was to be held.

However, the internal invitations were as wild as I had expected from my wild, imaginative youngsters, and served mostly to remind me of the gap in age, small though it was in years, between them and myself. Students whom I did not know provided the waiting services, recruited by members of the course from among their friends.

"They do it all the time in the Union, and some of them in jobs outside," I was assured. "They'll be fine."

And so they were, and so was the extensive buffet provided by the university's contract caterers, far better and more varied than the food they routinely provided in the cafeteria. That first edition of the journal was also fine. Huge reproductions of its startling cover hung on the walls all around the room. Copies were fanned on coffee-tables in profusion, with my name prominently printed above those of the rest of the production team. Within the covers, poetry, prose and even a couple of short scripts for one-act plays, to be presented at the forthcoming Festival Fringe, jostled irregularly, and attracted much praise. Everyone was amazingly complimentary. I quickly forgot my qualms about my new, short, bright summer dress and new hairstyle, both chosen on Flora's advice, as the last of the evening sun poured in through the tall windows at the end of the room.

"You're Hannah Lethbridge, I believe," I was repeatedly greeted. "I hear your name everywhere. Haven't you done a great job on this journal?"

"Oh, I did nothing, it was all the students' work, and the wonderful ambience of the Department," I kept saying until I almost forgot the long evenings of planning, and occasionally long afternoons of negotiation during which I'd had to rein in out-of-control enthusiasms and buoy up frustrated, stuck young authors and artists.

The only lacuna was Drummond's absence.

"No, no," he had said from the first, "I don't do parties at all well. You go and take your glory, Hannah. I'll probably be in the midst of an experiment in the lab which I won't dare leave. You'll not miss me, with all you'll need to do."

He refused to be moved, but he was quite wrong. I did miss him most terribly. How achingly I longed to be able to introduce him to everyone, to slip my hand into the crook of his elbow now and then, to feel his arm around my waist from time to time. I didn't want him to say anything. Indeed, he would probably have been unable to get in a word between the continuous congratulations, or to speak one that might actually be heard as the clamour grew. I just wanted him to be there, with me, mine, and I being his and seen to be.

142

I didn't even see him at the end of the evening. I hadn't known what time the party would finish, how much I would have to contribute to the tidying up, or when I would be able to escape. We'd agreed—well, Drummond had decided—to meet at my flat in Edinburgh the following evening for him to hear all about it. So I had to take all my excitement, my need to talk endlessly in relief at how well it had gone, this wonderful feeling of success, to the car, and then to the flat and sofa, of the Dundee colleague I hardly knew who was going to put me up for what remained of the night.

I was late getting to MacWhinney, Preston the following morning, despite getting the earliest train I could face from Dundee. Mr James was already behind his desk, apparently deep in yet another paper, but, unusually, he called out to me as I passed his door.

"Hannah, you'll spare me a minute, perhaps, before you go upstairs?"

I went into his office.

"Sit you down, lassie, sit you down," he invited. "And did you enjoy your party last night?"

I had greeted Mr James on his arrival at the party, and had seen him chatting to his friends and contacts at various points during the evening. Despite my best intentions, however, I had been unable to give him any more time in the press of people who had demanded my attention.

"Yes, thank you, Mr James," I said. "It was great fun. I hope you enjoyed it too. I kept trying to get across to you, but somehow it just kept on not happening."

"Oh, aye, you were kept busy. So was I. 'Is that your Hannah Lethbridge,' they kept saying to me, 'who's responsible for all this?' You've made a great success of it up there in Dundee, for yourself and, I'm glad to say, for the Firm. I was very pleased to see it, very pleased indeed."

"Thank you, Mr James."

"So much so, I understand, that my friend Archie MacAlister wants to have you back for next year, as well. The demands the man makes!" he said. He drew down his eyebrows in mock severity, but smiled.

"So I understand, Mr James."

"And do I take it you'd be willing to contemplate it, then?"

"Oh, yes, I'd be very pleased to do it again, if you were agreeable."

"Well, it doesn't seem to have reduced your productivity here too much, I believe, and I'm all for any free publicity the Firm can get, so I suppose you'd better do it, Hannah, if everyone's happy with the idea. You'll have less preparation to do for it the second time round, I presume?" he queried.

"I've some improvements to the course that I'd like to try, Mr James, but nothing that will require a lot of research."

"Aye, well, will you be telling my friend Archie that I'm willing, then?"

"Thank you very much, Mr James. I'll telephone him later on this morning, if I may."

Mr James smiled.

"No rush, no rush, from my point of view, lassie. Do it when you can. Off you go, now." As usual, Mr James had already picked up his temporarily abandoned paper and waved me out of the door.

***

Elisabeth was back at her desk as Hannah crossed the lobby to go upstairs.

"It was a good party in Dundee, I hear," she said. "Himself's been full of it this morning. And you'll be going up there again from September, we hear?"

"It looks like it, Elisabeth," Hannah replied, smiling broadly.

"And how's your young man?" she enquired slyly.

Hannah blushed deeply.

"He's very well, thank you, Elisabeth. But I didn't know you knew…"

"Have you not heard of this wonderful thing on the end of my desk, Hannah? It's called a telephone. And it's not just you and Mr James who have friends in Dundee, you know. So when do we get to meet him and size him up," Elisabeth pressed, "since he seems to be having such an influence on the prosperity of MacWhinney, Preston?"

"I'd love to bring him in to meet you all, Elisabeth, but he's very busy in his laboratory at the moment, and only gets up to Edinburgh for the odd evening. But I will bring him in as soon as I can get him here in office hours."

"Oh, several of us have a life after five in the evening, you know," Elisabeth said archly.

Flora telephoned shortly after eleven.

"Hallo, Golden Girl! It's Flora."

"Hi, Flora," Hannah replied, rather mechanically.

"Lunch," Flora ordered, as usual.

"I'll be there," Hannah replied dreamily. "I'm getting nothing done here this morning. I'm shattered."

"That sounds promising," Flora said. "Usual place, usual time?"

"Sure," Hannah confirmed, and the line went dead.

Once they were settled at their table, Flora's inquisition began.

"So the launch was the great success everybody knew it would be, then?"

"It was great fun, I think. The students did really well, making the most of their exposure, and networking madly."

"As you'd told them to do. And I want to see a copy of this famous journal."

"I brought you one. Put it in my bag before the party started, so you wouldn't miss out." Hannah reached into the bag at her feet and presented the journal proudly.

"Wow! Really striking!" Flora said admiringly, and flicked over the pages with an air of professional criticism. "Really varied. Who chose the fonts?"

"Oh, the students did all that, editing and all the production," said Hannah, as she seemed to have been doing for days.

"And you did nothing, just sat back and drew your money, I suppose?" Flora teased. "I can't see that, Hannah. I expect you dropped your usual tactful, tasteful hints and pointers at regular intervals through the preparatory process. Like, every thirty seconds or so."

"Well…"

"And how's Drummond?" Flora finally asked.

"Oh, he's fine, thank you. How are—"

"No, Hannah! How is Drummond? Properly!"

"Oh, he's lovely," Hannah confessed with a silly grin on her face.

"Has he…have you…?"

"Uu-mmm."

Flora squealed with excitement, drawing looks from all round the café. More quietly, she said, "Well, how was it? Was it wonderful? Did stars shoot across the sky? Do you want to do it again? Soon?"

"Uu-mm," Hannah replied, looking down at her sandwich and then up into Flora's face, to share her joy with her best friend.

"Well, come on! I need more than 'Um'. Hannah Lethbridge, you can be the most frustrating girl in the world, do you know that?"

"He was wonderful. It was wonderful. And he's coming over again this evening." Hannah giggled. "And I've changed the sheets, but I must buy another pair, if he's going to come so often. Getting them dry is such a chore in a flat, even in the summer."

Flora's face turned serious for a moment.

"And did you go to see my doctor in good time?"

"Oh, yes. I put it off and put it off, but really only for a few days," Hannah said. "And she was sweet, and amazing, and gave me a prescription and lots of advice, so I'm fixed up as well as I can be, I think."

"Well, it sounds as though that's a very good thing," Flora grinned.

"And how *is* Ian?" Hannah was at last able to say, "and Veronica?"

"Oh, Ian's fine. And, do you know, Veronica will start school in September. All-day school, well, most of the day, anyway, so I'll be able to take on more work. Kindly remember that, Ms Lethbridge, in your guaranteed-employment ivory tower in St Andrew's Square!"

"Of course I will," Hannah assured her. "Can I tell Mr James and Elisabeth, and Munro? They'll be really happy to hear that. They do miss you, you know."

"'Course they don't. They've got the gorgeous, talented Ms Lethbridge these days! Anyway, that's for September. I'm going to have to dash now and pick her up from her playgroup, and see which poor little boy she's been leading by the nose this morning. She does, you know."

"Can't think where she gets that from," Hannah rejoined, laughing.

***

Through that summer, I regained a comfortable routine. Drummond came down to spend an evening with me at least once a week, and often twice. I would have liked him to come more often. However, he claimed that the demands of his laboratory experiments precluded his devoting any more time to our pleasures, especially during working hours and including at weekends. We made love almost every time he visited, and it continued to thrill me.

It was such a new, wonderful experience of being cared for, of having another beloved person to appreciate and to give me compliments, to give myself to, wholly and completely, to lie beside and simply watch and touch and stroke as he rested, for however few precious hours, really minutes in fact, as often as could be arranged.

But I did so miss Drummond between his visits. For all my increasing ability to concentrate on my work for a couple of hours, I would find my mind suddenly break off and dream. Blind to the surroundings in my office, its stacked manuscript table and the view over the city from the window, for a few seconds—minutes, sometimes—I saw nothing but Drummond, his chest against the pillows on my bed, or dressed as always in his tweedy sports jacket—was it truly the only one he possessed?—coming into the cafeteria at Dundee. Then I would have to physically shake myself and return my attention to the work on the desk in front of me. But Drummond was seldom far beyond the periphery of my mind. My love for him had come to dominate my existence, and I was thrilled that it should be so.

I saw more of him from the beginning of October, of course, when I began my second year of teaching at Dundee. Saw him, but could not be fulfilled by him on campus. Drummond did not resist my need to touch him, or to put my hand into the crook of his elbow, or to walk closely beside him. However, he did not encourage more intimate expressions of my affection in places where other people, staff or students, might see them. He would not himself take hold of my hand, or put his arm around my waist as we walked on the campus.

Until the passage of the days caused the evening dark to draw in by the time we parted, he would avoid my arms being put around his neck, as I so longed to do as we separated, and would only allow what seemed to me a chaste-feeling kiss on his cheek before turning briskly, though smilingly, away from me for the next few days.

He had still not made time to meet my colleagues at MacWhinney, Preston. He had met Flora and Ian. That had been made almost unavoidable by Flora's increasingly insistent and persistent invitations that I should, then *must*, bring Drummond to supper for her inspection. The occasion had been delayed repeatedly. Ian, coming from a not dissimilar professional background, was understanding. "He'll be taken up with work that has to be monitored regularly and consistently. A chemist has to keep a close eye on what's happening in his wee pots and potions, for fear they'll boil over, or go off, or something," he said at first.

But, by late October, even Ian's excuses for his fellow scientist had started to peter out, and Flora was starting to look concerned each time she pressed me to "take him by the collar, if necessary, but just bring him. Whatever is the matter with the man?"

Eventually, early in November, Drummond agreed to accept Flora and Ian's invitation. As the occasion approached, I felt a mixture of pride and apprehension, but the evening passed without any undue difficulty. Drummond and Ian got on politely, if coolly, as two men without much in common will do on first acquaintance. Drummond, being a reserved city-boy through and through, expressed limited interest in Ian's climbing, or in Flora's devotion to Veronica.

He sketched out his laboratory-work adequately, indeed in more detail than I had previously heard from him, and had seemed quite interested in the practical details of Ian's work for the local authority. Despite Flora having taken some trouble to buy a decent wine to go with their supper, Drummond had preferred to drink beer with Ian during and after the meal, so Flora and I drank the wine between us. I had taken perhaps more wine than I was normally used to, and felt its effects by the end of the evening.

I had hoped that Drummond would come back to the flat with me afterwards, but he dropped me off with an excuse and a passionate kiss in the car, which did nothing helpful for my wine-enhanced, relieved, relaxed longing for rather more. But that's Drummond, I thought, only slightly mollified. Nonetheless, as the subsequent days passed, I became aware of a growing frustration. Not just for a more frequent fulfilment of my need for the physical expression of my love, but also simply to see him, to be with him, more often than seemed to be happening.

As December began, the annual MacWhinney, Preston celebrations of Christmas and New Year approached.

"Mr James has decided to have a Christmas lunch, just for the MacWhinney, Preston office staff," I told Drummond with quiet excitement. "Or at least, it's probably Elisabeth who decided it, and Mr James' only decision was not to oppose it. Anyway, Elisabeth told me to be sure to bring you." We were sitting, partly dressed, in my flat, nibbling the rough cheese and salad sandwiches Drummond had made from some leftovers he had found in my new 'fridge. "And I'd love to have you with me at the Firm's New Year party."

"Ah, Hogmanay's big for my parents, Hannah," Drummond replied. "They'll expect me with them in Glasgow. I knew you'd be with your Firm that night, so I hadn't told you before."

The disappointment cut sharply. Without conscious thought, I bit my bottom lip. He had not mentioned the lunch, and I foresaw another excuse looming.

"But you'll come to the lunch, won't you?" I said, trying not to beg.

"You know how difficult it is for me to get away from the lab. during the day. My client's really pressing me for some results before Christmas, Hannah. They badly want to know what they'll need to buy in order to launch their new biscuits. I doubt I can get away down here for a whole day before Christmas, and that's what it would be with the journey-time, and all."

I felt tears in the corners of my eyes, but was determined that Drummond should not see them.

"What about Christmas itself?" I asked, in as matter-of-fact, 'just making arrangements', a voice as I could manage.

"I expect I'll have to go over to Glasgow," Drummond said, "just for the inside of the day. The parents don't make a lot of Christmas, but the family is expected to gather around, you know."

Effectively having no family, then or ever, I did not "know", and Drummond should have known that I probably did not. I felt bruised again by his thoughtlessness. I waited, a tiny speck of hope lingering in the background of my mind, for an invitation to go with him to Glasgow to meet his family. I still had not been taken to be shown, let alone shown off, to his parents.

The invitation for Christmas Day did not come. Nor did any enquiry as to how I would spend the day myself. I wanted to sob, but habit, and the fear of upsetting Drummond, gave me the strength to hold in that need. He meant no harm, I thought to myself. He just doesn't think much about people, and would certainly be put off by tears. I should be grateful that he seems to love me, I thought, though why he should, I don't know.

Chin up, Hannah, I told myself. Be thankful for small mercies. At least I knew that he had no interest in anyone else. And perhaps his mother would demand that I should be brought to Glasgow for Christmas Day. Always supposing his mother knew of my existence, of course, which—thinking about it, after Drummond had left me that night—I realised was by no means a foregone conclusion.

***

The run-up to the Firm's lunch was difficult.

"Will you be accompanied, Hannah?" Elisabeth asked one morning, and, on receiving the negative response, she had raised her eyebrows and pursed her lips slightly before looking down to mark the list in front of her.

The other girls, Jenny and Tansy, would be bringing their boyfriends, they told me excitedly when we met to collect our morning tea and coffee from

Elisabeth's scullery. I smiled brightly and said nothing, and neither of them pressed me to add to the excitement of their conversation. At the lunch, however, they introduced their other-halves, both very nice, presentable young men who chatted pleasantly with everyone, but had eyes only for their own beloveds. For most of the meal, I talked to Phylida, who was also on her own, and apparently happy to be so. She entertained me with accounts of the latest doings of her pet cats, to which, apparently, I was able to respond satisfactorily.

Over the holiday, I worked. My student group at Dundee was by no means as lively as their predecessors had been in the previous year. They were dividing into definite cliques, and I was afraid that a lot more of the work for the production of next summer's journal would fall on me this time around. I welcomed the chance offered by the holiday to think up some additional components for the course which might bring the students together as a team. Drummond came down to Edinburgh twice between Christmas and New Year.

On one occasion, we went to a play for which I had been commissioned to write a review for the *News*. On the other, we went out for a meal, and back to the flat to go to bed, and I was dreamily satisfied by the time Drummond left in the early hours of the next morning.

The Firm's New Year party was as well-organised and well-attended as always. It was a major feature of the Edinburgh literary scene. Elisabeth was kept unusually busy this year adding to the guest list the names of more and more people who had succeeded in persuading friends to beg an invitation for them. This would be the sixth such event since I had joined the Firm, and they no longer held any of the fears I had felt before my first one.

I circulated comfortably and elegantly in a dress fashionably short and heels fashionably high, welcoming guests and contributing my share of MacWhinney, Preston's welcome to everyone who was anyone in the Edinburgh publishing industry. My mind went to Drummond now and then, of course—well, repeatedly—but I had forced myself to be reconciled to knowing that there would be no New Year's hug and kiss from him until the following night. Overall, I enjoyed the party, and went home afterwards, tired but content, to sleep late and dream that Drummond would be over to see me soon.

In fact, he did not come the following evening. Nor did he telephone. I began to worry that he had had an accident in the car on the way to or from Glasgow, or that one of his parents had been taken ill. Or even he himself, though I had never known him ill in all the time we had known each other. Drummond did turn up the next day, however, just before lunchtime.

"Oh, Drummond, where have you been? Are you all right," I cried out when I saw who was at my front door. I reached out for him, my arms going around his neck in a clasp that seemed unbreakable, my body pressed against him as though I were afraid I would never feel him against me again. He said nothing, but grasped me firmly and kissed me long and hard, and I never found out why he had not come the previous evening or where he had been instead.

Perhaps it's the winter's cold and snow which was lowering my spirits, I thought. Whatever it was, by mid-January I was beginning to wonder where I stood with Drummond MacKeagh. I was becoming increasingly aware that he was coming and going into my life as he alone saw fit. I did not expect to be central to his existence, as he was to mine. Who was I to expect anything from anyone? I had never known that role, in all my life. But he had seemed, if not to adore me as I adored him, at least to love me deeply, at least when we were together. He had told me he loved me, as we lay together, limbs entangled, in my bed, and when we were alone together elsewhere.

However, when we were apart, I was beginning to wonder whether I would ever be allowed to take a greater part in Drummond's life. What part did I have now, after all this time and all this giving on my part of loyalty and love, of body and mind and emotion? Did Drummond in fact need, let alone want, our friendship to be any more? I knew I had wanted more, from very soon after we had met.

These concerns were beginning to distract me. My concentration was beginning to fail. I was forgetting to buy things I had decided to get on my way home from the office. I forgot to collect dry cleaning. I was more brisk with one or two of my authors, and gentle queries began to be raised with Elisabeth, who fended them off without difficulty, but let me know that she was keeping a closer eye on me than before. Worst of all, Munro noticed the decline in the quality of my work. He came into my office one morning, carrying a manuscript he had asked me to take over on his behalf in a moment of pressure.

"Hannah," he said, looking at me over his spectacles, his expression even more stern than usual. "Would you go over this again, please? I've only looked through the first twenty-odd pages, but I think you've missed a number of basic errors in punctuation, to say nothing of points at which the grammar could usefully be re-examined." He sniffed audibly. "I know this is one of those authors who believes that his genius will show through if he just throws the words onto the page and leaves us to tidy it up afterwards. Nonetheless, we do have to tidy it up, having taken him on. That's what we're here for." He dropped the manuscript onto my desk heavily, turned away sharply and left the room without another word.

I was covered in shame and confusion. Munro had always been so patient with me. He was a bit stiff and humourless, but he had been treating me as a valued colleague in the past twelve months. This morning, he had treated me like an errant apprentice, with a coldness quite foreign to what I had thought of as our relationship, a coldness which was also foreign to the whole ambience of the Firm.

By the end of the afternoon's work on the manuscript, I had realised how right he was. My initial work on the manuscript had been superficial in the extreme, and my professional pride was deeply hurt by my failure. By the next morning, perhaps with the help of a distinct shortage of sleep, I had finally realised that the problem lay somewhere in the depths of my feelings for Drummond. At last, even I could see that our relationship was becoming somewhat one-sided, and that this issue would have to be faced and sorted out— which was not something that I felt equipped to do.

Over the subsequent days, my work improved. I drove myself to concentrate. In Edinburgh. I became more strict with myself, and in Dundee with my students, and both of us seemed to buckle down better to the work asked of them. And, eventually, I began to plan how to confront Drummond. The need could no longer be denied. But when and where, and in what words, was I to confront him? No, confrontation was too strong a term. It was too aggressive. I loved him, needed him.

And he had already made it very clear that he did not like to have his choices questioned. When I had asked, only once, why we could not meet as we had previously arranged, he had become cold and hard in his body as well as in his face. He had said that he could not meet me, and that was that. He had not withdrawn from me, exactly. He had been holding me close to him, his arms around my waist and mine around his neck, but his body had suddenly hardened, so that it felt as if I had been pressing against a rock rather than the human being I loved.

If I said what I felt, what I feared, as Margaret had taught me to do years before when I was in therapy, would he reject me? Would anger overcome whatever degree of love he felt for me? For me, love was a delicate thing, other people's love anyway. My own, I acknowledged, was centred on my gratitude for being loved, for having notice taken of me, for having someone else seem to admire and take pleasure in me. Margaret had led me to recognise how much I needed to be loved. Dare I risk damaging the regard, the love, which Drummond had seemed to feel for me? Could I live without him? Could I go on living if he were to decide that my demands exceeded his own desire, his own need? Could I bear to go back to the loneliness that had been all I had known before?

"For goodness' sake, girl," I said to myself, "get a grip. Whatever is all this talk of living? You lived perfectly competently before Drummond."

"But that was before I'd had him," my fearful self protested, "before I'd known what it is to have someone love me, to love someone above all other thought or feeling."

"But *where is this going*?" logic demanded. "Are you content to take crumbs again, after all you've been through?"

"No, it isn't like that. It is nothing like it was before. This is Drummond. I am a different person. I am an independent, professional woman, with more than sufficient income to give me a secure, independent life, materially at least. I can buy my own clothes, my own books, pay for my own home. I can go where I like, buy whatever catches my eye. I depend on him only emotionally, and I need to know whether his love is strong enough for more, for*ever*."

That last thought stopped me up short. Forever? Whatever was I thinking? Marriage? Flora and Ian's relationship demonstrated the validity of marriage in a way that no previous experience had indicated to me was possible. In London, all I had been shown, by my mother and the stream of men which had flowed through—no, past—my life, was that, for some people, relationships could come and go like summer clouds, puffing up for a while and dispersing inevitably at sunset.

As a result of that experience, I had no leaning towards marriage. Whatever was it, other than a formalisation of love? No one had given me any inkling of the nature of marriage, social or religious, until Flora and Ian's example seemed to indicate a permanence for which I longed with all my heart.

"Stop havering, Hannah," I told myself firmly. The key questions had still to be decided, those of when, where and how to bring Drummond to an explicit statement of commitment to me. It couldn't be done in bed, after love-making. That would look too much like blackmail. Nor in the Dundee cafeteria. Too public for him, and, truth to tell, for me. It had to be here, in the flat, in the kitchen, the nearest thing I had to a warm, intimate but neutral place. And it had to be soon. Enough was enough. Except that it wasn't. Also, what would I say to introduce the subject? In my inexperience, I could think of nothing better than cliché: "Drummond, where is this going?" How awful! Just like a bad film-script. But it would have to do.

***

One evening at the beginning of February, Hannah was in her flat waiting for, hoping for, Drummond. Her heart lifted when her entry 'phone rang, and she rushed to press the release on the outside door. She opened the door to her flat, heard Drummond's footsteps on the stairs, and all her nerves jangled. This was a new feeling for her, with her beloved on the stairs approaching her. It was going to be tonight. It had to be sorted tonight, and she had no idea how it was going to turn out.

Drummond reached her landing, stepped into the flat and reached out his arms for her as usual. Automatically, her own arms went around his neck, her lips reached up for his, and their kiss gave her strength. It would be all right! Oh, she did so hope it would be all right. His hands reached for the hem of her top, to lift it as he always did. He moved his feet to edge her towards the bedroom, as he always did, and Hannah had to fight herself not to let him have his way, and hers.

"No, darling, not yet," she said, her voice shaking with renewed fear. "Come with me."

It was the first time she had resisted him since they had first …

She felt his body harden, as she had known it would. She untangled her arms from his neck and stepped back, taking his hand and leading him into the kitchen. He was surprised. It showed in his face, but he allowed her to lead him to the upright chair on one side of the tiny table. She released his hand and sat opposite him on the other side.

"Drummond, darling," she began. With difficulty, she raised her eyes to look right into his. "I love you so much. You know how much I love you, but I have to ask. Where is all this between us going?"

Chapter Twelve

Drummond was not just surprised, he was deeply shocked. For several seconds, he did not reply, as though he were mentally trying out answer after answer, and rejecting each one in turn.

"Whatever brought this on?" he eventually said. "I thought we were fine. I love you, too, you must know that, and all of a sudden..." He stopped talking and simply shook his head from side to side as if he really did not understand what was happening.

For me, this was the moment of truth.

"Darling," I said, "it's wonderful when we're together, it always, really is. But we're not really together, are we? I mean, we're not recognised as an item. My work-friends know of you but don't know you. No one at Dundee knows we're together as we are, however much they suspect it." Suddenly, I realised, as I had not done before, that this was the crux of the whole matter. "You're sweet to me when we're together, but you make me feel as if I'm your secret, almost a guilty secret. I want to be known to belong to you. I want to be able to put my arms around you whenever I want to, and so often I feel you don't want me to do that, just there, just then."

Drummond's face hadn't changed. Had he heard me? I wanted to reach across the table and touch him, but was no longer sure whether I had that right.

"Hannah," Drummond said, "I'm...I'm not a public person. I ..." He clearly did not know what to say, let alone how to say it, and yet I needed him to say it, to take me verbally as he had taken me physically and emotionally. I said nothing, and waited for him to continue.

"Hannah..." he stumbled, "you are the best thing, the only thing, that has ever happened to me of this sort. I do so love knowing that you're here, that, while I'm working in the lab, I'll soon be able to come to you, and you'll be there, and you'll...love me, and kiss me, and let me hold you and feel you." For the first time, I was conscious that this was as difficult for him as it was for me.

155

"I look forward so much to coming to you," he continued. "I can't believe you have given me this…privilege sounds so heavy, but it's what I feel it to be. Hannah, where do you want us to go, because I have just been so much enjoying what we have, what you've given me…?" There was a note almost of fear in his voice, which was the last thing I had intended. Or, actually, was it?

"I don't know where I want us to go, darling," I cried out, "except I want us to go there together."

Drummond stood suddenly, stepped around the table and put his arms around me tightly.

"Is it marriage we're talking here?" he asked, sounding almost awed by what he was saying.

I leaned back slightly over his encircling arms so that I could look into his face. I kissed his lips, lightly and repeatedly, his chin, his cheeks, as if in reassurance, as if to dispel a dreadful fear.

"Sit down again, Drummond," I said. "This is important, and we have to know what we're saying here. I never know what I'm going to say when you're holding me. I just want it to go on forever. It becomes the whole world when I can feel you like this."

He released me slowly, and went back around the table to sit down.

"I don't know why people get married," I said. "I don't understand marriage. It doesn't have to be marriage for us. But I do need to see you more often, and to know I am near to you, or will be at a particular time. I know how important your work is to you—"

"Until you came along," he interrupted me, "my work was all I had, all I thought I'd ever have. I never had anyone—"

"Never a girlfriend before?" I asked, tonelessly, almost academically.

Drummond seemed to almost blush. Yes, it really was a blush. I was making this so difficult for him, but this was what needed to be faced. I was sure of it.

"No, nobody. At school, I wanted that more than anything," he murmured. "By the time I got to university, I was just convinced it wasn't going to happen. So I made my work central instead, I suppose as my father had done. I was good at my subject. Not great, but good enough." I did not dare to interrupt him, but my heart ached for his pain as he went on. "So I worked to make myself better than that, to build myself an achievement, a reputation, success of some sort. I put what emotion I felt into the work, I presume. And then, there was you, and suddenly…emotion…" He was struggling to say the word 'love', but, by sheer determination, overcame his difficulty. "I love you Hannah, I love you so much. Don't let us break up, please don't let us break up, not yet at least. Oh, Hannah…"

This time, I was the one who flew around the table to clasp his face to my breast, to kiss the top of his head, then his lips with long, passionate pressure. The minutes passed before I could release him reluctantly and return to my chair. Even then, I could not resist reaching across the table to take his hand.

"It isn't marriage I want," I said, "but…could we possibly live together, do you think? Then I'd know you were coming home to me at the end of the day, I'd know you'd be there when I got home, that we'd go back to what was ours rather than yours or mine after an evening out, or a holiday together, or …"

"I can't believe it," Drummond gulped. "I can't believe you want to. Oh, Hannah, yes, yes, more than anything else in the world." And then his old self took control of him again. "But your work is down here in Edinburgh, and mine is in Dundee, and it's an hour and more's journey between the two." There was a pause, and his face returned some way towards its usual professionally concentrated expression. "I can't be this far from my work permanently, Hannah," he said, and almost howled, "Oh, what are we going to do?"

Never, ever before had I been put in control of someone else's life, been given responsibility for someone else's happiness. Nor had I ever previously seen calm, confident, sometimes apparently almost cold, Drummond willingly—no, desperately—put his life in the hands of someone else. Sympathy was too inadequate a word for my feeling towards him at this moment. Pity was as far from my mind as poetry. He was crying out to me to solve a problem which he could hardly bring himself to face, but for which he knew the solution and did not dare to voice it out aloud.

But I dared. I wanted him so deeply, so very badly. Every fibre of me demanded that I comfort him like a mother, as well as like a lover, at whatever cost. Careful, so often wounded myself, I, who never stepped forward into anything without having rigorously tested the way ahead for potholes and pitfalls, without carefully making and repeatedly reviewing a plan until every potential ambush in it had been eradicated, said, without any further thought, "Then I'll have to come to Dundee."

Surprised, stunned into silence, we both sat back to think about what I had said.

"Would that be possible?" Drummond asked. "Would it be practicable? At least the spring is coming, even with all the snow outside at the moment, but what about next winter? Would Mr James stand for it? Could we afford it, with train-fares for you to commute, and two of us to keep."

"Yes," I said decisively, "it will be perfectly possible." Even to myself, and without any analysis at all, I felt, and sounded, totally confident. He was not hesitating over the idea of us moving in together, only over the practicalities. Well, I had dealt with practicalities all my life, making it happen when I could and making do when I couldn't.

Before, there had only been myself to extricate from someone else's messes. Now, there would be two of us. So what? I knew I could deal with anything anyone else threw at us as long as we were together, as long as he was truly mine to love and look after.

"I'll bring lots of work home from Edinburgh, and, with the teaching up here already taking most of a day, with the travelling, I could see if Mr James would let me do two days a week in Dundee and three in Edinburgh. As long as I keep up my work-rate for MacWhinney, Preston, I don't think he minds how I do that. And I know enough now to go independent, like Flora, if the worst came to the worst—but I don't believe it will." I could feel myself bubbling with happiness. "Oh, Drummond, come on," I said suddenly, standing up and beaming at him, "you're not usually this slow!"

***

Afterwards, in bed, wrapped around him, Hannah uttered nothing but sincere endearments. Drummond said almost nothing at all, in words anyway. It wasn't until they were sitting again at the kitchen table, more or less adequately wrapped against the late-evening cold, and stoked with recently finished toasted cheese, that they turned again to the practicalities of Hannah's move to Dundee.

"John and Jacqueline's lease is supposed to run until June," Drummond said. "Can you bear to move into my house, with them on the second floor?"

"Of course," said Hannah. She could do anything! Her beam had declined to a happy, calm, continuous, beatific smile, which she felt would still be there when she walked into MacWhinney, Preston in the morning – this morning, she realised. Drummond had never stayed this late before, but she was content that there had never been a day like this before in the history of the world. "I'll go and introduce myself to them next week, when I'm in Dundee, if you like, and if you'll tell them I'll be dropping in after I finish teaching."

"Um," he said, with his customary, slightly worried look back on his face. "I'll phone them. God, Hannah, it'll be all around the university within 24 hours." Hannah took a grip on her tongue. She did not say, 'But you live in the same house. Just tell them. I'm going to be there permanently as soon as I possibly can.' Poor Drummond had been through enough emotion in the last few hours and, for him, had handled it well, she thought. Well enough, anyway.

"I'll have to give notice on this place, too," she said. "Perhaps they'll find another tenant quickly, before the notice period ends." It was her turn to look regretful. "I don't think I could pay rent here and commuting costs from Dundee, even though I really badly want to come as soon as possible. Tomorrow would be wonderful, but we've managed so far. I suppose we can manage for a week or two longer." He didn't say, as she longed to hear, 'No, come at once', but she was neither surprised nor hurt. Enough was enough for today, and it was all lovely enough from her point of view. "I love you, Drummond," she said yet again. "I'm so looking forward to this."

By the time Drummond left her to return to Dundee, it was almost not worth Hannah going to bed, but she did. She sank her nose into the pillows, and snuggled into the sheets, that still carried the slight smell of Drummond, and she gloried in it. She knew she would not sleep but went off within seconds, and was thankful that her alarm-clock woke her at least in time to make it to MacWhinney, Preston just before nine o'clock, with a tell-tale carry-out coffee steaming in her hand, and her memories steaming in her mind.

"Late night, was it?" Elisabeth greeted her, "and no time for breakfast this morning? Are you fit to give us a good day's work, young Hannah, or will your mind be an hour up the road to the north?"

After so long, Hannah was no longer overawed by Elisabeth's teasing and actually giggled at her, to the delight of both of them.

"You'll no doubt be off to lunch with Flora directly, so I'll hear all about it soon enough," Elisabeth continued, with the slightly manic-looking grin that she kept for just such occasions. Hannah wasn't worried. She knew Flora would tell no one anything about her that Hannah wouldn't wish to be known. But she giggled again, because indeed one of her first jobs that morning was to arrange to meet Flora and tell her the wonderful news.

"Oh, Elisabeth," Hannah said, "could Mr James spare me a few minutes today, do you think?"

Elisabeth's expression dropped, but not her eyes.

"Hannah, you'll not be thinking of too big a change in your life, I hope?"

It took Hannah a moment or two to catch up. Then she beamed broadly at Elisabeth.

"No, no, I don't want to leave the Firm. You know I love it here, Elisabeth."

"Is it maybe…" Elisabeth glanced around the empty lobby, and dropped her voice. "It's not tiny feet we hear, is it?"

Hannah's face flushed brightly.

"Goodness, no," she denied, "at least…not to the best of my knowledge. No, it's nothing like that. Just, I'd like to talk to him about possibly reorganising my work a bit."

"But it's nothing 'like that'?" Elisabeth teased again.

Hannah giggled yet again. Whatever was happening to her this morning, they both thought silently, as Hannah headed for escape up the shadowy stairwell. She was many things, and always pleasant and friendly, she hoped, but surely could not usually be described as giggly!

In her office, Hannah flung her overcoat and beret at the hook behind the door, and her bags at the side of her desk. "I'm not a 'flinger' either,' she thought to herself. 'What *is* happening? You'll have to concentrate *very* hard this morning, my girl, or you'll make a right mess of everything you touch.' The first thing, though, was to 'phone Flora and fix lunch. She should be home again by now from taking Veronica to school.

"Oh, Hannah," Flora said, after offering a preliminary account of her daughter's latest achievements, "I can't do lunch today. I'm meeting a client. Business. But, is it news? Is it Drummond?"

"Um," said Hannah, typically.

"Well, come for supper. Probably just something light, since I expect I'll have eaten far too much at lunchtime. And so must you. And Ian's away in Aberdeen for a conference today, and won't be back until late-late. So come and tell me *everything*."

"You know I always do," Hannah replied appreciatively.

"About seven?"

"See you then."

Just before eleven, Elisabeth telephoned.

"The kettle's on down here, Hannah, and Mr James can't see you until about four o'clock. He's out to lunch," Elisabeth said, with a touch of disapproval in her voice, real or joking.

Everybody seemed to be lunching today, Hannah thought, as she tripped down the stairs. At least she would know where she stood with Mr James by the time she met Flora. By half-past four, Hannah had almost given up hope of seeing Mr James that afternoon, and was feeling increasingly frustrated. Elisabeth telephoned at a quarter to five, however, to say that Mr James had been 'delayed'—said with heavily exaggeration—but would see her now if she wasn't rushing off home that evening for 'anything'—more exaggeration, and a questioning lift of her voice at the end of the enquiry.

Carefully hurrying down the stairs to the lobby, Hannah tapped the door to Mr James' office, went in on his call and closed the door behind her.

"Oh, it's one of those calls, is it, lassie?" Mr James smiled at her from his customary comfortable slouch. "Elisabeth suggested something of the sort, but was frustrated that she couldn't prise any detail from you." This seemed to please him. No doubt this represented a minor skirmish in their continuous affectionate rivalry for control of the Firm and its staff. At least he seemed to Hannah to be in a mellow mood after his long lunch. Even in this sort of mood, however, Hannah knew he was not to be underestimated.

"Sit down, lassie, sit down, and tell me what I need to know," Mr James invited.

"I wanted to ask you for something, rather than tell you anything, Mr James," Hannah began delicately. "I've been invited…that is, it has been suggested…" This wouldn't do, Hannah thought. Mr James liked crisp, concise explanations. Get on with it, Hannah, she told herself.

He helped her out.

"This will be to do with your young man, I take it?"

"Yes, Mr James."

"I hear he's a chemist?"

"Yes, Mr James."

"Well, at least it's unlikely he's offering you a job, Hannah. Elisabeth tells me you've no idea even how to make a decent cup of tea."

He was teasing her without mercy.

"There's no question of my wanting to leave the Firm, Mr James. I wouldn't! I love it here. I so much enjoy everyone, and all the clients, well, almost all of them, and—"

He took pity on her, glancing at his wrist-watch at the same time.

"Aye, well, that's some relief, anyway." He twinkled at her, and said, not unkindly, "Out with it, then. Say it straight, and we'll know what we're dealing with." He slumped slightly further into his chair. "You've been invited…?"

"Um. My boyfriend…" It was too early to say 'partner', she supposed. "Well, we, that is, I…he wants me to be with him, live with him, in Dundee." This was terrible, and Mr James' silent, patient smile wasn't helping. "He can't leave his work in his laboratory to move down to Edinburgh. I'm already effectively in Dundee, and away from the office here, for a day a week. I wondered if I could do two days a week in Dundee, and the rest of the time here?"

She hurried on. "It wouldn't affect my work-rate, Mr James, I promise. In fact, with a whole day in Dundee, and Drummond out of the house at the university, I could well get even more done that day than I do here. And I'd have my telephone and computer. And I'd take plenty of work with me when I was away, so as to keep up with everything. And Elisabeth could pass on the number of my mobile to authors, and everyone else, so I'd be nearly as closely in touch with everyone as I am here, and…" She stopped. She had made her case, or as much of one as she could in her present state of excitement and trepidation.

Mr James thought for a second, and then said, "You're a good worker, and a valuable asset to us, Hannah. You shift a lot of work, and you're popular with our contacts and authors." He drew down his eyebrows, his usual technique when he was trying to look especially serious. "You know how important it is to us that you stay on top of the slush-pile. And that turnaround times are minimised when we do go forward with a manuscript into editing." He paused again for more thought. "How about a trial period of six months for your new arrangement? Then we'll review how we're doing. Just make sure you're not wearing yourself out with it all. Hmm?"

"That would be fine, Mr James," Hannah said with relief. "I really am very grateful, and I promise I won't—"

"I'm pretty sure you won't, Hannah. Now off you go, and don't waste the rest of your day in your excitement."

"Thank you, Mr James." He really was the sweetest man, and did deserve a big warm kiss. But she hadn't the courage to offer it, however fond she had become of him since she had first met him almost five years before.

***

Ian was indeed absent when Hannah arrived at Flora's front door for supper. Veronica was in bed, though her bedroom door was open. Flora put her finger to her lips in warning as she ushered Hannah through the front door and down the hall. Once in the kitchen, Flora said excitedly, "Well? What about you, my dear? Off to the nether depths of Scotland, I hear."

"I only told Mr James two hours ago!" Hannah protested, smiling. "Is there no privacy at all in the world?"

"No, of course not. Now. Drummond. Is there to be a wedding, or is this a less formal arrangement? And how did you get him to…?"

Hannah told most of the story, all the bits to Drummond's credit, anyway. Once she'd finished, Flora said, "Oh, well. I've been dreaming of being your matron-of-honour for the best part of two hours, but I didn't really believe you'd get him to go so far in one evening, even you, you little seductress!"

"You definitely will be my matron-of-honour, or Chief Witness or whatever, if it ever does go that far. But, apart from you and Ian," Hannah said, "and Elisabeth's hints, I've seen nothing yet to persuade me to consider marriage worth the risks."

"If you love him as much as you obviously do, Hannah," Flora said, "and you can be sure of his commitment, and are taking care not to have children for a while, you're probably right. But, was the big M mentioned?" Flora asked, with a wicked grin.

"Oh, yes," Hannah replied. "When I made my challenge, it's what Drummond thought I was going to demand. You should have seen his face, poor darling!" They burst into laughter. "He was so relieved that what I wanted was no more than him, and immediately began to be practical, and think about the impact on his test-tubes."

"Well, you've got a real man there, then," Flora said. "Typical! You'll need to be very patient with him, Hannah, for he must be allowed his work. He'll likely leave everything else to you, though, my dear. My advice there is, just do it and tell him afterwards." They both giggled, and Hannah squirmed slightly with delight at the prospect of giving her life to making Drummond truly comfortable and content.

"You're a careful girl," Flora went on, "and I wouldn't say this to a spendthrift, but take over his surroundings. Do it very gradually. Buy one cushion first. If he likes it, or more probably doesn't notice it, buy some more." She smiled, evidently at a fond memory. "If he objects, leave cushion-buying until he's forgotten the subject. Then try again. And don't expect him to want to go shopping with you too often. You and I can do that when we get the whim. Oh, and his clothes! Just replace. Don't force-innovate. You won't win."

"But Drummond always wears the same things. That awful old jacket, and his grey flannels. Mind you, I do love his jacket. It smells so wonderfully of him." Hannah sighed, and so did Flora, theatrically, to tease her. And they both giggled again.

"He must *have* a suit, I suppose, but I've never seen it, even when we've been to the theatre. And that old raincoat he wears is truly dire," Hannah ruminated.

"Well, you'll be able to poke around his wardrobe soon enough," Flora said. "But if he hasn't a suit, go gently, and give yourself plenty of time before it's needed." She raised her eyebrows in emphasis. "Don't try to just march him off to the shop. Suggest it no more than once a week for a month, then increase the intensity of the suggestions, adding the looming proximity of the event for which it will be needed, like a job-interview or a posh university event."

"But what if he just refuses to think about it?" Hannah was fascinated by all this man-management, which was totally new to her and her straightforward practicality.

"Oh, he will, until it's almost too late," Flora assured her, "and then there'll be the most almighty rush, so you'll need to know what he's looking for before you hit the shops. He'll likely buy the first thing the salesman suggests, otherwise, and he'll *hate* trying things on, and get very irritable." She almost jumped as the next important point hit her. "Oh, and ties. He must have *one.* Buy the rest he needs just like what he's got, for extra presents, birthday and Christmas, and so on. And anniversaries. So, when are you moving in with him?"

"As soon as I possibly can!" Hannah replied enthusiastically, "now Mr James has agreed. But there are so many practicalities. I must find out about a season ticket for the train, and …"

Flora looked serious.

"I'm not sticking my nose in where it isn't needed, am I? Tell me to shut up, Hannah dear, if I am. It's just that this is what I'll be telling Veronica in no time at all, I suppose."

"No, no," Hannah protested. "If I'd had a mother who'd been a mother, it's exactly what I would expect her to tell me, and a lot more too that I've had to learn for myself." She looked gratefully at Flora. "You're more of a mother to me than mine ever was, as well as a dear, dear friend, Flora, and I really am grateful for all this. Honestly."

"The biggest thing, though," Hannah said, seeking calm in practical matters, "will be carting enough work up to Dundee every week to keep my productivity up to Mr James' requirements, together with what I need for the course at the university, though much of that material can be generated, and can stay, there."

"You've your own computer in the flat, haven't you, Hannah?" Flora asked. "Do you have a printer as well? If you could scan a few manuscripts onto floppy discs to read in Dundee, you'd save yourself a lot of weight to carry on the journey up and down."

She noticed Hannah's look of blank puzzlement.

"Scanning's like making a photocopy of a document, for storage on a floppy disc, or at least a series of them, with your manuscripts. I do it all the time," Flora said, "when I need to take a manuscript to talk to an agent or publisher, or send one through the post. Lighter and cheaper, and the manuscript is less likely to be damaged and become tatty.

"But you need a special sort of printer, and a disc-drive for the computer. Ask young Kenny at MWP," Flora suggested. "He's a whizz at this sort of thing, and he loves to show off. Tell him what you want the kit to do, and get him to take you to his favourite supplier. He'll make sure you get just the right kit. It will be worth it, I guarantee."

Chapter Thirteen

The following two weeks were frantically busy, and expensive. My first task was to give notice of my wish to terminate the lease on my Edinburgh flat. This included blushes and giggles when I was asked why I was leaving. I had to admit that I was moving in with my boyfriend, and the assistant in the letting agency whispered that she was shortly to make the same move.

In preparation for the following Wednesday in Dundee, I telephoned John and Jacqueline, Drummond's tenants, to introduce myself. I was hardly surprised to find that, although Drummond had mentioned that I would be 'coming', it was clear that he had not told them why. They seemed to have no idea that I would be moving into the house on a permanent basis. I decided to let this go for now, without further explanation.

They would soon realise, as my 'stay' extended, just what sort of relationship existed between Drummond and I. But they both sounded pleasantly welcoming, and readily agreed that they would be pleased to see me at the house on Wednesday, when I had finished my work at the university. Drummond was under instruction to bring me a key to his part of the house when he came to my Edinburgh flat on Saturday, so that I could examine my new home. He would collect me from there on Wednesday, to take me to dinner in Dundee before driving me back to Edinburgh afterwards.

After careful consideration of the building society account in which I had been squirrelling what I could save since coming to Edinburgh, I invited Kenny to introduce me to his world. As Flora had foretold, he was ecstatic to be asked. At the computer shop, he talked to the sales assistant in what might as well have been a foreign language, translated what they had been saying into plain English for my benefit, and offered to set up my new system a few days later, when everything had been delivered. I just acquiesced, paid gratefully and, when Kenny had set up the equipment in my office, settled down to master the new mysteries.

***

On the Saturday, Drummond agreed that he would load all Hannah's belongings into his car the following weekend, and take Hannah home to Dundee. *Forever?* she wondered hopefully, but said nothing more than, "That will be truly wonderful, darling. I can't wait!" He was getting used to her endearments, though she was careful not to use them too often in Dundee company. Not yet, anyway. He no longer stiffened and looked around to check who else had heard them, in Edinburgh at least. And, from time to time, he called her 'honey', which she adored, and which made her knees wobble, literally. She so much enjoyed being loved, and being in love!

She would certainly deal with the day-to-day household expenditure, she decided, food and fuel and the water-bill. Sure that Drummond would not raise the issue, she determined to mention her decision to him casually if and when the matter came up, or just do it as Flora had advised, and put away whatever was left over at the end of each month for emergencies like repairs to the house and decorating.

And perhaps holidays, she mused, reflecting that she had never had a proper, do-nothing holiday in her life. There had never seemed any point when she had had no one to go with, let alone that much spare money. She suspected the same of Drummond, at least since he had left his parents' home, and wondered briefly how they would get on in each other's company for 24 hours a day. "Perfectly well!" she decided, and firmly put the idea out of her mind.

Under Hannah's guidance and encouragement, her student group was becoming more enthused and united, although they would never be as vigorous or as stimulating as that of the previous year. She had mentioned this view to Morag, who agreed on the basis of her own contact with them, but assured Hannah that this was normal. The quality, and qualities, of each year's group varied, and their members had to be encouraged differently. It was part of the challenge and the joy of teaching, Morag said. Hannah took heart, and put her mind again to considering what talents she had available to produce this year's Journal.

After the following Wednesday's session at the university, Hannah left her bags in Morag's study, and walked to Drummond's house. It was of three stories, with a basement below, in a 19th century terrace of similar properties. There was no garden at the front. However, railings protected the basement area from the street, and steps led up to the front door, and down to what had once been the tradesmen's entrance to the basement kitchen. For a brief moment, Hannah felt slightly dizzy. She had lived in such buildings before, in North London suburbs, in poor, drab rooms, when her mother had been between men. She shook herself free of the memory. This time was going to be different, totally different. She was coming here in joy, not desperation or mute acceptance.

The house was substantial, Hannah decided, and realised that she was considering it, for the first time considering anywhere, as hers, in part at least. The railings and doors had once been painted black, but could do with being repainted, she thought. The curtains at the front windows could do with a wash, even replacement with something bright and patterned and…happy!

That was it, she realised. It had once been a home, before becoming simply an investment in which to sleep for no better reason than bodily fatigue. Now it was going to be a home again, and needed to be cheered up, and Hannah would do that. Goodness knows when, she thought, but she would.

Out of deference to John and Jacqueline, she rang the bell, though she had the keys in her handbag. There was a pause, then the door flew open, and a young woman stood before her, puffing slightly from rushing down the stairs from the top floor.

"You must be Hannah," she said. "I'm Jacqueline. Come in, come in. We've been dying to meet you."

The hall was as long and dark as Hannah had expected, hardly lit by the single lightbulb hanging half way towards the back of the house in its somewhat dusty beige shade.

"Come upstairs," Jacqueline said. "John isn't home yet, but I've some heat on up there, so we'll be comfy."

She set off up the stairs at something of a gallop, slowing only on the second flight as Hannah climbed up more slowly after her. Did this girl do everything at the rush? Well, Hannah thought, she'd soon know, and it was quite an endearing characteristic if she did. Or was it just nerves? Did she and her partner fear the change in circumstance that Hannah's arrival might herald? Hannah determined to avoid seeming to be a new chatelaine, sizing up everything and ready to take over the house.

"Let me take your coat," Jacqueline said, leading Hannah into a cluttered sitting-room through the first door they came to at the top of the stairs.

"It'll be fine here, if that's all right," Hannah said, slipping it off and folding it over the back of a convenient armchair that was filled with books.

"Will you have a cup of tea?" Jacqueline invited.

"Do you have coffee?" Hannah asked. "I'm not a great tea-drinker, I'm afraid."

"Of course. Or a glass of wine?" Jacqueline offered. There was no sign of bottle or glass.

"I'd really love a cup of coffee, if that's OK," Hannah said. "I've been talking all afternoon, and I'm as dry as a desert."

"Come into the kitchen while the kettle boils," said Jacqueline, rushing back out of the room and along the landing to the next door.

Hannah followed her. The kitchen was cream-walled, clean and organised. The last of the evening sun came in through the window.

"What a lovely bright room," Hannah said admiringly.

"It's because it's at the top of the house," Jacqueline replied. "We love it. If you look out of the window, you can see the garden, and the gardens behind the houses on the next street. They're not terribly well kept—who has time, these days?—but they make space between the buildings for the light to get in."

Hannah walked over to look out through the window, and, indeed, the gardens were quite large. Summer sunbathing, Hannah thought, after a bit more tidying up? She'd had a little garden at the bungalow in Cambridge, but had never had either the energy or the motivation to do anything with it. I'll make this a home, she thought to herself, for all of us, recognising that she was beginning to like the other girl.

Jacqueline switched on the kettle, which was already filled, reached down beakers from a cupboard, and popped coffee in one of them and a teabag into the other. She drew a milk-jug from the refrigerator, looked Hannah up and down, and correctly decided that sugar wouldn't be needed.

"You're very comfortable," Hannah said. "How long have you been here?"

"Ever since John graduated, four years ago," Jacqueline replied. "We were looking for somewhere in Dundee, and Drummond's postcard appeared on the Union notice-board at just the right moment. We've been really happy. We don't see a lot of him, and try to bother him as little as possible, but we've always all got on fine together."

Their drinks made, they picked up their respective beakers and returned to the sitting-room.

"Do sit down," Jacqueline said.

She shifted the pile of books from the chair over which Hannah had left her coat, and put another pile of books onto the floor from another chair so that she could sit down herself.

"So what do you do?" Hannah enquired.

"I work in the university library," Jacqueline replied. "I did a master's degree in librarianship at Sheffield, and then came up here when I got the Dundee job. That was after the Christmas of John's last undergraduate year. We met in the library, of course, when I was very new and he was very patient, and we've been together ever since."

Her contentment was almost as obvious as Flora's. Would I start giving off the same signal soon, Hannah wondered? Do I look and sound like that already? Well, there could be worse things, by a long way.

"And what about you, Hannah," Jacqueline asked. "I've heard about your creative writing course in the English Department, of course. We've been selling your Journal all over the world since it came out last summer. What a success! We already have a big contacts list ready for when the second edition comes out next summer."

Oh, grief, thought Hannah, the expectation everybody has! This is worse than feeling the threat of writer's block at the prospect of a second novel. Jacqueline was continuing, "We heard you mainly work in Edinburgh?"

Hannah realised that Drummond really had told John and Jacqueline very little about her at all. What Jacqueline knew was no more than the gossip among university professionals.

Well, Hannah thought, I'd better say it all once, straight away. It really was not fair to leave the lodgers in any doubt about the situations, theirs or hers and Drummond's, any longer.

"I work for MacWhinney, Preston," she began.

"The publishers?" Jacqueline interrupted her. "How wonderful! How wonderful to have another book-lover in the house. I'd always wanted to be a librarian, never wanted to do anything else since I was quite tiny, though it's much more than sitting about all day reading, as I imagined then that it was going to be."

"So is publishing. I do get to do a lot of reading, of course," Hannah said, "but most of that is really just skimming the work of hopeful…er, hopeless…authors. But I edit, too, which is a fascinating process."

At last the ice was broken by their common love. They warmed to each other as they explored their individual likes and dislikes, in books and in their jobs. But Hannah knew that the rest of the story needed to be told, and preferably before the men arrived.

"I met Drummond by accident, in the cafeteria on the campus," she explained. "We started to go out, in Edinburgh mostly, and then we met after my teaching sessions here, and everything just grew from there."

"You've been noticed on the campus," Jacqueline said, smiling archly. "Are you actually an item, then?" Hannah could not help smiling back at her. "How exciting! Drummond needs someone to look after him. He's terribly quiet and devoted to his work. He doesn't seem to have made any close friends in Dundee, not drinking buddies, if you know what I mean. He needs someone to look after him properly, or he'll never come out of his laboratory. Is that why you're here, Hannah?"

"Um," Hannah replied, and felt herself bushing again. "I needed to see more of him, lots more, and it wasn't going to happen as long as we were so far apart. So I'm going to be here for my teaching-day and the one before or after that, and commute to Edinburgh for the rest of the week. That's what we're planning at the moment, anyway."

"Oh, you'll be here all the time!" Jacqueline was overjoyed. "It will be lovely to have another woman in the house, especially with the library being open until late into the evening, and we librarians working either a late shift or an early one from nine in the morning. I hate coming back to an empty house too often in the afternoon," she said excitedly.

"I shall probably go down to Edinburgh some weekends," Hannah said. "I suppose you have to work on Saturdays now and then?"

"Oh, yes, one week in three," Jacqueline agreed.

"So do I," said Hannah, "but only to keep up. When Drummond's busy with something in the lab. that he can't leave, it won't matter, of course, but, as you say, it will be lovely to have you here for time together now and then."

"I'm hoping to have a go at the garden, too, this summer," Jacqueline said. "I intended to set to in it last year but it didn't happen."

"Oh, yes, let's plan it and do it together," Hannah chuckled at that happy thought. "Are there any tools?"

"No, but my dad has more than he needs. I'll get him to bring us the basics. My parents usually come up and stay in Edinburgh at Festival time, and do shows," Jacqueline replied. She was telling Hannah all about her family and her undergraduate years at Exeter, when sounds of the opening of the front door, and of John's footsteps on the stairs, interrupted them.

The sitting-room door swung open to admit a well-dressed young man of middle height, wearing a suit and sober tie, and very shiny black shoes. Jacqueline's face broke into a beam as she said, "Darling, this is Hannah, who's coming to live with Drummond downstairs. Isn't that lovely?"

John kissed Jacqueline warmly and then turned to Hannah.

"I'm John," he said. "How very good to meet you, Hannah. You are very welcome. And is it to be a long stay?"

Hannah blushed, and Jacqueline giggled as she said, "It sounds likely to be pretty prolonged, from what Hannah has told me so far. We were just planning to attack the garden together as soon as it's warm enough outside." To Hannah, she explained, "John is a solicitor with Church, Landeman here in Dundee."

"A very junior one," John said modestly, "but learning."

"And a very busy one," Jacqueline added. "But at least he doesn't have far to go to work, or to come home after he finally escapes at the end of a day."

"No, that's a great blessing," John agreed. "I couldn't do those long London commutes. Or the London pressures."

"Neither of us would like that," Jacqueline said. "John likes to think everything through very thoroughly and calmly, but when he does act, he's very decisive and masterful." The couple smiled at each other, slightly dreamily, telling Hannah that it was not just in his work that John was 'decisive and masterful', and that Jacqueline loved it that way.

The front door opened and closed again, and Jacqueline went to the landing to look down the stairwell.

"It's Drummond," she announced back into the sitting room. "Hi, Drummond," she called down to him, "we've got Hannah up here. Isn't she lovely?"

Drummond's feet sounded on the stairs immediately, coming up at least two at a time. He's nervous about how they were getting on together, Hannah thought, and about what had been said in his absence.

"Hi, John. Hi, Jacqueline," he said, as he came into the room. "Hallo, honey," he greeted Hannah, as he bent to kiss her cheek and sit on the sofa beside her.

"Would you like a cuppa, Drummond," Jacqueline asked. "I'm making one for John."

"No, no, thank you," Drummond said, "we'll away downstairs. Have you looked around down there yet, Hannah?"

"No, Jacqueline brought me straight up here, to make me welcome," Hannah replied, hoping to reassure him a little. "I'm dying to see the rest of the house."

"Aye, come on then," Drummond said, gratefully, pushing himself upright. "We'll leave you two to your evening."

"Thank you for the coffee, Jacqueline," Hannah said warmly. "See you both soon."

"When are you …coming…" Jacqueline obviously wanted to say 'moving in' and 'permanently', but didn't want to make Drummond uncomfortable.

"At the weekend, sometime," Drummond answered for Hannah.

"When the test-tubes permit," Hannah teased, and they all laughed. Even Drummond smiled, if a bit tightly.

Hannah kissed his cheek lightly as they got to the first-floor landing.

"I do love you," she told him. "It's wonderful to be here."

He put his arm around her waist as they descended the stairs to the ground floor, and gave her a lovely squeeze.

"Let's start at the bottom," Drummond said, so, on the ground floor, they went along the hall to the back of the house, arms still around each other, and down the stone stairs to the basement.

"It was always the kitchen, here, when these houses were built," Drummond said, rather like a house-agent, "and it's been left like that here."

The stairs opened directly into a big space, floored in black, shiny bricks and dominated by a scrubbed deal table in the middle of the room. The room extended from the front to the back of the house. At the back, through a narrow arch, Hannah could see a small scullery, rather like Elisabeth's at the office in Edinburgh, with a similar ancient Belfast sink and wooden draining board. In the kitchen, a wood-and-wire meat cupboard was hung on the wall beside the doorway.

She was willing to bet it would have marble shelves, and that the shelves would be empty. A 'single-man' refrigerator stood in the adjacent corner, humming comfortably. It was too small for the needs of both of us, she thought, and would have to be replaced. However, in the corner of the left-hand wall, a big chest-freezer stood beneath a room-length wooden worktop, at one end of which stood a rather lonely-looking microwave oven. Above the worktop, shelves of a similar length rose almost to the ceiling. The shelves were sparsely occupied by crockery. There would be plenty of room for mine, and for more as I—we—added them, she thought.

No chatelaining down here either, she told herself firmly. *At least, not yet, for a while.*

There was even a reasonable-looking washing machine, Hannah was relieved to see, and an old-fashioned drier hung on pulleys from the ceiling. Thank goodness for that, she thought silently. No more launderettes.

She turned to see that an ancient gas stove stood in the left-hand corner of the front wall. It was in need of a good clean, but was located so as to catch as much light as possible from the rather grubby window in the door which would open—if it could be opened—into the basement area at the front of the house. What looked like a walk-in pantry had been built, floor to ceiling, in the opposite corner. Opening its door, she saw very little food inside, but said nothing. She'd make use of it, full use, given time.

It was a lovely kitchen, and it was going to be all hers, especially once they could get a couple of long, fluorescent lights fitted, to supplement the two inadequate single bulbs hanging disconsolately from either end of the ceiling. It would be lovely and warm in here, too, half-buried in the ground as it was, and with the insulating bulk of the house and its neighbours up above. That would be a lovely table on which to do layouts of the next *Journal*, Hannah thought.

Indeed, if Drummond didn't object, she could get her whole student group down here, if and when the occasion arose. Perhaps a change of venue would stimulate some of the less enthusiastic among them to let their minds, and their physical energy, run a little more freely.

"Seen enough?" Drummond asked.

"Yes, thank you," she told him, "for a while. But isn't it lovely?"

Drummond smiled down on her and gave her a squeeze, satisfied that she was contented, so far at least.

They went up to the ground floor. There, the hall and staircase ran along one side of the house, with two rooms leading off it. The back room was almost unfurnished, and the floor was uncarpeted.

"I tend to live in the kitchen or the front room," Drummond said, with a note of apology in his voice. "You could have this room for your work stuff, if you like."

Hannah saw, with a wonderful feeling of freedom, that, at the far end of the room, floor-to-ceiling windows looked out into the garden, separated by French windows leading into…

"A conservatory!" she exclaimed. "Oh, how marvellous! It'll be wonderful to sit out here in the summer, with the doors open, even in a Scottish summer, when the day's done and we just want to relax."

Drummond did not seem very sure about the concepts either of summer or relaxing, but simply looked happy that she liked what she was seeing and that she hadn't immediately demanded to be taken back to the civilisation of Edinburgh. He put his arm back around her waist and led her to the smaller, cosier front room.

This room was furnished. Indeed, cluttered. The upholstery on the sofa and three armchairs showed more than a little evidence of their age, but the seats themselves looked deep and comfortable. Hannah could see them curling up together here in front of the fireplace on a winter evening. There were overflowing bookcases on every available inch of wall, the books mostly stuck into the shelves higgledy-piggledy, with more heaps of books and journals in piles on the aged carpet within easy reach of one or another of the armchairs.

A small radio stood on top of one of the lower bookshelves, and a central coffee table bore both a coaster and a lot of rings, as well as more academic papers. A tall, modern, steel standard lamp stood behind one chair, its flex trailing across the carpet to a double power-point beside the fire. In the fireplace, an electric kettle and beaker stood on the tiles, the kettle's flex using the other socket. But there were no ornaments, no pictures or photographs, certainly no flowers.

Hannah had never had such things, either, except where they had been left in the furnished rooms by the landladies of her childhood. Margaret had such things, even in her very professional consulting room. Flora had lots of them, and even Jacqueline had a few. Hannah was determined that there would soon be some here, too. Eventually, lots of them. They were part of her dream of how a proper home should be furnished.

"There's no television," Drummond said. "You don't have one either, do you, honey?"

"No," Hannah confirmed, "but it might be fun to get a small one, just for us to watch a film, or part of one, with a hot drink on winter evenings."

"When it's too cold to sit in the garden and freeze," Drummond teased, and kissed her cheek. He seemed delighted at her evident appreciation of what he was offering her.

Four doors opened off the first-floor landing. Two were firmly shut and Drummond waved vaguely at them, saying, "There's literally nothing in there at all, though this one is a bit of a pigsty, I'm ashamed to say. I meant to tidy it up a bit, but…"

Going towards the back of the house, he said, slightly defensively, "This is the bathroom. It's not modern, but I've given it a bit of a scrub." He stood aside to let her look in. A splay-footed bath lined one wall, with a plastic soap-tray straddling it. The bath was a little stained but clean, with a shower-attachment suspended from its fitting above the old-fashioned taps. A handbasin with similarly aged taps was in a comparable condition, as was the tiny mirrored cabinet hung on the wall above it.

It'll do, Hannah thought, *to start with*. Again, it came as no surprise to her, and she had seen many worse.

With apparently even more trepidation, Drummond led her to the adjacent door.

"This is the bedroom I've been using. It's the biggest of the three," he said.

It contained a single bed, though there was room for a double, probably. Against a couple of walls stood a narrow wardrobe and a cheap, collapsing modern chest of drawers, from both of which spilled an assortment of clothes, mostly casual shirts and men's underclothes. For the first time since she had arrived, Hannah was taken aback. Wherever would she put her things?

Even given Drummond's restricted wardrobe, there couldn't be anywhere near enough hanging-space for both them, despite the fact that neither of them had a lot of clothes, thank goodness, compared for example with Flora's and Ian's. She quickly reviewed her savings account again. At least she could put washing-lines across one of the unused smaller bedrooms until she could buy more furniture. And a new double bed. And pillows and linen. And a pair of decent chests of drawers. She didn't want her tights snagged on the splintering furniture with which Drummond was managing, even if there had been any room in even one drawer in it for her to use.

"Is it too awful, honey?" Drummond asked quietly in trepidation.

"Not as long as you're here," Hannah answered nobly, and gave him a hug. "We'll manage fine, if you don't mind me getting some new stuff for my things."

"Anything you like," he said gratefully. "In fact, it'll be a huge relief to have you here for the practical things. And for just having you here, too." He grasped her and gave her a long, long kiss, which, though she knew it was partly to cover the embarrassment of his almost-*faux-pas*, she returned with all the warmth she could convey.

"We'll eat out tonight," Drummond said when they got back to the ground floor. "Are you all right to walk?"

"I need to collect my bags from Morag's office at some point," Hannah said. "Could we take the car and do that first, and then eat?"

"Fine," Drummond replied. "And would you like to come back here after we've eaten, and get the early train to Edinburgh tomorrow?"

She gulped slightly, but tried not to let it show. Surely he had some spare sheets for that tiny, narrow bed? She'd find a way to get him to let her change them when they got back. Whatever, she wasn't going to forego a night with him, even one spent among the rumpled sheets she'd seen during their tour of the house. And they'd be lovely and close all night, as they'd remain until she could replace the bed.

Over supper in a small restaurant, Drummond enquired with a worried tone, "Can you manage to live in the house, darling, and be happy?"

"It's beautiful," she cried with enthusiasm. "Of course we'll be happy! It's a home, a proper home. Oh, darling, I love it. All that space, and that lovely garden-room and conservatory, and that amazing kitchen! We'll be so very happy there."

To Drummond, a house was a house was a house. Just bricks and mortar, and something of a liability when anything broke down or needed to be replaced.

"There's almost no furniture, I suppose. Just enough for me, at present. But I haven't been there that much, you see, and I've not really noticed being short of anything."

"We'll build up what we need gradually. We'll colonise it," she said, "room by room. At least there's plenty of space for what I'll bring from Edinburgh, without you really noticing, I wouldn't be surprised."

Back at the house, she said gently, "Darling, would you like to make a hot drink while I change the bed? Just tell me where to find clean sheets, and it will be done before the kettle's boiled."

Drummond looked ashamed.

"I meant to do that," he muttered, "and then dashed off to the lab this morning without remembering it."

177

"Well, you don't have to remember now, my precious," she said. "You just get on and organise your enzymes and become famous and rich, and I'll look after the domestics."

"There's an airing cupboard on the first-floor landing. On the right. I should have showed you," Drummond apologised. "There's sheets and so on in there. I think that's where they are, anyway. I did get a bottle of coffee granules for you," he said, and she rewarded him with a hug and a kiss.

Given the width of the bed, they had a lovely first night together in their first home. In the morning, she was as happy as a lark, despite the hour, when Drummond's alarm clock roused them in time for him to take her to the station for her train.

"Roll on Sunday," Drummond said, pulling up the car in front of the station. "I'll be there as soon as I can."

***

Hannah stayed in bed for an extra hour on the Sunday morning. She was hardly up and dressed when, astonishingly, he arrived shortly after half-past eight.

"I couldn't wait any longer," he confessed with a smile as he hugged her inside her front door.

She kissed him warmly, and, on being released, suggested a cup of tea to warm him after his drive. Going into her sitting-room while she went to put on the kettle in the kitchen, he was impressed by how bare it was, how neatly the suitcases and boxes had been packed and assembled for loading into the car, and how many of them there were.

"Hannah, love," he called, "there's an awful lot to go, by the look of it. We may have to make two trips."

"Well, that's all of it," Hannah replied, "apart from a small box of things like the kettle and beakers, and a bag of last-minute washing. If there is anything left over when we've loaded the car, we could collect it later in the week, if you don't want to come back here again today."

"I've something going on in the lab that I must look at this afternoon or this evening at the latest," Drummond said.

"That's fine," Hannah decided cheerfully. "None of my stuff is essential, though I'd like the clothes and bits in that small suitcase for Monday and

Tuesday. I can gradually bring the rest of my clothes to the house after each day's work here in Edinburgh." Nothing was going to spoil today for her. She felt like a balloon inflated with hot air and ready to take off on its next adventure.

By eleven, they had carried everything downstairs to the car. Drummond had taken out the backseat. The only things that wouldn't fit in were one big suitcase and a small box, which could be moved to Dundee during the following week. Hannah dashed around the flat to check that nothing had been forgotten, and quickly stripped her bed. The bedclothes went into her black bin-bag of washing and she locked the door of the flat and ran down the stairs to join Drummond like a young child going off on its first real holiday.

At Drummond's house, the car was quickly unloaded and its contents carried up to the larger of the unused first-floor bedrooms.

"We'll just dump everything here for now, except the food," Hannah suggested. "I'll start sorting it out and putting it away after we've had something to eat."

"Can I leave you to do that?" Duncan enquired. "I really ought to go and see how—"

"Yes, yes, of course, darling," Hannah agreed. She would be pleased to have him out of the way while she decided where to put all her things. Childhood experience had taught her that that was a job best done by one person, or it took hours and neither could find anything afterwards. Also, she knew he'd been pining for his tubes and flasks all morning.

"You've been so good to give up all this time to getting me here," and she put her arms around his neck to give him a long thank-you kiss.

"Now," she said, "soup and a sandwich for lunch? Downstairs? I can do that in seconds."

Not giving him time to demur, she grabbed the cold-box and skipped down the stone steps into the kitchen to put on the kettle for the soup.

***

Life in Dundee quickly became idyllic. A new double bed was installed—Drummond wanted something bigger, but the dimensions of the bedroom would not permit it—and a small television set. The kitchen shelves and pantry gradually became more heavily populated, though by no means full, and the ancient gas oven was replaced by a smart but modest electric one. New carpets were bought and laid on the first floor and down the staircase, and, Hannah foresaw, would soon be needed in the ground-floor sitting-room.

She had established a work-space for herself in the ground-floor garden room, with a couple of fold-down tables for desks, and two decently-padded dining chairs. Although they soon wouldn't be needed any more until the autumn, the central heating boiler and all the huge old radiators throughout the house had been checked over, and declared to have a limited future life by an engineer who sucked his teeth constantly at what he found but said that the simple old systems were often better than these modern electric things, "hung with bells and whistles".

Hannah and Drummond decided to leave the major expenditure of replacing the boiler for a while, and perhaps get the job done next year. Their engineer, with an air of infinite wisdom, agreed that that would probably be all right, but that they shouldn't leave it longer, and he'd be happy to do the job for them "in a twelve-month or so, maybe".

Hannah's commute to Edinburgh quickly became routine. At first, the early start had been a bind, as had the task of fitting her working day and appointments to the train-timetable. But at least the platforms for her regular trains were on the side of Waverley railway station nearer to St Andrew's Square, so she didn't have far to walk to the office in a morning. Also, boarding the train at Dundee, she could always get a seat and find somewhere for her bags; and it was interesting to observe the other commuters sitting in the same seat every day, or glowering at 'irregulars' when their favoured seat was already occupied.

After a month or so, she struck up a gossiping acquaintance with a couple of young women who commuted each morning from Cupar, and another who sat near to them, when she could, from Markinch. For most of her journeys, however, she read manuscripts and was keeping up her work-rate at MacWhinney, Preston without difficulty.

Nonetheless, the season-ticket for the train was expensive and Hannah was beginning to think about learning to drive. She had never previously had either the opportunity or the need to have anything to do with motor vehicles, and would not pretend to know anything about how or why they worked. She knew less about them, and had had less interest in them, than in the computer equipment that was now so much a normal part of her life.

However, her move to Dundee had been made easy by the availability of Drummond's car. More recently, she had been struck by the convenience and pleasure of having Drummond drive her around in and beyond Dundee when they needed heavy shopping or could snatch the same day off to explore and be refreshed by the country inland or further up the coast. The value of her being able to drive was gently confirmed by the vagaries of her work-timetable in Edinburgh, and of the associated commuting.

Also, Drummond's car seemed to spend a large proportion of its existence parked by the pavement somewhere near the house, especially in the summer when he often preferred to walk to and from the university, "for the thinking time".

On one occasion, Drummond himself had even asked her whether she would like to learn to drive, to which she had replied vaguely, "Maybe, one day, perhaps", being at the time not a bit interested in the matter. Now, the idea was creeping around near the top of her unconscious mind, and becoming increasingly attractive.

She mentioned it to Flora at one of their Edinburgh lunches. Flora advised that, while Hannah might not feel the need at the present moment, being able to drive was undoubtedly an asset in emergencies, and did add increased flexibility to one's arrangements.

"Just don't let Drummond try to teach you, though," was Flora's last observation on the subject. "That's the quickest way to relationship-breakdown known to humanity. Get a professional, who won't shout at you or die of frustration when you make a tiny mistake. Best of all, get a woman. They've more patience, have stronger nerves than men and are more sensible about explaining everything to another woman."

At the university, her students were well on the way to putting together this year's Journal. It would not be as sparkling as last year's, but it would be more varied. Submissions accepted by the student editorial board, elected from within the group, included reviews and a couple of dramatic scripts, as well as poetry and short-stories. Some of the work was excellent, the rest adequate. Under Hannah's urging, contacts had been made with the students in the Art Department who had helped so enthusiastically last year, but were less enthusiastic this year. "Been there, done that, moved on" seemed to be a prevailing tendency. Nonetheless, the cover design and page-layout was acceptable. As Jacqueline had told her, the library was standing ready to release the *Journal* on to the literary world with press notices and circulations to an astonishingly wide contact-list.

Prof and Morag were content, and apparently "budgetary constraints" were going to preclude another big launch-party at the end of term, for which Hannah was grateful. However, her students were not about to admit to having been outdone by their predecessors in relation to organising a party. They decided to combine the launch of their work with a departmental end-of-year party, sell tickets around the university to fund it, and make Hannah their guest of honour.

This time, Drummond came, though he would not stay for the whole of the party. He spent much of the time he was there leaning against a handy wall, talking to someone when he had to, but looking very proud and happy when Hannah was again praised to the skies in her students' speeches, albeit in somewhat irreverent terms. It was clear that they had become fond of her after a dubious start, and had appreciated her energetic driving of them in the end. The final cherry on Hannah's cake was that, with Mr James' approval, she had been offered, and had accepted, another contract to repeat her course the following year, though nothing had been said about making her 'temporary' status any more permanent.

At home, she and Jacqueline were gradually bringing their garden under control. They had even managed to find a couple of opportunities to spread blankets on the now-subdued grass and sunbathe. The undergraduates would soon leave the university, the town would empty significantly, and she would be able to give more time to the house, their home, and to Drummond, and to MacWhinney, Preston and its needs. She was well content with life, even conscious of enjoying it.

Chapter Fourteen

Towards the end of October, the autumn was well-established. Hannah needed a hat and a warmer coat, and occasionally even gloves, when she set off for the train station first thing in the morning. Soon it would be winter, but Drummond and she had had a good summer. She had started driving lessons, "to take advantage of the light evenings and dry weather".

After a nervous start, and thanks to her lovely, calm instructor, Susan, she was by now reasonably confident in her steering and gear-changing, and was beginning to notice without undue effort the road signs, and what other drivers were doing around her. Also, she had finally been taken to meet Drummond's parents in Glasgow and, astonishingly, Drummond had agreed that they should go on from there to Fort William for a long weekend, which had provided quite a lot of useful driving practice for Hannah, on the outward journey at least.

Drummond's impatience to be back in his lab had excluded her from the driving seat for most of the return journey. All in all, the joys of her life with Drummond in Dundee, and with good friends in and around MacWhinney, Preston in Edinburgh, were easily displacing in Hannah's mind any lingering dread of the forthcoming cold and wet. After six years, she was ready to accept the Scottish winter as unavoidable, in the knowledge that it certainly wouldn't do her any lasting harm.

On that particular Thursday, however, a watery sun still glimmered gently between broken clouds, and the afternoon had been comfortably warm indoors for what she called that week's "Dundee day". She had combined a satisfying few hours of editing on a soon-to-be-published novel with skimming and rejecting five manuscripts from the slush-pile. She had invited Jacqueline down for a morning coffee in the basement kitchen. Now, with no one else in the house and one of her recently-acquired cookery books to hand, Hannah was trying for the first time in her life to make a sponge-cake. It was to be a surprise for

Drummond, if it turned out well, or could go into the bin without announcement if it were a total failure.

Neither Drummond nor John would be home much before six-thirty or seven o'clock. They never were, and Jacqueline was on a late shift and wouldn't be back before ten. Hannah was therefore slightly irritated when a shadow fell across the kitchen window from somebody climbing the steps to her front door. When the doorbell rang, she was tempted to ignore it, but her inherent consideration overcame her reluctance, and the cake would not need attention for another ten minutes, so…

She opened the front door, and froze.

"Hallo, darling," said the taller, older of the women on the step. "Hasn't it been a long time?"

Hannah slammed the door. Her fingers groped for the bolts, top and bottom, and slid them across. She couldn't believe it. She ran to the back door, which she had left open to let the last of the afternoon warmth into the house, and slammed and bolted that. Running down to the kitchen, she could hear the doorbell being rung again, once, twice, and then with prolonged, unrelieved pressure for ten or fifteen seconds.

She bolted the door from the area, and put her hands over her ears. She was too shocked even to cry. She could feel her body beginning to weaken. The shadows still fell across the kitchen window. The women must have heard the bolts slam shut, but were still expecting to be let in. Somehow, she staggered up the stone steps from the kitchen. In the hall, she heard her mother's braying voice, just as she still heard it in the occasional nightmare, or when she was particularly tired and alone.

"Come on, darling. Don't be a silly girl. I've someone here who really wants to meet you, and it's getting chilly out here."

From the back of the hall, Hannah heard in her mind the words, "Go away, go away", but she couldn't get them out of her throat. One of the women hammered a fist on the outside of the door, and her mother shouted with increasing anger, "Hannah. Let us in this minute, girl!"

Hannah screamed, long and loud. There were words in the scream, negative words, denying words, but they were totally indistinct. Her scream echoed round the hall, round the whole house, round the inside of her head, and Hannah collapsed slowly against the wall, tears coming at last, and she sobbed and sobbed and sobbed.

Coming up the street an hour later on his way home, Drummond noticed nothing of his surroundings. He saw the same parked cars and vans, the same house-fronts, every day, and his mind was still full of his work. There was a particular problem with his latest mixture, and he could not understand what it was or why it had arisen. Tomorrow, he would…

He turned to climb the steps up to his front door, raised his head at last, and saw two women apparently camped at the top, complete with two very battered suitcases and several well-filled black plastic bin-bags. Beggars, he presumed. Though common enough in Edinburgh, they got few of them in Dundee, except the one who was always near the train station. He could not recall having seen any in this street ever before.

"Away with you, if you please," he said, drawing himself up to his full impressive height, and putting on the face of authority he used if he found undergraduates acting the fool in one of the Department's laboratories. "There's nothing for you here." He stood aside at the bottom of the steps to allow them free passage, half-expecting to be offered a sprig of heather, *for good luck, darlin'* as they came past him.

Instead, the older woman, now standing, looked down at him imperiously, and said, in a very English accent, "And just who the hell are you?" The younger, more tousled and—truth to tell—rather grubby-looking one was still sitting, more accurately squatting, and sniggered.

"I live here," Drummond said, reaching into his jacket pocket for his telephone. "This is my house." He let the Glaswegian roughness of his youth into his voice. "Now away where you've come from, or it will be the polis for you."

The woman's nose rose higher into the air, and she smiled disdainfully.

"I'm Hannah's mother," she announced, "and Hannah has slammed the door in our faces, her own mother's, would you believe? Clearly, her manners haven't improved at all under your influence."

Drummond fought to prevent the surprise from registering in his expression. He thought quickly, dissecting the problem in the sort of practical terms he would use when something unforeseen happened in the lab.

"All right," he said decisively. "Now, you're going to go away, and I'm going to find out what all this is about. But not until you go and I can get to my own front door. You can come back at half-past eight. Not a moment before, mind! Then we'll see about all this. Come on. Off you go."

He still had his phone in his hand. The screen was glowing, and his thumb hovered over the emergency call button. The younger woman stood up and started to gather the bin-bags into her hands.

The older one began to protest again, and then saw how determined Drummond was to be rid of them, at least for now. She reached down for the handles of the suitcases and smiled, widely but artificially.

"This is all so unnecessary," she finally said, beginning to descend the steps. "We'll be back later then, as you have invited us."

Drummond stood well clear of the bottom of the steps. He did not know what was going on, but his instinct was not to trust these two an inch. Relieved, he watched them both go down the street and turn the corner at the end. He had no idea where they were going, and cared less. By half-past eight, John would be back home, he hoped, which would provide some legal experience to help deal with the matter, if need be. Drummond did not like the look or feel of the situation a bit, but he certainly was not going to have his home invaded by a couple of raggle-taggle women.

If Hannah had not wanted them in the house, that was good enough for him. He was perfectly capable of keeping them no closer than the front steps, though he couldn't make them just disappear completely. He only wished he could. He put his telephone back in his pocket, drew out his door keys, put the Yale in the lock as usual, and turned it. The door refused to open to him, and the scream which he heard from within frightened him. He knew at once that there was real trouble here.

Hannah had no idea how long she had lain, curled as tightly as she could, on the hall floor. The sound of a key being put into the lock, and turned, checked her sobs, and she screamed again. How had they got hold of a key? She gazed, transfixed, at the door, but of course the bolts prevented it from opening. Then she heard Drummond's blessed voice calling, "Hannah. Hannah, darling. It's me, Drummond. Let me in, honey. I'm here now, and those other two have gone. It's all right now, darling. Everything's all right."

After some seconds, he heard the bottom bolt slide across slowly. From behind the door, he could just hear a faint scrabbling of heels, as if a giant mouse were struggling to get to its feet. After a while longer, the top bolt slid, and he withdrew his keys and waited for Hannah to turn the lock. The door eased open slowly, and there was Hannah, a dishevelled mess, her lovely face redrawn by what had clearly been floods of tears.

"Darling," he said, and she began to subside again to the floor. Taking her in his arms, he drew her gently into the hall and kicked the door closed firmly behind himself. He let her down gently to the floor, not knowing whether, and if so how, and how badly, she was hurt. At least she was no longer crying. Deep, coughing sobs escaped from her every few seconds, and she seemed unable to speak or to support the weight of her slight body upright. He lowered himself to the floor beside her and hugged her gently to him, saying nothing and asking nothing, just giving her time to make any slight recovery that might be possible.

Drummond became aware of a smell of burning. It seemed to come from the kitchen, but he did not want to leave Hannah in order to investigate it. On the other hand... He took the stone steps into the kitchen three at a time, nearly falling at the bottom.

The smell filled the kitchen, but he could see no flames. One of the oven knobs was on though, and, when he stepped closer to turn it off, the whole oven was hot. Grabbing an oven-glove, he pulled open the door to the little top oven, which was empty, and then pulled at the big door to the lower oven, which resisted. Jerking it with all his strength, he opened it, and a cloud of sooty smoke billowed into the kitchen around his head. There were no flames in there either, he saw, though clearly there had been.

Whatever Hannah had been cooking had been completely consumed, but there was no immediate danger to themselves or to the house. He turned off the switch. He'd sort that out later.

Back up in the hall, he sat down on the floor beside Hannah and put his arms around her again.

"Darling," he said eventually. The sobs were becoming less frequent. "Whatever happened? Oh, Hannah, love, you've had the most terrible shock, but it's all right now, honey, it's all right now."

"Bed," Hannah murmured into his ear, almost a whisper. The only thing she could think of was to get into her bed and curl up and stay there, protected from the world, for ever. It was just like last time, and she remembered what a comfort, the only comfort, it had been to get into her bed and never have to think of getting out of it. She needed Margaret. Above all, she needed Drummond.

"Bed, oh, please, bed," she whispered again.

Drummond stood up, leaned over, and hoisted Hannah into his arms. She seemed in this condition to weigh no more than air. Careful not to bang her head on the stair-banister or doorframe, he carried her up to their bedroom and sat her on the foot of the bed while he folded back the neatly arranged duvet. With infinite care, he supported her as she laid herself down. Her back was already bending as she turned onto one shoulder, and her legs were coming up towards her chest as he undressed her.

He reached for the nightdress beneath her pillow, but she muttered, "No", so he just covered her lightly with the duvet and sat on the chair beside her head, stroking her hair and her shoulder as she curled into a ball and seemed to go to sleep.

He sat there for half an hour. He was conscious of the passage of time, of the fact that the women might well come back and startle Hannah again by ringing the doorbell and hammering on the door. They would surely come back at half-past eight. There was an hour yet before that time, however. He certainly wasn't going to have anything more to do with them until Hannah could tell him what was going on.

He felt at a total loss, unable to think coherently, hardly able to operate as a human being. It was a paralysis to which he of all people was not used, and, as well as Hannah's condition, it frightened him to realise it. He heard a key in the front-door lock downstairs, and stiffened, but it was only John's well-known footstep on the stairs. Drummond stood silently, and went to the landing, pulling the bedroom door toward him without closing it, as he met John at the top of the first flight of stairs.

"Hi, Drummond," John greeted him brightly, and then saw Drummond's face. "Is there something the matter, mate?" he said more quietly. "It's not Hannah, is it?"

"Aye, it is," Drummond confirmed, "and I think I need your help, or certainly your advice."

"Of course," John agreed, becoming comfortingly professional straight away.

Drummond led the way downstairs to the sitting-room, pushing the door open and kicking Hannah's heavy cast-iron cat into its place as a door-stop to keep the door back. He turned on the electric kettle which stood as always beside the hearth. Both beakers were cleaned and washed, and the caddy of tea-bags stood beside them ready to hand.

"Och, milk," Drummond said, irritated at his own oversight and standing up.

"Don't worry, I'll get it. In the fridge in the kitchen, is it? You just watch the kettle and listen for Hannah," said John.

The tea made and warming their hands through the beaker, Drummond had been woken up a little by the routine movements of tea-making and by John's welcome presence.

"So what's going on?" John asked.

"If I knew, it would be easier to tell you," Drummond replied mournfully. "I got home to find two women on the doorstep, and Hannah inside, sobbing on the floor and literally in a state of total physical collapse. I got her into bed, which was all she wanted, all she'd say, and let her sleep. She was breathing fine, once I got her into bed. She'd been sweating but, by the time you came in, she'd cooled and there wasn't a temperature, and I could see no external wounds. But I don't know what's the matter with her, what started it, what's happening at all."

"So who were these women?" John asked.

"They looked like hobbledehoys," Drummond said, "like beggars. They had suitcases and bin-liners, and they were none too clean. But one of them said she was Hannah's mother, and Hannah wouldn't let them in. Very English-snooty she was, with an accent not unlike Hannah's, but I got rid of them. Told them to go and not come back until half-eight. I'd hoped Hannah would have told me what it was all about by then, but I'm not sure she'll be able to. She hasn't moved since I put her into bed."

John thought for a few seconds.

"Has anything like this happened to her before?" John asked forensically. "Collapsing, I mean, for whatever reason?"

"No. Not as far as she's ever said, anyway."

"Maybe a doctor would be a good idea? Who's her doctor?"

"I don't know," Drummond said unhappily. "It's not something either of us have needed since we got together. I've never bothered registering up here. I'm not sure Hannah has, either."

"I...um..." John did not know how to put this delicately, especially to so private a person as Drummond. "Look," he said, "forgive me, but I presume she takes precautions, since you've been...living together. She must get her prescriptions from somewhere."

"That's not...something she'd discuss with me, I suppose." Drummond was embarrassed. What would John think of him? But there were more important

189

things than that to consider at the moment. "At least, she hasn't said anything about…all that. I just leave it to her, and it's been all right so far. I suppose." Drummond pulled himself together again. "But she has a special friend in Edinburgh. Flora. She'd probably know. They seem to tell each other everything."

"OK," John decided, "here's a plan. I'll phone Jacqueline, and get her back from the library, and you look in Hannah's phone, and see if you can find anything about doctors. If not, phone this Flora. I suppose her number will be in Hannah's phone, and I'm sure Hannah won't mind you looking in her contacts in this sort of emergency."

"I must just slip upstairs and make sure she's all right," Drummond said. "Then I'll have to find her bag with her phone in it. Probably in the kitchen. She was cooking something when all this started, apparently."

"Yes," John agreed. "The smell is still strong, but I tipped the remnants in the bin when I went down for the milk. Hope that was OK? I didn't see her bag down there, though."

"It'll be in her workroom, then." Drummond stood to begin his search.

Jacqueline was obviously away from her desk in the library when John phoned. When she did pick up his call and heard his voice, her first words were "Are you all right, darling?" It was so unusual for him to bother her at work.

"I'm fine," John assured her. "It's Hannah. Drummond got home to find her collapsed on the hall floor and…no, it's not that, apparently. She may have been harassed by somebody claiming to be her mother."

"I didn't know her mother was still alive," Jacqueline interrupted. "She's never spoken of her. I would have remembered if she had."

"Yes, well, apparently the relationship may not be good. This woman told Drummond that Hannah had slammed the door and refused to let them in. Anyway, is it possible you could come home, darling? We men are at a bit of a loss, and Hannah's asleep, we think, but it could be more. She's in a really bad state. Drummond's not much better, either. I've never seen him like this in all the time we've known him."

"I'll come straight away," Jacqueline told him. "Merry's still here, so she can put away the valuables and lock up, and I'll come in early tomorrow morning and do the rest. Depending on how Hannah is by then."

"Thanks, darling," said John gratefully. "We really need you. By the way, do you know if Hannah had a doctor in Dundee?"

"No, I don't think she does. She told me she's still registered with her doctor in Edinburgh, Dr…oh, I can't think of her name. Anyway, by this time of night, you'll only get a duty night-cover locum, so I wouldn't try too hard to find Hannah's own doctor just now. Just get somebody who will check her over and take any necessary immediate steps. I'm on my way, darling. Be with you in an hour at the outside."

Drummond returned downstairs carrying both Hannah's mobiles.

"Jacqueline's on her way," John told him. "How's Hannah?"

"She's just lying there with her eyes open, but she won't say anything," Drummond replied. "Her eyes didn't follow me when I went into the bedroom, or when I asked her about her phone. She seems to be getting worse, rather than better. I'm really worried, John."

"Well, Jacqueline said any doctor would do, just to make an initial assessment. Would you like me to phone our surgery and see if I can get the out-of-hours doctor?"

"That sounds good," Drummond said. "I'll try and get Flora, and see if she can give us any more background on this mother-person."

He bent over Hannah's personal mobile, soon found Flora's number and made the call.

"Is that Flora?" he said, as soon as she answered. "This is Drummond MacKeagh in Dundee."

"Drummond," Flora said, "It's good to hear you. How are you?"

"I'm fine," he replied. "But Hannah is in a bad way. She's had some kind of collapse, apparently. I'm trying to find her doctor. Do you happen to know the surgery with which she's registered?"

"Oh, yes, it's the same as mine. In fact, I introduced her there, ages ago, before she joined you in Dundee. But can't Hannah tell you?"

"She's in some kind of fugue," Drummond explained. "Something to do with a woman claiming to be her mother just turning up on the doorstep. I didn't know her mother was still alive, even."

"Oh, Drummond, keep her away from her mother!" Flora exclaimed. "Drummond, it's not for me to tell you about this in detail, but Hannah had a terrible time with her mother when she was a child." Flora was worried now for Hannah, and for how much she could properly expose of her background, even in Hannah's own, very pressing, interest. Nonetheless, Drummond was holding the baby, as it were, and needed at least minimal information. Flora made a decision.

"When Hannah went to university, she cut herself off from the woman, and has kept it that way ever since. Even the mention of the idea of 'mother' frightens Hannah. It makes her shudder, visibly. If you love Hannah, keep her mother away from her, for goodness' sake."

Drummond took in the urgency in Flora's tone. He wished Hannah had told him about all this before. However, the situation was as it was now, and it had to be handled. Flora was still talking.

"Here are her doctor's details, Drummond, but she's in Edinburgh, the doctor I mean. I suppose Hannah thought that wouldn't be a problem since she's here so much of the time." Flora gave the details to Drummond at dictation speed, and he scribbled them on the corner of one of the journals which were stacked beside his armchair. "But you'd do better at this time of night to get somebody local, in Dundee. And tell Hannah I'll be up to see her on Saturday. I've meetings in Newcastle tomorrow. And look after her, Drummond," Flora commanded him, knowing it was unnecessary but unable to prevent herself. "Hannah's a very, very dear girl."

John came back into the sitting-room from the hall, where he had been negotiating with his surgery's out-of-hours service to send a doctor round to look at Hannah.

"Someone will be around in about an hour," he told Drummond. "They wanted us to take her to A&E, but I told them she was in a state of total collapse and we didn't feel competent to move her. I had to lay it on a bit thick, I'm afraid, Drummond, since Hannah isn't one of their patients, but they accepted it in the end."

"That's really good of you, John," Drummond thanked him. He'd never been so grateful that he had decided to let his top floor to John and Jacqueline. "Flora gave me Hannah's doctor's contact details, but she's in Edinburgh, so I won't be able to contact her until tomorrow."

"If it's necessary to get hold of her tonight, the doctor who's coming can do it through the health service network," John said.

They had done all they could, or needed to do, on the issue of medical advice, and that matter could be parked temporarily. Time was passing. It was a quarter past eight already. Those women might be back on the front steps at any moment, and he and Drummond urgently needed a strategy to deal with them, for this evening at least.

"Drummond, when those women come back," John began, "and we have to assume that they will, you need to be prepared."

"I know it's a lot to ask, John, and you've done so much already..." Drummond was not used to asking for help from somebody else and found it really difficult. Now he was way out of his depth, however, and he recognised that John was just the man to help him. "Could we say, *we* need to be prepared for them to come back?"

"Are you asking me to act for you in this matter in my professional capacity?" John asked formally.

"I suppose I am," Drummond replied. "I really need some help here."

"That's fine, Drummond," John said, relieved, "but professional ethics require you to come out and say it, rather than me just taking over and doing it for you off my own bat. Which I would have done if necessary. I'm just glad we've sorted that out. All right." He gathered his thoughts. "I think the best thing we can do is to assume this is a matter of harassment, in which case, ultimately, we may need an order from the Sheriff Court to restrain them and keep them away from Hannah and this house.

"When they do come back, therefore, we'll need to know their names and where we can get hold of them to serve papers, if that becomes necessary. It would be good if we could also get them to say what is their purpose and intention in coming here. The first thing I'd suggest very strongly, though, is that those women are not on any account to be allowed into any part of the house. So, will you go around and bolt all the doors again, and I'll telephone Jacqueline's mobile to tell her to come to the back door and shout to be let in when she gets here?"

John reached for his mobile again and Drummond quickly went around the house to secure the outer doors. Slipping upstairs, he looked in on Hannah again. She had not moved, except possibly to have curled even more tightly under the duvet. Her eyes were closed, and her breathing was regular and easy, but she did not move when he gently stroked her head. There was no more he could do for her at this stage, so he tried consciously to restrain the concern that was growing to vast proportions in his mind and his stomach. Concentrate, he told himself, concentrate, on keeping the women out, on keeping his beloved Hannah safe.

Downstairs, John was standing by the window overlooking the street, as if keeping watch.

"When they do come back," John said, having clearly given this some thought, "will you come out onto the front step with me, but say nothing, nothing at all, however much they try to provoke you?" Drummond nodded, determined to try to control himself, difficult though it might well become.

"I'll present myself as your solicitor, and hint at a possible allegation of trespass, just to keep them out. Also, we won't let them know how they've affected Hannah. That would just give them a lever. The objective for tonight is just to get rid of them. Ah," he said, looking out of the window, "that looks like them coming down the street now. Here we go."

Letting themselves out of the front door, John and Drummond stood on the top step and watched the two figures and their baggage approaching the house. Drummond had let the Yale lock spring closed behind them, but kept his keys ready in his hand in case he and John needed to retreat inside hurriedly.

As the women reached the foot of the steps, John stepped forward and said firmly, "That's far enough, ladies. Please don't try to climb these steps."

"Good God, now there are two of them!" the older woman said in an arrogant tone, but she did not lift her foot to the bottom step. The younger one smirked again. That seemed to be her standard reaction to everything and, Drummond thought, it was not nice to see. It looked aggressive, a precursor to physical action on a lesser prey.

"So who are you to prevent me visiting my daughter?" The older woman put down her cases on the pavement, and the younger one followed suit with her binbags.

"My name is John Shields," John announced. "I'm a solicitor, and I represent my client Dr MacKeagh, who is the householder here and does not want you on his property."

"I have never heard anything so ridiculous in my life," the woman said, bending as if to pick up her suitcases. "I'm here to visit my daughter, and there's nothing in law to prevent me doing that, to the best of my knowledge."

"In Common Law, madam," John said with all the authority he could muster, "you have no right of entry onto this property without the householder's permission, which he is at present unwilling to give you."

The woman straightened again and met John's eyes, her mouth narrowing with determination.

"I know my daughter is here. I saw her this afternoon, before her spot of typical silliness. Now, let me in to see her. You two have nothing to do with this. I'm not here to see you, and I'm coming right past." She put one foot on the bottom step.

"No, madam, you are not," said John, "not without the possibility of consequences."

"Well," she said, "perhaps you think that making a fuss in the street will best serve your client's interest?" She laid emphasis on the word 'client'. "What is this place, anyway? Some kind of refuge or hostel? What has my daughter got herself into now? Clearly, if she is in trouble, she needs her mother's care."

"Not this evening, madam. Now, if you give me your name and that of your companion, and tell me where we can contact you, if that should become necessary, I will consult my client more fully tomorrow, and we'll see where we go then."

"Give them nothing," the younger woman muttered, barely audibly. "They'll only tell the filth."

"I resent and question your tone and your attitude, young man," the older one said to John. "I see no reason to give you any information, particularly after the way our time has been wasted. Goodness knows how we will find accommodation at this time of night, out here in this barbarian suburb of a grubby barbarian town. And after coming all this way out of motherly affection! It is too hurtful."

She composed her facial expression into what was obviously a practiced and totally artificial precursor for distress. John was unmoved. He had noted the women's unwillingness to give him any information about themselves, and decided to use it against them, in a legal ju-jitsu move.

"Well, I'll just note your names, if I may, anyway," he said, "and maybe a telephone number? No doubt you both have mobile telephones we can reach if we need to do so, though my client very much hopes that won't be necessary. I think, given that information, we can probably call the matter closed, for the present at the very least, and hope to see no more of each other, madam."

The ploy worked and the women picked up their bags and walked away down the street without another word to each other, or to John and Drummond. As they turned the corner, a car drew up outside the house and a tall middle-aged man got out, taking an efficient-looking flight-bag from the rear seat-well. Looking up the street after the departing women, the man carefully locked the car and approached the steps.

"Dr Klein," he announced, with a slight European accent, as he crossed the pavement. "Out-of-hours service. To see Ms Lethbridge, I believe?"

Chapter Fifteen

Drummond unlocked the front door and opened it for the doctor, while John introduced Drummond and himself briefly. Inside, Drummond said to the doctor, "Hannah's upstairs. Will you come with me, doctor?"

At the landing, Drummond carefully opened the bedroom door, and was about to enter. The doctor placed a restraining hand on Drummond's arm, and said quietly,

"I must ask you to stay here while I examine my patient, Dr MacKeagh. Tell me briefly what has brought her to her present condition, please."

"We're not clear, doctor. I got home at around 6.40 to find those two women, whom you will have seen outside, on the front steps. The front door was locked and bolted from the inside. I shouted to Hannah, and, after a few seconds, heard the bolts being drawn so that I could get in. I found Hannah collapsed in a heap on the hall floor, crying and obviously in a state of panic."

"What explanation did she give you?" the doctor asked.

"None. She just said, 'bed', but nothing else. I carried her up here and put her under the duvet. Then my upstairs tenant, Mr Shields, whom you've met, arrived, and those women came back…"

"And Ms Lethbridge has said no more since you put her to bed?"

"No, doctor. She closed her eyes and seemed to sleep at first. More recently, her eyes have been open, but she hasn't seemed to see me."

"And, to your knowledge, has this happened to Ms Lethbridge before?"

"Not to my knowledge, doctor," Drummond replied.

"And you have known her how long?"

"Two years, almost exactly."

"All right, Dr MacKeagh. Now, is there another woman in the house?

"Not yet, but Mr Shields' partner is on her way home."

"Please ask her to join me if she arrives before I finish examining Ms Lethbridge," the doctor said. "I will leave the door open enough for you to see and hear us, but you must stay here for the present."

Drummond nodded and the doctor went into the bedroom, putting down his bag just inside the door. He opened it, took out a pair of rubber gloves, which he pulled on, and turned towards the bed.

"Good evening, Hannah," Drummond heard him say quite loudly. "I am Dr Klein. Can you hear me, Hannah? Can you see me?" There was clearly no response from Hannah. The doctor put his hand on her forehead and gently rolled back one eyelid, then the other.

"Dr MacKeagh," the doctor said, "I need to lift the duvet to check for external injuries."

"I understand, doctor," Drummond replied.

The doctor lifted the duvet briefly, and then let it fall lightly over Hannah's quiescent body. Going around the foot of the bed, he did the same again to check her back, and the back of her head, touching nothing. Straightening, he stripped off the gloves and tucked them into his pocket. He turned back to the shape on the bed.

"Hannah, can you speak to me, please?" he said one last time, but Hannah's body neither spoke nor moved.

Picking up his bag, he said to Drummond,

"Dr MacKeagh, we will go downstairs."

At the bottom of the stairs, Drummond led the way into the sitting-room. John turned from the window where he had been looking for Jacqueline.

"Please sit down, doctor," Drummond said, and they all sat.

"You are not a medical doctor?" Dr Klein asked Drummond.

"No, I'm a chemist. At the university."

"So. Well, Ms Lethbridge presents no apparent sign of physical trauma or symptoms of illness. However, she is obviously a very sick young lady, and I would normally advise removal to hospital as a precaution. For observation, you understand."

"I'd much rather she stayed here, doctor," Drummond suggested, "unless there is something the hospital could actually do for her."

"No, I doubt there is anything to be done," Dr Klein replied, "until she regains consciousness of her surroundings and can speak again, or unless her physical condition changes. I believe that her condition is the result of a great psychological trauma. Ninewells Hospital has a psychological specialisation, as you probably know." The doctor paused for thought. "If we send her there, they may well attempt to bring her out of her fugue with drugs, which might help, but equally might simply complicate matters. Until we know her history, one cannot be sure either way. Also, for the time being, she would simply be occupying a bed, and they are already busy."

Drummond was shocked by the doctor's mention of psychological difficulties.

"If you are prepared to take care of her here for the time being, there is probably little point in subjecting her to a move which would result in her waking up in surroundings which are unknown to her," the doctor mused. "That might frighten her again. What we need next is her file, to enable me to see whether there is anything relevant in her history. Is she taking any medication regularly, Dr MacKeagh?"

"Not to my knowledge, doctor," Drummond replied carefully.

"Perhaps you would be so good as to check her handbag, and the bathroom cabinet, and so on, just to make sure?" Dr Klein requested.

"Of course," said Drummond, standing up, "though I'm pretty sure there is nothing."

He left the room, and Dr Klein turned to John.

"Mr Shields, I must ask this, and you must answer truthfully. Are social drugs taken in this house?"

"No, doctor, not by any of us," John replied firmly.

"Forgive me, Mr Shields, but I must press the point. Never, any drugs, of any sort at all? A little, grass, an occasional…?"

"No, doctor, nothing." John reached into the top pocket of his jacket and withdrew one of his business cards. "I know this is no guarantee of my truthfulness, but it may help to set your mind at rest."

Dr Klein glanced briefly at John's card, then slipped it into his pocket, as Drummond returned.

"This is all I found, doctor," handing over a small white box.

"Ah so," the doctor said, noting the name of the prescribing doctor on the label of the box of contraceptive pills and returning it to Drummond. "Gentlemen, we will leave Ms Lethbridge in your care for now, on the clear understanding that you call me immediately should any aspect, *any* aspect, of her condition change, at any time of the day or night. My colleagues will obtain her file as quickly as possible tomorrow." He raised his eyebrows slightly, and indulged in a small sigh at his own optimism on the subject of health service bureaucracy. "One of my colleagues will no doubt visit to see how she is. Are you content with that proposal, Dr MacKeagh?"

"Of course, doctor," Drummond said, relieved that he would not be separated from Hannah.

"Then I will wish you both goodnight," Dr Klein said, rising and picking up his bag to go.

As Drummond closed the front door behind Dr Klein, he heard the buzz of John's mobile.

"Hallo, Jacqueline," he heard John say.

As he re-entered the sitting-room, John was listening intently to Jacqueline.

"Come to the front door, then, darling. I'll be ready to let you in."

John broke the connection and looked up at Drummond with a serious expression.

"It sounds as though the women are camped in the Close. Jacqueline thought they were just a couple of beggars, so she's coming... Ah, here she comes," John said, looking out of the window and then hurrying to the front door.

Jacqueline reached out to hug John as she came through the front door. Pushing it firmly shut, he returned her hug warmly.

"Darling, what on earth is going on here," she demanded. "You sounded so upset, so...military, on the phone..."

"I fear we are under siege, sweetheart," John told her.

"Where's Hannah? Is she all right?"

"She's upstairs. She's very poorly, and the doctor has been."

Drummond came past them, on his way upstairs to check on Hannah again.

"Drummond, I'm so very sorry," Jacqueline said, disengaging from her partner. "Tell me what I can do? And somebody tell me what's happening?"

From halfway up the stairs, Drummond said, "John will explain everything. He's being great! I must see that Hannah's all right."

Jacqueline slipped off her coat as she went into the sitting-room, and John told her the story as far as he knew it. Drummond returned as Jacqueline was saying, "So those beggars are...well, they're claiming to be, well, one of them...*related* to Hannah somehow? And they frightened her into a coma, or something? Oh, this is terrible. Oh, poor love! Oh, Drummond, may I go to her? I'll sit with her for a bit. It might settle her a little."

She hardly waited for anyone's permission before she dashed from the room and up the stairs.

"John, you are both helping so much!" Drummond said. He had never been so grateful to anyone.

"No more than we can. Tell us anything we can do to help."

"Will you give me a hand to get the table in the kitchen across the door to the area?"

"Of course. Good idea."

It took the strength of both of them to shift the heavy Deal table. Marks on the floor-bricks showed that it had not been moved in decades. Maybe longer. When it was done, however, Drummond looked relieved.

"I'll sleep in the sitting-room tonight," he decided. "Well, in the armchair. They surely wouldn't try to break in, would they? But I'll feel happier where I can deal with them if they do."

"No unprovoked violence, though, Drummond, whatever happens," John warned, his lawyerly instincts fully active. "*If* they do take the matter so far as to try again to get in, phone the police. Keep your mobile out and ready. And plugged in, so it's constantly powered up! And, if they do get into the hall, stand two steps up on the stairs, if you can. If they touch you, minimal force, remember, but you're a braw laddie, and I'll be close behind you by then. Would you like me to stay with you or share watches?"

"No, no," said Drummond, "though the offer's appreciated. You've your work tomorrow."

"And ours, maybe," John said. "I'll certainly begin drafting papers for a possible non-harassment order. But until we know exactly why they're here and what they want and how they frightened Hannah so badly, we're on the back foot, I'm afraid."

The night passed without alarm. Jacqueline spent it on a chair beside Hannah's bed, and Drummond spent most of it patrolling from the front window to the back door. Every few hours, John came downstairs in his dressing gown, checked on Jacqueline and Hannah and on Drummond, and made tea and a sandwich for those who wanted them. By half-past eight in the morning, John had showered, shaved and dressed, and gone off to work. Drummond held a long telephone call with his assistant Isobel, to tell her that Hannah had been taken ill, he wouldn't be in to the lab until further notice and to give her detailed instructions on how to look after his current experiments and who to inform of his absence.

In the early light, Jacqueline reported, Hannah had finally stirred and opened her eyes. She had seemed to recognise where she was and who Jacqueline was, but her only words were to ask for help to get to the bathroom. In fact, she was so weak that Jacqueline had had to lift back Hannah's duvet, and more or less haul her body to the edge of the bed.

She found Hannah's nightdress, slipped it over her head and, with an effort, managed to get her arms through the shoulder-straps. Raising her off the bed by sheer physical strength, Jacqueline realised that Hannah's legs were incapable of supporting her. The journey to and from the bathroom exhausted both of them. For much of the time, Hannah's eyes had remained closed, and not a word had passed her lips.

When Jacqueline lowered her back onto her bed, Hannah simply curled up again and closed her eyes, not attempting to reply to Jacqueline's suggestion of soup, but not resisting the holding of a bottle of water to her lips. After three tiny swallows, she tried to withdraw her head fractionally and Jacqueline removed the bottle to prevent spillage.

Flora telephoned Drummond shortly before nine o'clock, but there was nothing to tell her. She sent her love, asked what she could bring when she came up to Dundee the next day, and undertook to tell Elisabeth Preston that Hannah had been taken ill suddenly from an unknown cause. Just before ten o'clock, Jacqueline 'phoned the library and cried off work, explaining her absence in relation to the serious illness of a close family friend who needed someone to care for her, at least in the short term. She would keep them up-to-date as the matter developed.

***

Drummond was dozing at about three o'clock in the afternoon, when the doorbell rang. Jacqueline rushed down the stairs to the door, hoping it might be a doctor with some kind of explanation for Hannah's collapse and wishing to prevent Drummond from being disturbed. She unbolted the door and opened it, to find a tall, dishevelled woman alone on the top of the steps.

"Thank God, a woman! Now we'll get all this sorted out," the woman drawled.

202

Jacqueline tried to close the door, but the woman had stepped forward, one shoulder blocking the door and a thigh pressing Jacqueline back into the house.

"Drummond," Jacqueline called. Then, as the woman pushed forward, Jacqueline screamed it as loudly as she could, "Drummond!"

"I want to see my daughter," the woman shouted into Jacqueline's face. "Where is the silly girl? Hiding from the inevitable instead of dealing with it, as usual, I suppose." She turned towards the foot of the stairs, crossing in front of Drummond as he came blearily out of the sitting room.

"Police first, and then John," Drummond said decisively to Jacqueline, who was leaning, shocked, against the wall of the hall. He started up the stairs after the woman, shouting, "Mrs Lethbridge, Mrs Lethbridge, if that is who you are, or call yourself. Get down here at once. I do not want you in this house."

The woman continued to clatter up the stairs like a runaway train.

"Hannah," she was shouting, "Hannah. Where the hell are you, girl? It's your mother, Hannah. Now get out here at once. We need to talk."

Reaching the landing, she turned unerringly into the bedroom and stopped. Drummond, now only steps behind her, lunged forward to grab at her shoulder, catching the woman off-balance and spinning her so that her face hit the doorpost. Deliberately, her eyes on Drummond's, the woman put her hand to her cheek and pulled her long, roughened nails down her face. Blood slowly welled, and then ran down to drip off her chin.

"You've done it now, haven't you, you bully," she shouted into Drummond's face. "Called the police, have you? You'll be sorry you did that, now you've drawn blood. And all I wanted was to be allowed to see my daughter." She was laughing at him, almost maniacally.

Appalled, Drummond let go of the woman's shoulder, and she slapped him, hard but carefully, so as not to leave a lasting mark. He stepped back a pace, enough to let Jacqueline pass them both and get between the woman and the bed. Hannah had rolled over, still curled, and was facing away from the door. She was now huddled into the corner of the bed as near to the wall as she could get, and she was emitting a strange continuous noise, a sort of "wooo, wooo, wooo", like an old-fashioned steam train pulling a heavy load up a steep banking.

Spinning around, Jacqueline had no compunction in slapping the woman in her turn. It caused the woman to pause. Drummond took quick advantage of this and again grabbed the woman's arms and pulled her hard out of the room and across the landing. Changing his weight, he gave her a hard push sideways, so that she staggered through the open doorway of the third, unused bedroom. Giving her another push, he slammed the door after her, turned the key—the fortunately long-ignored old key—to lock her in and slipped the key into his jacket pocket.

"The police are on their way," Jacqueline called, "but I didn't have time to phone John."

"I'll do that," Drummond replied shakily, "and I'll try to get a doctor around for Hannah."

In the bedroom, Jacqueline reached across the bed to pull Hannah towards her and enfold her again in her arms. They were both crying now and Hannah was still making her peculiar noise, but with long, gasping breaths between each sound. Her eyes were closed and her body was like that of an old rag doll. Her head and limbs flopped as if her mind was no longer exerting any will or control over them.

Getting through to John's office, Drummond took deep breaths to calm the panic that was threatening to consume him. The receptionist's routine enquiries as to Drummond's name and business tested his patience to the limit. He wanted to bawl at her, "hurry, woman, hurry", but managed not to give way to that need. The wait to be connected to John was only seconds, but seemed unending. Finally, John answered.

"John, it's Drummond. We've made a right mess of it here. That bloody woman got in, and we've called the police, but—"

"OK, Drummond," John said, "I'm on my way. Tell the police I'm coming and say as little as possible to them until I get there." He cut the call abruptly and Drummond called to Jacqueline.

"What's the number of your surgery?"

"It's in my phone," Jacqueline replied. "The phone's on the chair in here."

Drummond could scarcely bear to enter the bedroom. Hannah was no longer groaning, but she was still crying. Tears were flooding down her face and the front of Jacqueline's sweater, where Hannah's head was cuddled into her chest, was soaking wet. Drummond grabbed Jacqueline's 'phone and went back onto the landing. Bumps and bangs were coming irregularly from the third bedroom, but Drummond ignored them. The surgery telephone system was of course clogged. "Your call is important to us. You are third in the queue," the disembodied electronic voice told him, and he felt the rage of frustration rising dangerously in him. He must control it, he told himself.

Outside, a police car double-parked opposite their door, and its blue light began to flash in warning. Two police officers, one male, one female, got out and put their peaked caps correctly on their heads before climbing the steps to Drummond's front door.

"Call from Ms Vernon?" the male officer asked as Drummond opened the door. "You've a wee bit of trouble, is it? We'll just come in and have a quiet talk about it all, shall we?" He was already into the hall by this stage, his colleague close behind him.

"In here, is it?" the constable said, turning into the sitting room. "You'll not need that just now, Sir," gesturing to the mobile still bleating its plaintiff and useless message, "You are first in the queue", from Drummond's hand.

"I'm trying to get a doctor for my partner. She's in a terrible way upstairs and I've been trying to get through to the surgery for minutes."

"Aye, all right," said the constable, taking off his cap. "We'll just sit down, you and I, shall we, Sir, while my colleague goes and sees how things are upstairs?"

His female colleague gave him a brief nod, and Drummond heard her measured pace going up the stairs. This was clearly a well-drilled team. By the time he and the constable had sat down, Drummond was already responding to the calming effect of the officer's so-far gentle authority, and was able to deal with the surgery's routine questions. He explained that Hannah had had another severe shock, and tried his best to encourage them to send a doctor to her as soon as possible. They undertook to do this, but without promising when that would be. It was all he could do, and Drummond turned back to the constable sitting opposite him.

***

Upstairs on the landing, the female officer called, "Ms Vernon? Police."

"In here," Jacqueline replied.

The officer pushed open the door, but did not come into the bedroom. Looking around, she asked, "And who's the lassie with you?"

"This is Hannah Lethbridge."

Still cradled in Jacqueline's arms, Hannah seemed to have stopped crying at last and had returned to her former comatose state. Jacqueline could feel that

Hannah's body was gradually relaxing and her breathing was settling to a more normal rate.

"She's in a terrible state," Jacqueline said.

"Ms Lethbridge?" the constable said, gently. There was no answer.

"Can she speak at all?" the constable asked.

"She hasn't said anything sensible since that woman first arrived yesterday afternoon," Jacqueline told her. "When she came back this afternoon and rushed in here, the woman, I mean, Hannah just made noises and tried to hide in the corner of the bed. She was in a dreadful panic, quite out of control of herself, but she's calming down now. We really need some medical advice. Dr MacKeagh's phoning the surgery, I believe."

The officer nodded silently.

"And who is this woman, and where is she now?" she enquired.

"The woman said she's Hannah's mother." At the mention of that word, Hannah stirred slightly, but gave no other sign of involvement in the proceedings. "Drummond—Dr MacKeagh—got her out of the room, but I didn't see what happened then."

Jacqueline turned her attention back to Hannah and the officer nodded again.

"And what was that clattering from next door?" It had stopped now. Presumably whoever had been making all the noise was listening to Jacqueline's exchange with the constable.

"I don't know," Jacqueline replied, "but I don't think it's doing Hannah any good."

The constable turned towards the next door along the landing. Addressing it, she called out, "This is the police. Can you open this door, please, and identify yourself?"

A voice, muted by the thickness of the door, said indignantly, "Of course I can't open the door. I've been locked in here, unlawfully detained."

The officer tried the doorknob.

"And who are you, madam?" she asked.

"I'm Hannah's mother and I want to see my daughter. I have every right to visit my daughter, I presume?"

"Aye, well, we'll see about all that. I take it you're in no immediate danger in there?"

"No, but that's no thanks to that thug who pushed me in here. And injured my face."

"Are you bruised, madam. Or bleeding?"

"The bleeding has stopped now, but no doubt there'll be a scar."

"We'll get you out of there as soon as we can, madam. Just stay quietly in there for a minute or two, if you will, please."

She turned away from the door, taking her notebook and pen from a pocket in her tunic and returning to speak to Jacqueline again from the bedroom doorway.

"So who lives in the house permanently, Ms Vernon?"

"My partner, John Shields, and I rent the top floor. John is Dr MacKeagh's solicitor, and he's on his way home now, I understand."

The constable raised her eyes. Legal advisers tended to get in the way at the beginning of an inquiry, in her opinion, and often suggested that there was something to hide. They usually made things unnecessarily complicated, anyway, especially if they came on the scene before the first formal statements had been taken. This was going to be a hell of a domestic, she thought, and sighed gently.

"And Dr MacKeagh?"

"He's the owner," Jacqueline said, "and lives in the rest of the house with Ms Lethbridge. She's his partner."

"How long have you lived here, Ms Vernon?"

"John and I have been here about four years. Hannah joined Drummond something over six months ago or thereabouts. I don't know how long Drummond has been here."

"And had Ms Lethbridge mentioned any family to you before this woman turned up yesterday?"

"No. I suppose I imagined her parents were dead. She never said anything about them, anyway, either of them."

"OK," said the officer. "I'll leave you be for now and consult my colleague."

There was a muffled shout from the third bedroom.

"We'll not be much longer, madam," the constable called back, and turned to go down the stairs.

In the sitting-room, the male constable had been taking much the same information from Drummond, and recording it in his notebook similarly.

"Constable MacAllan," the female officer called as she got to the bottom of the stairs.

As they conferred quietly in the hall, the front door opened to admit John.

"Good afternoon, officers," he said. "I'm John Shields. I'm Dr MacKeagh's solicitor." He handed a business card to each of them and the officers stored them away carefully in their notebooks.

"Aye, Sir, so we understand," said the male constable. "I've seen you in Court."

"Now," John said, "before we go any further, I'd be glad if you'd let me consult with my client and see what's been going on here since I went to the office this morning."

"Aye, Sir, of course," said the constable, "but you'll mind there's a woman locked in a bedroom upstairs who's anxious to be out of there, and says she has a wound, so the sooner we get her out the better, maybe."

"Quite so, constable," John agreed. "We'll be as quick as we can."

John joined Drummond in the sitting-room, closing the door behind him.

"So she's in?" he asked, "And wounded?"

"She rang the bell about three, I suppose. I was dozing and the damned woman pushed past Jacqueline and ran up the stairs before I could get in her way. When I got upstairs, she was just going into the bedroom. Hannah had opened her eyes, wide. I'd never seen her look like that, or anybody else, thank God. It was horrifying to see."

Drummond shook his head from side to side at the memory. "It really was as if she'd seen a ghost, or witnessed a murder, or something. Her whole body was stiff, and her mouth wide open, too. Anyway, I grabbed the woman's shoulder, and tried to swing her out of the room, and her cheek hit the doorpost. It wasn't a hard impact. She didn't flinch, let alone show any pain or dizziness. She just put her hand up to her cheek and scratched down it, deeply, as if it were somebody else's, until the blood ran. And then she smiled."

It was John's turn to shake his head ruefully, but he let Drummond finish his story.

"Oh, and then she gave me a slap. Anyway, I managed to push her into the small bedroom, and lock her in. I was afraid of having to hit her in self-defence. There's nothing much in that room, and I didn't care what she did in there, as long as she couldn't get to Hannah again."

"How many times did you push her?" John asked.

"Oh, two or three, I suppose," Drummond replied. "Once I'd got her off balance with the first push, I tried to keep her that way, like hitting a moving snooker ball into a pocket."

"And on which parts of her body did you push her?"

"Oh, just her arms and shoulder," Drummond said.

"Quite sure?"

Drummond thought for a moment.

"Yes, as far as I can remember."

"And where was Jacqueline when the woman scratched her cheek?"

"Either coming up the stairs or on the landing behind me," Drummond replied.

"So she wouldn't have seen the scratch, or maybe the slap?"

"That's possible," Drummond confirmed.

"Hm," said John, concerned. "OK. Now, I guess the police will want you and the woman to go with them to the station to make statements. Jacqueline will stay with Hannah, no doubt. I'll be with you every step, so don't worry about it. It's your word against hers as far as the so-called wound is concerned. She's already in the wrong, so keep the indignation out of sight. This is a horrible incident, this woman tried to get into your house and seriously upset your partner, whom you used minimal force to defend. OK?"

"Aye," said Drummond. "What about that other woman? There's been no sign of her since Jacqueline saw both of them yesterday evening in the Close at the back of the gardens. If she's around and sees us going off with the police, will she try to get in independently, and …?"

"Well, I'll warn Jaqueline before we leave. And we'll tell the officers about the second woman. I'll see if I can get one of them to have a walk down the Close before they go, and make sure she isn't there. If she is, of course, they'll want a word with her as a material witness in relation to purpose at the very least."

He walked to the door, opened it and said, "Thank you for that, officers. I'm up to speed now. I hope we haven't taken too long."

As the officers came into the sitting room, the male constable said to Drummond, "We'll have that key now, Sir, if you please, and get that woman out of your bedroom."

John held up a hand to prevent Drummond complying.

"We'd much rather that you heard a brief summary from Dr MacKeagh of the events that have taken place here in the last 24 hours, before you let her out. We will suggest that she is not totally innocent in either her motives or her actions." He paused and gathered his thoughts. "You should also know, officers, that, when she first came here yesterday, she was in the company of a second woman. They were both seen by Ms Vernon later in the day apparently loitering in the Close behind this house. We feel that her continued presence nearby might well constitute a threat of further attempted incursion."

The male constable turned to his colleague.

"Mary, would you go and see what Ms Vernon has to say about this second woman?"

Before she could leave the room, however, there was an anxious call from the first floor.

"Drummond, can you come and help me, please? Quickly?"

The officers were up the stairs before Drummond could move, but he was close behind them. Jacqueline's head poked out of the bathroom.

"I'm so sorry," Jacqueline said, "but I just need Drummond, on his own." Turning to Drummond, she explained, "Hannah needed to come in here and I got her here, but afterwards she collapsed again and I can't lift her on my own."

Repeated crashes and thumps were coming from the third bedroom and muffled shouts of, "Let me out! Let me out now! I demand to be let out!"

"Soon, madam!" the male officer called firmly, but with little effect.

"Hannah was doing fine until *she* started all that noise. It was when she heard the woman's voice that Hannah's legs gave way." Going into the bathroom, Drummond found Hannah lying on the floor, trying and failing to raise herself on one arm. When she saw Drummond, she gave up her efforts, just gazed up at him with utter thankfulness and burst into floods of tears again.

"Oh, darling," she murmured. "Oh, Drummond."

He bent down, gathered her to him and carried her across the landing into their bedroom. There was clearly going to be a pause in proceedings as far as Drummond was concerned, while he reassured and quieted Hannah. The female constable took the opportunity to get Jacqueline's account of what had been going on, and made copious notes. Her colleague took John back downstairs to the sitting-room.

"Maybe you'd just give me the background, as you know it, Sir, not for evidence, but just so I can start to get a full picture of what's going on here. Ms Lethbridge is clearly in a very distressed state. There's more going on here than meets my eye, at present at least, I believe."

They heard the female constable and Jacqueline coming down stairs. Constable Mary Bows put her head into the sitting room to say, "Ms Vernon's very kindly going to make us some tea. I'll go with her." To her colleague, she said, "The kitchen's in the basement of course."

The other officer nodded.

In the twenty-five minutes it took Drummond to quiet Hannah, and Jacqueline to return to her bedside duties, John had set out the actions which had led to the present situation, as he knew them. Once Jacqueline had gone back to Hannah, and Drummond had returned downstairs, Constable MacAllan again demanded the key to the third bedroom, and, at John's nod, Drummond handed it over.

"You'll not let Hannah see her, will you, officer?" Drummond pleaded. "Or hear more of her than is necessary?"

"No, Sir. We'll talk to the woman in that room to begin with, and I'll close the door on Ms Lethbridge and Ms Vernon."

Chapter Sixteen

Reaching the first-floor landing, Constable MacAllan put his head into the bedroom, nodded to Jacqueline, and quietly closed the bedroom door. The noise from the third bedroom seemed to have ceased. Going to the door to that room, the constable rapped on it firmly, and said, "Madam, this is the police. We're going to come into your room. Kindly step right away from the door and stand where we can see you immediately as we come in."

"Oh, do get on with it, man," the woman said from inside.

Constable MacAllan unlocked the door carefully and pushed it open. The woman rushed at him, but the constable restrained her easily and spun her around so that he could grasp her hands behind her back.

"Now, settle down, madam," he demanded, "or I'll have to cuff you, and you won't like that one bit."

In the doorway, Constable Bows adjusted her feet and settled her weight, ready assist her colleague if necessary, but the woman relaxed and Constable MacAllan released her, as his colleague stepped into the room, closed the door behind her and stood in front of it.

"Now, there's a very sick young woman in the next room," Constable MacAllan said gruffly, "so we're going to have a quiet conversation in here, with no raised voices, if you please." Both officers drew out their notebooks. "So, first of all, madam, your full name?"

"I am Irene Lethbridge," the woman said, her nose back in the air as if the constable should have recognised her as someone of some importance.

"And your address, madam?"

"Until recently, I lived at 49, Baddington Drive, London SW15."

"And an address in Dundee?"

"Well, I expected to be welcomed here, of course, with my daughter. As yet, I have not arranged any alternative accommodation in Dundee."

"We understand you have been in the town for more than 24 hours, madam," Constable MacAllan said. "So where did you stay last night?"

For the first time, the woman's haughtiness was dented.

"Um…" she said, "I didn't note the address."

"So, did you camp out in the open air, then?" the constable asked.

The woman sniffed, but offered no other reply.

"When were you last resident overnight at the London address, madam? We'll be checking with our London colleagues, you understand, of course?"

"God, is all this really necessary, officer?" the woman said, gathering herself to step forward and then relaxing again as she saw the hard looks in the eyes of both the constables.

"Yes, madam. We need to know who you are in order to assess the claims we understand you to have made. Now, you were here yesterday with another woman, we have been told. And who is she, might I ask?"

"That was my other daughter," Mrs Lethbridge stated.

"Name?"

"Naomi."

"Address, Madam?"

"Most recently, with me."

"So," said the constable, appearing to write laboriously in his notebook, "both of no fixed abode at present."

Mrs Lethbridge appeared likely to expostulate loudly, and then relaxed in silence. Constable Bows had withdrawn slightly, and turned. She appeared to be passing information over her radio and asking for routine checks to be made.

"And where is your daughter Naomi at this moment?" her colleague asked Mrs Lethbridge.

"I've no idea," Mrs Lethbridge answered, dismissively. "She is a grown woman and has her own life, of course. We're not bound together."

"But how long have you been…together?"

"Six months, or so."

"And where was she before that, do you know, madam?"

"I really don't know, constable. She's never said, and I do not interrogate my children, especially not since they've been grown up and left home."

"I see, madam," said Constable MacAllan. "Well, it may be as well if you might remember something more about Naomi's likely whereabouts, since we'll be asking you to come to the station to make a statement about all the goings-on here, and she'll no doubt wonder where you've got to. You'll have made arrangements to meet somewhere later, no doubt?"

Mrs Lethbridge appeared to ignore the officer's implied question.

"There is no need for anyone to go to the police station," she began hotly. "This is all a misunderstanding. It can be cleared up at once, when Hannah stops playing the fool. Where is the girl, anyway?" She raised her voice. "I want to see my daughter. I demand to see her now."

"Enough of that!" Constable MacAllan raised his own voice in volume and tone just sufficiently to overcome Mrs Lethbridge's. "I said we'd do this quietly, or we'll be down the station faster than you can imagine…" pause …"madam. Now, tell me about that scratch down your face."

"That thug did it," the woman said indignantly. "He assaulted me. He hit me and pushed my face against the doorpost."

The officer raised his eyebrows and examined the wound closely from a safe distance.

"And that bruise on the other side of your face?"

"He did that at the same time."

"Um," the constable said, writing in his notebook. "Now, why are you here, madam? Why did you come to Dundee and to this house?"

"To visit my daughter, of course."

"When did you last visit her here, might I ask, madam?"

"We haven't seen each other for some time, officer. It was well time I came to see she was all right."

"Exactly how long ago were you last in each other's company?"

"Oh, I can't remember."

"Weeks, months, years?" the constable inquired helpfully.

"I can't remember," Mrs Lethbridge insisted. "Why ever does that matter? She is my daughter. I felt a duty to make sure she was all right. It looks as though I was correct to do so, too. She is clearly in the hands of a…a thug of some sort. She may even not be here of her own free will. Had you thought of that, officer?"

Dr MacKeagh did not strike Constable MacAllan as the sort likely to abduct a young woman and hold her against her will, and with a solicitor's connivance and support. On the other hand, you never knew, in this job. You really never knew what a body might do, once you put them under sufficient stress. He shook his head sadly at some of his memories. Anyway, it was time to make a decision.

"Right," he said, "we'll all go down to the station, and you can make a formal statement, madam."

The woman drew herself up.

"Are you arresting me, constable?" she said, as if surprised and shocked at the possibility.

"Not yet, madam, though I will if you don't cooperate with us, quietly and willingly." He recited the formal caution of suspects of a crime, to underline the seriousness of the situation as he saw it.

"You have no grounds at all for—"

"Oh, aye, I mind I have, madam," the constable said tiredly. Why did the hoity-toity ones always take that line? "When we get out of this room, now, you'll follow my colleague closely down the stairs. I shall be right behind you. If you make any attempt to go elsewhere, I will restrain you. Do you understand?"

"Don't you dare lay your hands…"

Constable MacAllan was becoming very bored with all this. The woman's cliched responses and her readiness to change her tone at will, like a rather poor actress on some television drama, suggested to him that this wasn't her first involvement with the police.

"Come on now, Mrs Lethbridge," he said. "You'll be going straight down the stairs, one way or another. Let's do this in a quiet, civilised manner, shall we?"

The woman shrugged, sniffed and her head dropped slightly. She said nothing, but seemed ready at last to accept the situation. Constable MacAllan nodded to his colleague, who opened the door, and stepped to the head of the stairs.

"May I not even just see my daughter before we go?" the woman asked.

"No," Constable MacAllan said, very firmly. "Get on with you."

In close company, a constable in front of her and another behind, Irene Lethbridge descended the stairs to the ground floor.

***

In the street, another car pulled up behind the police vehicle, and a well-dressed middle-aged man propped a "Doctor Calling" card against the windscreen. He got out, came around the car, and lifted a bag from the front passenger seat. He climbed the steps to the house and rang the doorbell. Constable Bows opened the door and blocked the entrance.

"Dr Fieldham," the newcomer announced himself, "to see Ms Lethbridge?"

"First floor, doctor," said Mary, "first door on the right. We'd like a word with you when you've seen Ms Lethbridge, if you please."

"Of course," the doctor said, and started up the stairs. Constable MacAllan put his head around the sitting-room door.

"May Mrs Lethbridge sit in the back parlour, Dr MacKeagh, while we wait for colleagues?"

"That's fine, officer," Drummond agreed, "though there's only one chair in there, I'm afraid."

"That's all she'll need, sir, thank you." Constable Bows moved past the woman and looked into the back room.

"That's OK, Hal," she said to her colleague. He gestured Mrs Lethbridge before him into the room and told her to sit down. Quietly, he said to his colleague, "Will you radio for backup, please, Mary? The street's getting blocked up. We need someone to look after the traffic and idle gawpers, as it's getting on for coming-home time. When the others arrive, take one of them around the streets and the back Close, and see if you can see this other woman anywhere. If you can't find her, put in a call to get the Sergeant to issue a "stop on sight and bring in" for her, but I mind she'll probably be long gone from round here, and probably from the town, by now."

He went into the back room and closed the door, stationing himself comfortably in front of it as a precautionary measure. Upstairs, Dr Fieldham greeted Jacqueline and Hannah.

"It's good to see you, Doctor," Jacqueline said. "I'm so glad it's you. Thank you so much for coming."

"Ah, you're a bit more awake this afternoon, then, Ms Lethbridge?" the doctor noted. Looking up at him, her face paper-white and her eyes wide and pleading, Hannah could only nod silently. Her chin juddered occasionally, but she was no longer crying. For her, doctors were trusted sources of comfort. She was so glad to see him and gratefully allowed him to check her vital signs, look into her eyes and take her blood-pressure.

"Is it like last time, Hannah?" he asked gently.

Hannah nodded again, but a little more vigorously.

"There, there," the doctor said, patting her shoulder. "And you've no strength?" Hannah shook her head, and Jacqueline said, "She can't get across the landing without help, doctor, a lot of help."

"Yes," said the doctor, "I'm not surprised. So we need to get food into you, Hannah, for strength. Soup will be fine to start with, Jacqueline. Try solids by tomorrow night or Sunday morning, maybe a little toast with lots of jam or marmalade. Sugar for energy. But don't force any of it on her. She'll eat all she can, won't you, Hannah?" Hannah nodded briefly. "And all the fluid you can get down her, especially water, Jacqueline."

"Yes, doctor."

"Call me if you need to do so. I'll be back on Monday afternoon to see how you're going on, Hannah. Good afternoon to you both."

Hannah said, indistinctly, "Is Drummond all right?"

"That's Hannah's partner," Jacqueline said. "He's downstairs, with—"

"I've not seen him yet," Dr Fieldham replied, cutting her off, "but I'll be having a word with him, no doubt, when I go downstairs."

"Take him my love," Hanna murmured.

"That I will, Hannah, that I will."

Downstairs in the hall, Constable Bows asked, "What can you tell us, doctor?"

"It will save time if I tell you all at the same time what little I know. Where's your colleague, officer?"

"He's occupied in the back parlour, doctor. But Dr MacKeagh and Mr Shields are in the front room. Let's go in there."

They went into the front room. Drummond introduced himself to the doctor, and invited everyone to sit down.

"Well, first of all, Dr MacKeagh, Hannah instructed me to bring you her love." Drummond smiled with relief.

"So she's talking again," he said.

"Hardly," the doctor explained, "only for the most essential things." He smiled, and gathered his thoughts. "Hannah has had a most dreadful shock and has suffered another collapse."

"Another?" Drummond exclaimed.

"Yes," the doctor continued. "I've spoken to her Edinburgh doctor, who has seen her file, of course, and is sending a copy up to me here, though I probably won't get it until next week. However, it seems that, eight years ago, when

Hannah was living in Cambridge, she had a similar incident. Complete collapse and subsequent prolonged psychotherapy, through which she was deemed to have made an excellent recovery. What has she been doing up here in Scotland, can you tell me?"

"She's a reader-editor with MacWhinney-Preston, the Edinburgh publisher," Drummond said proudly, "and teaches here at the university."

"Well, her recovery was indeed excellent," the doctor said. "That's a good sign in itself, though recovery from repeated incidents tends to become progressively more difficult. That's a generalisation, of course. Matters of the mind are aye unpredictable." He nodded his head from side to side. "Anyway, it will take her some days to gain enough strength and stability to get out of her bed, never mind out of the house. In fact, I would strongly advise against any such attempt in the immediate future."

He looked meaningfully at Constable Bows, who was writing industriously in her notebook. "I'll be able to suggest a positive way ahead when I've seen Hannah's file, and talked to her doctors in Cambridge." Turning to Mary, he said, "I'll contact you as soon as I've been able to do that, Constable."

"Thank you, Doctor. We'll need to take a statement from her here, then?"

"Yes, I think so," the doctor agreed, "but not for at least a week. She won't be coherent yet, and it will do nobody any good to press her. She'll just collapse again, and possibly with worse effects. Again, I'll let you know when she's ready for that."

"Aye, doctor," Mary said. She wasn't sure what her Inspector would say about that, but, well, that was a bridge to be crossed later.

"I'll come back and see her on Monday," the doctor said, rising to leave.

"No prescription, doctor?" Drummond inquired.

"Oh, no," the doctor said decisively. "Do more harm than good. Rest, total calm, increasing food and drink. I've briefed Jacqueline. Good afternoon to you all."

***

As the doctor was going down the front steps, another police car drew up in front of the first. Two more male officers got out, took in the sign in the windscreen of the doctor's car, and nodded to him before coming up the steps to where Mary waited to let them in.

"Aggravated trespass, with assault, maybe," she greeted them briefly. "Will one of you keep the traffic moving in the street, Hal says, and look after any idlers. The other, with me around the neighbourhood, especially the back Close behind these houses. We're after a youngish woman looking like a beggar, carrying black bin-bags. Might answer to Naomi Lethbridge. Might make off. Probable witness, if not co-conspirator. If apprehended, bring her to the station for interview. There's another witness inside for transport, too, when we've time. I'll just tell Hal you're here, and then we'll take a quick tour round the block from opposite directions."

One of the officers went back to the street. There were no onlookers yet, but, with two cars flashing blue light all over the front of the houses, it was quite likely there would be, as people came home from work.

Mary tapped on the door to the back parlour. Speaking to Mrs Lethbridge, Constable MacAllan instructed the woman firmly, "I'll be right outside this door, so just stay seated where you are."

"I need the bathroom," Mrs Lethbridge demanded.

"Soon enough," Hal replied unsympathetically.

The officer went out to the hall, closing the door behind him. Mary told him what Dr Fieldham had said.

"Also, Alistair and Willie have arrived. Alistair's looking after the street, and Willie and I are about to go around the block looking for this Naomi."

"Aye," Hal agreed. "Don't be too long. The sooner this one's at the station," he nodded over his shoulder towards the back-parlour door, "the better. She's full of self-confidence, and not a bit in awe of us."

The constables were soon back empty-handed. Willie went into the back parlour to relieve Hal, while Mary went upstairs to tell Jacqueline what was going to happen next.

"May I have a word, Ms Vernon, out here on the landing, so as not to disturb Ms Lethbridge?"

Very gently, Jacqueline disengaged herself from Hannah's arms, gave her a hug and whispered in her ear that she would be back straightaway. On the landing, Mary explained that the woman and Dr MacKeagh and Mr Shields, would be taken to the police station to make statements, "just routine, at this stage, but it might take a little while." Would she be all right here on her own with Hannah until the gentlemen could get back, or would she like a constable to remain on site, bearing in mind that there was as yet no sign of the younger woman? Jacqueline thought that it would be good to have an officer on the premises. He'd be welcome to help himself to tea and biscuits and so on, she said, and Mary returned downstairs to tell Willie he'd drawn a soft number for the rest of the shift.

Hal had explained to Drummond about the need for him to come to the station. There was the assault allegation to be sorted out, he said, apart from everything else.

"I'll be coming with Dr MacKeagh, of course," John said immediately, and would not be put off by the officer's half-hearted suggestion that it wasn't necessary. "I'll just slip upstairs and make sure Jacqueline's all right."

"Aye, but sharpish, now," Hal agreed.

"I've told her we'll be leaving an officer on the premises until you get back, Mr Shields," Mary said to his back as he went quickly up the stairs. Once John was back, Hal ushered the men into the sitting-room. With that door closed, Mrs Lethbridge was escorted out of the parlour and down to Alistair's car. Mary put her into the back seat carefully, and went around the vehicle to join her on the other side, and Alistair switched off his blue light and drove away.

"We'll follow you in my car, constable," John said to Hal MacAllan. "Then we'll not have to bother you for transport home afterwards," and Hal was happy to agree.

In the car on the way to the police station, John warned Drummond, "There is likely to be a lot of hanging about before you're interviewed. The constables will be writing up their notes, and trying to find out as much as they can about these women before they are formally interviewed. We're here, easily checkable around Dundee. The incident happened in your house, and we're being open with them, so they'll do the difficult stuff first. and they'll be hoping that one of their patrols picks up the other woman. So we'll just have to be patient. But there'll be loads of very stewed tea available, and Jacqueline and the other officer are with Hannah, so try to worry about her as little as you humanly can."

Drummond was worried, though. Of course he was. Hannah had not told him about her collapse in Cambridge, or that her mother had this power to terrify her. He wasn't hurt by the omissions. He was suddenly aware of how…well, withdrawn, he had been himself in the early days of their relationship. However, he was beginning to realise how much more he needed to know about the things she valued, the things she enjoyed, the things she feared and why. How else could he protect her as he so earnestly wanted to do, more than anything else in the world?

And no doubt she might well be feeling the same about his life before they met. They must talk, really talk, he decided. When all this was sorted out, they must go away together alone for a long time, perhaps months. Not for good, just for the thorough resetting of their love for each other.

At the police station, they were shown into an interview room, invited to sit at the table, offered tea ("Not yet, thank you," John said, and he and the constable smiled knowingly at each other) and left alone. Out of their hearing and sight, Mrs Lethbridge had been given similar treatment, which she had received with much less grace and a lot more bluster, but no different result except that a female constable was stationed, unspeaking, inside the door from the room. Two and a half hours later, two detectives came into Mrs Lethbridge's interview room and sat opposite her, the younger placing a thin file on the table before him.

"I am Detective Sergeant Fraser, and this is Detective Constable MacVey," the older officer said. "This is an interview under caution in relation to allegations of aggravated trespass and assault. And you are?"

"You know very well who I am, and—"

"I've not the time to waste on you, madam," the DS said quietly. He'd seen it all before. "You can sit here as long as I like, all night if necessary. I'm here till morning, and the day shift staff can take over if we're not done by then. I'd advise you just to answer our questions as straightforwardly as possible. Then we can all find somewhere more comfortable to be as soon as possible. Now, name?"

"Irene Lethbridge."

The sergeant repeated the words of the formal caution, and of Irene's rights at this stage.

"So, Mrs Lethbridge," he continued, "I understand that you have no address in Dundee?"

"I was coming…"she stopped as the sergeant looked up into her eyes. "No."

"And you claimed earlier to have last lived at …" He consulted the paper which his constable slid in front of him. "…49, Baddington Drive, London SW15."

"Yes."

"And that is the residence of a Mr Michael Journeyman?"

"Yes, it was when I lived there." She was visibly shaken to hear that name.

"And how long did you live there?"

"I don't remember exactly. Quite a long time. Why on earth…" She stopped speaking again.

The sergeant drew a deep breath, consulted the paper in front of him again and asked, "Now, why did you leave that address, Mrs Lethbridge?"

"I don't remember. I expect we had simply had enough of each other. Relationships do sadly break up from time to time, you know, sergeant."

"Who else was customarily living in that house at that time, Mrs Lethbridge?"

Irene was thinking hard. How much did they know? How much more did they know? Already. And how far away had Naomi run by this time? Not far, since Irene had never trusted her with more than minimal amounts of cash.

"Well, Mrs Lethbridge? Who else was living there?"

Irene looked down at her lap.

"My daughter, Naomi."

"Now, was Naomi—in your company, shall we say?—when you first moved into Mr Journeyman's house, Mrs Lethbridge?"

Irene said nothing.

"Was your daughter Naomi with you when you first went to live with Mr Journeyman?" the sergeant asked more firmly.

In the ensuing silence, the constable leaned forward, pen poised to make a note, and murmured audibly, "The witness declined to answer."

"I'm not declining to answer," Irene protested wildly.

"Then, was your daughter Naomi, or was she not, with you when you moved into Mr Journeyman's house?" the sergeant pressed.

"No." There was no way out of this. She was going to have to tell them at least a little more. In her turn, Irene drew a deep breath, recrossed her legs beneath the tabletop and said, "I hadn't seen Naomi for years, not since she was a baby." It wasn't worth waiting for the next few questions, they were too obvious. "She was taken into care when she was born. I was…going through a bad patch. I had nowhere to live, temporarily, at that time… Anyway, I came across Naomi in a café one day a year or so ago, or rather she came across me. She came in through the door, came straight across to where I was sitting, and said, 'You're my mother,' and I nearly died of shock. At first, I thought she was Hannah, but I couldn't believe she was so much changed. Anyway—"

"And what convinced you of her relationship to you, Mrs Lethbridge?" the sergeant asked.

"Oh, she had this grubby birth-certificate, and other papers from the social services, and fosterers, and so on. And she looked like her father, the bastard. He chucked me out of his house when I started to show with Naomi. Claimed she wasn't his, but of course, I knew she was."

"And so you took her back with you to Mr Journeyman's house?"

"She made me. She blackmailed me. She's been blackmailing me ever since. I may have been in a bad place, sergeant, just recently, but she's been in far worse ones and seems to think I'll always find a way to improve hers, however slightly."

There was a tap on the door of the interview room and Constable Bows put her head in.

"May I have a word, sergeant," she said.

The sergeant rose slowly and joined Mary in the corridor.

"We've heard some more from the Met," Mary explained. "They're interested in Mrs Lethbridge and Naomi in relation to the disappearance of Michael Journeyman. And the Transport Police got Naomi at Waverley, trying to board a London train without a ticket. They're bringing her here for us. She thumped one of their boys, so we've got her on a holding charge, for a while at least. She was carrying a blade, too, nasty bloody thing, apparently. Lucky she didn't have chance to use it."

The sergeant raised his eyebrows. More paperwork and complication.

"They'll have bagged and tagged the knife, no doubt?" he inquired. The constable nodded. "Good enough. It may be some use to the Met. Thank you, constable," he said and returned to interviewing Mrs Lethbridge.

"Now, what's all this about Dr MacKeagh assaulting you, Irene?" the sergeant said, sitting down heavily behind the table. Irene knew she was in trouble. No more, however ironic, 'madam', let alone 'Mrs...' Nonetheless, they seemed to have moved off the subject of Michael Journeyman, which was a relief to her.

"Yes, he pushed me against a doorpost and then imprisoned me in that poky little back room." Her hand went to her scratched cheek in dramatic emphasis.

"And you can't think why he might have wanted to do that?"

"Certainly not, sergeant." Irene was regaining a little composure and a little indignation.

"You'd been told by Dr MacKeagh that he didn't want you in the house, I understand? And by his solicitor, Mr Shields?"

"I had a right to see my daughter. She was so peculiar when I greeted her. I was worried about her."

"And how long was it since you'd last seen her?" the sergeant asked.

"I can't remember. Some time, I admit. Which was why I wanted to see her."

"And you were homeless, and fleeing the Metropolitan Police." The sergeant said it as a statement rather than a question. Irene blanched, but the sergeant continued. "Why did you think that your somewhat questionable 'right' to see your estranged adult daughter outweighed Dr MacKeagh's undoubted right to refuse you, or anyone else without authority, admittance to his property?"

He sat back in his chair. "Your appearance in her room clearly caused huge distress to Ms Hannah Lethbridge, Dr MacKeagh's partner. Can you tell me in what way Dr MacKeagh's actions might have exceeded the minimal force necessary to prevent further distress to Ms Hannah Lethbridge? Hmm?" Hardly giving Irene time to respond, the sergeant said, with some vehemence, "No. Well, I can't see it, either. Now, you'll kindly put this glove on your right hand, if you please, Mrs Lethbridge. Straight away please!"

Irene stared at the latex glove the sergeant had drawn from his jacket pocket. Reluctantly, she put it on as he had instructed.

"You see, Irene," the sergeant continued, "I have reason to believe that that scratch on your cheek was self-inflicted, for the sole purpose of incriminating Dr MacKeagh. We call that attempting to pervert the course of justice. Our forensic scientists can find no blood on the door or doorposts to that back bedroom, and I'm going to have them take scrapings from under your nails in a moment, as I have asked them to do with Dr MacKeagh, so we'll soon see whose flesh is under who's nails, won't we?"

Irene slumped.

"All right, all right, so I scratched myself to make it look better. But he did push me against the doorpost, and bruised my face, and it hurt like hell!"

"Stay there and don't move," the sergeant said to Irene. He raised his voice, and called, "Constable!" The female officer entered from outside. "She's to stay here and she's not to remove that glove, come what may.

"I still haven't been to the bathroom. I need to go, sergeant." Irene turned to her one very last resort.

"Soon. I'll take a chance you can wait a wee bit longer."

Back in the detectives' big office, DC MacVey asked, "How much of all that do you want me to type up, Sarge? I've plenty else to be doing."

"All of it," Fraser replied, "if only to cover ourselves. She's artful as the chimps in the Edinburgh Zoo, that one. But, aye, I'll talk to the boss and get them both sent down to London, and they can do what they like with them. Meanwhile, get the SOCO in there to check under Irene's fingernails."

"And Dr MacKeagh's, Sarge?"

"Aye, for the record, though I've no doubt about his story, or hers, and he's had more than enough time to wash his hands of any evidence that there might have been. And tell London we've got them both."

The constable reached for the telephone on his desk and the sergeant went in search of his inspector to bring him up-to-date.

Chapter Seventeen

Another half-hour later, DS Fraser reappeared at the door to the detectives' room.

"MacVey," he shouted, "has that Naomi Lethbridge arrived yet?"

"Yes, Sarge," MacVey answered, looking up from the computer screen in front of him. "She's in a cell, 'cos of the knife and the thumping of the Transport constable."

"Have the Met sent us any more on Journeyman?"

"Yes, Sarge," MacVey said, laying his hand on a well-filled file which was lying by his keyboard.

"So...?"

"Journeyman's sister made a fuss after she had gone around to his house. She hadn't seen or heard from him for six weeks, and their father's birthday was coming up, or some such thing, and it wasn't like Journeyman to go off for so long. Anyway, there was a lot of mail behind the door, and no sign of anybody, and none of Irene's stuff about, and the kitchen cleared out and smears on some of the surfaces, but she didn't think much of it 'cos she didn't think much of Irene, or her housekeeping..."

The DC paused to take a breath. The sergeant waited patiently.

"Anyway," the DC resumed, "the local police told her the usual and did nothing, except that Journeyman's boss is friends with the Chief Super. in that Division, and they're both in the Rotary..."

The pressure on the sergeant's patience was clearly increasing.

"Well, Journeyman's boss said to the Chief Super he'd a man missing, Journeyman, and what should he do, and the DCS mentioned the name to—"

"Aye, aye, lad. Eventually somebody went around to Journeyman's house, and they found...?"

"Well, the DC who went in with the sister didn't like the smears—"

"And the SOCOs found...?"

"Blood, Sarge. There'd been an attempt to clean it up, but..."

"Journeyman's blood?"

"They've sent it off for analysis by this new DN...something-or-other business, Sarge, which is supposed to be so brilliant. But there was a partial print in one of the blood-smears, which looked like Journeyman's, by comparison with those in his bedroom."

"I know how they do it, lad!"

"Yes, well..."

"Do they have a body?"

"In bits, in binbags, in the garden shed, Sarge. There wasn't a head. They must have dumped that somewhere else."

"Aah." The sergeant breathed out heavily with relief. At least there was some tangible evidence of Journeyman's death. He had not just exercised his right to go off somewhere without telling anyone.

"But nobody thought the smell was anything peculiar," the constable continued. "I suppose they all keep themselves to themselves down there, and why should the neighbours know what a man keeps in his garden shed?"

The DS nodded.

"And is there any background on this Naomi?" he asked.

"Oh, yes, Sarge. She's got a sheet as long as your arm. In and out of youth custody and then prison, since she was a kid. Thieving, assault, drugs, soliciting, you name it, almost."

"I'll take a wee look at all that, then, before we see her."

He took a beaker from beside the big metal teapot on a table at one side of the room, filled it, slopped in milk and two heaped spoonsful of sugar, looked at the resulting brew disconsolately, picked up the file from MacVey's desk, and took both to his desk at the end of the room.

Ten minutes later, Fraser looked up from the file, peered into his beaker with a look of slight surprise that it was empty, put it down on his desk and shouted to Detective Constable MacVey, "Tommy, get that Naomi into an Interview Room. We'd best check she is who we think she is before we send her down to the Met. Right fools we'd look if she wasn't. And put her under caution and read her her rights. And then go and do the same with Irene again, before we go any further."

"Yes, Sarge," MacVey said, reaching for his phone and pen.

Assembled with MacVey and a female constable in Interview 4, Fraser spent two minutes appearing to read the file again, while hoping that this would help the stress to get to Naomi. However, she showed no sign whatsoever of tension. Her customary smirk adorned her face, and she seemed to sit quite comfortably across the table from the police officers with one leg crossed over the other. Fraser looked up at her and wrinkled his nose.

"Been on the run, have we, Naomi. No washing facilities where you've been recently?"

Naomi ignored the insult.

"So what are you doing in Dundee?" Fraser asked her conversationally.

"No comment."

"Oh, it's going to be like that, is it?" Fraser said resignedly. "Ah, well. Name, for the record?"

"No comment." The smirk broadened slightly.

"Well, your wee bits of papers suggest that you are Naomi Lethbridge, daughter of Irene Lethbridge, whom we also have here. Is there any reason I should doubt that information?"

"No comment." She crossed her legs the other way, but made no other movement.

"Aye, well," the sergeant said again with his usual patience. "We'll be charging you with assaulting a police officer, whoever you are, and then sending you down to London. Our colleagues there want a word with you, you'll understand."

Naomi's expression remained unmoved. She showed no reaction to the news of this escalation of her situation.

"Wanna brief," she said.

"Oh, indeed," the sergeant sighed sourly. "Well, it's hardly worth bothering the duty solicitor here. You can see about all that when you get down South. Get her charged and fingerprinted for identification, Constable, if you please," he said, standing and collecting his papers back into his file. "And then get her back in a cell."

***

More used than Drummond to police routines, John had withstood better than his client the prolonged, lonely delay and was simply glad to see the DS back in the interview room at last.

"I'm sorry we've taken so long, gentlemen," the sergeant apologised, "but you'll think it worthwhile, I believe. I need formal statements from you both about your knowledge of the recent events at your house, Dr MacKeagh, and then you can both go home."

"And the woman claiming to be Mrs Lethbridge, sergeant?" John asked. "Will she be free to bother us anymore? Or her associate?"

"No, no," the sergeant assured him. "They'll be going down to London to talk to some of my colleagues down there, and we're laying charges against them up here before they go, anyway, so they'll not be able to bother you for a while."

Drummond was clearly not certain that the sergeant's assurance was sufficient. John placed a hand on his sleeve, however, and Drummond subsided.

Placing a pad of statement forms and a pen in front of each of them, the sergeant said, "By rights, I should separate you to write your statements, but I see no point in that tonight. Mr Shields' experience of all this will no doubt speed the process for you both, and you'll want to be getting back home as soon as you can." He gave a mighty yawn. "As will we all."

"Could this not wait until the morning?" Drummond asked.

"No, it's better done and time-stamped now," John explained to him, "to keep the procedure clear in case it's examined at some point in the future. It won't take long." To the policeman, he said, "Thank you, sergeant. I'll put my head out of the door and let someone know when we've finished."

Nonetheless, it was another hour before it was all done, they had recalled the sergeant and the statements had been signed and gathered into the sergeant's file.

"I'll be needing a statement from Ms Lethbridge, of course," the sergeant said tiredly. "In fact, until she writes that up, we've no precise idea of what happened when the women first turned up on your doorstep, Dr MacKeagh. However, that's of little consequence at present, as it happens."

"We'll get nothing coherent on any of that from Hannah for a while, sergeant," John said. "You haven't seen her yourself, have you? She's had a total collapse. She can't even get out of her bed by herself without falling on the floor and has said nothing more than a very few single words at a time since that woman arrived. I can get her attending doctor, Dr Fieldham, to certify that she is unlikely to be capable of making a formal statement for some days, without further detriment to her condition, if that would be helpful?"

The sergeant had no doubt that John would arrange for exactly that to be done, if the matter were pressed.

"Well, you'll let us know when she improves sufficiently, Mr Shields?" the sergeant said, accepting the inevitable. "We'll have to have something for the file sooner or later, but there's no great rush for it that I can see, where those two women are going."

"I'll bid you goodnight, then, gentlemen," the sergeant continued, rising and extending his hand across the table, "and I'm grateful for your patience. I hope you find Ms Lethbridge improving when you get back home. I'll have the constable who's there radio-ed and told to see you safely in, and then he can come back here and chalk off."

It was almost one o'clock in the morning. Drummond could hardly get out of the police station quickly enough.

Inevitably, at that time in the morning, there were no parking spaces on their street when they got back home. John had to park around the corner, and they hurried back from the car to the house, with Drummond setting a very brisk pace. Inside the front door, they found the constable had come into the hall as soon as he had heard Drummond's key in the lock, and was standing four-square before them, ready for anything.

"All's quiet, gentlemen," he reported, relaxing. "There have been no events and I've not heard the lassies upstairs, except Ms Vernon made me tea a couple of times."

They thanked him profusely, and let him out of the front door to return to the station.

"John, I don't know how to thank you for this evening," Drummond said, "or Jacqueline."

"Och, come on," John said. "And it's all worked out. Now, let's get upstairs and see how the girls are doing."

In the bedroom, Jacqueline sprang up from her chair beside Hannah's bed to receive John's hug and kiss.

"We are so very glad to have you both back," she mumbled, from within John's arms.

Drummond was bending over Hannah. In the dim light from the landing, he could see that her eyes were glistening, but at least they were open and her body was straighter in the bed.

"Oh, darling," she murmured, even more quietly than Jacqueline. "Oh, my darling Drummond." Very slowly, she stretched out one arm for his hand, and he took hers before reaching over to kiss her gently, first her lips and then her forehead and her eyes. Her tears wet his mouth and cheeks, but already she seemed better than she had been when he had so reluctantly left her earlier.

"Was everything all right?" Jacqueline asked, over John's shoulder. "At the police station?" There were still elements of deep concern in her voice.

"Yes, yes, indeed," Drummond said, hoping to calm both their girls as he might have done a pair of nervous ponies. "John was magnificent, and the women are in custody and are shortly to be carted off to the police in London, if they haven't already been despatched on their way. It's all sorted, my loves!"

John, without the blessing of Drummond's ignorance, knew that the details would drag on and raise their heads repeatedly in the coming weeks, like worms rising from their burrows after rain, but he said nothing. *Sufficient unto the day...* he thought. Jacqueline beamed, however, and gave him another enthusiastic kiss.

"My hero!" she told John, before taking her arms from around his neck.

"Come on, you," John told her. "Let's all get at least some sleep tonight. Thank goodness tomorrow's Saturday."

"Will you be all right, Hannah love?" Jacqueline turned to ask.

"Oh, yes, thank you," Hannah said. Was her voice already a little steadier, a little stronger?

As the bedroom door closed behind John and Jacqueline, Drummond slipped off his jacket and said, "I must have a shower, honey. I stink of that police station and the wait."

"No," Hannah said, quietly but very firmly. "I want you here, with me."

Drummond undressed quickly. Pulling off his socks, he heard Hannah struggling to move to the far side of the bed. Under the duvet, he rolled towards her and she moulded herself to him and held him as if she would never again let him go.

***

Flora arrived the next morning, just before eleven o'clock. Drummond was up but not properly awake. He had not dressed. His tatty dressing gown was loosely tied when he came to the door, and his thinning hair was all over the place. Opening the door, he stared for a moment at Flora in surprise.

"I am so sorry, Flora," he began. "So much has happened. I'd quite forgotten you were coming."

He stepped back to let her in.

"Is this all right, Drummond," she said. "Is Hannah all right? I had to come and see, and I've brought a few things in case you haven't been able to shop and so on."

"Of course, it's fine," Drummond replied, recovering. "And Hannah's still very weak and shocked, but she'll be so glad to see you! I was just making her some soup, which is all she'll take for the moment. Come down to the kitchen for a minute, and then I'll pop upstairs and give her room a tidy-up."

"Don't worry about that, Drummond. I know mess, even now Veronica's growing up."

"No, it's a shambles," Drummond insisted, remembering vividly how he had left his clothes scattered everywhere the night before in his haste to hold Hannah and comfort her. In the kitchen, he set Flora to stir the soup and dashed upstairs to make some effort towards dressing.

"Flora's here," he told Hannah, pulling a T-shirt over his head.

"Oh, wonderful!" Hannah said. "Send her straight up. She won't mind how the room looks. And open the window for me, Drummond, and let in some fresh air."

Hannah had not said so many words consecutively for two whole days. Drummond looked at her. She was indeed much better this morning. Her skin was brighter. The greyness of her cheeks and brow, and the rings around her eyes, were fading, and he was hugely heartened for her sake. Pulling on an ancient but clean pair of trousers, he threw last night's clothes into the bottom of the wardrobe, closed its door, grinned at Hannah with relief and rushed downstairs again to take over from Flora at the stove.

In the kitchen, Flora had found a bowl and spoon and poured the steaming soup. She had also unpacked her capacious bags, and the kitchen table was covered with parcels and packages of food, more food than had ever, for years, been in that kitchen at any one time.

"Now, where is she?" Flora demanded in her usual organising voice. "I'll take her soup with me, shall I?"

"First floor, first door on the right," Drummond directed her. "Hannah's…well, compared with yesterday, she's much better, and very pleased to hear you're here."

Flora swept up the soup bowl and spoon, gave Drummond a huge grin and set off towards the stairs.

"I'll be making some breakfast for myself," Drummond called after her. "Will you have some? Just a fry-up of some sort. I'll bring it upstairs when it's cooked, shall I?"

"Lovely!" Flora called back over her shoulder from half way up the stairs, and Drummond reached for the frying-pan to make a start.

As soon as she saw her visitor, Hannah said, "Flora! Oh, Flora!" She tried to raise herself on one elbow, failed and burst into tears.

Flora put down the soup and spoon on the bedside chair and rushed to enfold Hannah in her arms.

"There, there, my darling," she crooned. "There, there. I'm here now, darling. Whatever has happened to you, my love? No, never mind, Drummond will tell me."

Hannah could not stop her tears. They soaked the duvet where they dripped off her chin. Recovering slightly after a minute or two, she mopped at her face with the edge of the bedclothes, and muttered, "I'm so...o...o sorry to cry. It's what I do. I shall do it for weeks, I expect."

Flora pulled back a little and looked at her.

"You've been here before, haven't you, darling?"

Hannah nodded briefly.

"Ah, well, never mind that, now," Flora said. "We'll have a little of this soup and then I'll brush your hair. Would you like that?"

Hannah nodded again, and almost smiled.

"Drummond's marvellous, but—"

"He doesn't understand what a woman really needs," Flora finished her sentence for her. "Very few of them do, even the best. Men are just different, darling, aren't they?"

Lifting Hannah's shoulders very gently, she pulled at the pillows so that Hannah could be propped a little more upright. Then, taking up the bowl and spoon, she sat on the chair and began to feed Hannah a tiny spoonful of soup at a time.

By the time Drummond appeared at the door, Hannah had consumed all the soup she could manage and had relaxed back onto the rearranged pillows. But she was lying straighter than she had been able to do for the last two days, and Flora's ministrations with the brush and comb had calmed and comforted her. She looked much more Hannah and, truth to tell, felt much more herself, however weakly.

"There's breakfast for you, Flora. Shall I bring it up here or will you have it in the kitchen?"

Flora looked at Hannah.

"Shall I leave you to rest for a little, my love?" she asked.

Hannah nodded gratefully, so Flora rose, kissed Hannah's forehead and grinned at her.

"I'll be back very shortly," she said.

"Yes, please," Hannah murmured, almost asleep already.

Flora turned to smile at Drummond and to follow him downstairs again.

In the kitchen, Flora sat down at the table as though her legs, like Hannah's, would no longer support her.

"Drummond, whatever has happened to her?" she asked. "She's a different girl."

"That she is," Drummond replied ruefully, "but she's a great deal better this morning than she has been since all this began."

"That's your doing, no doubt," Flora stated firmly.

"No, no," Drummond protested. "I've spent most of the last two days defending the front step, or at the police station."

Flora looked even more horrified, if it were possible.

"We still don't know what exactly happened at the beginning," Drummond continued. "Hannah was here on her own, and hasn't been able to tell us yet. I only know the story from scene two, as it were, when I got home on Thursday evening and found these two women sitting outside and Hannah in a heap in the hall."

"And that was Hannah's mother?" Flora said, trying to move Drummond's explanation along. "But who was the other one?"

"Well, that's not clear to us yet, either, though the police said they were sending the both of them to London. Out of our way, anyway, and we're thankful for it."

Flora was sitting open-mouthed at all this. Drummond turned to the stove, and began to dish up two big platefuls of the breakfast which had sustained him every morning—when he had bothered to make time for it—all his life, until Hannah had begun to wean him onto something less unhealthy every now and then. He put down the plates, reached for cutlery and condiments and sat down across the corner of the table from Flora.

"I've not eaten properly since all this began," he said. She shovelled two bacon rashers across onto his piled plate and attacked a sausage.

"So now we've had the bones, tell me everything, in order, from the beginning," Flora begged, and he did.

"All the good bits have been down to John and Jacqueline, you see," Drummond said at last, mopping the remainder of the egg-yolk from his plate with a corner of fried bread, "and the police, though their bit took so long! Still, it has to be right, I guess, if the bad guys aren't to escape on a technicality of human rights." He switched subjects again, a sure sign of how tired his usually logical mind had become. "You haven't met John and Jacqueline, have you. You will, before the day's much older. Jacqueline will be down to see how Hannah is, as soon as she's up. We none of us got to bed until after one last night." He shook his head.

"Can I go back to Hannah?" Flora asked.

"Of course," Drummond agreed readily. "I'll be there myself once I've washed up. And, Flora, tell me what I owe you for all this food." He waved widely at the heaps on the other end of the table.

"No, no," she smiled, and hurried out of the kitchen before he could say any more.

Chapter Eighteen

A fortnight after it had all started, the telephone rang on John's office desk. Picking it up, he heard his receptionist say, "I have Detective Sergeant Fraser on the telephone for you, Mr Shields."

"Thank you. Put him through, please."

He heard the receptionist say to his caller, "Putting you through to Mr Shields", and then heard Fraser's voice.

"Good morning, Mr Shields. Sergeant Fraser, Angus Police, at the Dundee police station."

"Good morning, Sergeant. How are you?"

"I'm fine, thank you, Mr Shields. This is just to let you know that Irene and Naomi Lethbridge have been remanded in custody in London, so they'll be enjoying the hospitality of HMP Holloway for a while; and rather them than me," he said judiciously.

"Yes, indeed, Sergeant," John replied. "You'll want me to tell Ms Lethbridge and Dr MacKeagh, I take it?"

"Aye, sir, if you would be so kind. Not knowing how the lassie is, I thought, if you didn't mind, it would be better coming from you than me phoning the house and ...erm...setting her off again."

Clearly, the sergeant was not a man who was comfortable around what he probably still classified as 'hysterical' lady witnesses, John thought.

"It's early days, sergeant, but I'll tell them you asked after her."

"Aye, sir, thank you," the sergeant said. "I'll let you know if and when we hear anything more from the Met, but, as you're well aware, sir, it'll be months before this case is likely to come to court."

"I'm sure you're right, sergeant," John concurred. "Thank you very much."

"You're welcome, Mr Shields. Good morning to you."

John put down the telephone receiver. He'd tell Drummond the news this evening, and leave it to him to tell Hannah when he thought she was ready, or needed to hear it, or whatever. Poor Hannah, John thought. He'd never seen anyone in such a state of collapse, so vulnerable, and he gave thanks silently for the solid stability and apparently permanent good spirits of his Jacqueline, praying that, whatever it was at the bottom of Hannah's trouble, nothing like it would ever cross their own path.

Whether or not as a result of the news that Irene and Naomi were safely behind bars far away, and likely to stay there for a good long time, Dr Fieldham's corner was approached, if not actually turned, the following week. Drummond, taking advantage of Jacqueline having been at home for the morning, had popped down to the university for a quick visit to his laboratory. Jacqueline, believing Hannah to be sleeping, had gone upstairs to her own flat for a few moments when she heard movement on the landing below.

"Hannah, love," she called. "Are you all right?"

"I'm just going to the bathroom," Hannah replied quietly, in a voice which Jacqueline could only just hear.

"Well, leave the door open so I can hear you if you need anything," Jacqueline told her. "I'll just shake out your bed, so it'll be comfy for when you get back."

It was clear, when Hannah returned to her bedroom, that this first expedition had demanded a great deal of effort, but her eyes were clearer and more alert than before.

"I think I'd like to sit out of bed, if I may," she said to Jacqueline. "Just for a little while."

"Of course you can!" Jacqueline assured her. "You can do whatever you like, my dear."

"I wonder…" Hannah murmured, "I'd love a cup of coffee, if that wouldn't be too much trouble."

Jacqueline was over the moon. It was the first piece of initiative that Hannah had shown for two whole weeks. Jacqueline settled her into the chair, found a blanket in the landing airing-cupboard, tucked it around Hannah, and skipped up the stairs to make the coffee. By the time Drummond returned, half an hour later, Hannah had gone back to bed, physically tired but not sleepy, and Jacqueline was reading to her from one of her beloved books.

"Hannah's been out of bed. On her own," Jacqueline told Drummond, as proudly as a mother whose baby has said his first word.

Hannah smiled up at him from her pillows.

"Honey, that's great!" Drummond told her, kissing Hannah warmly.

"Only for a minute," Hannah said, "and I'm tired now, but it was all right. I'll do it again later, if I may."

"Whenever you like, sweetheart," Drummond assured her, knowing that Dr Fieldham would be very pleased.

By late November, the days were getting shorter and colder outside. Inside the house, however, it was warm and cosy, and its occupants' lives were returning towards what they had previously known as normal. Drummond was spending a few hours a week at the university now. Hannah herself was getting dressed for more and more of the day, and eating as she had habitually done, if even less. Much of the time, she was still tired. Her limbs continued to feel heavy and unresponsive, but she had been moving fairly freely around the first floor of the house. Dr Fieldham was pleased with her progress, and thought she would soon be ready for the next stage.

"I'm wondering whether we should soon plan for some more therapy, Hannah," he suggested gently, on one of his increasingly infrequent visits. He noticed Hannah's eyes widen and her head draw back as if in defence. "Perhaps after Hogmanay, if your progress continues so well?"

"I do wish I could get to Margaret!" Hannah said, and burst into tears again.

The doctor was used to Hannah's bouts of distress by now and gave her a minute to overcome it and dry her face and eyes.

"I'm so so...orry, doctor," Hannah apologised, recovering a little.

"Whisht, no, that's fine, Hannah. You know, I'm not surprised."

"It happens less frequently, these days, but I can't control it, when—"

"It's normal," the doctor reassured her, as he had been doing over the past weeks. "Your emotions are an indivisible part of you, and they have all been shaken up most terribly. They'll settle down, eventually, as you very well know."

Hannah nodded glumly.

"Now, I've been talking to your Mrs Turner, and Dr Walmsley, in Cambridge," the doctor resumed, "and Mrs Turner has suggested a colleague with whom she studied and who is now practicing in Edinburgh. Mrs Turner thinks it would be good, when you are able to do so, for you to consult him."

Hannah nodded again, but without either energy or enthusiasm. The only good news was that this man was a friend of Margaret's, one trusted by her, and therefore necessarily one to be trusted in his turn.

"I know you haven't been out of the house, yet, Hannah," Dr Fieldham said, "but no doubt, when you're ready, Drummond will drive you down to Edinburgh and back. It's not crucial to rush with this, but the sooner we can get you together with Dr Alder, the sooner your progress is likely to accelerate, I feel."

"I'm sure you're right, doctor," Hannah agreed. "Margaret was marvellous."

"Indeed!" confirmed the doctor. "Just look at all you did as a result of your work with her. It's a pity there's nobody as good in the same field here in Dundee, but Mrs Turner is quite sure Dr Alder is the man for you—"

"If that's what Margaret says…" Hannah interrupted him.

"Aye," Dr Fieldham said, smiling and rising, "I thought that's what you'd say. We'll talk about it again in January, Hannah. Meanwhile, go on just as you are."

***

It was to be quite a low-key Christmas in Dundee. Flora and Jacqueline were recruited to shop for such presents as Hannah wanted to give. Drummond was by now quite an accomplished and imaginative food-shopper, showing Hannah occasionally, on the wrappers of some of the tins he brought home, the arcane extended names of some of the chemicals included in their contents on which he or his professor, or a particular colleague, had worked. John and Jacqueline were going to be away for a week from Christmas Eve with Jacqueline's parents in Yorkshire.

For a week before, however, Hannah and Jacqueline made paper-chains and baubles from glue and crepe-paper and string to decorate the inside of the house. Drummond bought a much-too-tall Christmas tree which had to be placed beside the staircase in the hall for want of any other adequate ceiling-height in the house; and he bought a very handsome wreath to hang on the front door.

On Christmas Day, however, bundled against the biting wind but glad of the unseasonal, if thin, sunshine, Hannah began the next stage of her journey back to strength. With infinite care, Drummond helped her out of the house and down the frosty steps to the car, and they set off for lunch with his parents in Glasgow.

Arriving at his parents' house, he supported her to the front door with equal consideration. She had said almost nothing on the journey.

"How are you doing?" he asked, giving her a light hug before he pressed the doorbell.

"OK," she said, tentatively.

"We won't stay much at all after lunch," he promised, and she gave him a weak but grateful smile.

Drummond's family greeted Hannah very warmly, but there were so many of them! Though Drummond was an only child, his aunt and uncle were also at the family celebration, with one of their sons and his wife and their two children. Mrs MacKeagh was particularly welcoming. She gave Hannah a warm hug, and offered sensitive expressions of her shock at what Hannah had suffered, her happiness to see Hannah there with them all, and her hope that Hannah hadn't been too tired by the journey.

Once properly inside the house, and with their outdoor clothes removed, Drummond led Hannah into his parents' living room and made sure that she was comfortably ensconced in a big old armchair with several supportive cushions. Hannah had been tired by the journey, of course. She was still quickly drained of energy by any effort, but had learned to husband for as long as possible what strength she could muster between rests.

"What will you drink, Hannah?" Mr MacKeagh offered. "We've..." He and his brother-in-law were cradling shot-glasses of pale, peaty-smelling whisky, and the ladies had something transparent in taller glasses.

"Or would you prefer something to warm you both through?" Mrs MacKeagh asked thoughtfully.

"Might I have a cup of coffee, please?" Hannah asked. "It would just warm me up."

"Aye, and me too, please, mother," Drummond agreed.

"Ach, driving's the bane of enjoying good whiskey!" Mr MacKeagh grumbled, and his brother-in-law chuckled in support before taking another appreciative mouthful from his own glass.

The presents Drummond had carried into the house were soon unpacked and distributed, and the gifts that had been waiting for Drummond and Hannah were received and unwrapped with grateful thanks. By the time Drummond had put around Hannah's neck the pretty necklace that Mrs MacKeagh had chosen for her, Hannah was close to exhausted. She lay back on the cushions as Drummond perched on the arm of the chair beside her. It was all she could do to smile up at him and take his hand.

"I'm so very sorry to be like this, Mrs MacKeagh," Hannah said, once her hostess had returned with the coffee. "You'll have so much to do, and I know I should offer to help…"

"No, no, my dear!" Mrs MacKeagh assured her, patting her shoulder gently. "Of course you shouldn't. It's just wonderful to see you both, and looking so bonnie together. And it's Elspeth, anyway, and that's Patrick's sister Kattie."

Drummond and his father and uncle turned to the inevitable men's catching-up talk, on their work and the older men's hobbies and the latest news and prospects for the football. Elspeth and Kattie were talking about wool and pottery, but in abstruse technical terms which Hannah could not follow, and did not feel called upon to try. She just let herself recover a little strength, through the comfort flowing to her from Drummond's hand.

Eventually, Elspeth announced, "Now, everything's done, so I've just to dish up." She turned to the older men and raised her voice. "Do you hear that, you two? I'm going to dish up, so into the dining room with you all."

"What can I carry, Aunty?" The children turned from their occupations among the wrapping paper scattered all over the floor, their energy renewed, and dashed out of the room in Elspeth's wake.

Drummond took his hand from Hannah's and laid it on her shoulder. Bending, he whispered through her hair, "Don't rush, honey."

When everyone else had left the room, he put his arms around her in a massive hug and kissed her gently.

"Are you all right, darling?" he asked her, looking into her eyes with concern. "Not too tired yet?"

"No, I'm…managing, love," she assured him, "and I don't want to take you from your family, 'cos you don't see them often. But I'm not sure how long I'll last after lunch."

"We'll not be long, honey. And everyone understands. But it is good to have you here. My mum's very pleased with you, and the old man can't take his eyes off you either, and that makes me very pleased indeed!"

He kissed her again, before raising her from the chair and taking her across the hall to the dining room.

*****

241

Hannah and Drummond were back in Dundee by five o'clock that evening, and Hannah went straight to bed. She had slept all the way home, from the point when the car had pulled away from in front of the MacKeagh's Glasgow house. She had struggled to get all the way through lunch, or to do justice to the piled plates which, generously but misguidedly, had been placed before her.

She recovered by New Year's Eve, to the extent that she could dress and get downstairs again by 11.30 in the evening, in time for Sandy to come first-footing, with Isobel, the requisite piece of coal and a ten-pence piece.

"You'll do better next year, Hannah," Sandy professed, having asked the traditional blessing on the house and household as he came up the front steps. Hannah smiled at him. 'Surely, it can only get better from here?' she thought, but did not dare say. Drummond joined Sandy and Isobel in the appropriate dram and toast, though Hannah still did not trust the effect of alcohol on her weakened body and head. She drank their health just as sincerely in refreshing, ice-cold spring-water, however, and their visitors soon rose to leave.

"We've another two houses to do before we're finished tonight," Sandy said happily swaying slightly on his way to the front door. Isobel grinned, and took his arm.

"It's because he's dark. He always gets asked to first-foot, every year. He's dark all over, you know. And he never takes more silver than that ten p." She giggled, and the rest of them laughed as the door closed behind them.

"It has been a lovely holiday, darling," Hannah said, as she put her arm around Drummond to go upstairs to bed.

"They'll be missing you at MacWhinney, Preston's posh party," Drummond teased her.

"I do miss them all," Hannah agreed, "you know I do, but I could no more go back there yet, let alone to the Hogmanay bash, than fly; and I don't feel able to flap yet, let alone glide."

Tears threatened, but Hannah fought them back, as she had become increasingly able to do in recent weeks. But she was very glad to get back into bed, cuddle up to Drummond, and go to sleep.

Life for everyone in the house had achieved a routine approaching normality by the end of January. Drummond brought Hannah a cup of coffee in bed when he got up at about seven o'clock. He left for the lab. at about eight, unless there was something special in hand there that needed his earlier attention, and returned shortly after five on most days. Hannah got up when she fancied it, mostly about nine, pottered until noon, made a sandwich and returned to bed by two.

She slept until four or four-thirty, then got up to make Drummond's supper and something lighter for herself. Coffee with Jacqueline had resumed most days when Jacqueline was at home in the morning. Also, on her way upstairs when she got home from the library, Jacqueline always called in on Hannah, for a word if Hannah were awake or just to make sure she was all right if she seemed to be asleep. A Saturday morning fry-up brunch had become traditional for the four of them together, if and when they were all at home for the day.

Dr Fieldham's visits to Hannah were by now only fortnightly.

"And I can only manage that because my visits here are very quick," the doctor explained to Drummond. "There's nothing for me to do but assess her progress by eye, and I can see she's coming on nicely, aye, very nicely, Drummond." It was always a relief for Drummond to hear that news.

"Indeed," the doctor continued, "next time I come, I have it in mind to ask Hannah to allow me to make her a first appointment with Dr Alder in Edinburgh. Would that meet with your approval, Drummond? And you'd be free to take her?"

Drummond nodded firmly and assured the doctor he would—come what may!

"It'll take most of the day, of course, with the travelling, whatever is the time of the appointment, though his consulting rooms aren't right in the centre of the city, praise be," the doctor added.

Though the winter cold had not yet begun to ease, Hannah had forced herself to begin going outside again. First with Drummond or with Jacqueline, whose help in getting on her winter boots she more than appreciated, she began by walking the few steps around the garden, and then, with gradually increasing boldness, she went out into the street in front of the house.

On his visit two weeks later, Dr Fieldham reviewed Hannah's physical condition with approval. When he had completed his usual brief tests of temperature, blood pressure and breathing, and she had summarised her activities over the preceding few days, he said to her, "Hannah, I'm thinking you're about ready to begin to see Dr Alder. I spoke to you about him before Christmas, did I not?" Hannah nodded in confirmation. "Well, he's been talking some more to your Mrs Turner, and apparently they're both agreed that, subject to contra-indications, there's little point in going over what you did with Mrs Turner more than cursorily. She thought you had come to terms with your past at the point when you left her." Hannah nodded: she had thought so too, when she had found herself thinking about it a couple of years after she had come to Scotland.

"This recent event suggests, however, that there are still things in the depth of your unconscious that you and Mrs Turner didn't get to, those years ago, and they're still festering," Dr Fieldham continued.

Hannah turned paler, and the doctor noticed the sudden increase in tension around her eyes. He paused, and was gratified to see her relax again slightly.

"You'd realised this yourself, hadn't you?" he asked her gently.

"Um," Hannah said. "It seemed to be the only sensible conclusion to draw from the effect on me of last year's…business. I do remember very well what Margaret and I…talked about in Cambridge. She was so good to me," and this time she had to give way to the tears that welled up suddenly and overwhelmed her.

The doctor noted that Hannah's uncontrollable tears confirmed her need for more therapy, even though she had her emotions under greater control these days than in the weeks immediately after last year's incident. When she had mopped herself and taken several steadying deep breaths, the doctor went on, "Dr Alder's specialisation, I understand, is hypnosis. Do you know anything about such treatments, Hannah?" Hannah shook her head. "Well, very few people who have not undertaken it understand it. In fact, medical science has very mixed views on it." He dipped his head, as if in shame for his more closed-minded colleagues.

Looking up again, he smiled self-deprecatingly, and said, "I myself have never worked with it, but I have the greatest respect, from what I've read, for those who do. With the properly professional precautions, and a step-by-step approach, it has gained some very useful results in appropriate cases, where other approaches, on their own, have done less well. We all, Mrs Turner, Dr Alder and myself, think that you might well find it very helpful."

"Oh, yes, please, doctor!" Hannah said. "I am so fed up with being so stupidly weak, and I hate limiting Drummond's life as I do in my present state."

"You have no prejudice against hypnosis?" the doctor asked. "It's one of those things where the results can be heavily limited by a predilection against the process."

"No prejudice at all, doctor. If it's what you and Margaret advise, I really want to give it a go."

"Then I'll ask Dr Alder to give you an appointment and write to you. I'd guess you'll hear from him in a week or ten days, Hannah."

Dr Alder's letter arrived the following Friday, offering an appointment on the Wednesday next, April 3rd. Having checked Drummond's availability, Hannah telephoned to confirm that she would see Dr Alder then.

***

Drummond dropped Hannah in front of Dr Alder's imposing, stone-fronted building, and went off to park the car. Inside, and faced with a flight of stairs, Hannah sat on a handy chair at the bottom of the staircase to await Drummond's return. Already feeling the effect of the early start that morning, the journey to Edinburgh, and her unavoidable concern over how she would get on with a new therapist, there was no way she was going to try to climb the stairs on her own. Only a few minutes later, however, Drummond arrived and gave Hannah a reassuring hug.

"OK, honey?" he asked her.

"I…suppose so," Hannah murmured and looked up into his face. "I do wish it were Margaret, but…"

Drummond gave her another hug and a kiss, put his arm around her waist, and helped her to her feet and up the stairs.

In the polished varnish of Dr Alder's suite, the receptionist greeted them with a smile. "Ms Lethbridge?"

"Yes," Hannah said, feeling again as she had felt answering the class register at school.

"Do sit down, won't you?" the receptionist invited them. "Dr Alder won't be long now. I believe you were sent a form for you to record your medical history and current medication, if any. Do you have it with you?"

Hannah handed over the required form as the polished wooden door opposite their comfortable armchairs swung openly silently, and a slim, elegant man with short grey hair cut *en brosse* came out. He was wearing a well-cut, light grey three-piece suit, and carrying a pair of rimless reading-glasses in his left hand.

"Ms Lethbridge," he said, "I am Dr Alder. How do you do. And Dr MacKeagh." He had clearly been thoroughly briefed by Dr Fieldham.

The doctor shook hands with them both, his eyes searching their faces without intrusion but with keen kindness as he did so. He took from the

245

receptionist the form Hannah had brought with her, turned towards Drummond, and said, "Miss Evinton will make you a coffee, if you would like that, Dr MacKeagh. I hope you might find something of interest to occupy you for an hour?" He waved towards neat columns of overlapping professional journals on a well-polished coffee-table to Drummond's left, and smiled. "Ms Lethbridge, would you like to come this way?"

With Drummond's hand at her elbow, Hannah straightened her legs beneath her.

"I'll be just here, honey," Drummond whispered to her, hating to release her into anyone else's care, even that of a qualified doctor.

The doctor's hand unhurriedly replaced Drummond's at Hannah's elbow as he led her through the door into the consulting room.

"Here we go again, Hannah Lethbridge," she said silently and miserably to herself, as Dr Alder led her to the client-chair in front of his desk. He walked around his desk to sit opposite her, reached for his pen and case-notebook, already pressed open at the first recording page, and began.

"First of all, Hannah, Mrs Turner asks me to pass on her very warmest regards and good wishes."

"Thank you, doctor," Hannah said quietly, comforted by the name of someone whom she remembered with so much affection and respect, even after so many years and the recurrence of what Margaret had no doubt hoped she had helped to dispel for ever.

"Mrs Turner has told me in general terms about your time together," he continued, "but, as you will know, she is bound by the ethics of our profession to maintain your confidentiality as regards details, until you give your permission for me to know more."

"Of course you have that permission, doctor," Hannah said.

"Well, we'll deal with that formality at the end of our meeting today, perhaps."

He smiled again, and moved on.

"Now, this morning, we may not seem to make much progress, but everything we do is essential to my recognising how I may most effectively help you. So, mostly, it will be questions and notes, with any information either of us believe might be helpful, and anything more about which you might care to enquire and about which I am able to inform you. I trust that will be satisfactory?"

Hannah nodded.

"And I shall take every care not to overtire you," he said.

"I do still seem to tire ridiculously easily," Hannah admitted. "Thank you."

"Right, then," he continued. "Now, Hannah, I understand that you welcomed the opportunity to come and see me. Would you tell me what you are hoping to obtain from our meetings?"

"Oh, I just want to be released from my mother!" Hannah said with desperation. "I don't want to see her again, ever, but, if I do, I just want her not to make me collapse like this," and despite a real effort, inevitably, she could feel herself beginning to cry.

Unsurprised, Dr Alder pushed across the desk his box of client-tissues and waited for the phase to pass. When Hannah had recovered herself somewhat, she said, "I thought my time with Margaret had cured me of all this, and I haven't thought about my mother since then, well, only in passing, occasionally, and then she turned up on my doorstep and I was back where I was in Cambridge, as though I hadn't made any progress at all. And it's horrible! I'm not sure I could stand it to happen again."

Dr Alder waited again for Hannah to calm herself, and then said, with evident sympathy, "Even the thought of your mother clearly has a huge impact on you, Hannah, and we shall certainly address that in due course. So, may I say a few words about what we might do first in our future meetings? To begin with, something about the workings of the mind. Is this an area familiar to you, Hannah?" he asked.

"Not in any detail, doctor," she replied politely. "Please go on."

"Well, essentially, the mind is in two parts," he explained, "the conscious and the unconscious. The conscious mind is the part with which we perceive what is going on around us, of course. But it is also constantly busy sorting out those perceptions, and deciding which ones to deal with and what to do about them. It is where we reason, and apply logic and preference. The unconscious, on the other hand, is the storeroom for everything we have ever experienced, everything we have ever felt or decided, and its shelves are totally without order. The unconscious mind does not use reason or judgement or differentiation, it seems to believe that everything it stores is of equal value. Moreover, it keeps trying to push some of its contents back up into the consciousness, through which all those contents originally came."

He stopped to see if Hannah was following what he was saying. Content that she was listening with keen interest, he continued, "Now, both parts of the mind seem to learn, largely by repetition. When we have a happy experience, and respond to what that experience makes us feel, the mind remembers both the experience and the response. When we have a similar experience, the mind's first reaction is to respond as it did before, and it expects us to gain the same feelings as on the previous occasion.

"However, it may be that the mind expects, for example, a happy response to a remembered situation, but has made a mistake, as it often does. If, in fact, the outcome of the second experience is not as the mind expected, is in fact unhappy, there is a strong tendency for the mind to become confused."

In danger of becoming confused herself, Hannah asked, "Could you give me an example of that, please, doctor?"

"Of course," he replied. "There are always certain people whom one expects to provide security, support and affection. Teachers, carers, parents, for example. Sometimes, however, such people fail to provide what we quite reasonably expect. The mind will then react in one of two possible ways. It may ignore the difference in the outcome, insist that this *is* in fact a happy experience, and respond happily—which can of course lead someone to behave in an inappropriate manner which they afterwards regret. Alternatively, the conscious mind might recognise that the outcome is not what it was expecting, and become confused. It may well be disappointed, and even frightened, because it doesn't know what to do with the unexpected feelings that the disappointment and fear generate, so again it is faced with two options."

Dr Alder paused again and smiled briefly as his eyes checked Hannah's face. He continued, "One option is that the conscious mind can send the whole experience down into the unconscious, as if it were a piece of furniture we bring to a new house but for which we can find no place. We might then simply put it in the cellar out of sight, so that we can ignore its existence. The equivalent, in a confused mind, is to send it down to the unconscious, for the same purpose. We call that repressing the experience and the resulting feelings, and it is very common for the mind to decide to do this.

"On the other hand, if the mental confusion is sufficiently great, the conscious mind can simply give up trying to process what it is perceiving and feeling, and freeze, or effectively collapse. Furthermore, because the processes of the mind and of the body are inextricably related—effectively, our emotions trigger many of the messages which the brain sends out to direct the behaviour of different parts of the anatomy—a collapse of the mind can result in a physical collapse, as it appears to have done in your case, Hannah, in a perfectly common and ordinary response."

"So I'm not unusual or inexplicable?" Hannah said. "Oh, I am so relieved to hear that, doctor!"

Dr Alder continued his explanation.

"What I am intending to attempt," he said, "if all the circumstances are favourable, is to give your mind an alternative set of responses to the major issues which, in the past, have confused or frightened it, and my principal approach to such a process is through hypnosis. Do you feel any reservations about that suggestion, Hannah?"

"No, doctor," she assured him. "Dr Fieldham asked me that, and I told him that I knew nothing about the subject, but that I was happy to follow your advice."

"Thank you," he said. "Well, it will be a week or two before we can consider undertaking any of that. Nonetheless, perhaps it would help if I said a little about what hypnosis is, and how it is believed to work."

Hannah nodded again, so he expanded.

"In any one second, the mind is receiving a million or more pieces of information. However, the conscious mind is incapable of processing that volume of perceptions at anything like that speed. Therefore, it is continually ignoring the greater proportion of all the perceptions which are bombarding it. To do this, it is continually making choices as to which perceptions to notice, and which to allow to descend unnoticed into the unconscious mind.

"The purpose of the process of hypnosis is effectively to calm down the action of the conscious mind so that the perceptions then introduced by the therapist have a greater opportunity to become noticed. Furthermore, through the therapist repeating these perceptions, they will become so thoroughly learned that they become that mind's, that person's, habitual responses to the particular situations towards which these beneficial ideas have been directed. Is this making sense, Hannah?" he asked.

Hannah confirmed that it was.

"Well, just let all that introductory stuff rumble gently around your mind until we need it again," the doctor suggested. "For the time being, I need to know rather more about you, and about the main issues which you feel have shaped your life so far."

When he seemed to have asked sufficient questions, and made sufficient notes, for his purpose, Dr Alder put down his pen, leaned back in his chair and smiled kindly at her.

"Generally, Hannah," he said, "I am beginning to conclude that you are an unusually strong young woman who has suffered more than the usual series of slings and arrows which most human lives experience, and who, with Margaret's effective help, had been recovering from them very well until your mother's reappearance. Have you been administered anaesthetic on any occasion, Hannah? Perhaps by a dentist?"

"I had two fillings while I was at school," Hannah replied. "On both occasions, the dentists used local anaesthetics, I think. Injections, anyway."

"But never gas? You've never been put to sleep, as people say?"

"Oh, no, never, doctor," she confirmed.

"Good, good. Well, now, to the matter of the detailed records of your medical and psychological history. It would be of the greatest assistance to me if I could see those records, but I need your formal agreement to that,"

"Of course, doctor."

"Thank you," he said. "If you could just sign this release form for me, there, at the bottom of the page, when you've read it."

She was very tired by now, and this showed in the shakiness of her signature. But they seemed to have completed all that Dr Alder needed at this first meeting, and she felt almost as much trust in him as she had in Margaret Turner at the same stage. He let her sit quietly for a few moments, and lifted the telephone handset on his desk.

"Ms Evinton," he said, when his receptionist replied, "may we have a further appointment for Ms Lethbridge in, say, ten days' time? Perhaps you would coordinate that with Dr MacKeagh, and then ask him to come in to collect Ms Lethbridge?"

Putting down the telephone, he said to Hannah, "It would be helpful for us both, I believe, if, between now and our next meeting, you could begin to identify, and perhaps jot down, the feelings which you find yourself having that make you uncomfortable and upset you. If you can, explore situations that you can foresee arising in the near future, and those of the recent past, but not to the extent of distressing yourself unduly. This is not the time to court any sort of a setback. Bring the results with you to our next appointment, if you will, and they will form a valuable foundation for our discussion then."

Chapter Nineteen

Eighteen months later, I had benefitted greatly from my sessions with Dr Alder. He had given me many gifts, techniques which I could use to calm myself when my memories threatened to open the dam of tears. One such was when he said, "Hannah, today I would like you to envisage a particular place, a particular scene, which gives you feelings of peace, calmness and serenity."

I thought about this in silence for some time. He did not hurry me. I had not experienced many such places or scenes. After a couple of minutes, I asked, "Does it have to be a factual place, doctor? Could it be an imagined one?"

"Oh, yes," he replied.

"When I was in primary school," I said, "I often went to a local library to read. My favourites were A.A. Milne's books about Winnie the Pooh. I loved to read about Pooh's place at the Top of the Forest, on a little hill, with trees at the top and a sandy place to sit in among them and look out onto the surrounding open countryside. That always seemed to me to be idyllic, a wonderful, calm, peaceful, happy place and I always longed to have such place to go to."

For some inexplicable reason, tears were near again, but I managed to hold them back.

"That sounds like just the place we need," Dr Alder said. "Whenever, in our work together, we have undertaken an exercise under hypnosis, or whenever you feel stressed, here in the course of our discussions, or outside, when uncomfortable thoughts press upon you, I would like you to remember that place at the Top of Pooh's Forest, and go to it in your mind. Sit down in the sandy place for a little while, and feel its comfort. Can you do that? Do you think that might be helpful?"

"Yes, willingly," I agreed.

It turned out that I was easy to hypnotise, as many imaginative, literary people are, apparently. Together, we explored situations in which I felt insecure, issues to which I would refer with a euphemism ("we hide our fears behind euphemisms, Hannah, when we really need to face them down," Dr Alder said firmly, and at first frequently), and I was feeling much better. Not yet right, but on the way back from the dark hole into which I had fallen on that horrible autumn afternoon two years before. There was still a way to go.

We both knew that, Drummond and I, and since Dr Alder had offered no hint as to terminating my series of appointments, it seemed that he knew it too. We were all making progress, but it had cost Drummond and I dearly. In order to deliver me to Dr Alder's consulting rooms every week, the whole pattern of Drummond's working life had been completely changed. Gone were the days, those of his actual and emotional youth before he met me, when his laboratory was where he lived and his house was where he slept, if he and his team were not pulling an all-nighter on a crucial experiment.

Now, he headed a team which, he said, was becoming increasingly autonomous, contributing their own insights and their own directions, even their own strategies and marketing initiatives, to both the pure science and the increasingly essential fund-raising and sponsorship which was becoming the centre of university post-doctoral life. His role, he told me, was now that of co-ordinator, the one who kept track of what each member of the team was doing, or supposed to be doing, or were going to do next.

He was the one who kept the rest of the faculty happy, who ensured the flow of sufficient graduate students to maintain the team's productivity, and the flow of technical reports to clients as well as the academic papers necessary to maintain the Department's status among those of the other competing Universities across the British Isles and the rest of the world. And he was enjoying, it, he told me, bless him, though I was only just becoming relaxed enough to wonder if this were really so.

John and Jacqueline were still upstairs, and we had seen a lot of them through the summer. Even in the Scottish climate, we had gathered almost every evening in the garden, except for the evenings of my Edinburgh days with Dr Alder, as everyone tactfully called them, when I returned worn out and went more or less directly from the car to bed. They had been wonderful in looking after Drummond, as well as in looking after me, doing unasked tasks and favours, shopping, cooking and sharing food in our big, basement kitchen, and providing company for poor Drummond when I was going through a bad phase as a result of what my work with Dr Alder threw up for me to face.

The beginning of the winter was on us now, however, and we four gathered in the kitchen more and more often. John and Drummond often brought down folios and files of paper to lay across the big table after supper. Jacqueline would bring her latest finding from the eclectic shelves of whichever part of the university library was currently assigned to her oversight, or, if I was sufficiently rested and energised to make sense, she and I would sit and gossip from our chairs on either side of the oven.

In their care for me, we had become a real household, a real family, and it made such a difference to the comfort, perhaps even the speed, of my recovery by comparison with last time. Until, of course...well, perhaps the others had foreseen the possibility. John, I'm sure, must have done so, given his experience, but no one had said anything to me. I was perfectly fit enough to have foreseen it for myself, by this time, but was still liable to repress unpleasant thoughts now and then, so that, when it happened, it came as something more than a bit of a shock.

We were all of us home that evening, for a change. Jacqueline and I had cooked. Well, Jacqueline had cooked, with my contribution limited to stirring saucepans and greasing the dish. We had made a huge pasta-cauliflower cheese and simply put the dish in the middle of the table. I had eaten a morsel, Jacqueline had eaten healthily, and the boys had wolfed the rest as though they hadn't eaten for days. With the table cleared and the dishes washed, John's expression became serious as he said, "I'm sorry, but we all need to talk. I've had a call from London about the trial of those two women."

Drummond reached out to take my hand under the tabletop. I simply froze. My stomach felt as though I might be about to throw up what little of the recent meal I had consumed. But I didn't cry...yet. We waited for John to go on.

"The call was from the solicitor who is going to be supporting the prosecuting QC. Apparently, they would like you, Hannah, to attend the trial as a possible witness as to the character of...er...Irene."

Even now, nobody in the household referred to her as my mother, unless that were utterly unavoidable. For a number of months, none of us had referred to her at all.

"But the charge is that she...did away with that man, isn't it?" I clutched at the first straw I could think of. "I don't know anything about that. I hadn't been near the damned woman for years before they...did that."

I noticed that I couldn't bring myself to say the word 'murder', not in relation to my mother. She still was my mother. The psychological bonds put in place while she carried me in her womb, and just after, were still there in me, however weakly, however shamefully. Maybe the equivalent bonds were what had led to her association with that Naomi person, though who *she* was, and how and why, I still could not—refused to?—grasp.

"Irene's being charged as an accessory," John explained. "They've gathered a lot of forensic evidence, I was told, and they've charged Naomi as the killer. They're going to suggest that your...Irene assisted, but they've no evidence that she participated in the fatal act."

"When you say that the prosecution 'would like' Hannah to attend as a witness," Drummond asked, still holding my hand tightly, "does that mean that she can refuse? Especially on medical grounds, if Hannah doesn't yet feel sufficiently fit?"

"Well, that's possible," John said. "I'd have to make an application to the judge for your absence on those grounds, Hannah. You'd have to make a written statement, which Prosecuting Counsel would ask the judge to accept and allow to be read out in court. What they seem to want is a history of the relationship between you and your...mother, and its effect on your...health, to demonstrate...well, I'm not sure what they want to demonstrate, apart from perhaps to be able to counter a claim by the defence that Irene has always been too weak a character to resist being led into the business by Naomi."

"Do you mean, they think there might be a case to get her off?" I yelped, the panic rising from my stomach to my heart and head. "She'll come back! No! She can't come back!" Drummond had sprung up as soon as he heard the fear in my voice, to wrap both his arms around me and bend his body over me like a shield.

Jacqueline was kneeling at my feet to grasp my hands. I fought the panic down. I was *not* going to let it take control. Had I learned nothing from my doctors' patient care? Drummond and Jacqueline must have felt my body relax, for they slowly released me and, with a glance at each other, went back to their chairs.

"Sorry, folks," I apologised. "I'm OK now. Well, better. For a bit."

Drummond took my hands again and I gave him a smile and a quick thank-you kiss.

"Hannah, I am so very sorry to have to tell you about all this." John clearly was upset. "The solicitor who called me was sorry, too, she really was, but she has her job to do, and I understood that, of course. At least she allowed me to tell you, rather than having some clerk telephone you direct, out of the blue."

"Aye, that was thoughtful," Drummond agreed on my behalf and I nodded appreciatively.

We all took a few seconds to settle once again. John had more to say.

"Hannah, dear," he continued, "the impression my contact gave me was that they don't think there's a hope in hell of Irene getting off. What the defence is no doubt intending to do is to minimise the severity of her ultimate sentence, but the prosecution is confident that she will get a long custodial sentence, come what may."

I heard what he was saying, but wasn't greatly comforted.

"I need to discuss this with Dr Alder next week," I said.

John's expression stiffened.

"There's something else, I'm afraid, Hannah," he said. "Now that you've been given notice that you will be a witness, you mustn't have any more psychotherapy."

"Whyever not?" I protested, horrified.

"It's a standing rule," John explained. "There is a fear that such treatment might give rise to false memories. Indeed, it may well be that the defence will try to suggest that your evidence is unreliable because of the treatment you have already had. My contact realises this, but said that it couldn't be helped. It will be sufficient that the prosecuting counsel will be able to place your evidence in the juror's minds, to make of it what they will."

"This is a minor aspect of the prosecution case, after all, isn't it?" Drummond suggested. "Surely the major part will be to do with the forensic evidence from the scene of the …crime?"

"I'm sure that's right," John agreed.

"So what do I have to do now?" I asked.

"The major thing is for you to compose a statement recording the evidence the prosecution will expect you to present to the court. I'll give you the prosecution solicitor's telephone number, and she'll tell you exactly what they are looking for. The first thing, however, is for you to decide whether you wish to simply submit a statement to be read out in court, appear at the trial on video-link, or appear in person," John explained. "Take a couple of days to consider that, and then we'll go on from whatever you decide."

"So when's the trial to take place?" Drummond asked.

"It's scheduled for February," John said, "give or take a week or two. It's too early yet for them to be more precise."

"That gives me another several months," I said. "A lot can happen in a few months."

We broke up then, subdued. Jacqueline gave me a big hug and whispered how sorry she was about it all, and she and John went off to their own part of the house. Drummond turned on the kettle again for more coffee, and I began to summon my strength to face the next step in dealing with the burdens my mother seemed repeatedly to heap upon me.

***

I thought of nothing else for the next two days, of course. We did not see much of John. I presumed he was keeping out of the way so as not to interfere with my freedom of decision. Jacqueline also stayed upstairs most of the time when she was at home, apart from popping in now and then to make sure I was comfortable and had enough to eat and drink. Drummond was deeply concerned for me. He went to the university for a few hours each day, but I doubted that he was doing much real work. When he was at the house, we talked round and round the arguments for and against each of the options I was facing.

I had quickly come to one firm decision. If at all possible, I was determined to appear in the courtroom from the beginning to the end of the trial. Drummond was not happy about this.

"Darling, are you sufficiently strong?" he said. "It'll do no good to anyone if it's too much for you."

"Well, we'll have to see, say two weeks before the beginning of the trial," I insisted. "That gives us enough time to go down an alternative route if I'm not fit enough by that point. But that's the strategy I really want to adopt. I need to see her put out of my life, our life, beyond question." I nearly cried again, but a cuddle from Drummond strengthened me. "I must be there when the judge passes sentence. It will be a sentence for her and a release for me, you see. Also, if I were to claim to be unfit to appear as a witness, I can hardly turn up as a spectator, can I?"

"I suppose the same arguments apply if you went for the video-link idea?" Drummond suggested, "though it might reduce some of the stress."

"No, I won't be doing with all that technology stuff. It would make me so nervous, more even than being in court. At least in court, I'll be able to see whoever is asking me questions, and the judge and jury, and know where the questions are coming from, and what effect my answers are having. I'm not confident I could concentrate sufficiently with the distraction of having to think about the camera, and worrying about whether they could hear me in the courtroom."

Gently, Drummond continued to try to dissuade me, but I was as determined as my limited strength allowed, and that was what we told John and Jacqueline after supper on the second night.

"You do realise what an exhausting experience it can be to appear as a witness in court?" John said to me. "And it is possible that the defence will want to question your evidence, of course."

"We've been over all that," Drummond told him, "but she's fully determined to be there, John, so that's the plan, for now, anyway."

For me, the biggest difficulty was going to arise from having to postpone any more therapy with Dr Alder, at least until after the trial. I reviewed how much progress Dr Alder had made with me, how much more stable, and almost happy, I had been feeling before John brought us this terrible news. I spent quite long periods at the Top of the Forest. When Drummond noticed my absence up there, however, I still couldn't tell him precisely what I had been doing. This issue of total trust and totally open communication was something else I needed to sort out, but that was another matter altogether.

I telephoned Ms Evinton the next morning and explained that, as I had been called as a witness in my mother's trial for murder, I could not receive any more treatment from Dr Alder. She understood the issue, and its importance, straight away.

"Would you like to convert your next face-to-face appointment into one on the telephone?" she suggested. "I know the doctor will want to talk to you, Hannah. I could speak to him shortly and telephone you back to let you know what he says."

That was more than I expected and I agreed immediately. It was in fact Dr Alder who telephoned only half an hour later.

"This must have upset you terribly, Hannah," he said. "How have you been minimising the impact over the last few days?"

I explained that, by remembering the advice he had given me, using Margaret's mantra, and by frequent visits to my safe, calm place, I had been able to keep control of my fears, more or less. There was a short silence, then he said, "As you now know, hypnotherapy is essentially a matter of the subject achieving a deep degree of mental relaxation. Many people can do this more or less at will. Do you think you could manage that in the courtroom, Hannah?

"Well, doctor," I replied, "I've been reviewing not only what we've done, but how, so I think probably, on a good day, I might be able to do something useful in that way."

"I'm sure you can," Dr Alder said reassuringly. "Try to fix in your mind the conviction that, in the courtroom, your function will be no more than as a source of information. All you say will be the truth as you see it, and no more can be asked of anyone. Whatever you are asked, know with absolute confidence that you will be walking out of the courtroom afterwards with the respect of all who hear you. Try, also, to build on Margaret's very helpful mantra so that you know beyond doubt that the proceedings are not about you, and are concerned with matters for which you have no responsibility, either for their commission or their results."

"Oh, doctor, that is exactly what I need!" I said gratefully. I ran through the words in my mind. 'I am not my mother. I am not responsible for her actions or their consequences.'

"I am so sorry you have this additional situation to face, Hannah, but you and Drummond know where I am if you need me," he meant, if I collapse again, but neither of us said that, "and let me know just as soon as the trial is over."

I thanked him and we said our goodbyes. Once again, the practicality of his suggestions had given me new strength, and therefore confidence, with which to face what had to be done.

***

The next thing was to telephone the solicitor for the prosecution, and see what had to be included in my proof of evidence. I explained to the rather curt receptionist why I was phoning.

"Putting you through." An earful of Vivaldi. Then, "Marjorie Watson."

"Good afternoon, Ms Watson," I said. "My name is Hannah Lethbridge. I understand that your QC might want to call me as a witness in the case against

Irene and Naomi Lethbridge, and that I have to let you have a proof of evidence. I'm calling because I have never had anything to do with the criminal law. I've no clear idea what a proof of evidence is, or even, really, why you need me, and I'm hoping you can tell me."

"Oh, yes, of course, Ms Lethbridge. We would normally invite prospective witnesses into the office here in London, but I believe you are in Dundee and none too well, so no doubt we can do it over the 'phone in this case, as I told Mr Shields the other day. Clearly, he knows the ropes and can advise you on any aspects of the procedure which may not be clear, and you can always 'phone me again should you wish to do so." She gave me her extension number. "That will get you through directly, which might help."

I thanked her. She sounded very experienced and efficient.

"So, to begin at the beginning. A proof of evidence is a statement of the evidence you will be giving in court, contributory to the prosecution case. It is a written statement, so that it can be disclosed to the defence, who have the right, in court, to question you on relevant aspects of what you have said. Having seen your proof, they can plan their questions. Are you with me so far?"

"Yes, I think so," I said, beginning to realise more clearly what I had got myself into through my stubborn determination to give evidence in person.

"Now, your mother is being charged with being an accessory to the murder of Michael Journeyman. She is apparently claiming always to have been dominated by an overwhelming need to give and receive love, and to have been perennially weak-willed and easily led in her search for affection. In other words, her daughter Naomi demanded her loyalty before and after the act with which they're charged, and, characteristically and against her better judgement, your mother's love prevented her from withholding it."

I gulped, and must have made a noise audible even over the telephone.

"Ms Lethbridge? Are you all right?" Ms Watson enquired.

"Yes, thank you," I said. "I'm just…I shouldn't be surprised, but…"

"What in particular surprises you, Ms Lethbridge?"

"The contrast between that story and the truth about my mother's barefaced, life-long selfishness," I said. I was so angry…and no doubt I sounded it, because Ms Watson left me a gap in which to get control of myself.

"Aah," she said slowly after a moment or two. "Can you tell me a little more about that?"

The anger swept me along.

"As long as I can remember," I began, "She's been a scrounging, thieving, cheating, totally self-centred…woman, and as hard as nails. Until I went to university, we lived either in poky rooms or in the lush houses of the men she manipulated for a few months. In the one, there was often not enough to eat, in the other there was no attention for me. I was simply required to be out of sight. She never had an employed job or any regular income. She said that would be beneath her. She left me with anybody who was willing while she went out man-hunting. She put me in dreadfully humiliating situations at school…"

Suddenly, I was crying again in great deep sobs. I couldn't breathe sufficiently to go on.

Ms Watson paused again.

"Ms Lethbridge," she said, "I realise that this is going to be much harder for you than I had foreseen."

I took several deep breaths at last, although the tears still flowed uncontrollably down my cheeks. Ms Watson asked, "Are there other people who witnessed these behaviours of your mother, and who might support your assessment of her?"

"I presume so," I said. "Some of my teachers, and the landladies of our rooms with whom I was left, and so on. And my therapists, of course, after my collapses."

There was another pause.

"Ms Lethbridge…may I call you Hannah? I'm Marjorie, of course…Hannah, none of us here had any idea about all this. What I am now wondering is whether asking you to appear in court is going to do you more harm than the good your evidence will contribute to the case we will be attempting to present."

"You mean, will I collapse in a blubbering heap on the floor of the witness box and nullify the value of anything I might be able to say by opening it to charges of emotional unreliability?" I replied, my tears drying at last. "All I can say, briefly, is that I understand the trial isn't going to take place for several months yet, my condition and control are both improving rapidly, and I shan't be taken by surprise in the courtroom as I have been today. I badly want to do this, Marjorie, and I shall do my very best not to let you down."

"That is very brave, Hannah," Marjorie said. "Well, why don't we go on talking for a little longer so that I can compile an outline of what evidence you may be able to offer. If at any time it all becomes too much for you, don't hesitate to tell me."

We proceeded on that basis. Now I was under control again, I was able to recall easily all the incidents and examples I had enacted in Margaret Turner's consulting room. We were on the telephone for an hour that day, and I found it very tiring, as it was on the other two days shortly after that Marjorie called up and I filled in some more gaps.

Finally, she said to me, "Right, I'll pull all that together into a draft formal proof, and post it to you for review and signature. If you wish to change anything in what I write, please don't hesitate to telephone me and talk about it. Your solicitor will help you with the formalities. But Hannah, there's just one other thing I really must say to you.

"If the defence wish to undermine your evidence, their most obvious line of attack is emotional. They might try to present you as an unnatural daughter with no love for her mother at all. Are you confident that you could sustain and repulse such an attack without further detriment to your health?"

"I'll confirm that to you shortly before the date for the trial, if I may," I replied, "but at the moment, the answer is still 'yes'. I can and will give evidence. It simply has to be done, for everybody's sake, and especially for my own."

Chapter Twenty

In fact, the trial did not open until April 4th, and it seemed that I was not required to be at the court until the 6th. Even then, I had been told, I might not be needed until the following day, depending on how the case was going by that point. Indeed, if Irene and Naomi were to plead guilty, I might not have to appear as a witness at all, John had told me, but, from the start, I had prepared myself for the worst, so as not to have to suffer the dashing of futile hopes.

Drummond and I spent the night of the 5th at an hotel in East London, a taxi-ride from the Old Bailey where the trial would take place. Inevitably, I had not slept much, which meant that Drummond had not either. Whenever I woke up, I found him awake, too, to reach over and fold me in his arms for a cuddle before I went back to sleep.

It was a brief taxi-ride to the Old Bailey the next morning. As we were not due there until 9.45, we did not have to rush in the morning. We took a room service breakfast, or at least Drummond did, and I had a piece of tepid toast and a large cup of coffee. Our taxi-driver clearly knew the courthouse well, since he asked, "Public or witness, governor?" and, being told 'witness', took us past the long queue at the public entrance and deposited us at a smaller door further along the building. John had warned us that, on arrival outside the courtroom, we would be separated, and I wouldn't see Drummond again until either I was called to the witness box, or the court rose at lunch time and at the end of the day.

Drummond gave me a long kiss before we went into the building, and a tight hug, whispered, "Good luck, darling. See you later," and I turned from him more reluctantly than ever before, I think, to find the clerk who would be looking out for me. Inside, two women wearing badges which said 'Witness Service' were scanning the people entering. One of them approached me, smiled and asked, "Are you a witness here today, Ms…"

"Yes, I'm Hannah Lethbridge," I did my best to reply.

She glanced down at the list on her clipboard, and said, "Ah, yes, I'll take you up to the usher for Courtroom Four. Will you come with me?"

She turned towards a broad stone staircase, and said, "Can you manage the stairs, Ms Lethbridge? Perhaps you'd like to take my arm?"

I took the offered arm gratefully, grasped the banister with the other hand and wished fervently that Drummond had been there to help me up with his arm around me, as he still did regularly at home.

At the top of the stairs, the corridor was filled with a vast crowd of people, many in ordinary clothes and a large number dressed in formal black and white, with forbidding gowns and grey, plastic-looking wigs. My companion led me forward into the crowd, and I felt overwhelmed. "Help! Help!" I wanted to shout, and the urge to turn and throw myself down the stairs grew within me.

As we came up to another woman with a clipboard, this one wearing a black gown but no wig, my companion said to her, "This is Ms Lethbridge, for your case. Ms Lethbridge, this is the usher for your court. She'll look after you from here."

She smiled at me, turned and was gone before I could thank her for her kindness. The new woman ticked me off on her clipboard as present and said, "If you'd like to follow me, Ms Lethbridge?"

Before we had gone a step, however, a very attractive young woman detached herself from a huddle of the formally-dressed people and spoke my name.

"Ms Lethbridge? I'm Marjorie Watson, solicitor for the prosecution. We talked on the telephone. How do you do?"

"How very nice to meet you at last," I said. "You were so kind to me on the phone."

"Not at all," Marjorie said. "How are you?"

"I'm fine. A bit wobbly on my legs, still, but fine, thank you."

She led me to a long, already crowded, padded bench against one wall of the corridor, opened a gap for us by sheer weight of personality, it seemed, and we sat.

"I know this won't be easy for you," Marjorie smiled. I recognised that she was a serious young woman with many more important things to think about than my welfare, and that she was doing her best to put me at ease. She continued, "When you are called into court, it will all be very much as we have discussed. My principal, Mr Hornsby—the big man in that group over there, twirling his wig on his hand—will establish you as a young woman with an impressive intellect, and a very successful professional career. He will clarify the circumstances of your collapses, and the influence of your mother, especially in the most recent one. He will ask you to describe to the court some illustrative incidents from your childhood, as you told them to me. All you have to do is to answer his questions as fully and clearly as you feel able."

"I hope he won't feel it necessary to make a lot of my collapses," I suggested.

"As little as possible, I promise you," Marjorie assured me. "But the QC conducting your mother's defence, Ms Gansthorpe—forties, looks less, frilly blouse, lots of teeth, on your right—will be questioning your judgements of those incidents, and may well refer to them having been made at a young, impressionable age, and recounted to the court by someone who has suffered significant mental distress.

"Mr Hornsby will need to negate that impression in advance, though that won't stop her giving it a try. The defence hasn't got anything else of any value to say, in the light of the definitive forensic evidence. Mr Sandiman, the QC for your half-sister, probably won't ask you any questions, as you'd never met Naomi until she appeared in Dundee. Anyway, once all that's over, you can go back home."

"So what do I do now?" I asked her.

"I'll find your usher, and she will take you to the Witnesses' Waiting Room."

We smiled at each other, she confidently and I no doubt shakily. She stood up, disappeared into the crowd briefly and then returned to her gaggle of barristers, and I was taken back into the care of the usher.

Further down the corridor, the usher opened a door marked 'Witnesses', stood aside to let me pass, saw me seated on one of the hard office chairs at the side of the room, and left me there to look after myself. Although I had a book in my handbag, it was to be the most boring, as well as the most terrifying, day of my whole life. The other witnesses seemed to be experts, dressed in suits and earnest expressions, with thick files of papers which they opened on their knees for last minute revision, as if they were about to face a college viva. From their points of view, I suppose that's just what it was.

Lunchtime came in the world outside that waiting room. On being released by the usher, I went downstairs and met my patient Drummond, who had already been out and collected coffee and a sandwich for each of us. We ate leaning on the wall outside the courthouse, warmed by the weak spring sun, and then I returned to incarceration.

We were released for the day just before 4.30, with a repeated warning not to talk to other witnesses, the press, loved-ones or bus conductors, and to be back before 10.00 the next morning. I walked out stiffly into the corridor and carefully down the stairs to find Drummond, who gave me a huge hug and a kiss, and we eventually stopped a taxi to take us back to our hotel.

I slept better that night, and felt refreshed the next morning, even though the prospect of having to appear in the witness box still appalled me. Inside the witnesses' entrance to the Old Bailey, the lady from the Witness Service recognised me.

"Good morning, Ms Lethbridge," she said. "How are you today?"

"I'm …OK, thank you," I said.

"You had some breakfast to line your stomach?" she asked, with a warm smile.

"I had some porridge," I said. "I thought that would be the easiest to digest." I meant, to hold down, of course, and I saw her eyebrows twitch as she took in that implication. "It wasn't like porridge at home, as my partner makes it, but it served its purpose. Or, at least, I hope it will."

She smiled again and took me upstairs to the usher, who returned me to the Witness Room, and I began another long morning of sitting, dozing and reading without absorbing any of the words on the pages of my book. In common with some of the others suffering their own long-term waits, I took the occasional, short wander around the room to stretch my legs.

I was not called that day, either. Some of the suits were called and left the room as the day progressed, but it wasn't until the third day that the usher put her head around the door and said, "Ms Lethbridge, please follow me."

I suddenly realised that I was totally alone. I felt the shakes return to my stomach and then to my legs and hands. "Come along, girl, stop being so silly!" I told myself, and took as firm a grip on my courage and my limbs as I could manage.

Outside the witness room, I took a deep breath, tried to remember all that Dr Alder had taught me and walked forward unsteadily after the usher.

"I'll put your bag in a locker for you, shall I?" she offered. "It will be quite safe there until after your appearance."

I surrendered my handbag, and she opened an imposing door on which the brass plate said 'Courtroom'. She stood aside from the door, smiled and said, "There is a chair in the witness box. Please do not sit down until you are invited to do so," and I walked through into the witness box.

I seemed to have found my way into an almighty cave. Everything was dark, reflecting the heaviness of the stained oak panelling all around the walls, and the vast timbered surfaces of all the furniture. The ceiling was almost lost in the gloom which seemed to gather far above me. To my right, the judge sat, a huge red and grey blob of colours against the wood of the panelling on the front of his Bench and the walls behind him. Immediately in front of me, like people drowning in the sea off a steeply shelving shore, were heads, rows of heads, all grey under their tightly dressed wigs, above black robes.

My knees were still trembling. I grasped the broad wooden sill of the chest-high wall in front of me with both hands, and thought, '*Oh, Drummond, get me through this, just get me through this without...*' I did not know without what. Just that I was terribly, terribly afraid of ending up in my characteristic, stupid, sobbing heap on the floor. I said to myself again, silently, the mantra which Margaret had given me so many years ago, "I am not my mother. I am not responsible for her actions, or their consequences", and felt a little better.

I thought of Margaret's wonderful, come-what-may calmness, and felt strengthened. I turned to look for Drummond in the public gallery, seemingly so far away. I couldn't see him! Until...yes, I could, I could see the bright, un-Drummond, multi-coloured tie which I had bought him for just this purpose. At first, he had said, 'No, he couldn't possibly wear something like that', until I kissed him in front of the shop-girl and told him, "It's for me, so I know you're there," and he hugged me and let me buy it, and now it had worked.

My knees straightened and my wrists relaxed. I knew I would be all right now. And then, inevitably, my eyes dropped below the balcony of the gallery and, for the first time, I saw the defendants in the dock.

The dock was unmistakable, of course, as was the status of the two people sitting behind the spiked bars around the top of another oak wall as impregnable as the side of an Elizabethan fighting ship. Mother, and that other woman whom John had told us was claiming to be my sister! Behind them stood four uniformed people, two powerful, stern-looking women and two big, calm, watchful men. I knew I must not let my attention be captured by the sight. With an effort, I made my eyes sweep over them all, and return to the face of the man in his black robe standing on the floor of the courtroom below me.

Looking at a piece of paper in his hand, he peered at me piercingly, and asked, "Are you Hannah Lethbridge, of..." he gave our address in Dundee, and I said "Yes".

"Take the book in your right hand and read the words on the card in front of you," he said.

I looked at the small white card. Its words meant nothing to me, this talk of God and truth, but it was required, so I did it in as strong a voice as I could muster.

"Please sit down, if you so wish," he said, and, very thankfully, I sat. He came across to me again, tipped the head of the microphone down, looked at me enquiringly and turned back to his place in front of the judge, who took off his spectacles and said to me, "Ms Lethbridge, the Court understands that you have been very ill and are still in the process of recovery. I am sure that all here with any influence on the matter will do everything possible within our overall purpose of achieving justice to make your appearance as brief as possible. Should you at any time in these proceedings feel the need to pause, please indicate that to the Clerk promptly and clearly. There will be no purpose in your continuing to the point where your evidence cannot be heard."

I said, "Yes, My Lord. Thank you."

"Mr Hornsby?"

The portly man who had been twirling his wig in the corridor two days earlier rose smoothly from the front bench of figures before me, and began.

"Ms Lethbridge, the Crown understands that, at the time of the alleged offence with which your mother, Mrs Irene Lethbridge, is charged, you had not had any contact whatsoever with her for some twelve years, and that, at the time, you were living some four hundred miles from the scene of the alleged offence. Would you tell the court, if you please, how and why this prolonged separation came about?"

"I separated from my mother to go to university in 1990," I said.

The Clerk got up, came over and tilted up the tip of the microphone.

"Speak up, please," he whispered.

I nodded. Mr Hornsby was speaking again.

"And which university did you attend, Ms Lethbridge?"

"Cambridge."

"No doubt you performed creditably in such a very demanding environment?"

"I was given an upper second class degree."

"Indeed. And what employment did you take up on graduating, Ms Lethbridge?"

"I became a personal assistant to the drawing office manager in a local factory."

"And what was the general scope of your work in that position?"

"Typing, filing, running messages to other departments…"

"Just so, Ms Lethbridge. But will you tell the court why you took such employment?"

"I understand now that I was deeply depressed at that point in my life and did not believe myself capable of anything more. Also, I needed an income, and the factory was the first employer to offer me a job."

"How many other applications had you made at that point to other possible employers, Ms Lethbridge?" Mr Hornsby asked next.

"None, actually. I saw the post advertised in the local paper, telephoned, obtained an interview and was grateful to be given the job."

"And how long were in that employment?"

"Almost a year."

"Why was that position terminated?"

"I had a total mental and physical collapse, from which it took me three years to recover."

"And the diagnosed cause of your collapse, Ms Lethbridge?"

"Principally, the abuse imposed by my mother throughout my childhood."

There was an audible collective intake of breath in the public gallery. The judge looked up from his note-taking and glowered, and silence returned.

"Would you please recount some instances of that alleged abuse, Ms Lethbridge?" Mr Hornsby asked.

I described a number of the instances I had acted out in Margaret Turner's consulting room. I was getting tired now and I could hear my voice weakening.

"Thank you, Ms Lethbridge," Mr Hornsby said. "And so, by the age of eighteen, what was the nature of your relationship with your mother?"

"There was no relationship as such. I had left my mother behind and was grateful for the relief."

"And after your recovery from the collapse you suffered while working at the factory?"

"Through the goodness of a number of people, I obtained a post as a reader in a publishing house in Edinburgh. I learnt to be an editor, and was also invited to take up a teaching post at the University of Dundee."

"And how would you characterise that career, Ms Lethbridge?"

"It was…closer, I suppose, to what my time at Cambridge had prepared me to do."

"Were you happy in Scotland?"

"I have become immensely happy."

"And have you formed a happy social relationship?"

"Yes, I met and fell deeply in love with my partner, who is my rock and with whom I am living very happily indeed."

"So, after twelve years, how did you feel about your mother, Ms Lethbridge?"

"I almost never gave her a thought until she turned up on our doorstep in Dundee."

"And what was your reaction to her reappearance, Ms Lethbridge?"

"I collapsed again, and am still recovering from that event," I said, and swayed. If I had not been sitting down already, I might well have collapsed all over again.

"Thank you, Ms Lethbridge. I have no more questions, My Lord."

I trusted that I had done enough to fulfil Mr Hornsby's purpose in bringing me here. I had given him everything I had, at that stage. But there were still the defence lawyers to come, of course.

"Mr Sandiman?" the judge said.

A tall, thin, bent and balding man half-rose from the front bench of barristers, said indistinctly, "No questions for this witness, My Lord, thank you," and sat down again.

"Ms Gansthorpe?"

The woman that Marjorie Watson had pointed out to me in the corridor on my first day here stood elegantly and flashed her teeth briefly at the judge, and then at the jury.

"Thank you, My Lord." Her expression became severe as she turned to face me, not to say fierce.

"Ms Lethbridge, do you love your mother?"

Despite having had several years with Margaret and Dr Alder in which I had repeatedly asked this question of myself, I was still unsure how to answer it. Finally, I gave the only true response I could summon.

"I...don't know."

"Come, Ms Lethbridge," Ms Gansthorpe said. "This is your mother we're talking about. The person who gave you life and, within the scope of her character, nurtured you until you ran away after your own ambition. Well then, Ms Lethbridge, will you tell us how you felt about her during your...separation from her?"

"I didn't miss her when we were apart. I would have been content never to have seen her again."

As always, when I addressed this question, as I had done so often over the years, I felt a deep sense of guilt at having to say this, but I had sworn to tell the truth, so what else could I say?

"Well, Ms Lethbridge," Ms Gansthorpe almost sneered at me, "from your own account, it appears that your mother, with all the failings of character which you have implied, never caused you to suffer the extremes of poverty. You did not suggest that she had ever dragged you down into homelessness, did you, Ms Lethbridge?"

"No, that is true, but we were always unnecessarily poor and never had our own house. We always lived in rooms or rented flats, or in other people's houses."

"What sort of 'other people', Ms Lethbridge?"

"Men friends of my mother," I replied. "Always men friends. I don't remember my mother having any women friends."

"None at all, Ms Lethbridge?" Ms Gansthorpe gave the impression of finding this inconceivable, though John had told me that no barrister worth their salt ever asked a question to which they did not believe they already knew the answer.

"None that I ever met," I replied.

"That might suggest," Ms Gansthorpe said, "that it would be surprising if she should associate with Ms Naomi Lethbridge, your half-sister, in any significant matter, might it not?"

"I wouldn't know," I said. "I had never seen that other woman..."

"Ms Naomi Lethbridge, your half-sister?" Ms Gansthorpe insisted.

"So I understand," I said. "I had never seen her before in my life until that afternoon when she turned up on our doorstep in Dundee with my mother, and I have not seen her since. I don't know, at first hand, who she is, or why she came, or anything about her. I had no idea that I might have had a half-sister, or any other relation in the world apart from my father, and I haven't seen him since I was six!"

I was feeling increasingly upset. I could feel the panic rising in me again. I said Margaret's mantra to myself quickly, and then again, and it helped. Ms Gansthorpe paused to glance down at the papers spread before her.

"So, tell us about these men-friends of your mother, Ms Lethbridge," Ms Gansthorpe demanded when she looked up.

I'm sure I looked as flabbergasted as I felt.

"Come, Ms Lethbridge," Ms Gansthorpe pressed. "You lived with these men for months at a time, did you not? They must have left some impression on an intelligent young girl."

"My mother lived with them," I struggled. "I simply…occupied space in the same house. My mother instructed me to…minimise my presence. I avoided both of them as much as was possible, and those men seemed content for that to be so."

"So, what conclusion did you eventually draw as to your mother's motivation for taking up with this string of men, Ms Lethbridge?"

"I have hardly bothered to think about that. I…did as I was told, and tried to be invisible. I suppose they provided her with cash and comfort for a time, but it never lasted for very long. And they made her the centre of attention, and gave her access to social occasions, which made her happy for a while."

Ms Gansthorpe looked off into the distance temporarily, as if seeking inspiration, or a particular *mot juste* which I knew she had probably chosen days before. I strengthened myself against her coming thrust, though I could not yet foresee from what direction it was going to come.

"So, could your mother, at that time, have been described as…how may I say it, Ms Lethbridge? Feckless? Undirected?"

"Such descriptions might well have been considered applicable," I said judiciously.

"And in those circumstances, you abandoned her to herself, having by now reached years of some maturity? You did not just go to Cambridge University, but you stayed there, and withdrew any support you might have offered your mother from that day to this?"

I was trying to say, "No. No. I never had had any influence over my mother, and could not, and cannot, believe that I ever would have done. I was escaping to Cambridge from my mother's abandonment of me!" but Ms Gansthorpe had had enough from me for her purpose and had turned away towards the bench, saying firmly and loudly over my voice, "Thank you, Ms Lethbridge. I have no more questions for this witness, My Lord," before she sat down.

It was almost as if I were a marionette and someone had cut my all strings with a huge pair of shears. I did not pretend to understand what Ms Gansthorpe thought she had gained from all that. No doubt she would try to make something of it during her closing speech, but I could not see what. Anyway, I had almost had enough. *Please, please let it end*, I thought.

"You are free to go, Ms Lethbridge," the judge said.

I think I muttered, "Thank you, My Lord."

I heard the door behind me open. The usher was there, bless her, and she extended a hand towards me as I struggled up from the chair. I could look at nothing and no one. I needed all my available concentration simply to get to the door and to the usher's waiting hand. All I wanted now was Drummond, just Drummond. Out in the court corridor, the usher led me to another padded bench, and let me sit down to gather myself while she opened a locker and retrieved my handbag.

"When you're ready, Ms Lethbridge," she said. With her hand under my elbow, we made our way back to the corridor outside the doors to the courtrooms. The usher handed me over to the lady from the Witness Service, and, with her help, I made it to the top of the stone staircase to the ground floor. And there was Drummond!

I wanted to run down the stairs, to fly down them, but I could not. At every step, I needed to steady, first my feet, and then my body. My head was beginning to spin. I felt totally out of control. Drummond came rushing up the stairs and took over from the Witness Service lady, thanked her briefly and more or less carried me by my free arm the rest of the way downstairs.

I remember nothing of the taxi-ride back to the hotel or, once there, of getting back to our room or into bed, and, once Drummond was there beside me, I gave way and sobbed uncontrollably until I went to sleep, hugged in his arms.

Chapter Twenty-One

I slept through most of the following day. It was a Saturday, thank goodness, and whenever I woke up, Drummond was there in an armchair beside the bed, the floor around him littered with the remnant dishes of the room-service meals on which he had existed. We would smile at each other, and he might make me a cup of coffee or a mug of packet-soup from the supply we had brought with us, and I would go back to sleep. My behaviour had become so well-known to us now that we accepted as routine that any mother-related stress would result in a mini-collapse, and planned accordingly.

By the Sunday evening, I was sufficiently recovered for us to have a shower together and for me to get dressed. We ate in the hotel restaurant before I returned to bed, and Drummond to his armchair, where he watched a muted television screen and I went back to sleep. All that sleep was essential, because, despite gentle protests from Drummond, John, Jacqueline, Flora…in fact, virtually everybody I knew, I was determined to be in court for the climax of this whole horrific business.

Dr Alder understood, of course, and referred to my decision as 'a need for closure'. All I knew was that I needed to be there when the jury found those women guilty so that I could be sure that they would not return to bother me for a very long time.

On the Monday morning, our taxi dropped us off at the public entrance to the Old Bailey. Quite a crowd was already filing into the courthouse. As I came out of the taxi, I could also see men with long-lens cameras, and a couple of women holding microphones on the end of long leads which snaked out behind them in the direction of vans parked further down the street. Any hope of being ignored by the press was quickly proved to be misplaced. As soon as they saw me, the women left the queue and rushed across towards us. Drummond put his arm around my waist and virtually lifted me towards the door.

"Ms Lethbridge," one of the women squealed, "how did you feel to see your mother in the dock yesterday?"

"What verdict are you hoping for in your mother's trial, Ms Lethbridge?" the other one cut across her, both of them thrusting their microphones towards me like daggers.

None too gently, Drummond shoulder-barged the first woman to clear a way for us. I simply put my head down into my chest, said nothing and let his momentum carry both of us forward, with Drummond shouting loudly at the crowd around the door, "Excuse us, please, excuse us, please."

Widening a gap with more pushing, he managed to get us inside and turned sideways to block the journalists from following us. The crowd closed behind us as he said a hurried, general thank-you to them, and that part of the ordeal was over.

"Haven't had so much fun since playing rugby at school," he grinned at me. "Are you all right, honey?"

I told him I was, though I was shaken. I was also frightened at the intrusive determination of the journalists, even when accepting that they, like Ms Gansthorpe on Friday, had had a job to do and a living to make.

We found seats at the end of one of the benches in the public gallery. Below us, the courtroom looked completely different from how it had looked from the witness box. The dock and the jury box down one side of the room were empty. The judge's bench and the clerk's desk in front of it were unoccupied. There were a handful of barristers in the benches in the body of the court, and some suits, male and female, whom I assumed to be solicitors.

There was plenty of room for more of them, however, and I knew their seats would fill up before the proceedings opened. For the first time, I noticed narrow oblong windows high up near to the ceiling at one end of the courtroom, through which a little morning sunlight was brightening the room. A minute or two later, first Naomi, and then my mother, appeared in the dock again, each followed by their pair of prison officers. The Clerk appeared, stood behind his desk and said loudly, "All rise," and the judge entered from one side of his bench, like an actor entering stage left. He bowed, and sat down, and the jury filed into their places.

It was still a shock. I suddenly realised why everyone was there. The previous week, I had been too concerned for my own ability to get through my appearance in the witness box to appreciate anyone else in the courtroom as 'real people'. Now I had no more part to play in all this, but she did. My mother did! She was going to go to prison, John had said, "for a very long time", at least for a period as long as a half of my life so far.

Then I thought of some of the scenes of the half of my life during which I had been effectively in prison under her control, dependent on her whims, shamed by her irresponsibility, denied of anyone's interest, let alone understanding or love. And yet, those memories still did not stimulate any wish for revenge. I was not there in that courtroom for payback, only for the confirmation of release. I said Margaret's mantra to myself again.

"I am not my mother. I am not responsible for her actions, or their consequences."

At last, I could begin to accept my separation from my mother, past and future. I snuggled closer to Drummond to watch the action on the floor of the court below.

"Am I to understand that you wish to present no more witnesses, Mr Sandiman? Ms Gansthorpe?" the judge inquired.

Sandiman did his stooped half-rise and said, "That is correct, My Lord."

He sat down again, as Ms Gansthorpe rose, but only to concur with her colleague.

"Then Counsel will present their closing speeches today," the judge announced, "and I will sum up tomorrow. If we can keep to this timetable, I anticipate the case going to the jury tomorrow afternoon." He paused, but no one among the barristers moved, so he concluded.

"Mr Hornsby, your closing speech for the prosecution, if you please."

Hornsby stood, adjusted his robe, his spectacles, picked up a sheaf of papers from the desk in front of him, breathed in visibly, and turned to face the jury box.

It was the first time I had taken any real notice of the jury. They had been there last Friday. Indeed, they had necessarily been there all last week, but I had grasped their presence only as another block of people in the courtroom. Now, I looked at them. These were the people who would decide my mother's guilt. And Naomi's, of course, but I was still assuming that there was no question but that they would convict Naomi, and anyway she was of no particular interest to me.

Who were these people who, primarily, would give me freedom from my mother? They were a mixed bag. Ordinary-looking. Tall. Short. One, a worried-looking young man, was particularly skinny, but the rest were within the ordinary range of sizes, except for one woman at the end of the back row of jury-persons, who was...well, very large indeed. Three females and nine males. Of the men, five wore suits and ties, two apparently comfortably and three uncomfortably, as if they were unused to the constriction of their buttoned shirt-collars. Five jury-persons were wearing spectacles. Everyone in the jury box looked serious, and most of them looked tired, as if they hoped this business would not go on much longer and they could return to their normal lives. Beyond that, however, neither their faces nor their bodies gave any indication as to how they might judge the evidence with which they had been presented. I turned back to look at Mr Hornsby. Anywhere other than at the dock!

Mr Hornsby began, "As Your Lordship pleases."

He drew in another deep and portentous breath, before looking up into the jury's eyes.

"Ladies and gentlemen of the jury," he began, "of necessity, you have been required to hear the horrific details of what the Crown contends to have been a particularly vicious and cold-blooded act of murder!" He paused to let his emphasis on his last word sink into the jury's minds. "Throughout the distressing experience of the last week, you have displayed exemplary attention to the evidence which has been placed before you, and your duty is nearly done. However, the last phase of this trial is the most important for all concerned, and the most testing for you, ladies and gentlemen of the jury. You are required to pronounce upon the guilt or innocence of those who are accused of this evil act. It is my function today to seek to assist you in this onerous task, to the best of my ability."

He paused, ostensibly to look down at his sheaf of papers. Having successfully focused the jury's attention back on himself, Hornsby looked up again and continued, "The Crown contends that the lack of detailed explanation for the motive for this act is of no particular relevance to your considerations. The act was done, and the forensic evidence you have heard points unquestionably, the Crown would suggest, to the perpetrators having been the accused, Ms Naomi Lethbridge and Mrs Irene Lethbridge, whom you see in the dock before you." He turned to glower disparagingly at the dock, and the heads of several of the jurors turned in the same direction.

"Most of the dismembered body of the late Mr Journeyman was found in binbags in his garden shed. The whereabouts of his head has not yet been discovered. That eventuality will no doubt fall upon some innocent person at an unexpected and traumatic moment in the future. Like the lack of a clear motive for the killing, the lack of Mr Journeyman's head is also irrelevant to your concerns today. What does matter is the clarity of the forensic evidence which has been placed before you."

"As you have heard, ladies and gentlemen of the jury, from the numerous highly qualified and experienced experts who have testified in this case, no trace of any sort was found in Mr Journeyman's house, after the discovery of his…remains, of the recent presence there of anyone other than the deceased and the accused. You have also heard that superficial and incomplete attempts were made to eradicate splashes and spots of blood consistent with that of Mr Journeyman from the kitchen and ground-floor shower-room in his house, among which partial finger and palm-prints of both the accused were found.

"Samples of this blood, together with the other material of which you have heard, have been secured from living rooms and bedrooms in the house, and has been subjected to the most modern analysis by reference to the characteristics of its deoxyribonucleic acid, its…DNA. Those analytical procedures, ladies and gentlemen of the jury, are, as you know, of the most modern technology, and, so it is widely accepted, are of almost unquestionable accuracy.

"Tracing the patterns of those…materials through the house and garden, forensic science officers have been able to demonstrate to you a sequence of events in which Mr Journeyman was killed in the kitchen, butchered," Hornsby paused again for emphasis, "and bagged in the shower-room, and his body, or most of it, at least, was carried to the garden shed by Ms Naomi Lethbridge. You will recall that no trace was found to indicate that Mrs Irene Lethbridge had ever, at any time, been in the shed.

"Traces of both women indicate their cooperation in the attempt to remove the evidence of their deed from the kitchen and shower-room, however, and of their attempts to cleanse themselves and their clothes of the inevitable additional evidence, in the first-floor bathroom.

"They then fled the scene!" Hornsby roared at the courtroom, and allowed his voice to echo around the otherwise silent courtroom. After a number of seconds, he continued.

"You have heard, from the witnesses from York and from Newcastle-upon-Tyne," Mr Hornsby went on, "that women answering to the descriptions of Ms Naomi Lethbridge and Mrs Lethbridge sold or attempted to sell a number of valuable items of gentlemen's jewellery, notably dress studs and solid gold cufflinks, for which, as these witnesses have attested, the vendors could provide no adequate proof of ownership. According to the evidence given in this court by Ms Gemma Journeyman, the deceased's sister, there was at one time in Mr Journeyman's possession a collection of a great deal more, equally valuable, jewellery, of which no trace was to be found in the house after the discovery of Mr Journeyman's…remains.

"On the basis of this evidence, and in the absence of any firm alternative suggestion, you may be drawn, members of the jury, towards the conclusion that Mr Journeyman's murder was occasioned by simple, indeed casual, greed."

Hornsby glared derogatively in the direction of the dock, and several members of the jury turned in that direction with similar expressions.

"Ladies and gentlemen of the jury, you have heard of the many repeated difficulties which all three of the women in this family have faced during their lives. You will no doubt draw your own conclusions from the contrast between the determined response to those difficulties displayed by Ms Hannah Lethbridge, as opposed to those of her mother and half-sister. The Crown would suggest that that contrast underlines the fact that, tragic though such difficulties are, they cannot form any reasonable excuse for the ruthless selfishness demonstrated by whoever perpetrated the murder of Mr Michael Journeyman."

Hornsby paused again to fix the jury with a stern gaze, and then, after a few seconds, continued.

"The Crown contends, ladies and gentlemen of the jury," Hornsby's face now took on the expression of a humble, reasonable seeker after truth in a puzzling world, "that, on the basis of this evidence, a rational person might also reasonably approach the view that, having fled the scene of their crime, the murder and posthumous robbery of Mr Journeyman," another crescendo and pause, "the perpetrators progressed gradually further and further from London until the proceeds of their actions were exhausted. So, where could they go next? To whom could they possibly turn for assistance, shelter, a place to hide?

"Their only living relative was Ms Hannah Lethbridge, long separated from her birth-mother but, according to the evidence you have heard from Ms Naomi Lethbridge, apparently traceable with no great difficulty through the increasing volume of personal information on, I believe it is called, the 'World Wide Web', and ready access to that information through what are known as 'Internet cafés'."

Hornsby paused again, shook his head briefly in seeming despair at the sad erosion of personal security in the modern world, appeared to refer to his papers, and then went on, "Accordingly, the accused turned up unannounced on the doorstep of the house where Ms Hannah Lethbridge was living, and attempted repeatedly to force entry into the house."

My stomach turned over again, and I reclaimed the comfort of Margaret's mantra, and of the strong solidity of Drummond's body to which I pressed my own.

Mr Hornsby continued, "You have heard of the literally traumatic effect on Ms Hannah Lethbridge of these attempts to enter her home, members of the jury."

Mr Hornsby again indulged in a moment's silence to allow this point to sink into the minds of the jury.

"Tragic though that might be, however, the Crown contends that this aspect of the evidence placed before you is also irrelevant to the main issue with which you are required to deal. Are the accused indeed guilty of the murder of Mr Michael Journeyman? The Crown suggests that they are, on the basis of the following argument:

— One: the absence of any evidence whatsoever that any other identifiable person or persons might have had reason or opportunity to commit this terrible act
— Two: the evidence that the accused attempted to clean up the evidential aftermath of that act without bothering to make known Mr Journeyman's disappearance to any competent authority
— Three: that, when apprehended, Ms Naomi Lethbridge was carrying a knife commensurate with one which would have been capable of imposing the wounds found on Mr Journeyman's body
— Four: that she had been found to have been carrying such a weapon when she had previously been apprehended by the police in other, separate contexts—thus indicating that the carrying of such a weapon was habitual on her part.

"Should you conclude that these women were indeed Mr Journeyman's assailants, his murderers and his robbers, ladies and gentlemen of the jury, you have no alternative other than to find them guilty, thoroughly guilty, of this dreadful act!"

Mr Hornsby sat down, apparently satisfied, and the judge called on Mr Sandiman to present his closing speech on behalf of Naomi.

"Ladies and gentlemen of the jury," Sandiman began, looking far less collected or confident than had his predecessor. "This case does indeed turn on the interpretation of the forensic evidence purportedly discovered in Mr Journeyman's house. My learned friend and I have presented to you equally expert evidence in refutation of the Crown's contentions in this regard. Those experts have emphasised to you, however surprising it may be to the lay person, that finger-prints and palm-prints, especially partial ones, are actually very difficult to relate to a particular person. DNA analysis is in its youth, as a tool of forensic science.

"One day, in its maturity, it may become as certain as the Crown's witnesses have attempted to suggest it is in the present case. Both my learned friend and I, for the defence, contest that view."

Sandiman, in his turn, paused, took a deep breath, looked briefly at his papers, and resumed his speech.

"My learned friend and I believe that we have shown you that very reasonable doubts do remain in relation to precisely who murdered Mr Michael Journeyman. My client, Ms Naomi Lethbridge, has readily admitted that she has, on occasion, carried a knife for self-protection. That is, perhaps, a regrettable if reasonably understood response to the troubled life she has led since her mother, Mrs Irene Lethbridge, abandoned her at birth to the series of arguably less than adequate, even less than safe, foster and care homes of which she has informed you.

"She, and incidentally, her mother, claim that, on returning to Mr Journeyman's house after an afternoon's innocent shopping, they found a scene of frightening ferocity and gore. Ms Lethbridge, mindful of the implications of her past…experience of the police service, prevailed upon her mother to join her in avoiding, so far as it might be possible, any repetition of inappropriate blame. They cleared up as best they could, and as quickly as they might.

"Furthermore, they had for some months been dependent on Mr Journeyman for all their financial resources. Over that period, they had had no cash of their own whatsoever beyond what he had freely given to them, and they had innocently spent. Accordingly, in desperation, they gathered what few trinkets might support them in the immediate future, and did indeed, in their confusion and fear, flee.

"That is the Defence's contention, ladies and gentlemen of the jury, as it is our contention that this narration should seem, to the disinterested lay person, as reasonable and indeed incontrovertible as any other. My client, Ms Naomi Lethbridge, we put it to you, is innocent of the matter of which she is accused in this court, and we encourage you, in the strongest possible terms, to find her so today."

Sandiman sat down looking exhausted, as well he might. For me, a little more light had been cast on Naomi's history, but nothing like as much as was still to come.

The judge glanced at his wristwatch and announced a welcome adjournment for lunch. On everyone's return, he invited Ms Gansthorpe to offer her closing speech.

"Ladies and gentlemen of the jury," she began, with a subdued flash of her excellent teeth, "I shall not bore you by reiterating the interpretation of the evidence before you which my learned friend Mr Sandiman has explained to you in all the necessary detail, except to emphasise," she paused meaningfully, "that there is no evidence that my client, Mrs Irene Lethbridge, was in anyway involved in the killing of Mr Journeyman."

After a further brief pause, she said, "The defence maintains that both women came home to Mr Journeyman's house to find a scene of carnage. They were filled with horror and panic, cleared up as best they could and fled for their liberty and their lives, not knowing, but readily imagining, under what unseen threats of violence they stood while they remained in that house.

"What I do want to recall to you, however, is the sad story of Mrs Lethbridge's life, which goes so far to explain her very reluctant involvement in the sequence of events of which you have heard. She has recounted to you, with remarkably courageous frankness, her totally inadequate childhood. It was marred, from an early age, she said, by the inappropriate attentions of her alcoholic father and the lack of any normal, let alone loving, attention from her hypochondriac mother.

"Forced to leave school at the earliest possible moment, in despair, and without any useful qualification by which to support herself, poverty eventually caused her to quit the home which had barely merited that name. Seeing no practical alternative, she decided to make her way in what she saw as the only way available to her, as a courtesan. In her ignorance, she soon became pregnant with her daughter, Naomi. Recognising the tenuous security of her lifestyle, she despaired again.

"Concluding, rightly or wrongly, that her daughter might almost certainly enjoy more opportunities without her mother than in her company, she fled once more, in the pattern which has become characteristic of her history. When faced with overwhelming problems, Mrs Lethbridge habitually runs away. This is a weakness, but what chance, you might ask yourselves, has this woman had to learn any more effective response?

"Falling pregnant again some few years later with her daughter Hannah, however, she did attempt improvement. She kept Hannah with her, and brought her up as best she could, given the inheritance of desperation and unhappiness which Irene has carried all her life. Only when her daughter Hannah in turn abandoned her, as so many people in her life had done, did Mrs Lethbridge more or less shrug her shoulders and get on with facing the urgent need to preserve her own life in the only way she knew how to do."

"Mrs Lethbridge was therefore surprised and shocked when a woman claiming to be her daughter Naomi accosted her in the café that morning. Members of the Jury, please do your very best to imagine the degree of surprise, the impact of the shock, that this meeting must have imposed on Mrs Lethbridge. I am sure that anyone who has enjoyed a normal life, even a life with perhaps more than its fair share of significant difficulties, would not find it easy to identify the full measure of the emotional impact which such a meeting might impose.

"We might suppose that Mrs Lethbridge's normal response would have been to flee again. However, at that time, the kindness and generosity of Mr Journeyman argued strongly against that—until Naomi appeared at the Journeyman house shortly after, threatened her mother physically with her knife, and blackmailed her with the ruin of the relationship which Irene had so carefully constructed with Mr Journeyman.

"As a result, Irene has said she was forced to persuade Mr Journeyman to allow Naomi to join them in the household, until the fateful day of Mr Journeyman's death," Ms Gansthorpe's voice increased in volume, "in which Mrs Lethbridge played no part!"

When she continued, it was in the same vein.

"After the event, what was she to do? She had no doubt of the reality of Naomi's threats to her physical well-being. She had nowhere to turn. Her last remaining hope, in the weakness of habit, was to flee. When Naomi discovered the whereabouts of her younger half-sister, her mother saw no option but to go along with the plan of seeking sanctuary, perhaps reconciliation, with their last remaining relative, Ms Hannah Lethbridge.

"And there, too, she was again rejected. Her own daughter refused to receive her, to acknowledge her, to provide even the least support of allowing her to try to make up for whatever deprivations she had had to ask her daughters to share so many years before. This is the woman, my client, on whom you are asked to give judgement, members of the jury. Putting yourself as well as you can in her place, her Defence asks you to recognise her weakness, the sad, inexorable history which has led her to the situation in which she finds herself today, and to grant her the basic human charity of understanding how she became involved in the matter on which you are called upon to decide."

Ms Gansthorpe sat down and, in the public gallery, I was shocked and appalled. As the story had continued, I had unconsciously sat up straighter and more tense against Drummond's shoulder. I only realised this when the flow of Ms Gansthorpe's words ceased and the courtroom's silence filled the vast space below us. Now I realised why Ms Gansthorpe had subjected me to this…torture. It was to support a flimsy charade! Surely Mr Hornsby had done enough to dispel his opponent's cobweb of untruths? I could only hope so and wait for the jury to announce its conclusion.

Chapter Twenty-Two

At this point, the court was adjourned for the day, with dire warnings from the judge to the jury not to begin their consultations, however informally, until they had received his detailed instructions. At precisely half past ten the following morning, the judge began his summing-up of the evidence. There was nothing more I wanted to hear at that point and I dozed with Drummond's arm around my waist comfortably until he woke me with a gentle squeeze. The judge was about to give his advice and directions to the jury.

"Members of the Jury," the judge began, "you have three primary groups of decisions to make. Firstly, are you led by the evidence you have heard, and by that evidence alone," he stopped and frowned emphatically at the jury, "to be convinced beyond reasonable doubt that one, other or both of the accused together caused the wounds from which Mr Journeyman died? If one or other, but not both, which of the accused are you so convinced committed the fatal act?

"Secondly, are you led by that evidence to be convinced, again beyond reasonable doubt, that one, other or both the accused together, knowing of the killing of Mr Journeyman only minutes before, acted to hide evidence of that event? Thirdly, on the basis of that evidence, are you led to be convinced that one, other or both of the accused had indeed thus acted of their own free will, and were at the time capable of judging whether their actions were reasonable and appropriate responses to the situations in which they found themselves, as those situations progressed in that house on that day?

"If you are so convinced, in regard to all three groups of decisions in relation to one, other or both of the accused, then you must return to this Court a verdict of guilty on that person or both of those persons."

Most of the people in the jury box looked relieved as the judge paused again. They seemed exhausted already, after a week of sitting more or less still for hours and being asked to listen continuously, and supposedly with concentration, to the words that had been thrown into the air around them.

Nonetheless, the judge resumed, "I shall shortly ask you to retire to consider your verdicts, and to continue with your deliberations until at least four o'clock this afternoon, unless you reach the decisions required of you before that point. If you have been unable to reach those decisions by then, I shall adjourn the court until tomorrow morning, when you will continue your deliberations."

Expressions in the jury box demonstrated that the jurors had heard that part of the judge's address, at least! Every emotion from dismay to horror was evident. I dozed again as the judge completed the technical parts of his instructions to the jury about electing a foreman and seeking unanimity in their decisions, and was brought back to the scene below by the sound of the jurors filing off-stage under the direction of the usher. The Clerk called sharply, "All rise!" as the judge bowed to the court, and left through his door to one side of the bench.

"How are you feeling, honey?" Drummond asked me, "and what do you want to do now?"

"Coffee!" I replied with feeling, "but quickly. I don't want to…I can't miss anything here!"

"You look really tired," he said with real concern. "This could go on for hours, and almost certainly will."

"I can rest when it's all over," I insisted. "Coffee! And then back here."

Outside, Drummond and I found sandwiches and takeaway coffees in a crowded café on a shady side-street below St Paul's Churchyard. We parked ourselves to eat them among a crowd of others in weak spring sunshine on the low wall of an open area in front of city office buildings.

"You're not talking, honey," Drummond said.

I knew he was worried about me, and about the impact of all we had heard, but I hadn't yet completely absorbed it all. It was my family's history, such as it was a family, and I had heard none of it previously.

"I don't yet know what to say," I tried to explain, "but I promise I'll talk when I've sorted it all out in my head. I'm fine for now, though," and I took his hand and gave him a very sincere kiss. He didn't seem to mind. We weren't the only ones doing that on our piece of wall, so perhaps that helped. Or perhaps he was comforted by my reassurance, and just enjoyed it. This whole, horrible, dragged-out nightmare was nearly over, and the excitement of that prospect, and the remaining dregs of uncertainty associated with it, gave us an urgent need to return to the Old Bailey.

When we got back to the corridor outside Courtroom Four, it was much less crowded, though there was still a considerable number of people standing about or sitting on the benches against the wall. As we sat down, Drummond said wearily, "Well, the jury should at least have chosen their foreman by now," and we grinned weakly at each other in memory of the initial manoeuvrings of all the other committees we had both ever known.

I was undeniably tired as the time crept past. I dozed again, with Drummond's arm around me the only thing that prevented me from sliding off the bench onto the marble floor. Suddenly, shortly before four o'clock, people started to stand up and look more alert. A whisper began to go around:

"The jury's coming back. It looks as if there's a verdict."

The door to the public gallery was opened, and those who were waiting were let in. At first, nothing seemed to have changed in the court below us. Counsel and solicitors were still standing in groups, or adjusting the piles of papers on the desks before them. The bench was empty, but, as we sat down, the Clerk was coming in to take his place in front of it, and the defendants were back in the dock. The robed, wigged barristers took their places, and ceased whispering.

"All rise!" the Clerk barked, and everyone obediently stood up as the judge came in, bowed to the court, and sat down at his bench. The door through which the jury had disappeared earlier swung open to let its members file back in.

When the jurors had sat down again, the Clerk asked their foreman to stand. The woman on the end of the front row of jurors nearest to the judge's bench rose, looking collected and confident. Clearly, the progress of the jury's deliberations had been accelerated by the influence of a sensible, experienced woman who had no doubt led many a committee to a quick decision in her local community.

The Clerk asked, "Madam foreman, will you please answer yes or no to my first question. Members of the Jury, have you reached verdicts on which you are all agreed?"

"Yes," the foreman answered.

"In relation to the murder of Michael Journeyman, do you find the defendant Naomi Lethbridge guilty or not guilty?"

"Guilty," the foreman replied firmly.

"And is this the verdict of you all?"

"It is."

"In relation to the murder of the said Michael Journeyman, do you find the defendant Irene Lethbridge guilty or not guilty?"

"Guilty," the foreman replied again.

"And is this the verdict of you all?"

"It is," she confirmed.

"Please sit down," the Clerk said. The usher took from the foreman the formal written record of the verdicts and walked across the courtroom to give it to the Clerk. He turned to bow sketchily to the judge, reached up and put it on the Bench.

The judge glanced at the record, pushed it aside and said, "Ladies and gentlemen of the jury, you have completed your duties fully and effectively. The Court thanks you."

The jury stood at the usher's whispered direction and left the courtroom. The judge looked up at the convicted prisoners in the dock.

"Naomi Lethbridge, Irene Lethbridge," he said, "you have been found guilty of heinous and thoroughly irresponsible crimes, for which you might reasonably expect to receive substantial custodial sentences. I will consider what sentences are appropriate, and will hand them down...Mr Clerk?"

"Twenty-fifth of May, My Lord?"

"At ten am on the twenty-fifth of May. Until then, you will both continue to be remanded in custody. This Court is adjourned!"

The Clerk called yet again, "All rise," and the judge stood, bowed to the assembly in the body of the court and, without a glance at the now empty dock, disappeared through the door to the Chambers Corridor.

***

In the hotel, I slept that night, more or less all Wednesday, and only got up at lunchtime on the Thursday, but it was a relieved sleep, a happy sleep, totally different from any experience of sleep I ever remembered having had. I awoke on the Thursday feeling light and needing to be generous. Once we were showered and dressed, Drummond and I got a taxi to the top of Oxford Street and bought thank-you presents for our wonderful friends. Drummond chose handsome Italian leather wallets for John and Ian, and I bought necklaces for Jacqueline and Flora, and a very pretty little summer dress for Veronica, which I hoped would fit.

I went back to sleep on the train North from King's Cross on Friday morning, and didn't stir again until, Drummond told me, we were beyond York and well on the way to Scotland and our home. I remember, not really awake, stretching up so that I could whisper in Drummond's ear, "Do you think it's time we had a baby?"

He stiffened momentarily, then turned slightly and grinned down at me.

"Oh, yes, I think it's high time," he said. "But not here and now, perhaps."

"Fool!" I said and went back to sleep until the train reached Edinburgh and I really knew I was almost home.